LOST KINGDOM

A book by Nick Gibson

First Edition 2025
0 9 8 7 6 5 4 3 2 1

ISBN: 978-1-967199-84-6 (Paperback Edition)

Critical Blast Publishing
624 Sunnyhill Drive
Belleville, IL 62223

Distributed by Critical Blast Logistics - CriticalBlast.com / PRINTED IN USA.

This book is dedicated to
the memory of

Harold R Cosby

A man who taught me
what unconditional love
truly feels like.

R.I.P.

It is also dedicated to
the memory of

Christopher "Xevious" Roberts

A man who made me feel like a true
pro even when I very much wasn't,
and whose art adorns not just this
book but many of my comics.

R.I.P.

Contents

1
Something Ends

"All Castle forces, Elrick's troops have breached the inner walls. This is our final stand!"

Not for me, it isn't. My mind is still coming to terms with the betrayal as I look down at the carnage around me, and once pristine halls are now littered with rubble. Remnants of a battle I was supposed to fight in. A battle I was honor-bound to die in. Not today, today I live.

Taking one last look at the place I had called home for the past 5 years, my eyes intentionally drifted past the brothers with whom I had laughed just hours prior. None of us was prepared for this, I thought with a shiver. The magnitude of destruction a mere shelling could cause washed over me. I should have trained them for this.

With my head hanging low, I marched through the halls. My destination has long since been decided upon. I wept silently as I walked, for there was nothing more I could do here...except to die. I am the first, I reminded myself, the oath ringing inside my head as loudly as the day I uttered it. I am the first sword our enemies see.

The closer I got to the courtyard, the louder the sounds of the battle raging outside became. Our King is my consort, my body his shield. Those words I was once so proud to say now stung hollow as the screams of the men who once looked to me now looked onwards to death.

I never asked for this, I reminded myself. I was happy where I was—loved, respected.

But now was not the time to assign blame. I can hate myself later. Even now, the two halves of my heart wage a war for my fate. I knew the pain that was in store for me. I knew full well what my actions today meant. "A traitor," I whispered to myself, stepping over the body of my captain—a man I had personally raised up, now a corpse under my boot.

"No more," I uttered as I keyed in the access code. Warm, sticky air rushed to greet me; the scent of the courtyard's cherry blossoms filled my nostrils. But beneath that nostalgic sentiment was a tinge of pain and suffering. Our King is my faith, his castle our Temple.

Entering the courtyard, a place where so many moments call their home, I could not help but feel a sense of longing wash over me. This is where it all began, I recalled, remembering the first time I had stepped onto the landing pad. Said landing pad currently housing the royal starship Eventide.

This is where things shall end… My mind went blank as the reality set in. The only company my racing thoughts had was the clatter my boots made while I walked on the metal grating. The ship... no, my salvation, was in sight.

"Okay, you can do this, Jayce," I said to no one. Trying in vain to psych myself up. "It's not like you are betraying everyone and everything you once held dear."

Shaking my head, I banished such wretched thoughts, then took one step onto the ship's ramp and…

"SIR JAYCEN LAMONT! WHAT IN PLUTO DO YOU THINK YOU ARE DOING?!"

In an instant, my mind and body froze. Not her, I thought with a shiver. Anyone but the Queen.

Having no other choice, I turned around to face her. The Queen Brianna Shinkar was decked out in all her regal glory. A fine green petticoat along with matching trousers, the ancient blade Windseeker at her waist. "From the first," she said, looking down at the near-matching blade I wore at my waist, Earthbringer. Its orange gemstone glistened in the flickering firelight.

"To the last," I returned with a sigh. My eyes, of course, were drawn to Windseer's pale blue gemstone. So pale that in a certain light you would swear it was white.

The Queen stared at me for a moment, as if trying to process what I had attempted to do. "So you aren't brain dead after all," she said after what felt like an eternity.

Not wanting to deal with this, I set aside long-held notions. Turning my back on the woman who means so many things to me, I began marching up the ramp. Up towards…

"Jayce, turn around and face me like the man you once claimed to be!" she roared, her words stopping me in my tracks once again. My body went rigid in accordance with my training. Years of hard-earned reflexes were now at war with my present dissatisfaction.

Fighting what both my heart and body desperately wanted to do, I made up my mind to turn and face the soon-to-be ex-queen. "It's over, Your Highness," I said, finding the mental strength to protest the inevitable.

Her eyes met mine, full of steely resolve and iron-clad will. "You swore a vow," she said, as simple as ever. Her words were nothing if not sweet yet firm. Years of training and courtly politics coming forth. Making a woman in her 20s seem decades older. A queen until the end, it seemed. "An unyielding vow. You, of all people, should be by my side."

"What does that have to do with anything?" I asked as I slowly inched backwards up the ramp. My arms cast outwards to the battle beyond us. Breaching the walls of tranquility, the sounds of shellfire surrounded us. I could still make out the screams of my brothers as they died fighting a lost cause. So pointless.

"Everything," she responded, waving her hand to someone I couldn't see. Then, from out of the shadows, came The Queen's personal servant, Grump. But it wasn't Grump that made my blood begin to boil. It was what he was holding that angered me so. Him.

That wretched child- it hurt to even look at him. Who knew so much guilt could come from such a small package? None of this would have even happened without him. My mind started to think dark thoughts. So much death...avoided.

"I can't do this," I said, my voice betraying just the hint of a quiver. Many times, I have let The Queen get her way. Her words had a power over me that few could hope to match.

"Why?" That was all she asked of me; her words nearly broke me in the process. For the briefest of moments, I was transported to a simpler time when everything was right and made sense.

I was such a lost whelpling when I first came here. Memories of a rough transition flooded back to me. Going from hotshot pilot to a courtly statesman would ruin almost anybody. But she wouldn't allow me to fail, she...helped me. But now I must break her.

With tears of regret, I cast my eyes towards the many fires going on around us—so much destruction over something so small. "Things... change," I said, my voice choking on the words. It hurt my soul to speak it aloud. As if admitting the truth made it reality at last.

Not wanting to suffer any longer, the time seemed finally at hand. My ears continue to pick up the screams of my dying brothers. I can't listen to this a second longer! My eyes finally landed on my feet as I said, "People...change."

The Queen's eyes widen with shock at my words. She stood there for a moment, mouth agape, before quickly covering her grief with a mask of concern. But like all things in the King's court, it wasn't for herself.

"If you are so determined to leave, then at least take him with you," she said, picking up the little babe into her arms. Barely a few months old, yet still old enough to tear a 300-year-old dynasty to pieces.

Looking at him, I could feel the anger start to swell up inside me once again. Giving rise to a boldness I had forgotten. "He's the cause of all this!" I said, waving my arms in frustration. Memories of the past year flashing before my eyes. The confusion, the frustration, and ultimately the revolution can be traced back to this little one. "If he had never been born, the transition would have been peaceful, my brothers would still be alive!"

Not wanting to hear her answer, I stormed the rest of the way up the ramp and into the ship. "Probably just more excuses," I said to myself, still grasping for ways to justify what, in my heart, I knew to be a bad decision. The ship's systems hummed to life as I entered.

"Welcome, Your Highness. Where to?" The ship's AI greeted me with its usual cheerfulness as I entered the bridge. Looking around, it astounded me how a place could seem so familiar yet so alien. I had spent countless hours in this very room. My mind was running through all the scenarios I had been put through.

The thing is, none of the ninety-nine scenarios I had been trained in came close to covering what I was about to do. A lone soldier fleeing the post he was honor-bound to die defending. "Guard override, nickto-vega-niner," I finally replied, the coldness of my words surprising even me.

"Acknowledged, where to?" A.I. said before I quickly cut it off, not wanting to hear another syllable of its cheerful tones. Just listening to him sickens me, I thought with a shiver. Part of me wondered if I was really sick of its voice or if my guilt had become overwhelming. "Alpha Centauri System. Planet 3," I sputtered.

"Confirmed, would you like to depart now?" A.I. cheerfully replied, ignorant of both my anguish and the chaos surrounding it. First thing I am doing is changing that damn voice box, I thought to myself— the idea giving me at least some measure of comfort.

For a moment, I let myself get lost in the monotony of launch prep. The pre-ordained sequence of tasks allowed my mind to run on autopilot—anything to get away from this guilt. Sadly, my peace was not to last, for as I looked out the window to check on the ignition, I saw the Queen, still standing in the spot where I had left her. JAMES seemingly long gone.

Defiant as ever, it seems, I mused to myself. I didn't really believe what I was seeing. She is risking life and limb, but for what? I wondered.

"Hold launch," I said to the computer, my curiosity somehow overriding my rising sense of guilt. Stepping back down the ramp, I did something I never thought I'd do. An act that even I did not think possible. I was going to talk to her...again!

"What do you want from me?" I yelled to her from the ramp, the roar of engines revving up and pounding my eardrums. Sadly, even two engines spooling up, not even 10 meters away from me, was not enough to drown out the battle beyond us. I must get out of here soon, lest I go mad.

The Queen stood there in silence at my words. Not a drop of emotion crossed her face. Her eyes were simply taking me in. Marveling at the man I was becoming. "For you to do...YOUR JOB!!" she yelled back. Holding the young prince out to me. No threat shall pass my sight, lest my life be made light.

I looked at... the thing softly cooing in The Queen's arms. It had no idea of the conflict raging around him. The battles being fought in his name. How can such a little thing be so innocent yet so guilty at the same time?

Then I looked at her, our eyes meeting in the middle and staring at each other for what seemed like an eternity. I could sense the confidence radiating from her. She thinks she will win this battle, just as she has in all our other battles before. Digging deep down, I mustered up courage I didn't know I had. My gaze finally pulled away from her. I would not be snared by the eyes again. Those that had trapped me so many times before.

Not a moment too soon, for if I lingered even a passing glance longer, the Queen would have gotten her way again. In my rush to get away from her snare, my gaze found itself lingering on the boy in her arms. What kind of life does he have to look forward to? I wondered. Even if Elrick didn't kill him, his childhood would be one on the run, never knowing permanence.

Now that I knew what I had to do, I looked back up at The Queen. Our eyes met, and the battle began. For the briefest of moments, my heart yearned to yield. Seeing my flash of insecurity, her mouth formed what looked to be a smile. Not the usual smug 'I win' smile, but a smile of relief.

Sadly, that relief was short-lived. Her smile was torn from her face when I ripped my badge from my chest and threw it at her feet. "No" was all I said, my actions doing most of the talking. That one word rang louder than any mortar shell throughout the halls, for I am the Captain General.

We both stood there a moment, the two of us frozen in disbelief at my audacity. She's not used to me standing up for myself. At least, not this publicly. Slowly but steadily, my senses returned to me. Not sure what to do, I did the only thing I could think of: I ran, racing up the ramp to flee like the coward I now knew I was.

I didn't turn back to look at her; I couldn't. The guilt washing over me proved to be overwhelming. If I stopped to think about what I was doing for even a moment, my knees could buckle under me.

"You bastard!" The Queen screamed, her desperation finally breaking through her court-trained facade. "Curse you to all nine hells!"

"I already am," I replied, not bothering to look back as I finished walking up the ramp. So deep was my despair that I could not even bring myself to look at her as I closed the door. My eyes so weighed down with tears, they stared at the floor as I closed the bulkhead, sealing my fate. All things end with me.

So strong was this moment that it managed to haunt my nightmares. Playing out inside my mind every night for the next fifteen years…

BEEP! BEEP! BEEP!

As usual, the first thing I feel upon being jolted awake is the uncanny sensation of cold sweat running down my back. The air compressors have long since shut off, leaving only the kind of general haze one's body heat can muster.

Sitting up to wave on the lights, fifteen years of dangerous situations and bad decisions rushed back up my spine at once. As usual, the location may be different. However, the pain persists.

It wasn't the years on my body that hurt me the most. No, while my back bore the burden of the past decade and a half of bounty hunting. My heart bore the greatest strain. For it wasn't every day that a man abandoned his post, leaving behind not just everything he had sworn to protect, but also the honor that had once been a cornerstone of his very being.

Jaycen Lamont, Captain-General of the King's Royal Guard, died that evening. What replaced him...is something else entirely.

What even am I anymore? I wondered. The years of constant survival flashed before my eyes. The countless jobs I had taken just to not starve a blur before me.

"I can't keep doing this," I muttered to myself as I poured whatever lukewarm water remained from the skin I had purchased the previous night. That and this room were draining what remained of my meager funds.

Which beckoned the obvious question: Where can I find myself some work? Knowing full well the answer to the query.

Leaving my semi-permanent home at The Dead Space Lodgings, I made my way through the cold, hollowed-out halls. It was next to impossible to keep a repurposed asteroid fully lit. Thus, my journey took me through gloomy outcroppings. These were doing a good job of reflecting my mood, probably why I chose to settle here a few years back.

Said Rock in Space was one of many orbiting a planet, I couldn't for the life of me remember, out in the farthest reaches of known space.

When I fled here all those years ago, Alpha Centauri was a far-flung settlement just at the beginning of its life. As lawless as it became, the new frontier attracted not just all the worst sorts but also all manner of lost souls searching for a place to disappear.

Now, it's a slightly less lawless place. Order has made several attempts to impose itself upon it over the years, achieving, at best, partial success. Time sure does have a habit of standing still when you stop moving forward, I thought, connecting the static nature of this place to my own melancholy existence.

No point in looking forward, I reminded myself while staring through one of the few windows on this rock. The void before me reflected the vast emptiness that was my heart. Why bother when your course was set in stone so long ago?

My mind lingered on that thought of the choices I had made. Was it possible for one man to undo a lifetime of sin? No, it's impossible.

What was possible, though, was the threat of new work. For it was that moment my comm decided to go off, interrupting my pensive depression. "Only one person in range has this number!" I said to myself, my words echoing all across the empty halls. There was hardly anyone out at this hour. The party people were either sleeping off a hangover or getting laid, and the early risers had yet to be jolted awake.

Reaching down to my wrist to check it, I was greeted with the only man it could be, Ross. My one contact on this gods forsaken sphere of shite. Probably another drug run. Those seemed to be the only gigs a Fixer of his caliber could secure with a mercenary of my standing. Hard to trust someone who refuses to talk about their past.

But a job was a job, I reminded myself. Those were in short supply these days. So with a reluctant sigh, I opened my comms.

Surprisingly, it was not a job offer, but an invitation—an invitation to meet him at an all-night diner. Not that there was anything even close to a day/night cycle this deep in space. It was just the pretense that mattered to most people. "Jayce, meet me at The Noodle Boodle at 0600. Order the wings, they are divine," was all his message said.

Very subtle, Ross. The man was never the brightest bulb but at least knew how to screw one on. Still, though, the instructions were clear if not as subtle as a Stryo-Brick.

The Noodle Boodle, the only establishment of its kind on this lifeless rock they call a moon. As such, it is a mecca for the type of scum and villainy that have inhabited this part of the system since its founding. Scum such as myself

Being a regular at an establishment like this did have its perks, though. One such privilege included not having to worry about being jumped the moment I stepped inside. I sighed as my mind began to ponder such a folly—best of luck to the would-be hood who tried to 'frisk' me. I kinda wish they would, though, I thought to myself, my hands grazing over my almost-healed knuckles. Been a minute since I've had a good scuffle.

Said fantasy was quickly dashed as I remembered the holding cells on this rock—an almost second home for me.

Thankfully, the restaurant was at least reasonably close by. Arriving close to the assigned time, I could see the early risers were having a late go of things, for only a single soul sat at the bar.

"Hey, Royce, hair of the dog again?" I said to the drunk as he nursed his White Claw.

Royce was known far and wide as the drunkest drunk who ever could get drunk, with a crippling White Claw addiction. The man is single-handedly keeping the company afloat. "Alwayssss," he slurred before taking another sip. Realizing it was empty, he slammed it to the ground. "Bartender, another!" he shouted, the can landing among the 18 other White Claws he had consumed over the previous evening.

Ignoring the fool with the seemingly iron liver, I flagged down a nearby waitress. Well, the only waitress really. Didn't really need more than one at this hour. "GOOOOOOOOD MOOOOOORNING SIR!" The waitress, Alicia chimed, her voice extremely high-pitched and peppy. Almost as if she took every drug that one could get their hands on right before coming to greet me. Which, given the rock we lived on, probably wasn't too far from the truth.

"Morning," I replied to her with a gruff tone. My vocal cords not really used to uttering anything other than gasps of pain these days. "I'd like an order of Wings?"

Alicia initially stared at me as if I were crazy. Well, I was crazy, but not in the way she thought. Realizing that Ross was cleverer than I originally thought, I quickly followed it up with "I heard they are divine?"

"Oh… ohhhhhhhh!" she said, her eyes widening at the realization, before she quickly darted into the back, leaving me alongside the so-called Iron Knight, the best of his age. At least, that's what he keeps calling himself anyway.

Now, I sat alone at the bar. Even Royce had gone in search of more White Claw, and I was left with no one but myself for company. As per usual

That left me pondering all the choices that led me here. Is this job really worth it? I asked myself. Looking around, I took in the cheap green neon lights that filled the room. I could just walk away, right now.

While that was indeed an option, it was the consequences of that choice that really tied me to the chair. Consequences are something I should have considered so long ago, I mused, my face going long at the idea.

Sadly, my pity party was cut short dreadfully when two rather large and imposing men crept up behind me. "Follow us, Mister Lamont," the dude on the left said, jolting me from my inner turmoil. His voice had an icy chill, sending shivers down my spine and filling my already addled mind with even more dour notions. Not wanting to start a scuffle, I stood up. My back was going rigid as a board in compliance with their demands.

Falling behind these brutes, they swiftly led me past the curtain. It was only then that I realized I had never actually been to the back room of this establishment. I have seen every place on this rock, I thought to myself, my mind racing as we stepped beyond the curtain and into the unknown. Every crack, crevice, and corner. But never here.

The back room they led me to was truly unappealing. What little care they seemed to put into the front of house all but disappeared upon entering the back of house. Dry goods were haphazardly placed wherever there was room; the walls themselves were just bare rock, the restaurant having been built into the rock itself. Even the chairs and tables looked to be at least a thousand years old. Hell, every surface I could see was caked in two inches of dust. Did anyone ever clean in here? I wondered.

That answer would sadly never come as the burly guard who ushered me in here almost immediately sat me down at a table. Sitting to my left was my contact, Ross Johnson. His dirty, mangled dreads marked him as a member of a tribe most had forgotten about with the abandonment of the Old Earth.

Who was this tribe? I wondered as Ross and I locked eyes. The two of us were accustomed to conducting business over comms, but meeting in person always felt a bit awkward. Who knows? I finally concluded, my eyes drifting rightward. Doubt even he knows at this point.

Not that the man actually cared, of course. He wore a crazed smile, well, as much of a smile as he could make with only three teeth. As soon as Ross saw I was secure, he took the sleeve of his mangy black petticoat to wipe some dust from the table.

By "some," I meant a huge cloud of dust. A cloud that almost swallowed up the room. Instantly, tears rolled down my face to protect me. "Ross!" I yelled in frustration before covering my mouth with my sleeve.

It would be a few moments before all the dust finally settled. Giving me time to check out the other guest we had sitting at the table. A boy no older than fifteen, whose golden locks and fierce eyes looked oddly familiar to me.

Where have I seen you before? I wondered, marveling at how oddly overdressed the Kid was. Given his current company, at least. Probably the financier of this whole thing, I concluded as the last of the dust settled around us, finally allowing this...whatever it was, to begin.

Seeking to set the tone of this little affair immediately, I blurted out, "You know, Ross, you could do well to clean the place more than twice a decade," before anyone else could speak.

"Can it!" Ross blustered back, shooting some spit in the process. The man was clearly not enjoying my candor. "You know why you're here." His head gestured to the well-dressed pauper beside us.

I didn't respond at first. Instead, I smiled to show him I got exactly the response I was looking for. It's so easy to get under this man's skin, I thought to myself, my smile widening even further.

Finally, I decided to get down to the matter at hand, leaning forward and staring intently at Ross before saying, "I assume this is some sort of transportation job?"

"Sharp as ever, Sir Jayce," Ross replied, adjusting himself in the seat in a vain attempt to make himself look taller. The man was trying to maintain some dignity now that he was in full business mode. "May I introduce you to...?"

I gritted my teeth at Ross's insistence upon referring to me by my old title. Bastard found the one thing that never fails to get under my skin, I conceded, raising my hand to silence him before he could further aggravate me. "I care not for the personal details," I said, making a point of not even looking at the Kid. "Just point me where I need to go and tell me when, I'll be on my way shortly thereafter."

Ross took a few short breaths to calm himself after my interjection. The man simply did not like getting interrupted. My lack of formalities did tend to ruffle some feathers, I reminded myself. Probably why jobs are so scarce nowadays.

"I figured as much," Ross said, slipping a thick manila envelope across the table. A huge dust cloud billowing in its wake. "I had this dossier prepared just in case you get bored one night."

Picking up the folder, I could feel its heft. It definitely had cash inside; the question is how much? "Half now, the rest upon completion," Ross said, as if reading my mind. Or at least the sour expression I was giving him, "per your usual."

Not wanting to waste a second longer, I quickly scooped up the envelope and stuffed it into my vest pocket. "Fine," I said to Ross, not even bothering to look at the Kid. "I'll leave within the hour. Where is the cargo?"

Upon my saying that, Ross's once-dour expression turned into a devilish smirk. Motioning to the blond boy who had been beside us, silent the entire time. His head remained down during the entire meeting. "He's sitting right next to you."

My head instantly snapped over, looking over the Kid with renewed vigor. He was an overall twitchy little thing, but he looked well-fed and taken care of—a rare combination for sure, I thought, my gaze going upward. His eyes, though, looked …familiar. Drawing me in, making me question things I had long since put to rest. Shaking my head, I refocused on the moment. Now's not the time, Jayce.

"I'm no babysitter." I huffed, reaching back into my vest to fish out the envelope. I had sunk low, I thought to myself, about to throw the envelope back onto the table. But Human Trafficking is a depth even I refuse to sink to! "Get someone else to be your nanny," I said, slamming it on the table before pushing my seat out from me. I will not stand for this!

"There's 20,000 in that envelope, Jayce," Ross called, causing me to freeze in my tracks at the mere mention of such a high number. My morals quickly going out the window. "You will receive an additional 5K from our contacts on Drifter Colony 17. Another 5k will come from an agent on Europa."

That's a lot of money, I thought to myself, my previous moral fiber quickly decaying.

"The final 10 will be rendered unto you when he is delivered safely to The Spartan Alliance."

Well, guess I really am the scumbag they claim I am, I mused, realizing it hit me hard. The promise of lots of money turned out to be a welcome salve. "40,000! The Spartans must be truly desperate to pay that much!" I said, looking over at the Kid again, our eyes locked. Eyes that pleaded with me, a very familiar plea. Why do I feel like I know him? "What's so special about the Kid?" I asked after shivering for no reason.

"Like I said before, it's all in the dossier," Ross replied, that crap stained grin now a permanent fixture on his face. He's enjoying this way too much. What did I do to piss this man off?

Shaking my head, I made a mental note to check whatever was in that godforsaken envelope once we had gotten off-world. "Fine, whatever," I said with a sigh, my body in a mad rush to get out the door.

I was about to cross the threshold back into the main room when I realized something. Where's the Kid? Only by looking back was I able to see the Kid still standing at the table. Stubborn little brat. "You coming or not, kid?" I asked him, throwing up my arms in frustration.

"I have a name," the Kid replied, his voice quivering with false bravado as he looked me straight in the eyes. "Orion"

Having long since passed the point of giving any sort of care, my response was a simple "Whatever, Kid." Who the Skeletor does he think he is? I pondered the audacity of this blonde-haired little shrimp, which caught me off guard. "Just get your stuff together and try not to slow me down, okay?"

"Yes, sir," he responded, his voice cold as ice, but his body rigid as a board. An action that seemed to be as if by reflex.

In an instant, I saw red. The Kid was pushing what I thought to be my only trigger. He just had to say one of the few things that could send me into a blind rage! "Rule #1," I shouted, my screams amplified as they bounced around this small room. "Don't EVER call me 'Sir!'

The Kid stood there, looking up at me, lost for words. I probably should have taken this as a cue to let off the gas but I was pissed and wanted everyone to know it. "I am no 'sir.' Something you shall soon find out."

The Kid continued to stand there, still seemingly taken aback by the harshness of my words. "I thought you said he was a knight?" the Kid said to Ross after a very awkward moment, somehow catching me off guard. "He carries himself more like a scoundrel than anything else."

How dare he? I thought to myself, my anger returning in full force just as it was starting to subside. My face was going red in the process. This kid needed to learn some manners. I began to rub my knuckles behind my back. Where did Ross find this brat?

Sensing the danger quickly brewing between The Kid and me, Ross quickly jumped up and got in the middle. Even he could see the rising anger painted upon my face. "Jayce has a past that is... complicated," Ross said, his usual dry diplomatic flair cutting through the tension like a hot slicer through lube. "He prefers to dwell in the present and not dig up old bones, isn't that right, Jayce?"

I sighed, taking my first breath in what seemed like forever, the anger finally leaving my body. "Sounds about right," I replied, still not wanting to even look at the boy. "But Rule #2, no questions about my past, we clear, Kid?

Now it was the Kid who sighed. He struggled to form civilized words. It was clear the boy was not used to being told what to do. "How many more 'Rules' must I abide by?" he asked at last, those cultured words finally finding him.

"Depends on how much you piss me off," I fired back. This Kid's pompous tone is seriously grating on my nerves. I thought, my teeth grinding in response to the frustration. Thankfully, it seemed his confidence was razor thin, as his eyes fell almost instantly. All it took was the simplest of pushbacks to get the Kid to crumble. Not too tough in the end, it seems, I thought gleefully.

The Kid stared at me for a moment. I could see the wheels turning in his head. He's deciding if I'm worth the trouble. The very notion that I was pleased with showing a 15-year-old kid who the boss was went straight over my guilt-ridden head.

Finally, after what seemed like an eternity but in reality was only a half-second, the Kid put his head down—officially admitting defeat. Yes! "Very well, lead the way, good..." he said, his voice trailing off at the realization of the final word. The Kid is learning.

Flash forward some 45 minutes; the ship was prepped and finally ready to go. The Kid was even strapped in, if not unwilling so. I was just about to hit the button to start the engines when I looked down to see Ross come running up onto the launch pad. "Son of a Mera!" I screamed, cursing the sheet-staining demon.

"Hold launch," I commanded A.I as I stepped away from the controls and began making my way off the ship. Whatever could the old codger want now? I wondered as I stepped off the ramp. "You do realize that you were five seconds from being roasted, right?" I yelled at the fool, the sounds of my footsteps getting louder as I increased my pace. "What is so blasted important?"

"This," he states simply, his wrinkled hand holding out some sort of data wafer for me to take.

Snatching it from him, I held up the thin piece of plastic between my two fingers. 'And what exactly is 'this'?' I ask, shoving the thing in his perfectly manicured face.

"The coordinates for Drifter Colony 17," Ross replied, his sick smile somehow growing even larger. "Figured you'd need them."

"And why wasn't this included in the briefing dossier?" I ask, glaring at him. How could he forget something so crucial?

Ross shoots me a sly wink. His face was as plain as crackers, but I could tell he was holding in a massive fit of laughter. "It is," he says with an even tone—the strain of doing so causing tears to start raining down from his eyelids.

Our eyes met, and at once neither of us could hold it in any longer, years of camaraderie breaking through our thick walls. The two of us descended into a fit of laughter that would make Lord Williams himself blush. Finally, after the ever-so-brief respite, I shot that old fool a death glare, roaring with all my might, "Get out of here, I have work to do!"

Knowing his time was done, Ross began to back away from me. Even the ones I know best, I keep at arm's length, I thought, a sigh escaping my lips. "Safe travels, good sir. Best of luck on the job," the fool says with another wink as he closes the bay door behind him. That bastard, he got in the last dig!

I'll need it. I turned my back and walked up the ramp. As it closed behind me, I felt a sudden shiver run over me as if this was the start of... something. What that 'thing' is, I had no idea, or even if it was real. It's just a job, Jayce, I reminded myself.

Nothing whatsoever important is going to happen as you transport this nobody.

Feeling better about myself, I went straight to the bridge so that I could properly start the ship, as well as this adventure.

2
Inn To The Fire Pit

"Are we there yet?" the Kid asked for what had to be the fifteenth time this hour. Does this thing have any sort of off switch? I wondered.

For two weeks, the Kid and I have been in space, two hellish weeks. The only thing he seemed interested in was following me around, asking questions about anything and everything. Did this boy ever leave his mother's bosom? I asked myself. My sanity was quickly slipping away from me.

To the Kid, all things seemed new to him. My first instinct was just to try and ignore him, but still, he persisted. Eventually, my sanity finally broke, and from there, I simply started to scream at him anytime he got close. That seemed to do the trick, but it only scared him off for a short while. Where have they been keeping this thing? I wondered, his extreme levels of naivety confounding me. No reasonable person, not even one his age, would act in such a way.

"Are we there yet?" he asked again, the Kid picking absolutely the worst time to pester me. At that moment, I was going over the Nav charts, a very important task that required my complete concentration, lest we get lost in space.

I can't do this, not a second longer will I suffer. My blood was boiling, and the anger inside me had finally reached its peak. "NO!" I roared, my patience having now well and truly been spent.

The Kid shrank back from my high-strung words, but he did not move a millimeter from where he stood. Bloody Hell, I thought to myself, staring at him in disbelief. Hell, in another life, I might have even been impressed. This kid is relentless.

The air between us grew cold and tense upon the conclusion of my tirade. The two of us were just staring at one another, begging the other to speak. "At least tell me what we are doing," the Kid asked after a long and deafening silence.

Maybe if I indulge him a bit, he'll shut up, I thought, taking a few moments to collect myself before speaking. "I'm checking over the Nav charts to see if we are still on course," I said to him, pointing to the rolls of paper that the computer had already spat out.

"Why are you doing that?" The Kid shot back almost instantly, causing my jaw to lock up almost instantly in frustration. It was either that or smack the tar out of him. I realized with a shudder.

I was not abusive by nature, or at least that's what I try and tell myself. But this Kid, he...brought certain emotions out of me. He has to be a punishment for my past misdeeds. It's the only explanation for my current misery.

"The Nav plots our course through Slip Space," I replied, attempting to maintain an even tone, given my current mood. "But even it can sometimes make mistakes."

I then gestured to the rolls of logs that my Nav computer had already generated. By this point, they had begun to spill onto the floor. Should have sprung for the wireless upgrade ages ago. "By checking over it and comparing it to the plotted course, I can correct any errors before they cause us to go too far off course." Finishing my speech with a sigh, I looked down at The Kid to see if his curiosity had been satiated. Please just shut up now. Please?

There was a long pause after I finished my speech. The two of us were just staring at one another, waiting for the other to blink. After what seemed like an eternity, the Kid smiled a sly smile, pausing for a moment to take it all in before saying. "What's Slip Space?"

Dammit, I thought to myself, scorning my weak will and empty stomach. You just HAD to take this job, didn't you, Jayce? I tried to turn away from him and get back to work. Not wanting to blow up on him, but knowing how close I was to doing so.

"Jayce, Jayce!" he said, poking my back with a steady rhythm. Each stab of his index finger took a year off my life. "You gonna answer my questions?"

"ENOUGH QUESTIONS!" I roared, my heart pounding with a steady mixture of stress and frustration. This Kid will just not shut up! "Room. NOW!" I screamed, practically pushing him out the door. Pressures from the prior weeks were finally boiling over.

Oddly enough, he did not budge, choosing instead to give me that same intense stare. The stare that seemed oh so familiar to me. One that, a lifetime ago, almost broke me. Where do I know that from? This Kid is getting weirder by the second. "Screw this" I say, throwing up my hands in frustration, and stomping out of the bridge in a huff. "I'm getting a drink. Don't follow me!"

Turning back, I gingerly looked over my shoulder. I was thankful to see that he hadn't followed me. Taking my softest steps in the hope that the Kid would not be able to trace me to the kitchen. My wish seemed to be granted when I noticed that he indeed had not entered the kitchen with me. Maybe The Kid finally got the hint? I wondered, knowing full well how wrong I was.

Taking in the fleeting silence that was still there, I enjoyed the peace I had worked so hard to obtain. If only for a few moments, all was right once again.

Not wanting to waste a single second of this blissfully serenity, I proceeded to grab a bottle of Phobos Hellfire Whiskey. Dem traitors sure knew how to brew a good swill, I thought before raising my glass in a toast. But who to toast? I wondered. Everyone I ever cared about is either dead or hates my guts...

"To the Emperor! Long may he reign!" I proclaimed to no one before downing my glass in a single gulp. The liquid brown irony burned its way down my throat as if it were doom eternal. "Ah, that's the good stuff," I said to no one before reaching over to grab the bottle so I could pour myself another glass.

As if on cue, The Kid walked in on me. Somehow, choosing exactly the wrong moment. Hearing everything I had just said, his face wore a mixture of confusion and disgust, taking one long look at me, then at my now-empty shot glass.

The Kid stood there in silence for a moment. His eyes squinted at me in disgust. "Why do you drink to that monster?" he shouted before spitting on my freshly cleaned floor. Disgusting, I thought to myself, shaking my head. I had this entire ship scrubbed clean a week before takeoff!

I sighed a long sigh, not to relieve stress but to prevent myself from strangling this mongrel. Just a few more weeks of this, and then you're home free, I reminded myself. The money I was earning and its temporary nature were the only things that were preventing me from murdering him on the spot. A notion that on some level sickened me to my core.

I never liked the person I became after the sacking. While I know it was a necessary evil to deal with the immense grief and the guilt that always threatens to consume me, I knew this rage fueled jock of a man was never me. The real me never left, it just got buried deep beneath the brimstone.

With my rage finally kept at bay, I turned to confront The Kid head-on. My own face now wearing a mask of its own, a mixture of confusion and disdain. "First off, you're cleaning that up," I said, tossing him a rag and a bottle of cleaning fluid. The Kid easily caught both in each of his hands. How the heck did he do that? I wondered before finishing my sentence. "Secondly, have you ever heard of the word 'Irony'?"

"I have," he replied. The Kid's words conveyed confidence, while his baby face betrayed the fact that he still had no clue what I meant. No kid can be this sheltered, I thought to myself while The Kid stared at both the rag and the bottle as if he had never seen them before. I'm starting to think perhaps he hasn't. Shuddering at the thought, suddenly a second drink sounded much more appealing.

"Then you have just answered your own question," I responded in an attempt to catch The Kid off guard. Taking another swig before he could answer, and quickly making my way out of the room. The plan was to do my rounds in relative peace, leaving him to clean up his mess in a state of confusion. Hopefully, that takes him a while, I thought, knowing somehow it wouldn't.

"You drink too much," the Kid shot back from the kitchen. My fast footwork proved insufficient to outrun his quick wit. Of course, he had to try and get in one last parting shot. My footsteps were getting shorter and louder at the mere thought of such insanity. Wanting to try and regain some face, I gave a huge belly laugh—a totally fake reaction in an otherwise effective attempt to offset his weak endeavor at an insult.

"When you've done as much as I have, kid, you tend to want to forget some of the finer details," I said, yelling back in the general direction of the kitchen. My eyes were neither looking back, nor my legs breaking stride in the process. How can someone be so fluent in Sass but not have any actual, real-life experiences? I wondered, the mystery of this kid getting ever so deeper.

What have I gotten myself into? I wondered, finally stepping back onto the bridge after having to deal with The Kid's sudden arrival of a spine. The greeting from Nav's computer as I entered the room filled me with glee. It's lovely chime being my sole source of comfort at the moment. The beeping signaling that we were close to our exit point. At last! I thought to myself, my confidence returning to me in an instant.

"Finally!" I exclaimed, shooting up from my seat at the Nav station. "Time for some real excitement." I was so happy to be doing something finally, I practically skipped over to the front of the bridge before hopping into the helmsman's chair like a kid on their name day. Looking over my shoulder, I smiled at the still-empty bridge. Happy to see that The Kid was nowhere in sight. I think I got a few minutes before...

"What's going on?" The Kid asked, his head popping up from behind the corner as if by clockwork. What the hell? I thought, flabbergasted at his seemingly uncanny timing. How does he do that?

Shaking my head, I turned forward, deciding it was better to focus on the task at hand. "Strap in, kid. We're about to exit Slip Space." I said in response, not even bothering to look at him this time.

A sullen silence washed over us as I began the exit procedures. The Kid is being way too quiet, I realized. Turning to look over at The Kid, hoping he had done what I asked. I was relieved to see that, thankfully, he had. Well, wonders never cease, I thought to myself, happy that he at least had some compliance in him.

Sadly, I did not have time to dwell on this minor victory. For that was work to be done and a job to do. Forcing myself to push that happy thought to the back of my mind. My attention returned to getting the ship out of Slip Space.

Pushing back on the lever, I felt the familiar jerk forward. Except this time it was accompanied by a very loud "Ow!" from off to my side. First time, huh? I mused to myself, a sly smile cracking across my face.

"Oh, by the way," I said to The Kid as he scrambled to get back into his seat. My face was not even trying to hide the joy at the sight of his suffering. "There is a slight jerk whenever you come out of Slip Space." My voice rose in pitch as I spoke.

I really shouldn't be deriving such perverse joy from his suffering, I thought to myself in a failed attempt to rationalize my shitty behavior towards the Kid. A cold wave of dread enveloped me as, for the briefest of moments, I saw just who I had become.

But on the other hand, he's just so annoying, I reasoned, the sudden wave of guilt washing out of me as quickly as it came in. All it took was the thinnest of excuses to absolve my mind of any guilt. Truly, I am a wondrous being.

"How come you didn't warn me beforehand?" The Kid asked, throwing some venom my way and clearly catching on to the fact that I messed with him on purpose. I still didn't care, really. His reaction annoyed me more than anything else. The Kid sure makes hating him so easy.

"You never asked," I replied, wearing yet another huge grin on my face. Outwardly, I was portraying the cold-hearted bastard I wanted everyone to see me as.

Mentally, however, I was struggling with self-disgust. No matter how many excuses I give myself, no matter what logic I try and apply. There has never been a thing in the past 15 years that has ever gotten rid of that feeling. That nagging nub in the back of my mind, telling me that I was wrong.

Well, there is one thing, I remembered drawing the hip flask from my waist. It's warm, tepid, haze quickly soothed my guilt.

Now self-medicated at the required levels of slosh, I realized I had been ignoring the squawk box for the past few minutes. Probably should answer them.

"Unknown ship: Identify yourself and state the purpose of your visit," a voice squawked over the loudspeaker. Its tone conveyed they were at the end of what little patience they once had. "You have 30 seconds to comply; otherwise, we will open fire." These people certainly don't fool around, do they?

"What?" The Kid exclaimed, his head whipping back and forth. Trying to find the source of the noise, "Who said that?" Has this kid ever gone off-planet? I wondered, his naivety was quickly becoming yet another source of annoyance.

"Relax, Kid," I replied, calmly flipping the switch for the outgoing transceiver. "This is standard procedure." I finished, shooting him a dirty look. "Now be quiet."

"Hello, this is Virgil Alligries of the Sindel." I squawked back at the announcer. My voice took on the most agreeable tone I could muster. "I got stuck with my nephew, Ed Dantes," I continued, reciting the spiel I had rehearsed weeks ago. "I'm taking him to a drifter colony so that I can show him the seedier side of the universe."

Rolling my eyes at the last bit, I couldn't believe that's what I had come up with. Who in their right mind is gonna believe this crap? I wonder, my hands instinctively moving towards the button that would warm up the weapons.

There was a long pause after that, my hand starting to cramp from hovering over the weapons switch for so long. Then, all of a sudden, "Whatever, maintain your current course and speed," the announcer said, and my hand instantly shot back from the switch.

My mind was not able to comprehend the level of passivity on display. H...how? "Follow the escorts when they intersect. They will guide you to the landing pad," the man said before promptly cutting the line. Letting out a breath I didn't know I had been holding, relief once again flowed into my body. Finally! Something goes off without a hitch!

"A warrior and a poet," the Kid said to me out of nowhere. "You truly are full of surprises, Jayce."

"What?" I replied, my neck craning over to look at the Kid. He had a puzzled look on his face. That made two of us, because for the life of me, I had no idea what he was going on about.

"The Count of Monte Cristo," he finally shot back after a few seconds of confusion. "The story of a man who takes on a duel with destiny to exact revenge on those who have wronged him." I didn't take him for a literate person. Shocked at his sudden outburst of competence.

Upon considering his entire comment, I realized only now what he had done. The Kid did not just work in a subtle jab with that compliment, did he? I asked myself, feeling that same old frustration begin to work its way back.

This kid might be more clever than I originally thought. I finally concluded, a sly smile cracking across my face. I'm gonna need to be more careful around him.

"There are many things about me that you don't know," I said, turning my head to look over at him, my expression shooting daggers straight at his heart. "And I prefer it to stay that way. I'm here to do a job, nothing more, and nothing less." My tone was chill, and my voice was even colder—the need to set the pattern of our... relationship becoming oh so clear to me.

The Kid's eyes dropped a bit with my words. And when they did, a sudden pang in my stomach quickly followed. What little remained of my humanity was screaming at me. Telling me I shouldn't be so cold.

As much as I tried to ignore it, I couldn't help but start to feel sorry for the Kid. Well, 'started' to the extent I was gonna allow myself anyway. Catching feelings for someone in your charge is never a good idea, I reminded myself, memories of past dangerous liaisons flooding my mind. The last time I did that, an entire kingdom fell at my feet.

"I see," he said after a long pause. The Kid seemed defeated. I was about to turn my attention back to the matters at hand when, out of the corner of my eye, I caught him. I caught The Kid muttering to himself under his breath. Something to the tune of "...far you've fallen...". That little shit did not just....

"What did you say?" I yelled. The frustration that had been building over the past few moments finally reached its peak, as my insecurities took full control at last. Did he just say...

"Nothing," The Kid meekly replied, before putting his head down, seemingly catching on to the rising tension, the tension he himself had caused.

Yeah, that's right, enjoy my good friend, shame. Feeling at last relieved, I breathed one last sigh before looking at The Kid. "Keep it that way, okay?" Besides, we are almost there," I said, turning back to him so that I could look at what was in front of me. "Not a peep, understand?" Looking at his reflection in the view screen window, I could see that he nodded in compliance. Good.

Gazing upon the colony, I could see that it was far larger than I had expected. This, of course, was understandable, as a drifter colony was nothing more than a mishmash of different parts from dozens of different worlds. What was once considered junk by some is now a vital part of a whole. Each piece is interlinked and heading towards a common goal.

Their doom, I mused to myself as I watched the ship complete its final docking procedures. At this point in the process, everything was automated, so I had very little to do. With nothing else to occupy my mind, I found myself thinking about the path I was on and whether I would make it out of this. I'm not gonna make it out of this one alive, am I?

To be fair, though, does anyone make it out alive? The finality of that last thought lingered upon my mind. Like a cancer, it would sit there in silence while the ship clicked into its final resting place.

"Sindel, you and all of your passengers are to proceed to processing." The same voice squawked over the comm. Its tone is still as cold and disinterested as ever. "You will receive temporary ID badges there. You are required to wear these at all times, with no exceptions." And just as quickly as he came on, he was gone.

Wow, these drifters really don't mess around. I mused to myself, the final steps in our docking at last taking place. Not even the Palace had this much security. And I ran it! A sly smile escaped my lips as I remembered better times.

"Best to do what the person says," I told the Kid, finally allowing myself to unhook from the pilot's seat. "Sounds like they enjoy their job a bit... too much." Reminds me of Anders. My mind recalled, pulling up memories of a person I had not thought about once since the night I betrayed everything I once was. How that sick bastard rose to the third seat is beyond me.

The Kid did not reply to my warning, at least not verbally. His response was to simply get in line, silently following me as we stepped off the ship. So he can be corralled! I thought, this realization gave me a much-needed boost as we took our first steps onto the station.

The first thing that greeted me was the smell. Oh god! That was my internal reaction. My nose instinctively crinkled in an effort to stem the tide. Sadly, it was for naught, as the smell of literally thousands of cultures mixing into one giant cesspool hit my senses in a putrid moment. How do people live like this? The mask I would now call a face was adopting a look of neutrality so as not to betray my actual feelings. Drifters tended to be a proud but delicate people. It wasn't my intention to start a conflict as soon as we arrived. That will come later, mark my words. So I figured it was best to do as the drifter does. At least for now. Reminds me of the Royal Court. They would cut off their finger if it offended their hand. Best to be cautious.

Ahead of us, I could see the customs office. Where we'd get processed and eventually let out on our way. A useless entity, but one good for appearances. Some things never do change, do they?

The Kid, in all his eagerness to move things along, attempted to sprint past me towards the office. "Wait just a minute!" I said to him, grabbing the boy by the scruff of his collar. Even though I was lifting him, the Kid still tried to run. His feet were dangling in the air like some sort of ancient cartoon. "You actually cleaned the kitchen, didn't you?"

As if to continue this comical display of ineptitude, the Kid turns his head to me and gives an awkward smile. "...Kind of?" He said it in the most drawn-out way he could manage.

Sighing a long sigh, I let The Kid go. "As much as I wanna kick your ass right now, we don't have time for that," I said to him, barely even noticing the crumpled heap that was his body.

"Were you always this big of an asshole?" The Kid said to me, gazing up towards me with disdain. His words cut me deeper than I realized they could.

"Not always," I responded, reaching down to help him up in a rare gesture of kindness. He did not take it. Instead, he opted to march towards the office on his own.

Perhaps I've gone too far? I wondered, The Kid's defiance waking something in me. No, it's The Kid who is wrong, I reassured myself, squashing back down that spec of humanity I could never seem to get rid of.

"Names and reason for visit?" The woman at the counter said to The Kid in a dry monotone voice.

"I am Virgil Alligries," I began, my breath heavy from having to double time so that I could catch up to him. "And this is my nephew, Ed. We're here to see..."

A bright flash engulfed me, followed by a mechanical whirl. What the Hades was that? I asked myself, seemingly blinded. My eyes took their time adjusting back to normal. When my vision at last cleared, two plastic cards were sitting on the counter in front of me. How did she print those so fast?

"Enjoy your stay. NEXT!!" The person behind the counter said, their voice as uncaring as ever. The two of us were quickly rushed out the door like the pieces of meat we were by two wiry fellows. I could probably take them, I thought, sizing up the two gentlemen beside me.

But with The Kid and I being on a timeline, fun was sadly not on the menu. Besides, I'm supposed to be here incognito, remember? I reminded myself. Fighting guards for no reason kind of defeats that purpose.

Upon crossing through the checkpoint's threshold. As I entered the station proper, a putrid smell assaulted my nostrils all at once. A smell that only seemed to intensify once we stepped onto the streets.

"I'd plug my nose if I were you, Kid. Kid?" I said, only to turn around and find him darting around the stalls like some damn pinball, leaving mess after mess in his wake "Oh for fracks sake!" I yelled before breaking into a sprint to chase the Kid down. I need to get a leash or something for this mongrel.

"Do you have Mushu p... He...Hey! What gives?" The Kid exclaimed as I grabbed his arm and dragged him off. The shop owner was shooting me a stare that conveyed a mixture of frustration, relief, and, somehow, empathy. She must think I have to do this all the time.

"Not here!" I told him, giving The Kid a dirty look of my own for good measure. Taking him aside, I looked around to see if anyone was staring at us before continuing. Thankfully, it seemed the two of us were in the clear, at least for now. "We will be there soon. Just shut up till then."

"Don't have to tell me twice," the Kid says, cowering behind me. His eyes cast into the alleyway off to our side. The Kid's rapid shift in demeanor caught me off guard, forcing my attention and bringing me out of my delusions and straight into guard mode.

Did he see something or… I wondered, my eyes darted back and forth up the busy street. Scanning it in a way only a seasoned member of the Royal Guard could. Something's not right, I concluded, going into high alert. But the question is...what?

I wouldn't have to wait long for an answer. All I had to do was look over my shoulder. Behind us, way out in the distance, were two men. Men wearing the costume of the Imperial Guard. Those two thugs were currently distracted with their favorite pastime, beating up a helpless shopkeeper. Ah, that explains a lot.

My first encounter with the reformed Shinkar Empire is going exactly as I thought it would. Looking down at The Kid, I could see the fear in his eyes. This is not his first time experiencing Imperial brutality, I realized. "Good Eye," I said to him, figuring a small compliment and a hand on his shoulder would help ease his nerves. It did, at least to some extent. His shoulders eased up, but the rest of his body remained rigid. "Quickly now," I whispered, gesturing to a nearby inn a few blocks away.

Somehow, we were able to make it. No sooner had the danger passed did The Kid resumed his usual shtick. Only this time, he added copious amounts of complaining to the routine. Who knew there were so many variations of the word "When"?

However, even with the Kid's best efforts to expose us, we managed to reach the Springfield Inn.

It must have been an especially slow day as the proprietor stood at the door to greet us. A solemn person at first blush, the woman's kind face was sharply contrasted by her bright outfit. She seemed on a lifelong quest to be covered head to toe in every shade imaginable.

Leading us to the front counter, I was surprised by the smell. The smell was… actually quite pleasing. Whatever was wafting into my nostrils was a most welcome change of pace from the petri dish that was this station.

Without missing a beat, she took my hand in hers. Catching me off guard with the kindness. The many beads around her neck quaked as she passionately shook my hand. Either I'm her first customer ever, or I found the nicest lady in the system.

"Hello, good sir!" The woman greeted us with a very pleasant voice. Her inflection washed over me like ultra-soft velvet, instantly putting me in a state of ease. "Welcome to my Inn, how may I serve you?" Her kind eyes looked up at me as she finished. A shade of watery teal, it evoked the sense of the most luxurious depths. This woman had surely seen things, but it was clear that she refused to let it dampen her spirit. I like this one.

My nose wrinkled at the mention of 'sir'. Usually, I'd say some sort of curt remark to regain the pecking order, but the woman's gesture so took me aback that I pushed that thought out of my mind. I chose instead to concentrate on the lovely lady in front of me. "My nephew and I will be staying with you for the next night or two," I said, once I had taken a long moment to regain my composure. An action I am sure she picked up on.

"Splendid!" She cheered, her eyes squinting as she put her hands together in excitement. Turning to look over at The Kid, he seemed just as enraptured with the woman as I was. His mouth agape, his posture rigid, and his eyes watery with admiration. It seems it's been far too long for us both since we last heard the voice of a good woman, I concluded.

While my head was turned and my attention distracted, the lady leaned in close. Whispering into my ear, "Be nice to serve a set of honorable folks such as yourselves." My attention instantly kicked into high alert.

How did she know? I wondered, my mind spiraling into panic. I knew the impression I gave off, and I would bet a considerable sum no one would say I was 'honorable' at first blush.

"Your boots," she said simply, probably catching on to the sheer terror quickly spreading across my face, and gesturing downward with her eyes. I looked and saw that the tips of my Royal Guard boots had the royal seal embossed on them. A detail that almost no one would care to notice. No one except her, it would seem.

I smiled at the compliment, my face going flush. "My pleasure," I said. I couldn't help but glance at the Kid, though. His hand was involuntary rubbing his stomach. We did skip breakfast... and lunch, I reminded myself. "Now, could you show us to our rooms?" Oh, do you serve Mu Shu Pork?"

To my surprise, it was not the Kid who instantly perked up in excitement, but the lady. For a brief moment, I thought she was going to scream in recognition like the waitress back at the Noodle Boodle.

Apparently, she was smarter than she let on. All it took was a short moment of silent excitement before her face returned to its normal, joyous state. "I'll have a plate sent up within the hour," she said, her face remaining cold, but her eyes betrayed the excitement of meeting new people. She motioned for us to follow, and follow, we did. Finally, some progress!

With that initial burst of excitement now past us. The walk up the Inn's many stairs was oddly quiet. "Your arrival was well-timed, good sir," the woman said as she led us up the many stairs, clearly trying to break the silence between us. "The Emperor himself is here for an inspection of the station." He's what?

Her words stopped me dead in my tracks. The mere mention of that name was enough to send me into a panic. My entire body went rigid in the process. "The Emperor is here?" I exclaimed, my voice cracking while I was still visibly shaking. Probably letting out more emotion than I should.

"I know, right?" she replied, the cheer in her voice being almost unmistakable. Thankfully, it would seem she mistook my apprehension for admiration. "Most of the Inns are booked up with guards." The lady continued, not missing a single beat. "We have our fair share, but I still have a few rooms left."

Of all the places he could be, why here? I wondered, that thought lingering in my head. Like a splinter of the mind. "Will he be here long?" I asked. My voice was still quivering somewhat. There are few people in The Traverse, I fear. Emperor Elrick is damn near top of that list.

The woman didn't answer right away, my anxiety growing as she seemed to concentrate on her task. Leading the Kid and me down a rather long hallway. How big is this place? I asked myself. Going by the distance traveled, we must be three to four doors down by now.

Finally, after what seemed like a five-minute walk, we had arrived at what appeared to be our room. "Not too much longer," she replied, her hand moving down her apron as she rummaged for the key. "I believe he will be delivering a speech tomorrow."

"A... a speech?" I stammered. This is quickly becoming the worst-case scenario. Against my emerging emotions, I forced a smile. Trying not to give away any more suspicion than I had to. Just play it cool, Jayce.

"Yup, the entire station is currently on high alert," she said, seemingly oblivious to my behavior. Oh, thank Bowie! The woman smiled as she found the key she was looking for. "The guards are really on edge. The whole lot seems like they are just waiting to shoot someone."

We're doomed.

The woman sighed at the thought, holding up the key in front of us. "Better mind your Ps and Qs!" The lady said with a wink and a smile, before handing over the key.

"I'll take that into consideration," I said with a wink of my own, gently grabbing the key so that I may at last take possession of it. What the Hades am I gonna do now?

Looking around the empty hallway, the woman searched for something to say to break the tension. "This is where we part," she said at last with a quick flourish of her hand. "Have a wonderful night, gentlemen!" And then with nothing more to say to either of us, she promptly turned and left.

"Come on, kid, get in," I told the Kid, ushering the boy inside once the woman had left. Shows over… for both of us. "Best we turn in soon, got an early morning start ahead of us."

"Yes s..." the Kid said as he entered the threshold of the door. Did he just? Catching himself, The Kid turned around to look at me upon realizing what he had said, putting on his best impression of a cute kid. He really thought wearing a forlorn look was an acceptable apology?

"Kid, you'd better learn quick," I said in response, heading in so that I could conduct a quick survey before he arrived. "I'm not going to play around much longer."

The room was a spartan affair at best. With just two beds, each with a trunk at its foot, and a tiny desk in the corner being the only adornment. Reminded me of my pledging days, I thought, a warm wave of nostalgia washing over me as I looked over our accommodations. My mind drifted back to the time when I put myself through literal hell—all that pain just for the hope of joining such an elite squadron as The Shadow Hawks.

Things are nothing like it is now, I mused, once again casting myself back to a simpler time—a time when I knew what was right and could tell what was wrong. Back then, we had honor, oh, how naive we all were.

"Jayce, I'm taking the window bed," the Kid proclaimed all of a sudden, yanking me away from a trip down memory lane, remembering the embrace of the woman who made it all bearable. Oh, how sweet things once were.

"You will do no such thing!" I said to him, mostly out of reflex. At this point, I was beginning to get used to his shenanigans. Am I getting...familiar? I wondered, shuddering at the thought.

While I was lost in my own delusions, the Kid seemed to have wasted no time whatsoever. Looking over, I saw that he had already unpacked half of his things into the trunk. With a huge shit eating grin, he motioned to the trunk, then to his bag. "You sure about that?" was all he said. Judging by his expression, he knew he had already won.

Damn it.

"Fine, whatever, just keep it down," I said to him, too tired to really care any longer. "Lights out in 20." The Kid is learning.

At this point, I just want the day to be over more than anything. Thus, I began to unpack my belongings as quickly as possible. Leaving out the things I knew would be needed for tomorrow's... excitement. The Kid has no idea what's in store for him. How could someone go so long in this Traverse and still be so ignorant?

Glancing over at him, I wondered who coddled him before me. It was only then that I caught him staring at a photo, tears streaming down his face. "What's the matter?" I asked more out of curiosity than actual concern. "You miss your favorite hooker?"

"MIND YOUR BUSINESS!" The Kid roared, his nostrils flaring with indignation, before promptly turning his back on me.

I wasn't intending to insult him; I was just curious, I thought, though even I knew what came out was anything but friendly.

"Am I interrupting something?" A familiar voice broke me from what remained of my guilty conscience, causing me to sit up on the bed and confirm who had just entered the room. I was happy to see the lady from before, the one who had led us up to the room. She seemed to be beaming, holding out a tray of steaming hot food. "Your pork," she said, her voice calm as ever. The woman's eyes gestured down towards the glistening food in her arms.

Part of me in that instant just wanted to jump up and hug her. Haven't had a decent meal in years. My stomach, at this point, was more used to scraps than proper nutrition.

"Thank you for retrieving it so quickly," I said, trying to play it cool, but my rumbling stomach betrayed how grateful I was for the food. "Put it on the desk, we'll start on it momentarily."

"As you wish," she replied with a smirk, putting the tray down in its requested place. I think she's caught on to my infatuation, I thought with horror. Then, as if she read my mind, the woman gave me a very obvious wink. She then promptly curtsied and left, leaving me in an utter state of confusion upon her wake.

"She's nice. Don't kill her," the Kid said to me, his back still turned, snapping me out of my nostalgic daze and bringing me back into the present. I already want to go back.

Still, though, I was not expecting any kind of comment from him. Where the Hades did that come from? I wondered. "Don't be silly, Kid," I said, shooting a death glare back at him before sitting down to eat my food. "I very much doubt she will get in our way."

Taking the covering off, I breathed in a big whiff so I could take it all in. The tray itself was lavishly decorated. Not only was there the finest pork, but also a bowl of lentil soup and the requisite crackers. To wash it all down were two cans of some generic cola, and finally, for the grand finale, two bowls of sweet custard sat on either side. Truly a feast for a prince.

"Wasn't that sent up for me?" the Kid asked, his mouth mere inches from my ear, causing me to nearly jump out of my skin in the process.

The mistake I made was, in my indulgence, I had failed to notice the Kid come down from his bed and make his way over to me. Clearly attracted by the smells on display, he somehow managed to sneak up on me. Placing his head on my shoulder. Easy to sneak up on someone when they are so deeply distracted. I concluded.

Reluctantly, I gathered all the food and handed it to him. Portions that, in hindsight, were clearly meant for two people. In the moment ignorance or willful withholding? I thought to myself, wondering if I had held food back from The Kid without even thinking about it. Truly, you can't be THAT monstrous, Jayce.

In my defense, I rarely got to eat this good. Being a mid-tier merc definitely didn't leave me the lap of luxury, so I certainly made sure to savor every bite.

To my surprise, a note had been sandwiched between the cans of cola. Upon finishing my last gulp, I turned my attention to it. The thing was surprisingly short, consisting of only two lines.

Pig's Belly: 2:00 PM TST

Bring the Kid.

Seeing that last line, an exasperated sigh escaped my lips. My hopes to lock the Kid in this very room seemed to have been dashed. Instead of stuffing him here while I went to the meeting, I'd have to bring him along. This... complicates things.

Sighing again, this time in discontent, I quickly disrobed before jumping into bed. More than anything, I was eager to end this evening. "Lights out, kid!" I said, clapping twice to shut off the lamp in the corner.

"Sleep well, Jayce," the Kid said with a surprising amount of sincerity.

I didn't reply because I really didn't know how. Kindness was a long-forgotten concept to me. Thankfully, I wouldn't have to dwell on it for too long. The long-sought sleep soon took hold of me.

3
Escape From The Frying Pan

"Morning, Kid," I said to him. Watching as he barreled down the stairs. His balance wavered a few times, mere moments from a crippling accident. The Kid was clearly not looking where he was going. How does he not trip over his own feet? "I was wondering when you'd decide to get up,"

"I... I didn't see you when I woke." The Kid said, stammering his words. His eyes filled with panic as he looked over at me once he stepped onto the ground floor. "So I started to freak out."

"I'm your escort," I replied, my voice not showing even the slightest bit of concern. Right now, I was more concerned about the food in front of me, taking another bite of the delicious omelet I had ordered long before The Kid decided to wake up. "Not your nanny." I finished, taking another bite in order to hammer my point home. "Man up." Does this kid even have a mother?

The Kid stared at me, his brain seemingly dumbfounded by my response. After a good solid moment (His brain rebooting perhaps?) His eyes finally looked over at the food in front of me. The Kid looked as if he had never before seen food in his entire life. What the?

Instantly, his mouth began to water. His face took on the look of a ravenous dog, staring at its favorite treat. "Where's my food?" he asked me after a very uncomfortable silence. His eyes fixated on my eggs. This is starting to get a bit...weird.

It's way too early for this. I thought, a sigh escaping my lips. "You tell me, Kid," I said after allowing myself a few free bites. Shooting him a look of contempt right back at him before he sat down in front of me. "Did you want to order anything?" I asked him, trying to break The Kid from this ravenous visage sitting in front of me.

"I have no money." The Kid replied, his mind suddenly snapping back to reality. His ears turned a bright shade of red as he suddenly developed an intense fascination with his shoes.

He can't be serious! The mere notion that I would be paid to protect someone who didn't have any money themselves seemed practically preposterous to me. "You're messing with me, right, Kid? Kid?" I said to him, panic filling my voice before quickly being replaced by rising anger.

The Kid's face went utterly catatonic at my words. His eyes adopted the same thousand-yard stare that I often did. The Kid is clearly remembering something traumatic. I realized, empathy somehow filled the void I once called my heart. "I lost it all that day. The money, mother, everything." The Kid said in repose, his voice barely more than a whisper.

That answered that question, I concluded; my hand was developing a sudden urge to reach out and comfort him. But why? Why do I even care? "What day was that?" I asked, doing everything in my power not to make a fool out of myself while at the same time my curiosity getting the better of me.

"NONE OF YOUR BUSINESS!" The Kid roared in anguish, his outburst taking me by surprise. Must not have been too long ago if he is reacting this way. Part of me wanted to rip his head off, the other half wanted to hold him. But before I could do either, he stomped over to sit at a table on the far side of the room.

Well screw you then! I thought, watching The Kid finish his display of immaturity. To my surprise, though, the anger I felt inside of me quickly subsided. Replaced with a slight sense of pity, a foreign feeling for sure.

Looking over at The Kid in the corner, he seemed lost and unsure. Like a lamb unknowingly sent to the slaughter. Don't want the pipsqueak collapsing on me at the worst possible moment. So against my better judgment, I flagged down the waitress who had served me earlier. "Coffey, could you send a bowl of oatmeal over to the poor fool in the corner? Put it on my tab."

"Of course," she replied, her smile as sweet as ever. "That's very kind of you to do so, sir."

Kind, I thought to myself as I watched the woman walk away. Now that is a word I have not heard describe me in some time. Not since...

"Yikes!" I yelped in surprise. Glancing down at my watch once the waitress had fully left to fetch The Kid's food. The hands showed the time: 12:36. No more food for me! I thought before scrambling off to make the final preparations.

Ten minutes later, with my tasks complete. I barreled down the stairs with a skip in my step. That will be a new record, I realized. Not since my boot days have I cleaned myself up so quickly. Elias would be proud of me.

My joy was soon to be shattered, sadly. For as soon as I stepped back onto the ground floor, The Kid was all I saw. Still in the corner, except this time he had Coffey for company. "That boy sure does love him some attention," I said under my breath in between some very heavy sighs.

"So there I was in a street not unlike the one outside, now I'm all alone. Finally, I turned and yelled...Hey! I was just getting to the good part!" A very startled Kid yelped in shock as I grabbed his arm and dragged him out of the Inn. We do not have time for stories!

"Loose lips sink ships," I said to The Kid, opening the door for both of us. Does this kid know anything? I wondered, his naivete quickly becoming a liability. "While I am sure it's a riveting story," I told him, the two of us crossing the threshold. "We gotta go." The bright light assaulted us as we stepped into the artificial daylight.

Knowing what we were heading into. I gave The Kid a final once over, his blonde hair arrayed in its usual curls. Now that I had a chance to actually look at him, I was aghast to see what he was wearing.

The Kid had picked out a garish metallic gold speckled jacket over a light blue tunic. *I will burn that thing once we leave port.* I noted to myself. Trying to swallow the fury that was currently welling up inside of me. At least his brown cargo pants were of a more pedestrian variety.

"Why the sudden interest in my appearance, Jayce?" The Kid asked. "Are you starting to actually care?" Chiding me as I finished inspecting him.

"Not really, Kid," I replied coldly, trying not to give away that I did care. If only in the slightest. "I'm just making sure that you look presentable."

"You finally read the packet!" The Kid said sarcastically, "Congratulations!" His voice was practically dripping with glee. *Big mouth for someone who would die without me.*

"Not really," I responded with even more chill in my voice. Desperate to regain control of this situation. "I've just dealt with a lot of people in my life."

I paused, looking around to see if anyone was watching us. Thankfully, there was not. "I know how these sorts of things go." Giving him a look as I finished up, hoping that this time he'd get the hint. "Come on, Kid, let's get this over with."

With that little inconvenience out of the way, it looked like we were finally able to set off. With only having an hour to get to the destination, it was best we make haste. *I just hope it isn't too fa-*

"MY NAME IS ORION!!" The Kid roared, breaking me from my train of thought. What now? I thought, looking around to see where he had gone off to now. He lose a button or something? My question was soon answered as I looked back to see The Kid standing just over 15 paces in the distance.

Is he TRYING to piss me off? I wondered, furiously marching back. With the gap closed, I grabbed The Kid by the scruff of his collar. Dragging him kicking and screaming into a nearby alleyway.

"We do NOT have time for this!" I said, snapping at The Kid. It took every ounce of my willpower not to explode. No matter how much I wanted to, I knew I needed to maintain at least some semblance of control.

Of course, The Kid tried to open his mouth to protest. Enough of this, I thought to myself. Feeling the dark urges inside of me, finally starting to win over. An unwilling smile formed at the side of my mouth as I gleefully wrapped my fingers around the boy's tender neck. Lifting him upwards for all to see.

"Let's get something straight, kid," I said, the raging inferno burning a hole in my eyes. "I am getting paid damn good money to transport you which means that you are hot property." The Kid looked down at me. Fear finally filled his eyes as he at least realized what he had awoken.

Oddly enough, I drew no satisfaction from his fright. My desire is not to harm him. But to make him understand. Some tyrant I am, can't even torture someone correctly. Taking a deep breath, I returned my gaze to him. This time, wearing a less angry but still dead-serious expression. "You carelessly telling the entire station who you are will only serve to get you killed," I said, still holding him high.

"Now you see, I get paid regardless, dead or alive," I said, the lie coming off my tongue easily while I continued the spiel. Oddly, though, my fingers found themselves losing their grip on his throat. The motivations are more driven by guilt than a desire to make a point.

"Since I stand to gain more from you still being alive you sack of shit, I am inclined to keep you that way," I said as our stares locked. Both of us were waging a silent battle for dominance. "But don't think I am not above taking the easy way out of this." That last bit sealed the deal, The Kid's eyes going downward in defeat. "Grunt twice if you understand."

"Fronk...WOOO!" The Kid gurgled, attempting an insult.

"How cute," I replied, my smugness reaching an all-time high. "I'll take that as a yes," I said before releasing him.

The Kid crumpled to the ground in a heaping mess. It's almost as if he had been partially cut off from oxygen for the last few minutes. I thought to myself, a gulp escaping from me. He looked at me and got up, defiance creeping back in while he cradled his neck, his only response to my violence being "You are a horrible person."

Huh, he finally caught on. I thought, feeling pretty good about myself, until the realization of what I had just done hit me like a two-ton pipe. Shame washed over me, my head lowering itself, staring at my hands with internalized horror. What have I become? I wondered Have I truly fallen this far?

But at least you are getting results. I thought, feebly trying to justify my actions and looking back at The Kid, wondering if he had truly fallen in line (he had).

With that little bit of nasty business taken care of, I could actually start doing my job and checking the streets for anything iffy. The realization of what exactly I had gotten myself into finally hit me. The Verse truly hates you, Jayce. You are being forced to protect that which you hate most, yourself. As a result, I could not help but expel a very nervous laugh at the irony of it all.

"Kid, one thing you will eventually learn is that in this world..." I said to him, still desperately trying to justify my shitty behavior, gesturing to the filth around me. "...is that to be kind is to be dead, only the strong survive, compassion died out nearly fifteen years ago." Along with my honor, "Now come, we are running late."

Upon the two of us finally reaching the establishment, I could see the thing was aptly named. The place truly did look like the inside of a pig's belly. The smell alone would be enough to give it its name. A putrid odor that could only be described as if every lowlife in the station had gathered in one place at the same time. Then

The smell, OH MY LORDS the smell! Let's just say that it made the rest of the station seem like a basket of freshly cut roses by comparison. It seemed as if every person on the station collectively defecated at the same time, in the same place.

Of all the times to leave my hanky back on the ship, I choose now, I thought to myself in disgust. Cursing my lack of foresight. No use dwelling on what should have been Jayce. I shook my head to bring things back into focus.

With my head now back in the game, I made a beeline for the bar. "Scotch on the Rocks," I said to the bartender, flipping him a gold coin—anything to drown out this smell.

"Right away, sir," The Bartender replied, the sarcasm practically dripping from his mouth as he spoke. Not wanting to start a bar brawl, at least not so soon, I reluctantly gritted my teeth. "And what for your companion?" The Bartender continued, gesturing to the side of me.

It was only then did I realized that The Kid had planted himself on the stool right next to mine. His dopey face stared up at me like some sort of hungry dog. I wanted to say something mean and nasty to him, but I found that I didn't have the heart to do so. The only reaction I could manage was to roll my eyes in frustration.

For a brief moment, I contemplate smacking The Kid upside the head. Might as well get him something to shut him up at least, I finally concluded, the thought being that if he were too busy burying his face in a drink, he'd be too busy to bug me.

"Sarsaparilla," I say to the Bartender. The need for secrecy was winning out over my unhealthy thirst for violence. Well, that, and I'm also getting really tired of playing the asshole. I thought, but sadly, what I wanted and what needed to be done were two very different things.

"Thank you so much, Jayce!" The Kid said with glee, his innocent enthusiasm breaking through my walls ever so slightly. Causing me to chuckle, even if only a little bit. "I've never had alcohol before!"

Turning to look at him, I felt a devilish grin break out over my face. He truly doesn't know, does he? Thinking of all the different ways I could mess with him. I figured just saying to him straight would have the greatest effect: "It's root beer." I said, making sure to give the boy a cocky smirk to make sure he got the message.

His eyes went wide at the reveal. For a moment, he just stared at me in disbelief as I simply shrugged and kept drinking. After a few awkward seconds he seemed to snap back to his usual cocky self. Taking a huge swill while he looked at me, giving me a wink before saying, "Still tastes good."

With the Kid satiated and an oddly wholesome moment shared between us, I finally had the time to seek solace in my drink. That turned out to be the worst thing for me, as no sooner did I have a moment to myself, I started pondering my lot in life.

Staring into the kind of abyss that only scotch could provide. My mind went to thoughts I had always tried very hard to avoid. How did things get this...bad? I wondered, the aches and pains of fifteen years on the run always present. How can one choice lead to a lifetime of misery? That one question was one I asked myself so often, but could never really answer.

Will I ever know? I wondered, these...concerns were never far from the surface of my mind as much as I tried to run from them. All it took was a strong drink for them to come back and confront me. This is why I try to get smashed as little as possible.

The world before me seemed bleak and uninviting. Sadly, it was cowardice that kept me on this mortal coil. The same cowardice that had caused me to flee, abandoning all that I ever knew and loved. Will I ever find that person I once was? I wondered, that fear was threatening to swallow me whole. Thus, with seemingly no other option. I dived headfirst into my drink.

It was in the process of drowning my sorrows that my gaze seemed to take on a life of its own. Without knowing exactly what, they seemed to be drawn to something... no, someone else.

Who is this angel? I wondered. My mouth stopped agape as I stared at her, not sure if it was the cut of her dress or her general demeanor. My eyes could not help but be sucked in by her grace. Even The Kid seemed taken aback by her. His head did a double-take as she passed by. He looked at her as if he knew the woman, but couldn't place where he had seen her before. She does seem oddly familiar.

At this point, my mind was made up. In a room full of beautiful women, this person was an angel. As she marched towards the bar, she glanced back and forth, working the room like the pro she was. Everyone and everything fell to her touch. Drinks were offered, pleas were made for pleasure, yet she rejected each and every one of them. Then her eyes met mine, and time itself stopped. I didn't know they still made woman like her.

All at once, my world turned upside down as she made a beeline for... me. The entire time she approached me, our eyes never left one another. What is happening to me? I thought, my body clearly not used to being this lovesick. I haven't felt this way since… my thoughts trailing off as they rang through a now empty head. I shouldn't be falling like this...

"Hey, stranger," said the Dame, her voice smooth as silk, greeting me as she walked up to the bar. She looked at me, my mouth agape like an idiot. Then she looked down at my drink. "Good, it's working," she said with a smirk.

What does she mean by that? I wondered, part of me starting to get worried about what was happening. Much to my growing dismay, her mere presence was somehow enough to force out any sense of logic I could grasp. "You look out of place." She asked me, her hand lightly brushing up against my thigh. "Need a guide? I am...very helpful to have along."

For a moment, I stood there in a stunned silence, not sure how to respond. Part of me was still panicking at this clearly artificial feeling. Another part of me just wanted to know what the Hades is going on. "I'm sure you are," I replied, not exactly sure where I was going with this. "The question is, how much?" What the hell, Jayce? THAT WAS YOUR RESPONSE?

"S...sure." I stammered, my mind seemingly going blank in response. Wha...what's happening? I wondered, my mind starting to fuzz over. It was only then that I looked down at the drink and saw the nearly spent tablet at the bottom. Of course.

"Splendid," she said, grabbing the drink from my hand. "We won't need this anymore." She gently pulls it away from me. Then, without saying another word, she crooked a finger, and like the drugged-up dog I am, I followed.

The fog of bliss did not last long, sadly, for it wasn't even five steps in before she turned back to me, saying with a puzzled look on her face, a look that by no means she had per-rehearsed for hours the previous night, "And what about the boy?"

What boy? I asked myself, my mind almost completely fuzzed over. As if by instinct, my eyes darted to my side, seeing a young man look at me with a troubled expression. Oh, him… For some reason, this caught me off guard. Why is he looking at me like that?

"The Kid?" I said after taking a moment to gather what little of myself was left. "He'll be fine while we're gone." At that moment, what remained of my good sense started ringing alarm bells. Part of me was content to stay in this hazy dream state, marveling over my good fortune. The other part was wondering how I could so easily fall under the spell of a woman's beauty. Or was it something else that has me so taken?

"Dammit" She said, glancing over at The Kid, seeing his concern for me. Looking down at the glass, panic seemed to set in for a moment.

Putting herself back together at record pace, the Dame looked me deep in the eyes, running her fingers softly through my hair to draw me in close. "Hun, you need to know something."

"And what is that?" I asked, still not sure what to make of the moment. The reality was painfully put in place as the Dame grabbed my hair, using it to pull me even closer to her face. The pleasure of the moment suddenly turned stark. What the? What's happening? I thought, my faculties coming back to me all at once.

To my surprise, a face that mere moments before had been a beautiful maiden now showed only the hardened glare of a soldier. "Listen, bucko," she said to me, the eyes that once shot hearts my way now only brought steel. "One: You're late. Two: We need to do this as quickly as possible." She took a breath before motioning to the bar around us. All eyes were now on the two of us. "We are attracting too much attention already, understand?" Not knowing what else to do, I nodded in compliance. How did this just happen?

"Good, now go grab the boy." She said, managing to eke out a slight grin among a face of sheer frustration. Who is this woman? I wondered, the whiplash of the situation still leaving me reeling. Knowing the answers weren't going to be found here. Plus, it's best not to upset her further. I quickly did as she 'asked'. The Kid, after seeing the display, had no objections to being collected. The two of us were quickly ushered towards a small room off the main hall. Waving us in, all of us quickly entered.

The room seemed quaint when compared to the hustle and bustle of the bar just outside, its comfortable arrangements conveyed a space built more for pleasure than simply…

"HOW DO THEY BREATHE IN THESE THINGS!?" The Dame screamed, shaking me from my musing and causing my attention to focus back on her. My inner rambling was interrupted mid-thought to see the woman who had just, mere moments ago, almost made me a monk.

Now this same woman stood before me, half naked. Having ripped off her corset as soon as the door was shut, leaving not a stitch to cover her upper body. "Ah, much better." The woman said, seemingly relieved. Taking in what seemed to be some very deep breathes.

"Shall we begin, mister...?" She asked, before she noticed my wanting eyes. "Your eyes drift any lower than my chin, I'll knife you." She quickly added, twirling the blade around her neck.

"The names Alligries, Virgil Alligries." I responded, trying to sound all suave and sophisticated, but ended up just stammering in response to her threat.

The Dame stared at me for a moment. Trying to figure me out. It was clear she knew somebody would be accompanying the Kid, but she did not know who. But whoever she expected, I was certainly not it. Am I ever what people expect?

"Riiiiight," she said at last after finally checking out every inch of me. "Well, anyway, Mr. Alligries, I am sure you know why we are here," she continued, walking right past me in order to sit on the bed.

"Um, actually no," I said, earning a dropped jaw for my reply. She definitely was not expecting that! I thought to myself as I swelled with a sense of unearned pride.

As she continued to stare at me in utter disbelief, I could feel my rapidly rising ego just as quickly shrink. This isn't going very well. My nerves are at last catching up with me, causing me to shiver. "You should have gotten a packet when you picked up the boy." She said at last. "Surly you must have read through it by now?"

Panic instantly set in as I realized exactly what it was that Ross Johnson had given me a few weeks prior. "I did…" I said hesitantly, my mind scrambling for an excuse. "I just haven't gone through it yet," was all I could come up with. Jayce, you moron!

Somehow, her jaw managed to drop even lower at my words. "You have to be kidding me." She replied, her voice starting to growl as it rose in both anger and pitch. "No one is that lazy."

I wasn't sure how to respond, so I just stood there. A mixture of guilt and fear freezes me in place. "How can you call yourself a Merc if you can't do the required prep work?" The Dame asked me after taking a moment to gather herself.

Not knowing how to handle the situation, I intrinsically fell back into the only role I knew how to play—the one role that people had come to expect of me the past fifteen years: The Asshole. "I prefer the term 'serial procrastinator'," I replied, a sly smile escaping from the corner of my lips.

Her arms shot up into the air in frustration at my comments. My words have their intended effect. The Dame then marched over to the nightstand in a huff, fishing out a fancy box. "I really shouldn't be doing this." She said, still rummaging around in the drawer.

"But I really don't have a choice in the matter." She said, shoving the box into my arms as hard as she could. I'm sure she intended for me to flinch, but I did not move an inch. "This box contains sanitized identities that will get you past any Imperial checkpoint," she said to me, looking straight into my eyes as she did so, just daring me to say something. Instead, I just continued to smile, which somehow just made her even madder.

"Luckily, there is one not too far from here," she said at last, finally admitting defeat in our impromptu stare down. Her eyes broke away from me, drifting out to the window, gazing out into the depths of space. "Probably why we get inspected so often."

I wasn't really interested in her sudden realization. So instead of being a decent human being and attempting to comfort her. I chose the easy route, ignoring her completely. Looking down at the ornate box she had shoved into my arms, I started to study it.

The thing seemed to be made of some sort of heavy, dark wood. Golden leaves are embossed along their edges. The box itself fits neatly into my palm. Definitely expensive, I thought to myself, looking down at it. However, all that studying still left me feeling lost and confused.

I was just about to open my mouth so that I could question the gift. But the Dame was quick to beat me to the punch. "On this station," she began, placing a finger over my mouth. Her eyes locked into mine, staring at me with burning intent, "It is customary for whores to give out a token of affection for a 'job well done'."

She placed her hands over mine, closing my grasp on the ornate box. "It's supposed to help promote repeat business or something equally ridiculous," the Dame said, pausing for a moment as she saw my face, guessing my next question before quickly adding, "Yes, your pay is inside." After which, she rolled her eyes.

"Thank you so much," I say in the most sarcastic tone I could manage. I took one last glance at her breasts before looking at the door. "I guess we'd better be off then."

At my words and my gaze, the Dame sprang into action, eagerly opening the door to show us the way out. "And not a moment too soon, the Emperor's speech will be starting soon," she said, giving me a death stare the entire time. You two should be able to slip out fairly easily."

"Till we meet again, milady," I replied to her, tipping the brim of my hat like some sort of arrogant self aggrandizing moron while we all filed out.

Her eyes go wide at my insult. The Dame clearly looked like she wanted to slug me, but the importance of the mission won out over her desires. Instead, she vigorously shook her head and grabbed my hand into her own. Squeezing it tight, almost to the point of pain." I am no lady, the name's Fur," she said as I just looked at her with the same dumb grin I had the entire time. Seemingly oblivious to the pain she was trying to inflict.

Returning her gesture. I took her hands into my own, holding them tight. "Alright then, Fur," I replied to her, squeezing her palms together something fierce. Fur leting out a yelp as the three of us reached the door to the common room. "Farewell." Don't start something you can't finish, I thought to myself, swelling with macho pride.

While the three of us had only been gone a few moments, the room itself… looked just as jam-packed with people as it did before, if not more so. The big difference was that they were all fixated on one thing, that being the Emperor's Speech. Crap, I forget he was here, I thought to myself with horror. I could not escape Emperor Elric's face. The thing was being played out on every screen.

Judging by the man's cadence, he seemed to be in the middle of his speech. "As I say this to you all, the lives you lead will continue to flourish under my rule. The regulations my father placed will hinder you no more!" Are they really gobbling up this grek? I thought to myself, casting my eyes upon the now captive audience. "Freedom is the operative word! And freedom is what I have granted you!" Humanity is forever a sucker it seems.

Shaking my head in amazement, I could not help but think to myself, That prick always did have a gift for the gab.

Figuring it was best to take advantage of the situation, I made a beeline for the door with the Kid in tow... wait? Ah, hell, he's over by the bar staring at the screen.

"Come on, kid," I said, grabbing The Kid's arm in an attempt to drag him away. He didn't budge. "We need to go." Instead, he just stood there, solid as a stone, transfixed by what the Emperor had to say.

"I've never actually seen him before." The Kid mumbled, His eyes and ears glued onto the screen. Seemingly transfixed by whatever that rat bastard had to say.

"We need to go, NOW!" I replied, trying again to steer him away, jerking his arm a bit harder. But it was no use. The Kid just stood there, unmoved by even me.

"Who are you to deny him the voice of the Emperor?" A drunk man said out of nowhere. The fool stumbled up from his stool to get in my face.

"I'm his caretaker," I replied calmly as I could. Not trying to escalate the situation any further. "And we have an appointment to make."

The drunk did not take that well. His nostrils flaring, his eyes glaring. "The Emperor's word goes above ALL!" He yelled, winding up his arm and clearly preparing to try and take a swing at me.

Before I could fully take in the situation, my training kicked in almost instantly. Without a second thought, I nimbly ducked under his reach. Needing to end this quickly, I gave the fool a quick punch to the gut. Any food or drink the idiot had consumed quickly came back up. The chunks falling from his mouth like the sad sack of crap he was. His body soon joined as he collapsed onto the floor in a very messy heap.

With that minor nuisance dealt with, I hurriedly ushered The Kid out of the door. Despite the scene I had made, oddly enough, there were no other disturbances. Thankfully, allowing us to exit without any protests this time.

Gotta get back to the Inn before the guards catch up to us. I thought to myself, knowing full well the barkeep would have called upon them the moment things went down. My only hope was that the two of us could be out of there before they showed up. That is, if they even showed up at all.

"That was very dumb of you, Jayce," the Kid said as we turned a corner, clearing ourselves from the immediate scene. "You put undue attention upon us."

OK, that's it! I thought to myself, my body filling up with an unbridled rage. It was bad enough that I had to deal with that drunk. But now that we are in an emergency, NOW the Kid decides to judge me? Enough is enough!

Squeezing the Kid's shoulder, I made sure I was holding it extra hard. "Alright, Kid, enough is enough!" I roared, dragging him into the same alleyway we had been in not even an hour prior.

"From here on out and until we board the ship, I will hear not a peep out of you." I paused for a moment, looking the Kid over to see if he had gotten the message, giving him an extra squeeze for good measure. "Do I make myself clear?"

The Kid did say a word, instead choosing to glare at me in response. Not having the time or patience to deal with his childish behavior, I applied even more pressure to the shoulder in turn. The Kid tried to hold out, doing his best to endure the pain. "Crystal," he finally grunted, no longer able to hold back his displeasure. He lasted longer than I thought, I'll give him that.

"That's more like it," I said to the Kid. A look of smug satisfaction broke across my face. "Not a word, remember that." Putting my hand behind his back, I led The Kid back to the inn.

As soon as we stepped into the inn, Rebecca Snow's eyes brightened. Nice to be missed, I guess. Little did I know how quickly that hope would turn sour. "Virgil, you are popular today!" she said to me, waving the two of us over.

"I beg your pardon?" I replied, looking around to see what she was referring to, the moment we got near her. The confusing in my voice could not be more obvious. What is going on here?

"Some men in black and gold coats came by asking for you," she replied loudly. A shiver went up my spine. I'm sure the entire common room could hear what she was saying, her voice was that loud. Please quiet down! I thought, looking around to see if anyone was paying attention to us. "I told them you were out. They then left without another word."

A shiver went down my spine as the realization of who she was referring to hit me. Inquisitors. The memory of the atrocities that Aery's, now Elric's, secret police did in the name of 'The Greater Good' slammed my senses at once. It took me back to a dark time in my life. Instinctively, I grabbed my wrists. The burning sensation I felt for days on end was coming back to me. And that's what they did to 'vette' me in the eyes of my king.

Not good, I realized, the full gravity of the situation becoming oh so clear to me. We have to get out of here...NOW! "Thank you for looking out," I say to her in a hushed tone, pressing a rather large gold coin into her palm.

With a smile, I followed up with "I am afraid we must depart with haste," before leaning into her ear and whispering as urgently as I could, "Going forward, I would appreciate a certain level of... discretion."

Rebecca looked at me, and a mixture of confusion and fear spread across her face. She's probably never had to deal with anything of this magnitude, I thought to myself, realizing I must do something to remedy the situation, and do it quickly.

"This should help things, I think," I said to the woman, taking her hand in mind, and passing along a few gold coins I kept for just such an occasion. "A token of our appreciation." I smiled as I saw her face soften. The feeling of the coins pressed against her hand took its desired effect.

"Of course," she replied, taking a moment to pocket the money before speaking to us further. "Thank you for staying with us. I'll have my men bring down your things at once."

"No need," I responded, already halfway to the stairs. "I prefer to do things myself." We need to get out of here as soon as possible. There was no telling when...they would arrive.

Once out of the Rebecca's sight, I broke into a sprint. The needs of the moment quickly took over my need for secrecy. I just hope the Kid is keeping up. I thought, dread washing over me. Deciding to look over, I expected him to be at the bottom of the stairs. But much to my surprise, the Kid quickly followed suit. His stride matched mine, but just two steps behind.

He looked up at me with confusion showing on his face. Kid is clearly looking for an answer. Sadly, I had nothing to say to him. My mind was too focused on not dying a horrible death. At least he is capable of learning. My mind dwelt on the Kid as the two of us rounded the last flight of stairs, landing on our floor.

The Kid was as eager as I to enter, even going so far as to try and push past me. "Wait a moment," I whispered to him, holding him back. I had to make sure the door hadn't been disturbed. Checking for any cracks that would show signs of forced entry.

As best I could tell, the door looked clean. Glancing over at The Kid, though, I could tell he was growing increasingly worried about what was happening. I need to say something to him, I realized, seeing his deepening signs of concern.

"In situations such as these," I said to him, putting my hand on his shoulder...for no reason whatsoever. "The two prerogatives you must abide by are caution and swiftness."

My speech did little to calm his swiftly beating heart. Nor does it do little to calm mine, the ole ticker beating at such a pace it would be right at home in an Electro Show. We really need to wrap up things and get out of here. I thought to myself, knowing full well what those two could do.

Opening the door, I was shocked to see that our room was tossed. What the? I thought to myself in shock, my head turning back and forth from the clearly disturbed room and the pristine untouched door. The situation is worse than I imagined. A cold shiver went down my spine.

"Alright then," I said with a long sigh, finally realizing the full stakes at hand. At once, I could feel my entire body kicking into overdrive, darting around the room as I furiously began to pack. "Screw caution," I said to the Kid, my face now full of passion and determination. We've got no time for trepidation. "We leave in 30 seconds."

Twenty-eight seconds later, we were out the door. The door of us barreling down the stairs, only stopping when we were on the verge of entering the common room. From out of nowhere, some of my long-forgotten instincts kicked in, said instincts making me pause in place.

This situation must be especially dire for them to kick in, I mused to myself, motioning for The Kid to remain quiet. Putting my ear around the corner, I listened in to the growing commotion in the common room, hoping to hear something useful. Why does it feel so cold all of a sudden?

"You just missed him," the Inn Keeper said to two people whom I at this moment could not see, but had a dreadful inclination as to who. "He and the boy checked out about 15 minutes ago." Whoever they are, she's covering for me. What did I do to deserve such loyalty? I asked myself, watching things go down from afar.

I have to know for sure who they are, I thought, carefully craning my neck into my common room. I must know who is chasing us.

My worst fears turned out to be true, Inquisitors, I realized with a shiver. The dread was washing over me like the coldest of waves. While still in their infancy during my time back on Mars, the Inquisitio Insurrectionis is a shadowy arm of the crown, well, now the empire. They live to enforce Emperor Elric's will. And right now it seemed that will was our captor.

While Rebecca was busy staring down the two Inquisitors, the one closest to her returned her gaze.

For a moment, the two seemed locked in an invisible war, neither side gaining ground. Then, without warning, its jaw muscles cracked into a facsimile of a smile. "You speak lies," it said. The thing seemed to delight in playing with its food. "It is all over you."

Looking over to the smaller one standing beside them, its eyes went wide, somehow getting even crazier as a crooked finger pointed to its brain. "Tell me, brother, what do we do with those who displease us?" The thing asked the smaller one, who at that point hadn't even been paying attention.

The smaller one's head slowly turned to face its kin. A wicked smile cracked out from its thin lips. "We show wayward souls the way," it replied, the thing's expression now matching its "brother". Judging by the cadence of their delivery, I thought to myself, staring at the two and trying to figure out what the Hades was going on. What it said was probably a quote from some text. My heart dropped to my stomach as I realized what was about to down.

At this point, all I wanted to do was look away, knowing what was to come next. "Quickly now," I whispered to the Kid, hustling him out of sight, not wanting him to see what I knew was to come. "Out the back while their distracted." He looked up at me in confusion; his mouth began to form words. All I wanted to do was shield the boy, and all he wanted to do was resist. Why do I suddenly care so much?

Sadly, the realization that I indeed still possess a heart had to be cut painfully short. For before The

Kid could utter another word of protest, there was a sudden BOOM along with the inevitable accompanying THUD. Neither of us said anything for a moment; we both knew well and good what had just transpired.

Our silence continued as we both slipped out of the back door. The two of us were in too deep a state of shock to really be able to say anything. The women really did not deserve to die. The irony of losing someone while attempting to save another was not lost on me.

When will death stop following me? I wondered, looking at The Kid. The full weight of my responsibilities crashed down upon me at once. For now, just focus on the mission, Jayce.

Surprisingly, we made it out to the alleyway unseen. That's what happens when someone gets murdered in a more than ok area of town, I mused to myself. Everything else suddenly becomes secondary.

Reaching the outside, the Kid puked up his last six meals while I did the Lord's Cross. The full weight of the situation finally coming forth. "You can mourn later," I said, desperately trying to pull things back together. I grabbed the Kid's arm so I could keep dragging him forward. "Right now, we need to focus on getting the hell out of here."

The Kid did not protest, nor did he resist, now knowing the stakes we were in. Sad that it took the murder of someone we cared about to get him to start listening, I thought with a heavy heart. Though

I guess I should be thankful he's good in a pinch, I told myself as we crossed over to the next alleyway, the sound of the Inquisitors giving their orders to the Inn's clearly panicked patrons ringing in my ears.

Someone will give us up soon, I thought to myself, as much as I wanted to remain hopeful. Reality always has a bad habit of seeping in. They always get what they want in the end, I remembered, their effectiveness was just about as infamous as their brutality. What did we do to draw their ire?

I wanted to figure out what we had done so much, anything to distract from the guilt. But we had not even a moment spare, not a second to dwell on such a notion. Focus on the Kid, I reminded myself. Focus on the mission. I told myself, shoving that piece of the puzzle out of my brain. The Kid and I approaching a city street. Two blocks till we get to the hangar, we can do this.

"Hang on to me, Kid," I said, grabbing his arm so that I could keep him close. The two of us crossing over together, into the light. "Things could get rough." I finished, scanning the streets. My fingers hover over the claps of my gun holster.

Heeding my words, he held onto me extra tight. Waddaya know, he does listen, I marveled, the two of us making our way across the street. The entire area is filled with all the trappings of a noonday hustle. Merchants in every corner hawking their wares, street performers doing what they do best in the hopes of earning another meal, and of course whores in shape or size imaginable. Each and every one of them beckoned you to quench your thirst for pleasure.

Right now, my thirst is all dried up, I thought, my mind laser-focused on getting the Kid to safety. Part of me was in awe at how easily I slipped back into the protector role when things got rough. It's almost like you once did this for a living, Jayce.

Of course, the world surrounding me was meaningless. For at that moment, all I could see was the path I needed to take... "Hey! Watch where you...you're him!" Startled and shaken from my thoughts, I look up from my pathfinding to see a very angry Imperial Guard with Proto-Kaff spilled over his jacket. "Come with me!" he roared, going for his weapon.

Apparently, they sent the dregs out to sniff us out. I thought, my mind scrambling to figure out what I should do in response. I practically walked up to the very people who are looking for us and said, 'Here we are!'. Idiot, I thought, chiding myself for my stupidity. Gotta think fast or we're both dead.

"I am so sorry, officer," I say to the man, attempting in vain to dry him off. "My nephew and I were just heading off to the station after hearing the Emperor's wonderful speech." There was an extended silence between us as the officer studied me. "Long may he reign," I added, trying to sweeten the pot.

"Long may he reign," the man replied, as if by reflex. "It definitely was a good speech, sorry for the mix u..." The officer continued. My head was zoning out of the moment while the dreg finished up his spiel. Ok, next alleyway, then three doors down to the right, I thought, attempting to ready myself for what was to come next. I got this.

Except we didn't, because of course, things weren't going to go that easy for us. The chaotic element I call 'The Kid' just had to do the stupidest thing in the history of stupid. "Come on, Jayce! Let's go already!" Why, oh why, did he have to say that?

The dreg's head snapped to attention at the mention of that name, breaking it from the conditioned reply. Elric's propaganda truly is that strong, huh? I mused, a reprieve from this rapidly devolving situation. "Jayce? As in Jaycen Lamont?" he said, eyeing me up and down as if finally seeing me for the first time. "You are so dead, buddy!"

At this point, I was mentally done with all of this. Screw it, I thought, casting aside any previous need for secrecy and deciding just to go for it. I figured it was best to let the officer know I was done playing around. So I threw a left hook at the guard's chin. Unsurprisingly, the man crumpled like the rag doll that he was.

They really will select anyone these days… I thought to myself, a small chuckle escaping me. Looking down at the fallen officer and then at the growing crowd around us. I knew I had to do something and do it quickly.

"RUN!" I yelled, firing a few rounds into the air in a desperate attempt to scatter the mob that was quickly surrounding us. Thankfully, the gambit worked. If not a bit too well. As soon as I found the path before us opening up, it was blocked by hundreds of people. All of them seemed to run in a thousand different directions.

Wading through the throngs of panicking people, it all felt rather...familiar, like sifting through the mud flats of Titan. Good Times, I thought to myself. The memories of home and the life I once lived flooded back into me. But this is no time to get nostalgic.

Taking my own advice to heart, I pushed my way through the crowd. One hand was wafting through the chaos, the other held tightly onto The Kid. The sea of bodies pressed tightly against me. Practically suffocating me. It will all be worth it in the end. My mind cast towards the ship while I breathed some somewhat fresher air. I was free from the threshold of bodies that had just a moment ago surrounded me.

"Not too much farther," I said to the Kid. Scanning the area to find our final destination. "Yes!" I exclaimed after a moment, having finally spotted the port entrance. "Victory is in sight. Let's go, Kid. Kid?" I said, looking back to see the hand that had once grasped onto my lifeline was now empty. "Aw dammit!"

Frantically, I retraced my steps back to the alleyway we were just in. Desperately searching around for any sign, but the Kid was nowhere to be seen. DAMN! I thought to myself, the weight of my misdeeds lying heavy upon my heart. I failed...again!

Knowing that the Kid's safe passage was my last shot at doing anything substantial with my life. I was well aware there was only one thing left to do. It's time, Jayce, I thought, my emotions running high as I put the gun against my temple. Let this be the end of it all. That was all I was able to think, my finger on the trigger.

Feeling at the end of my rope, with nothing more left to lose, I...Wait, I hear a voice, I said to myself. Feeling something unusual filling me up, warming my once-cold, dead head. His voice! It was then that I knew exactly what I was feeling: Hope.

Now is not the time, Jayce, I thought, releasing my hand from its death grip, fingers mere moments from ending it all. Now is the time to fight. I now knew exactly what I had to do. Find him, find the boy.

With a renewed sense of both purpose and vigor, I smacked myself silly. Anything to put me in a better headspace while I searched for the Kid. Tuning my ears to filter out the fluff, his cries for help could not be that far away. Only then can I save his life.

Thankfully, my search did not have to take very long. I barely had time to round the first corner before I spotted something. Not even 20 yards out lies a dog pile of people. A casualty of the recent stampede. But it was not the pile of people that interested me. What caught my attention was a single hand reaching out from the top. A well-manicured hand…

"Jayce!" the Kid cried out; his screams muffled from beneath the pile. He must have seen me approach, I realized. Knowing that I didn't have much time before the crowd crushed him. I did something really stupid.

In one swift motion, I drew my pistol from its holster. Once again, raising it high in the sky. This was stupid the first time, I thought to myself as I pulled the trigger, sending another shot into the air. Now it's just ridiculous.

My folly had its intended effect, causing the people piled on top of the Kid to scatter to the four winds. Not wanting to waste this chance, I dived headfirst into the throng. "Take my hand!" I screamed to him, his hand instantly reaching for mine as if by reflex.

Surely we can't have built up such a report already? I wondered, my sweaty hand grasping his. Together, we were able to pull one another away from the pits of despair—a problem of my own making, but a solution we achieved as one.

"That was close." The Kid exclaimed, catching me off guard by drawing me in close. Hugging me with all his might. "Thank you so much!" What is this? I thought to myself, clearly not used to such affection.

Unsure of how to respond to such a situation, I awkwardly returned his hug, though not without some hesitation on my part. "Just doing my job, kid,"

I replied, pushing him away once my capacity for compassion finally ran out.

I looked around to see if anyone saw us. Scared someone will see your softer side? I thought, my insecurities ringing loud and proud. Seeing that everyone else was concerned with their own personal dramas, I found myself able to breathe a bit better. Slowly peeling myself away from an ever more attached Kid, I scanned the area and properly assessed our situation.

By the looks of it, the crowd I had pulled him from was stilled riled up. The shots that had been fired before had a larger effect than I could have foreseen. At the very least, the group was thankfully showing the signs of slowly coming back to order. Perhaps our luck is turning around!

Not wanting to waste the opportunity, I decided to make haste. Grabbing the Kid's arm, I led him to our destination...whether he wanted to or not. It seemed by now he had gotten the memo, as the Kid made no protests. Miracles do happen, I thought to myself, happy for his cooperation.

Getting up to the gate that led to the port. All that stood between us and freedom were two men dressed up as Imperial Guards. Choosing the sneaky but confident approach, the two of us ducked under the gate. Attempting to walk right past them as they stood at their posts outside the entrance

At first, I was convinced it would be easy. The two guards seemed engrossed in their conversation. "So I was telling this broad." One of the guards said to the other, practically puffing out his chest in delight, "'Yeah, I know the emperor personally.' You should have seen the way her eyes li...Hey, what gives?" the man says, looking down to see the Kid smiling up at him, having just knocked into his shin.

My eyes met those of the two men. Clearly, neither of them had expected anything to happen. The action was blocks away. Surely none of it would come there. Let alone so quickly. But as unfit as they were for us, they were still formidable foes and should be treated as such.

If you are going to do something, Jayce, better do it quick, I thought to myself, my body rousing itself from its musings as I saw the guards starting to do the same. Not wanting to shed any more blood than I had to, my initial response to this sudden encounter was a full-on sprint down the corridor. Sadly, it would seem the guards reacted about as I expected them to. The two of them gave chase, following us down the corridor. Slowly at first, but quickly picking up pace to match ours.

I signed a long sigh, not wanting to do what I knew must be done. If we must end it, best end it quickly. I reminded myself, my hand reaching downward. "So much for subtlety," I said, drawing my pistol from its holder, aiming down the sights, and firing off two shots. Shots that instantly hit their mark.

No sooner had the shots rang out, than two meat bags were lying on the floor. The blood from their bodies hadn't even had a chance to spew forth before the Kid went crazy. "Holy shit!" he exclaimed. His head darted back and forth between me and the bodies that lay before us. His face a mixture of horror and astonishment, "Where the hell did you learn to shoot like that?"

I shrugged, not really wanting to respond—a mixture of embarrassment, coupled with the desperate need to move things along. But knowing the Kid needed some sort of response, otherwise he wouldn't shut up about the matter. I simply replied, "A story for another time," before gently putting my hand on his back and not so gently shuffling the Kid into the control room.

Waltzing into the room, the Kid and I were greeted with a bit of a disturbing sight. To say that the operator was caught with his pants down would be a bit too literal for my tastes. His face went pale as he tried to hide the rather lewd magazine that mere seconds prior, the fool was clearly pleasuring himself to.

Not wanting to waste any more time, I leveled the shaft of my gun onto his cheek almost instantly. The tech was so shocked at this sudden turn of events that all he could let out was a very soft squeak.

Pressing the gun harder into his cheek, I looked down to see that the floor beneath him could use some mopping. Good, I thought to myself, feeling rather quite satisfied. That will make things easier: "Lower the locks on platform 934 and start the departure sequence," I quickly said, my eyes fixed upon his and nowhere else.

Thankfully, the man was too thoroughly embarrassed to resist, so he complied quickly and quietly. I pushed the button to release the locks on my ship. The wet spot on the floor was a testament to his sadness more than anything else.

While seeing the poor sod cowed certainly put a smile on my face. I had to double-check to confirm he had done as I demanded. Wouldn't be the first time I fell for a fake-out, I reminded myself. Looking at the camera, I saw my ship. Thankfully, still in one piece. I smiled at the man, happy that he had done what we wanted. He weakly smiled back, not knowing what was to come next. Good thing he didn't because not even a split second later, the butt of my gun met his lower jaw. Knocking him out cold.

"Was that really necessary?" the Kid asked, his arms folded across his chest, looking at me, most disapproving.

"Necessary? No," I replied with a devilish smile, not breaking eye contact while I put a charge underneath the console. "It was fun!"

The Kid just rolled his eyes. "Whatever," he said, looking just about done with everything. "Can we please get out of here already?" I nodded to him, the two of us breaking into a sprint as we made a mad dash for the ship.

With the two of us finally united, we ran down the hallway in near lockstep. Our quick pace put the platform into our view in record time. Needless to say, the lack of resistance on the Kid's part felt a bit...odd. This is almost too easy. My head looked back and forth as the Kid and I took the final steps onto the platform.

There she stood waiting. My home, my comfort, my ship: The Eventide. Needing to give myself a moment, I stood there, basking in her beauty before walking up to the entrance ramp and punching in the access codes. I don't deserve her, I mused to myself. Unsure of exactly who or what I meant. The list is much too long. I shook my head in an attempt to rid myself of such recollections. Now more than ever, I needed to focus on the task at hand. Why is my past just now coming to haunt me?

"Jaycen Lamont!" A voice called out. Shaking me from my complacency. A voice of someone from my past. No, it can't be. I thought, a potent mixture of dread and anger filling me. "Stand down or be put down!" It's him, I finally concluded, sure in the knowledge that the voice behind me could only belong to one such person—the weasel and general waste of a human being who called himself Anders.

As the third most senior Royal Guard, Benedict Anders was always an upstart. He came from nothing, and he never failed to let everyone know it. The cretin saw his rise to the top as some of manifest destiny. One can only imagine how much of a slap in the face it was when I was chosen to lead the King's Guard. A man 10 years his Junior. To say that I was not surprised to see him here in this position would be an understatement.

"Kid," I whispered to him, having an idea of what was about to go down. "Put in these coordinates and prep for departure." I shoved the boy a slip of paper in his palm.

The Kid looked up at me then, looking for some guidance on what was happening. My eyes shot over to the whelp pumping out his chest in front of us. The boy soon followed suit. "You sure?" he asked me, his eyes starting to show some understanding of the situation.

"Leave without me if you have to," I replied. The Kid nodded. Based on his expression, I could tell he now knew the score. This isn't good. We are starting to build a...rapport. I shuddered at the idea.

As much as the thought of letting another person in. I forced myself back to the present. You see, while the Kid went to do as he was told. I, on the other hand, went to greet an old friend. "Anders!" I said to the upstart warmly, extended my arms to offer up a hug. Knowing full well he wouldn't take me up on the offer. "It's sure been a while."

"It sure has," he replied coldly, his voice practically dripping with animosity. It's like the last 15 years never escaped us, I thought, enjoying the irony. We're right back in the Palace.

Anders could clearly see I wasn't taking his bait. The frustration on his face would be almost delicious if I weren't trying to get the heck out of here. Eyes on the prize, Jayce, I reminded myself. Ander's looking around for something else to stall me with.

His eyes lit up as they drifted toward the ship. "Never figured you for the sentimental type," he said, pointing his middle finger to The Eventide.

"What can I say?" I shot back, my voice a bit shaky as I wasn't expecting him to call me out. "Good tech is hard to come by these days."

I knew full well the authority he now wielded. Ander's was now the right hand of the Emperor. The position I once held was his to covet no longer. Only took a full-scale coup for you to get what you wanted, I thought with disgust. Still, the man wielded institutional power, and I had a ship. Best be cautious.

Anders paused for a moment to take me in, not quite sure which version of me he was dealing with—the honorable vanguard of old or the bitter sellgun of the present. "Yeah, well, I guess it doesn't matter," he said to me, his sneer turning into a wicked smile. Clearly figuring me out, knowing he had the upper hand. "For it will soon be returned to its rightful owner."

He then turned to look at me, or well, to be more accurate, through me. "Though before that happens, I have one question for you," he said. The man looked lost in thought, his eyes glazed over. He's looking into our past, I realized. "Why come back after all this time?" Ander's asked me, his tone indicating a rare honesty. "Do you believe yourself to be worthy of redemption finally?"

His words hit their mark, cutting me down to my core. Man, knew exactly which nerve to strike, I concluded. Casting my eyes on the floor, feelings of shame and confusion flooded me all at once. I'm sure they all wish I had disappeared and died, I thought, the despair washing over me like the fiercest of waves.

But here you are. I realized the initial rumblings of the ship's engines were reverberating inside me, filling me with the fierceness I hadn't felt moments prior. And you ain't dead yet.

Feeling like my head was finally back in the game, I steeled myself and adopted a cocky smile. "It's just a job," I said to him, coating my words with as much sarcasm as I could muster. "Nothing more, nothing less."

Tension filled the air as an uneasy silence stirred between us while he took it all in. For a moment, I just stood there. Desperately trying to figure out what was rattling around in that tin can he called a head. The man was truly a personification of chaotic ambition. One day he'd be buttering you up, the next he'd put a knife in your back. Or in my case, at least try to.

Just when I had resigned myself to not knowing what would happen next, the little weasel burst out laughing! "You don't know, do you?" Anders said, practically snorting in between fits of laughter. "You honestly don't have a single clue who you are carrying?"

His words ended up cutting me deeper than I thought they could. The anger, all the frustration, all the...everything started to rise from the surface, awoken from its fifteen-year slumber. I was feeling something I had not felt in a very long time.

That feeling, to which its absence has kept me in place this entire time, was desire. To be more specific, it was the desire to prove myself to my doubters. Feeling the fire being lit inside me, I marvel as all the pessimism I felt years prior was washed away in an instant.

Looking at Anders, his smug expression slowly disappearing as he sees me straighten my posture. Once again, I stood tall, adopting the stance I held oh so long ago. I was well aware of the chaos that was soon to come.

Tricking myself back into my old ways, I put on that same cocky smile I had worn prior. The one that had won me the loyalty of royalty. "Perhaps," I say, the two of us looking back at the steam beginning to pour out of the engines. "But I am bound to find out eventually."

I actually didn't care about whatever this grand revaluation was. I just wanted to piss off the backstabbing bastard who made every day of my life as a guard hell. That is, until she saw me anyway. "In the meantime," I say, the steam getting so thick it almost enveloped me. "I advise you to exit the platform."

Anders started getting the gears going in his head, looking first at the engines, then at the flashing lights around him, and finally, his stare came back at me. His face drooped into some sort of dumbfounded expression as the idiot finally realized exactly what was going on. "You wouldn't." That was all he managed to squeak out, the panic truly starting to set in.

"I am," I replied, letting the mist fully consume me as I swaggered my way up the ramp. You are so dramatic, Jayce, I thought to myself, reveling in the unnecessariness of it all.

I stopped my march upon reaching the door. "If you don't wish to be atomized in about 15 seconds," I said to my former underling from beyond the veil of steam, hovering my hand over the button that controlled the entry ramp, "I advise that you leave right now."

At this point, the steam was so thick it had enveloped the entire room. I could barely see Anders amidst the obstruction. What I could see was enjoyable, at least. The man seemed to be doing his best not to panic while he looked around, taking in the current situation.

While I couldn't see it, I was positive the man at that moment was weighing the choices in his head. At first, I wasn't sure what he would do, but then thankfully, he made the first correct decision in his life. The vague outline that I was sure was Anders promptly stormed off without saying another word. I still couldn't see anything, but I was sure he gave me a dirty look for our troubles.

With Anders cowed and the launch pad now filled with toxic engine exhaust, I did the only sensible thing and dove into the ship. "Whew, that was too close!" I said, pressing the button to retract the entry ramp.

My feeling of safety would prove to be short-lived, sadly. For no sooner had I pressed the button than the hull sealed itself and I was knocked on my ass by the force of the ship blasting from its cradle and out into the wild blue yonder.

What the hell? I thought to myself, bracing against the railing for the inevitable second blast as we cleared the atmosphere. Is the AI in fits again or… I wondered, thinking it had bypassed the manual launch input and just put us in space. But that was impossible, I had taken out the bypass almost as soon as I "got" the vessel, which left only one possible solution. Oh no no no, he better not!

Now officially pissed off, I ran the length of the ship, practically storming onto the bridge. I was already angry as hell, but being greeted with the sight of the Kid in my chair? That…that was a step too far!

"The AI was too slow to respond, Jayce," the Kid said to me as soon as he noticed me on the bridge, completely oblivious to my obvious rage. "So I took the liberty of...whoa!" His joy at having an independent thought soon turned sour. His face looked up at me in confusion as I tore him out of my chair. That look of confusion quickly turned to one of shock as I threw him across the bridge. My vision has now turned fully red.

"What gives?" the Kid said to me, propping himself up with one hand while nursing his bruised jaw with the other. His tone reflected the fact that he still had no idea what he had done wrong.

With my vision somehow taking on an even darker shade of red, I rushed up to The Kid, putting myself practically nose to nose with him and feeling no need to hold back now that we were safely back within the confines of the show. I allowed my inhibitions to be finally free. Soon, I set my fire loose upon the boy.

"You're the one who just stood there gobsmacked at the Emperor," I screamed down to the Kid. All the anger, all the doubt, every insecurity I had held back came forth all at once. The raging inferno needed a target, and sadly, the Kid was the only victim in the vicinity. A part of me knew how wrong this was, but at this point, I really didn't care.

I was so angry at this point that I just put my face even more into his orbit. The two of us were so close, I could feel my breath spit landing on his face.

"You forced me to knock that drunkard out." I continued, my screams echoing off the walls of the bridge, "You're the one who called me by my name, my real name, to the guards!"

At this point, The Kid well and truly broke. Tears began to roll down his cheek. Oh no! The consequences of my rage were starting to seep in. Not the water works!

The part of me that was still honorable. The part of me I desperately tried to deny was starting to feel like a real piece of work. What have I become? I wondered, finally looking at myself for the first time.

Sadly, this revaluation was not to last. For my rage was quick to overrule any sense of morality I could have had. "Might as well have said 'We're right here! Take us!" I screamed, starting to poke him in the chest. Trying to get a response, any response, other than what I was currently getting. "You're the one who got caught underneath that mob."

The Kid did not react as I continued screeching at him. His sobs are now coming in full force. "You forced me to save your sorry ass," I said, desperately trying to justify my unjust reaction. "No more," I said, feeling my rage starting to burn itself out.

His sobs took a pause, looking at me with a face somehow redder than mine. His eyes are full of false hope. A hope that I felt compelled to dash. I truly am the monster they claim.

"No more," I started, part of me not wanting to continue, but my insecurities were once again winning over. "No more will you be taking any 'liberties'," I said, the Kid's dreams dashed before my eyes. "From now on, you will do what I say exactly as I say it."

Feeling my fury at last truly spent, I slumped my shoulders in defeat. Once again, I had let my worst self take control—the weight of everything bearing down on me at once. Perhaps best to get some shut-eye. I thought, figuring it might be best to retire for the time being.

Oh, what a rest that wi- "But Jayce!" the Kid interjected, courage finally finding him while his face was still red and puffy, bearing the marks from my verbal assault.

At this point, I thought my anger had been well and truly spent. But this interruption to my train of thought renewed me in a way I didn't think possible. I felt a new fury bubbling up once again. This time I tried to resist it, but of course, I failed miserably.

"No buts!" I screamed, grabbing the Kid's collar. He tried to follow me back to my room, but I just wasn't having it. "We will be at the checkpoint in less than two days," I told him, holding my hand out to bar him from entry.

"Until then I don't want hear so much as a fart from you," I said, pushing the button to close the door. Once again, putting my barriers up. "You hear me? A FART!"

4

A Rock

"Alright, Kid, take it from the top," I said to the boy. Once again, I looked down at him, acting confused as he stared at the piece of paper in his hand. For the past few hours, the two of us had been going over what were to be our assumed identities. And now, with mere minutes to go before our exit point, we were still reviewing even the most basic things. It would be an understatement to say the panic was real. I swear, if things go south, I'll rip this kid apart piece by bloody piece.

Sadly, I had no time for an existential crisis, because once the moment the ship exits Slipspace, the show would begin in earnest. The two of us would have to put on the performance of a lifetime. Just a single mistake would be enough to give us away, costing us everything. I have to be sure.

"My name is Robert Thorn…" The Kid began, laying out the spiel I had prepared for him. His voice still a bit shaky. "I was born on Oberon in 2 KE. My parents died when I was 2, Ow!" he exclaimed, letting out a small yelp as I smacked him upside the back of his head. "What was that for?" the Kid asked, looking up at me in confusion. "I had the year right!"

Has this kid received any formal schooling? I wondered, unable to believe what I was hearing. "First off, you gave the wrong era," I said, correcting him. My eyes were on fire as I glared down at The Kid. He must remember this, I thought, the panic starting to really set in. Otherwise…

"You said Kingdom Era," I continued, taking deep breaths between each sentence so I wouldn't fly off the handle completely. "It's actually the same period we're in now, the Empire Era, or EE for short." Everyone knows this, I thought, his lack of such basic information astounding me. How could he not know?"

"Why does it matter?" The Kid said, rolling his eyes for good measure. "Why do I need to…Ow!" He exclaimed, rubbing his head in the same spot as before, as I struck him again.

No one is this thick. At this point, I was half convinced he was doing it intentionally to get my goat. At least if he's mocking me, he's doing something proactive for a change. "Everything!" I replied, my voice dripping with barely contained fury as I continued with my rant. "Secondly, although you correctly stated the year of your father's death, your mother died years later."

The Kid seemed to have gotten the message. His eyes lowered onto the floor as I finished correcting him. My jab has truly hit its mark, it seems. Let's see him mope about this, I thought to myself, the idea of making an obviously still grieving child cry filled me with some sort of twisted glee.

My sadistic delusions were soon cut short, sadly. The Kid wasted no time, quickly responding to my jab with one of his own, not so quietly muttering, "Just like in real life," as if he were answering my thoughts.

His sudden boldness caught me by surprise, leaving my jaw proverbially on the floor. 'Just like in real life? ' What the hell does he mean by that? I wondered, only just now realizing I knew next to nothing about The Kid's backstory.

Not knowing what else to do. I sheepishly looked over at him. My eyes were searching for some sort of answer. He simply returned my gaze, looking at me with a newfound sense of confidence. His face gave me absolutely nothing.

"What was that?" I asked, trying and failing miserably not to play into this little scheme of his.

"Nothing," he responded in a vain attempt to hide his very apparent pain. The little squeaks in his voice showcased how miserably he had failed.

"Look," I said, heading over to the console so I could check up on things. My ability to handle the Kid's nonsense is running almost on empty. "I don't know your trauma, and right now we don't have time to care." Turning my back on him as I finished.

Through the reflection in the window, I could see the Kid's response was to slump down in his chair, his depression plain as day. A pang of...something coursed through me. Guilt perhaps? I wasn't quite sure, as I wasn't used to thinking about anyone but myself. The idea of my having empathy for another was such a foreign concept to me.

That being said, if The Kid was moping about. He'd be more likely to make a critical mistake, costing us everything. I can't have him going into all of this feeling like a wet noodle. I thought, sighing to myself, before returning to him. Not really looking forward to what I was about to do. "Look." I started, trying my best to adopt a more pleasant tone. The Kid's ears were already perking up at my words. Is the boy that starved for positive attention? I wondered. I wanted to dwell more on this, but sadly, our time was running short, so I'd have to stick to the essentials. "I need you at your best for this," I told him, trying my best to be as even-handed as possible. "If you play along, I promise to hear your story, deal?"

The Kid stared at me for a moment, looking at me in utter confusion. Clearly not sure how to take my sudden onset of decency. The air hung with tension; I wasn't really sure how this would go. Would he comply with me or reject me altogether?

The answer to that question came to me sudden and swift. The Kid galloped up to me, quickly closing the distance between us and giving me a big hug. Needless to say, I was surprised at this sudden outpouring of emotion. I wasn't really sure how to respond, so I did the only thing I could think of: I returned the hug.

The two of us stood there awkwardly for a few seconds, holding each other in an embrace. Neither one of us had a single clue as to what we should do next. Thankfully, or perhaps regretfully, the choice was made for us. The alarms going off signaled our immediate exit from Slipspace. "Showtime, Kid," I hollered at him. Breaking the hold we had between us, I headed over to the front of the ship so I could man my station. "Buckle up or pay up."

Taking one last look at the Kid, I saw that he had safely secured himself. A brief wave of relief washed over me. Here goes nothing… I thought to myself, desperately trying to ignore the pool of emotions swirling inside of me. "Exiting in 3...2...1..." I said, pulling down the lever, feeling the familiar rush as I was pushed back into my seat. That never gets old. I thought, enjoying the rush of returning to normal space.

"Unknown ship!" said the person on the other side of the Squawkbox. "You have entered Imperial Airspace." Their tone was neutral and firm, but with a hint of underlying threat. "State your business and prepare to dock." Straight to business as usual, I thought, remarking on déjà vu: Doesn't matter if it's Kingdom or Imperial, some things never change.

Showtime, I thought to myself, letting out a huge breath to calm the nerves I felt bubbling up from within me. "Just follow the script and we'll be fine," I said to the Kid, trying to tame my nerves just as much as his.

Let's just get this over with. I thought to myself as I flipped the comm switch. "This is Virgil Alliegries, Captain of The Singularity," I said into the mic.

Rattling off the speech I had been practicing the past few days. This has to work, or else... "I've been tasked with taking my companion, the other person on this ship, to his Aunt on Europa." The best lies have an ounce of truth to them, I mused to myself, hoping to high heavens the person on the other end of the line would buy my story. The moments passed like moussaka as the person in charge of our fate mulled over what I had just said.

"Okay, fine, whatever," a female voice chimed in, breaking the tense silence. What the? A part of me feels let down by all this build-up leading to just...nothing. That can't be it. "Have your documents ready for inspection when you get off your ship," she continued, her tone conveying a level of disdain that could only be achieved by someone who did this multiple times a day.

While I sat there, waiting for her next instruction. My mind wandered over to the notion of her voice. It was seemingly deeper than one you'd normally expect to hear. While her tones were distinctly feminine, they'd more in common with a voice you'd associate with a short, stocky bodybuilder than with any sort of woman. Odd, I mused to no one.

Stop fretting over insignificant details, Jayce. I thought, trying to keep myself on the level and forcing myself to file that nugget of information away for later. Focus on what's in front of you and The Kid. You'll be out of here in no time, don't worry. I said to myself, hyping myself up for the troubles that were sure to come.

Flipping the switch to respond, I took a sharp breath to steady myself. "Thank you, milady," I replied, actual genuine gratitude escaping my lips—surprising not just myself but also the Kid.

There was a long pause, almost as if the other person was considering exactly how to respond. "I'm no Lady." That was all she said after a few minutes of very confused silence. I tried to open my mouth to reply, but she cut off the communication before I had the chance to do so.

I guess 'smooth sailing' is no longer on the weather report. I thought with a shiver, the idea of all my carefully laid plans sinking before they even had a chance to swim, it truly terrified me. Not wanting to give myself away, I clenched my teeth. Pretending to be grateful while flicking off the switch and shutting down our outbound feed in turn. That could have gone better, I guess.

I knew this privacy we had would be short-lived. Not wanting to waste a single second, I turned my chair around to face The Kid. My face was a thinly veiled mask of utter confidence. "Alright," I said, my body rigid, but my hands were visibly trembling. One can only fake so much. I said to myself. Trying to steady myself before continuing, I said, "So we've got a few minutes before we've to leave the ship." Any last-minute questions that you want to ask?" Breathe, I thought, trying in vain to calm myself. I did, but it didn't help one bit.

The Kid sat there for a moment, his mind clearly lost in thought. "Just one," he said after a few seconds of pondering. Please don't be something stupid. Please don't be something stupid… I mentally pleaded, really not wanting to deal with his crap. Not on today of all days. "Why do we have to go through a checkpoint? Can't we just sneak in via Slip Space?"

Dammit! I thought, practically screaming in my head while outwardly laughing to myself. I did this even though I knew I really shouldn't have. The Kid's naivete, while frustrating, was, in a way, endearing. It certainly did much to break the tension between us. The idea of which sent me off into a bit of a mini-panic. Was I beginning to...like this boy? I thought, the notion sending a shiver through my system.

Despite any trepidations I may have had, I really needed to move things along before it was too late. "There is a field that surrounds the entire Sol System," I explained, choosing to answer The Kid's question while keeping one eye on the Nav screen. We can't afford to screw anything up. "Any craft that crosses it is instantly ejected from Slip Space."

Slow down, Jayce, I said to myself, taking a quick pause to catch my breath and inhaling a huge gasp of recycled air. Everything's gonna be ok. Feeling a bit better now, I looked down at the Kid, noticing he was about to chip in.

Not wanting to delay things any further, I quickly followed up with, "And before you ask, The Great Dark is a huge place. You'd run out of fuel long before getting anywhere even close to something solid," I said to him, knowing full well the question he was gonna ask me.

The Kid's eyes widened with my response. He definitely wasn't expecting that, I realized, a smirk cracking out from the corner of my mouth. The boy stood there for a moment, thinking over his next words before finally blurting out. "How'd the Shinkar Kingdom find the resources to build that?"

How sheltered was this kid? I wondered, my exasperation reaching an all-time high. The moment of joy passed me by. His naivety swiftly shifted from its comfortable, endearing place to a point of annoyance. "The Empire's resources are vast and large," I said, my voice completely neutral because any emotion added to it would be that of anger. "Why do you think he controls such a large area?" I concluded, making sure to emphasize a certain word.

It took a moment, but the truth of my words finally dawned upon the Kid. His mouth opened wide in shock as part of the process. He stared at the floor for a moment. Seemingly letting everything sink in before looking up at me. The Kid more than likely prepared to ask another stupid question. Not wanting to answer any more of his questions, I was prepared to slap the shit out of him to shut him up but thankfully my actions were cut off by the squawk from the comm box.

"Singularity," the gruff lady said, her voice as dry as any desert, yet still conveying a hint of annoyance. "You are now under the dominion of the Shinkar Empire. You will obey all laws while occupying our space; ignorance is no excuse. Now step off your ship and present your papers." She then cut off the feed as abruptly as it began.

No turning back now. I thought, taking one final gulp in an attempt to swallow my terror. "Come on, Kid. " It's Showtime," I said to him, the nervousness in my voice now fully on display. Slinging the satchel that held our forged papers over my shoulder in a vain attempt to hide my concern. But it was a useless gesture, for at this point, I was so on edge it was impossible to hide it.

Things were so obvious that even The Kid was picking up on it. His eyes filled with concern as he looked over at me quizzically. "Jayce, you do realize it's okay to be scared, right?" he replied, clearly trying to be empathetic, but the boy couldn't help having a knowing smirk on his face.

Flabbergasted at his two-faced audacity, I grabbed The Kid by the scruff of his collar. Dragging his sorry ass straight to the exit bay. I shot him a nasty look as I pounded the button to lower the ramp. "Quiet," I hissed, putting a finger to my lips in order to silence him.

This has to go off without a hitch. I said to myself. At that point, I was so nervous that my breath seemed almost spent as the door to the outside rolled up. The two of us were walking down the ramp as casually as possible. At the base stood two very imposing people. They were waiting for us.

The two people who greeted us could not be any more unlike. On the left was what I can only assume to be the 'lady'. The one on the comms stood there waiting for us right at the foot of the ramp. The only word I had to describe her was "Solid".

The woman's broad shoulders silhouetted a rather boxy frame. The little skin she had on display revealed muscle upon muscle. This girl clearly works out. I thought to myself before containing my assessment. Lil Lady stood at about half my height, though, giving her burly physique, I had my doubts as to whether I could take her.

Swallowing what little pride I had left, I bowed deeply. A proud race, dwarves were. They'd sooner cut your throat for the slightest offense. Didn't realize the Emperor employed them, I thought, the very idea being not too surprising to me. The only other thing dwarves were known for besides their pride was their immense loyalty. Well, that and their cruelty towards those they hate.

"Greetings, servant of the Emperor," I said, my tone reserved, my body shaking like a leaf due to the sheer terror coursing through me. "Long may he reign."

The two of them just stared at me silently. Having seemingly failed my attempt at flattery. The dwarf was the first to break the silence. "Got any weapons?" She asked, looking me up and down in the process, as if she were sizing me up.

I don't like this. I thought with a shiver. The dwarf's elevator eyes looked me up and down, as if I were some sort of meat meant for slaughter. I really don't like this. My concern grew deeper as I looked into her eyes. They were practically watering, not with desire, but with hunger. The woman wanted to devour me.

"Not on me," I replied sheepishly, doing my darnedest not to look her in her ravenous eyes. This isn't how I planned it at all. I thought, the dwarf's demeanor having truly thrown me off my game.

"What do you have on the ship?" she shot back, not wasting a single beat. Her eyes didn't even bother to meet mine, skipping past my sheepish stare and going southward.

"Just a few pistols and some knives," I said in response, my voice cracking a few times in the process. You shouldn't break this easily. I said to no one, wishing now more than anything I could just take a moment to psyche myself up.

But that didn't happen, so I had no choice but to press on. "A guy's gotta protect himself," I said to her at last, taking as long as was socially acceptable to reply.

The 'lady' stood there, staring at me, clearly lost in thought, pondering what I had just said for the briefest of moments.

Then, just when I thought it was safe to relax, even if only a little bit, the Dwarf strode up to me. Reaching down to feel my man parts up without warning. Naturally, I tense up, the feeling of her hand probing every inch of me most unpleasant.

This is excessive, I thought; my tolerance for all this was about at its limit. Does she really hav...OW! "Not bad," she said, squeezing my package. A smile broke out on her face once she saw the effect she had on me. Her hands had found their mark. But part of me felt it wasn't just the physical assault that pleased her. No, it was plain as day, my wincing in pain as a result of her press. That was what she truly desired.

"Follow me," she said, standing up after her deed was done. The dwarf gave me a certain look. A look that all but dared me to object. I did no such thing.

"The two of you will be placed in a holding room while we strip and search your ship, all awaiting your entrance interview," she said breathlessly, never breaking eye contact the entire time. "Unless either of you objects to anything, that is."

"No objections," I replied, my voice suddenly taking on the characteristics of a 7-year-old. "Lead the way." She snickered at my response, then turned her back to me and began heading out. The Kid and I fell in line behind her. Her movements conveyed the confidence of a woman who had won and was used to it.

You need to pull yourself together, Jayce. I told myself, feeling just how quickly the situation was spiraling out of control. I shook my head to clear myself of the nonsense. Letting out a large grunt in the process.

The Dwarf's head instantly shot back at the noise. Giving me a stare of utter bewilderment. All she got in return was one of my patented sly smiles. See, I can play the game too!

I could see why he used these old mining sites, I thought to myself, looking up and down the hallway that the Kid and I now found ourselves in. I marveled at the boundless corridors of featureless brown stone. Endless shafts mean endless places in which to hold secrets, I concluded, making a mental note to be extra cautious.

Venturing further into the rock, the Dwarf paid us no mind as she led us through similarly lit hallways. I attempted to memorize our route, but sadly, even with the best of my abilities, I could only capture a fifth of it into memory. Better some than none, I concluded, clinging to that thought hopelessly.

"Here we are," the 'lady' said, the three of us having reached what was obviously to be our holding room. "Get in," she ordered, her voice as chill as the air surrounding us.

With neither of us looking to start any trouble, the Kid and I followed her orders without a word of protest, quickly shuffling inside.

The joint itself was more like a cell than a room, with the exposed bare brick glistening with moisture. The beads of condensation came dripping down from the vents above. The room itself was a rather spartan affair, with two metal chairs sitting in the corner. A first glance, they looked rather unremarkable. However, upon further inspection, I could see scratch marks and what appeared to be dried blood splattered all over the concrete floors and ceiling. This is what passes for decorations in this pit? I wondered, my old friend fear started to creep back in.

"Settle in." She said, standing at the door, preventing us from leaving. "Someone will be with you sh... I can't even finish that sentence." The Dwarf broke out into a fit of laughter mid-sentence before slamming the door behind her. The sound of her exit echoed through our room for quite a long while.

Looking over at The Kid, he seemed equally unsettled as we both sat down in these very uncomfortable chairs. It was clear as day that the boy wasn't enjoying this experience at all. Neither am I, to be honest. I thought with a shiver, this time not because of any feelings but more because of how cold the room was.

The Kid finally opened his mouth to speak. His breath hung in the air for a solid three seconds before disappearing. Not wanting to deal with any of his nonsense, I put a single finger to my lips, giving him a death stare worthy of the entire Pantheon.

Thankfully, The Kid seemed to get the message. With that little distraction out of the way, I cast my eyes about, looking around for some sort of recording device. I knew they wouldn't just leave us alone. No, they had to be monitoring us somehow.

It was at this point that I was glad for my years of training as the Captain-General of the Royal Guard. For my eyes instantly shot up to the air grate. Lo and behold, as I took a look inside, I was greeted by a very obvious red light, and said light was coming from what could only be a security cam.

Why bother putting it all the way up there if you aren't even going to try and hide it? I mused to myself. The lack of effort leaves me a bit miffed. "If you're going to hide something," I said under my breath, just loud enough for the mic to pick it up. "At least put some subtlety into it." From there, the Kid and I sat in an awkward silence. How long are we going to wait? I wondered, not knowing how long this would take. I wouldn't have to wonder long, though. 'Cause out of the blue, as if they had read my mind, two guards stepped in. One of them was the 'lady' from before.

The other was the lanky man who had originally stood beside her at the landing bay. Now that he was up close I couldn't help but notice what a pock-marked face the cretin had. The only thing about him more ugly than what I could see at a glance was his teeth. Well, at least the lack thereof, man had more gaps than molars.

"Come." That was all the lanky man said, his lisp more evident up close than when I first saw him from a distance. Not wanting to cause any issues, at least not yet, the Kid and I complied without any resistance. Both of us instantly fell in line without a word between us. Neither of us really wanted to draw their ire.

The cold corridors the lanky man led us through were about as devoid of life as they could be. The sterile nature of the rocky walls and their bare metal framing made me feel a bit mad. The shadows pocketing every crevice danced before me. Almost as if they were given life by the few light sources that were there to begin with. Calm thyself, I thought, reminding me to keep my wits in check. We will surely arrive at the next place soon.

As luck would have it, our sterile journey would soon come to an end. A lanky guy pointed to the door as The Kid and I approached it. Our journey was capped off with an active Shock Stick being pointed mere centimeters from my chest.

"Not you," the lady taunted, throwing her head back for a deep chuckle that reverberated for miles down the twisting hallways. Your playtime will be coming soon. She said before turning to head into the room. The lanky man quickly followed her lead, sending a few sparks my way to drive home the point.

As if by instinct, I jumped back in reaction to the sparks. The Dwarf acted as if she hadn't seen a thing, quickly pushing me across the hall and into the open room behind me, closing the door behind her before I could get a word in. Giving me a wink as the door closed. She just had to dig it in, I guess. I thought to myself, sighing in frustration. Great, just great. What am I going to do now? I wondered, looking around at a room more featureless than the one I had been in before. Wait, I guess.

Now all alone, I was left with nothing more than to stew in my bad thoughts. Mulling over the choices I had made to get here. Thank Hades, this job pays so well. Because I certainly ain't doing this for the 'Honor'...Honor, been so long since I had any. Will I ever be able to regain it?

That idea lingered in my head, like a splinter I could not get rid of. I had abandoned it long ago and had not given it another thought since. However, upon taking on this most recent contract, it seemed to be the only option I could think of. Whether or not you do regain it doesn't matter right now. I reminded myself. Right now, all you can do is wait for the next event.

So, I waited, and waited. Then, just when I thought I could wait no longer, eventually the lock turned. Freeing me after what to my mind seemed like an entire cycle. I was expecting the Lanky One to fetch me, but instead, the lady opened the door, a devilish grin cracking across her face. "Follow," was all she said, giving a quick jerk of her head to indicate where to go. As before, I quickly complied and got in behind her. The Dwarf was leading me through many of the same, similar-looking corridors.

She struts through like she owns the place, I mused, taking note of her confidence in navigating the various twisted passageways. She must be on some sort of long assignment here, I realized. But where exactly is here? I wondered, trying to map out where we have gone in my head.

Seeing as this was to be my second go-around, I found myself having a much easier time memorizing the layout. Everything is connected, I thought to myself, the layout clicking into place inside my head. It's all slowly coming back to me. Sadly, my sudden revelation was cut short, as the two of us had been stopped in front of an aggressively nondescript door. That doesn't look ominous at all...

Before I could say anything, before I could even make an offhand comment, the Dwarf opened the door ever so slightly, then motioned for me to enter. Still trying to play the amicable one while also still not wanting to piss her off, I quickly scooted in.

Looking around, the room seemed to be the same barren affair as before. Why even bother moving me if... I wondered, only for my thoughts to be rudely interrupted without notice. The Dwarf was yelling "Have fun!" before slamming the door right in my face.

I could feel the wind rushing past my face as she slammed the door in front of me. My nose was practically touching the cold stone. A resounding THUD echoed through the tiny room once it had found its way home.

Wanting to access the sticky situation I found myself in, I took a step back so I could soak it all in. My eyes went wide in shock as I saw the three long claw marks that marred the door. Not good, not good at all, I thought to myself, letting go of a rather fearful gulp.

Not knowing what else to do, I turned around to check out the rest of the room. It was only then that I realized my situation had gone from bad to worse. She hadn't been speaking to me. I realized, staring straight into a set of very terrifying eyes. Eyes that could hardly be considered human.

Behind me this entire time was a man, well, not exactly a man. More of a sort of beast. It certainly isn't the lanky one from before! I thought in an attempt to make myself feel better. It didn't work.

No, that was no man bearing before me. Before me sat a beast, taking court atop a plain wooden table. His body was covered from head to toe in hair. Where nails once were, claws now took root. His bloodshot eyes stared straight into my soul. The pupils reflected exactly the kind of fury he was just dying to unleash.

The thing was so massive that two chairs were required for him to sit down properly. When did the empire start employing Warwolves? I asked myself, mentally going through everything I knew about the experiments. Which admittedly wasn't much.

As if by instinct, my hands went down to my sides. Feeling my thigh to make sure "it" was there. Relief washing over me as I felt what very well could be the tip of my salvation. Oh, good, I didn't forget it.

"Please... sit," Was all he said to me. The beast seemed to be taking some sort of perverse pleasure in watching me stand there, frozen in shock. "Sit." He said with a short growl in his voice. Foam began to form at the corners of his mouth. "I will not say it a third time."

Feeling the fear begin to well up from inside of me, I did as he 'asked'. Having no desire to be mauled by this savage beast. "Mr. Conway." He asked, his beady eyes looking me up and down. As if eyeing a piece of meat. "What is your reason for entering the Shinkar Empire?"

Ok, Jayce, you got this, I said to myself. Knowing full well it was my time to put up or shut up. Feeling the pressure but charging forward anyway, I took a deep breath before I spat out what I had prepared on the ship. "I have been contracted to take Mr. Thorne to his aunt on Europa." I said as 'casually' as I could. The Beast sat there stone-faced while I spun my tale.

Perfect, I thought, the fear I felt starting to ease up a bit. Just as I rehearsed. That relief I felt was proven to be only a momentary reprieve. For as soon as I finished, the Beast's mouth broke into a huge Cheshire grin. A grin that could not mean anything good. Maybe it was a bit too perfect?

"Your companion said something similar, quite similar in fact," The Beast said with a most sinister tone. Pausing for a moment to gauge my reaction. "That is, until I broke him," he concluded, taking his sweet time to relish every syllable.

Knowing all the Beast wanted was a reaction out of me, I sat there motionless. Giving him exactly nothing. On the inside, though, my body was screaming in sheer utter panic. The Beast knows! I thought, the words practically screaming in my head.

Seeing straight through my facade. The Beast just chuckled before continuing. "Please, tell the complete story, Captain-General Jaycen Lamont," he said, looking me straight in the eye while delivering the gut punch. "Well, former anyway." The Beast was chuckling as he finished the final sentence, reveling in the power he felt over me and giving his words a special relish for dramatic effect.

I tried to quickly hide my shock behind a mask of anger. I was able to do so, but only just. Thankful for the fact that I didn't have to reach too far down in order to find it. Yes, anger, use it for all it's worth, Jayce, I told myself in an attempt to keep my wits together.

"Where is he?" was all I could manage to eke out. The anger was beginning to truly boil inside of me. Using that fire, I leveled a burning gaze upon him. Trying to match his intensity.

The Beast caught my gaze and matched it with his own. His eyes beckoned a challenge that I knew better than to answer. "Far from here," he finally responded, a snarl escaping his lips. "That is for certain," The Beast said, his eyes still fixated on mine.

Without breaking his gaze, the Beast began flexing his fingers, the claws that he kept inside popping out one by one. "Now we can do this the easy way," he said, his claws glistening in the low light. "Or the..."

Whatever it was he was about to say, I was not about to let him finish that sentence. At that moment, I sprang into action. Kicking the table out from under us. Before I knew it, the Beast was already leaping towards me, his claws bared as if he had sensed my desperate move before I even made it. Knowing that this fight would be over quickly, regardless of the outcome, I decided to make every moment count. Using the momentum from his leap, I threw himself across the room. A little trick I had learned from some visiting monks back in my Shadow Hawk days. That wasn't the only trick I had just pulled off, as The Beast was soon to find out...

I smiled a bit as I watched this mass of fur and muscle hit the wall. The Beast slumped to the ground, his eyes groggy. The hit seemed to have done its job, leaving him seemingly stunned. The trail of blood following in his wake was an added benefit. The stun sadly seemed only momentary, as his eyes quickly lit back up in a renewed blaze of fury.

"I was hoping you'd pick the hard way," the Beast said, looking me straight in the eye as he spat out excess blood onto the floor. "Been spoiling for a good fight."

If you are going to do something, Jayce, best do it quickly. I thought, my head quickly taking stock of my options. He's wounded, I realized, seeing the Beast clutching his side, panting like the injured dog he was. Though the bloody smile he swore told a somewhat different story. But that looks to be invigorating him.

It was only then that what this animal truly was hit me—a berserker. I thought with a smile. I can work with that, but first, I need a weapon. I thought, looking down at the floor. Out of the corner of my eye, I saw the Beast standing up, preparing to lunge at me once more. It's now or never, I realized, the panic well and truly starting to settle in. DO SOMETHING!

But I don't have anything to fight back with! I realized, feeling the panic about to overwhelm me completely. A fate that would have doomed not just me, but also the Kid. Thought it would seem death was not in the cards for me at that moment. My hands hit my sides, reminding me of the sharp salvation I had stowed away in a hidden pocket of my pants. At this revelation, a light bulb went off in my head. Or do I?

"You certainly are skilled." The Beast said, spitting out two bloody teeth while he crouched back onto all fours, preparing his finishing strike. "It's a pity you had to choose the wrong side." His words rang in my head as he lunged towards me. Wrong side? I wondered, but that thought had never really occurred to me. That would have to wait, for in that brief moment where I pondered a new crisis, The Beast proved that he was too quick for me. Before I could even register the hit, I found myself pinned to the ground. My fingers fruitlessly grasping at tufts of his fur.

Gotta find my mark, I thought desperately. My hand eagerly reached into that hidden pocket where I had stashed a rather toxic surprise. As you can feel, Mr. Lamont," the Beast said with a cruel smile. His claws started to dig into my chest. "I was made to be a weapon," he said, digging his talons so deep into me, blood began to pour out. "I can hurt you in ways you can hardly imagine."

The Beast's brutality took me by surprise, even if he was part animal. One shouldn't act so giddy. When violence is your favorite delicacy, I concluded that situations like these must be a veritable feast.

"It is useless to resist." He said, his jaw so close to my ear, I could feel his hot breath going directly down my ear canal.

At that moment, resistance was all I could think of. I hadn't survived fifteen years just to be ended on my first honest job, I reminded myself, carefully taking my victory from its hiding place. I will not run from what must be done!

"Well?" He said with another smile. This one someone more sinister than the last. The Beast was clearly enjoying this. "What is it gonna be, give up already?"

Giving up? I've had so many chances to do just that. So many people wanted to see a coward like me fail, but I proved them all wrong. Now, of all times, I wasn't about to change that. But why is he like this? I wondered, seeing the Beast for the dark reflection he truly was. A reminder of the path I could have taken. A reminder of the person I could be.

I know what I have to do, I realized, grasping the hilt of my salvation firmly. Kill the coward, let the man live on.

"Never!" I yelled, sinking the dagger I had hidden this entire time deep into the Beast's side. His wicked smile soon turned to pain as the poison I had coated the blade with did its job. The Warwolf looked at me in shock before he quickly rolled over. Silently slumping to the floor before twilight soon took him. "I too was made to be a weapon," I said to the now corpse, returning the blade to its hidden chamber. "But unlike you, I choose not to let it consume me."

The shadows soon overtook him as I slumped to the ground. The full weight of what I had just done hit me all at once. "That was way too close!" I said, sitting there for a second, letting out a breath I didn't know I had.

Looking around, the only thing more strange than the eerie silence surrounding me was the odd bloodstain on the wall. What was worse is that I had no idea if it belonged to me or The Beast. Best not to dwell on such things. I told myself, pondering what my next move would be. The musing was suddenly interrupted by The Beast taking in a sharp breath of air. Oh, come on!

I had thought the poison did its job, but it would seem he was too strong for it to fully take him. What was supposed to be potent enough to kill the fiercest foe only served to stun him briefly.

Knowing full well I had only mere moments before The Beast awoke from his slumber, I had to act quickly. Using the knife again would be fruitless, so instead I quickly searched him for anything I might need. On his furson, I was happy to find a bunch of things that could help me. Coming across guns, cuffs, an ID card, and most surprisingly, a med kit. All of this was just there for the taking.

While I did all this, I could hear his breathing begin to pick up in its pace. The Beast is gonna wake soon. I concluded, pocketing all I could before making a beeline for the door. Quickly slamming the door behind me as I left, I took extra care to ensure it was securely locked.

It was good that I made haste. The moment I turned the lock and bolted the door shut, I heard a roar, all but confirming my worst fears. That toxin should have been strong enough to kill a man five times his size, I thought, knowing this was coming, but still having a hard time believing it. How is he still alive? I wondered, jumping in fright as I heard a second roar. This one was more powerful than the last. Let alone back to full strength?

What kind of man does this? I wondered, feeling the panic start to seep into me swiftly. I looked on in terror, the roars soon being followed by slams. Slams that somehow shook the entire surrounding area. All I could do was look on in terror. Watching helplessly as the door in front of me took the full force of the man's rage. Its hinges barely contained its might. Then again. I concluded this beast is no man.

"I'll kill you!" the Beast yelled in pure rage, practically howling at me. The fury in his voice was so loud the door could not even hope to damper it. "No one gets the drop on me, no one!" The Beast continued, and the foam from its mouth began to cover the tiny window. Obscuring him from me.

Feeling a sense of smug satisfaction, as if I had all but won, I didn't reply to his calls. Instead, I dashed away as quickly as my legs could carry me. I knew not to push my luck. But more importantly, I knew the door would not hold out for much longer.

Where is he? I thought to myself, in an attempt to refocus my mind on the task at hand. Running full tilt through the corridors. Initially taking turns at random, I came to a full stop once I realized that my surroundings looked to be exactly the same. That was by design. I recalled. Looking around to see if there was anything I recognized.

Knowing they wouldn't have taken the Kid too far, I began to retrace my steps, looking out for any possible signs of life. He can't be too far off, can he? I wondered.

My search, however, did not go unnoticed. Off in the far distance, I could hear a roar. A roar that seemed to echo throughout the station's halls. A yell so fierce yet also displayed a sense of not only hunger but... intent. I am being hunted. I realized. The door didn't last as long as I thought it would.

With the game of wolf and prey now set, I realized I'd have to find the Kid, and I'd have to find him fast. With that, I doubled my efforts, hoping to hasten the result.

My search soon yielded a single fruit, or, rather, a step. An impression in the soft floor that could only belong to...The Kid. Finally, some progress! I thought to myself with glee. The Beast's roar will still be far off, but I knew that wouldn't be the case for much longer. Following the direction these footsteps took me led deeper into the rock. It wasn't long before my ears began picking up on a certain...whine. A whine so intense it could only belong to The Kid. Got 'em!

Without even a hint of irony, I followed the direction of the whine. Well, perhaps maybe a little. I thought to myself, my eyes squarely set forward. I may not know how far this would be, but I was determined to see it done.

Thankfully, the path I chose proved to be a short one, as the whine was turning into actual words. Words I could actually recognize. "I'm telling you!" The Kid yelled, obviously in pain. "I don't know anything." His cries of desperation echoed amongst the halls, stilted silence. After that burst of emotion came a crash, followed by a scream. Then, finally, silence.

Shit!.

While the Beast was not currently in sight, its presence was still very much felt. The slight tingle on the back of my neck alerted me to its vicinity. While its nose may have long since lost my scent, that really didn't matter; the Beast knew exactly where I intended to go. He has known this entire time I would seek out The Kid. I am a victim of my obligations, I thought to myself, knowing full well, The Beast had the pick of the litter. All he had to do was wait for the proper moment to strike.

I took only one step before the massive weight of everything I was doing at last hit me. And hit me it did. I'm risking life and limb for a kid I honestly hate. I thought to myself, the low rumble of The Beast's far-off growls reverberating all along the stony caverns. Why am I doing this?

Screw it. I thought to myself, finally feeling a moment of clarity. NO amount of gold is worth this trouble. I concluded, turning my gaze back towards where I came from. It's not as if my reputation isn't already stained beyond repair," I thought, looking down at the tattered remains of my royal guard jacket. I'd kept it all these years, utilizing it well beyond its intended lifespan. Why have I held onto it? I wondered, knowing full well I could have ditched it at any time. That thought burned bright as ever in my brain, my body shaking uncontrollably as I slipped through the hall, trying as hard as I could to be as silent as possible. The steps I took were making no pattern. My form itself melds with the shadows.

This was the rhythm I found myself in as I snaked my way through the halls. I could tell the Kid's torture was closer to the front of the rock. Closer to our...I mean my ship. This is too easy... I started to think. My justification was interrupted by a scream, one that was now familiar.

Those cries for help stopped me dead in my tracks. The Kid's scream broke through not just the silence of the halls, but also the walls I had built up around my heart. His pleas seemed similar on the surface to the last one. This time, I could easily tell they were more guttural and… more desperate.

My body froze in an instant, my mind fracturing itself in two. It's not like he's my own child, I thought, I owe him nothing. The desperation was practically pouring out of me at this point. He's just some kid, I justified, trying to move my feet, but my long-dormant conscience forbade it. Feelings I had long since buried deep were choosing this exact moment to come up and make a stand. He's just a kid. Someone else's kid. He means...NOTHING!

Once and for all, after much wrangling with my better self. Greed at last won out, my foot finally complying, stepping out and over into the next hallway. The Kid's screams, of course, trailed behind me, mocking me for my cowardice.

Once, I was a protector, I reminded myself, my mind filling with memories of better times—a time when I actually stood for something. I failed in that mission. Now I was able to see in my mind's eye the fires of that night, stepping over my dead brothers who died for a lost cause. A cause I could no longer support. While it was never my choice to serve with the Royal Family, I still chose to serve with distinction.

Now I am nothing more than an Oath breaker. I realized that part of me had always known how deeply my betrayal had affected me. But never before had I admitted out loud the crime I had committed against myself.

I knew all this self-destruction would have to wait. Thus, I did what I have always done. I stuffed whatever negative feelings I felt and focused on what lay in front of me. Which, thankfully, was beginning to look more familiar. The ship is close, I thought, the Kid's screams still lingering on in the distance, taunting me with my next failure. He will break soon. I reasoned, wishing more than anything that it would be the case. Sadly, reality always won out over fantasy. That or die. I eventually concluded that I was not happy at all with the outcome. Either way, the screams will stop.

I shook my head to clear myself of such dreary thoughts. I took a moment to assess my surroundings. Before me, I see a light. A marker of a well-traveled corridor. The ship is in sight, I realized, squinting to see it far off in the distance. My freedom practically gleaming off in the yonder.

Taking a single step towards my liberation, the Kid's screams continue to echo through the halls. His cries of pain could not help but resonate within me. He is stronger than I thought, I mused, trying in vain to rationalize this latest betrayal. Stronger than I. That's for certain. That last thought lingered deep, like a splinter in my mind. Tearing my morals in two.

While it wasn't the right time or place, I couldn't help but take a moment to reflect on myself. The path that had gotten me here. Each choice, a cobblestone on the road. Am I just the end result of the choices I have made? I wondered, realizing I was about to make the same mistake I had made fifteen years prior. Or can I choose to be the better man?

In this case, it would seem that the choice was made for me. Or at least, that was the excuse I chose to tell myself in the moment. Looking around the corner, I checked if the coast was clear, and I saw him. Staring back at me from the other end of the hallway were two red, glowing eyes--the eyes of The Beast, the eyes of my doom.

It never lost track of me, I thought with a shiver. Fear once again returned to me as I realized the game we had been playing all along. The notion hit me like a sack of bricks. It wants me to run, I thought to myself, the panic well and truly starting to set in.

Weighing the choices put before me, my eyes darted back and forth between the freedom that beckoned me and the Beast, whose only desire was to play. Do I even have a choice? I wondered, gazing upon the foam forming under the Beast's mouth. The idea of fresh meat sends it into a frothing frenzy.

Screw it. I thought, throwing down my Royal Guard jacket onto the ground. The symbolism of which was not lost upon me in the slightest. "Come on, little doggy," I yelled to that mongrel, breaking out into a trot. "Let's play!" My legs were tearing down the hallway as fast as they could carry me, heading straight towards my freedom.

My sudden dash towards liberation had exactly the reaction I expected. The blood may have drained from my head in lieu of my legs, but I could still make out the rhythmic THUMP THUMP of all four of The Beast's paws hitting the floor, his pursuit of me now clear as day.

What caught me off guard was the Beast's pace. The pace was not a fast one as I had originally thought. Instead, it turned out to be a slow and methodical one. He's playing with his food. I realized, the taste of that thought was a bitterness on my tongue.

You got this, Jayce, I told myself, my gaze now pointed forward. Hope began to swell within me once I realized I was halfway to my goal... You can do this, I thought, mentally hyping myself up. Knowing it's the only way I'll make it. Just keep pouring it on!

As with all things you focus deeply on, I quickly fell into a rhythm. The pitter-patter of my feet on the millennia-old rock began to be like music to my ears. I can do this!

Turning my attention backward, I was shocked to see that my pace was quicker than that of the Beast, who wanted nothing more than to make me his supper. The stride I chose was not meant for long distances. A fact that my lungs were quickly informing me of. My breath was coming in a steady rhythm of heaves, some of which gave me sharp pains.

No pain...no GAIN! I told myself, my mind screaming in determination. I was so close to my goal; there's no way I could lose now. Freedom shall be mine!

My second wind secured, I felt the sheer willpower coursing through my veins. I redoubled my efforts, pouring all my strength into my legs so I could push myself forward. I still had some lingering doubts; old honor was always hard to shake. But I was too committed to dwell on what I was doing wrong. The mistakes I was inevitably repeating. I'm too far gone, I said to myself. Redemption is no longer in the cards.

My eyes began to tear up when I saw the threshold coming into view. Well, it was either that or my exertion finally taking effect. Almost there. I thought, trying as hard as I could to keep myself on task.

The rhythmic pain I felt in my lungs was now a constant struggle. Feeling how close my salvation was, I ignored what I could—burying the rest of my suffering along with my pride.

Feeling the rush of cool air across my skin, I knew I had reached my goal. Smiling to myself, looking down at the tips of my toes crossing the line into the hanger, the breach to freedom at last. Finally! I gloated to no one but myself. I did I...

WHAM!

Everything, all at once, came to a sudden halt. My pace, my vision, even my mind. They all just… ceased to function. Still in a haze, I reached up to my now aching forehead, trying to feel out what had just happened. Pulling my hand back, I was greeted only with a warm, wet sensation. "Wha?" was the only thing I could manage to say, my mind and body still wobbling in a fog.

"Stupid man," a now-familiar voice replied. The Dwarf, I realized. I heard a deep chuckle, then felt a small rush of air pass upon my face. At that point, I was so far gone that I felt nothing as darkness soon enveloped me...

5

A Hard Place

It all came back to me very slowly. First, I heard the words "Wakey, wakey, eggs, and bakey," filling my eardrums. Then came touch soon after, feeling the cold wetness beneath my skin. Smell quickly followed suit, the dank aroma of centuries-old sewage drifting up towards my nostrils. Taste was next, and I noticed that my tongue was coated with a thick layer of long-dried blood. Lastly, sight was my final sense to return to the fold, seeing a familiar set of sharp teeth mere inches from my eyes.

"Sir Jayce!" The Beast greeted me with applause. "So good to see you finally awake!"

"Wha... What's going on?" I replied groggily, taking stock of my surroundings. The air was... musty, the walls... damp. We must be even deeper into the rock now, I thought, my mind still not fully clear. Rock? Are we on a rock? We? I thought, still reeling.

"I am no Sir," I said, mostly out of reflex, taking a quick breath to gather myself before saying, "Also, my name is not Jayce, it is Virgil Alligries."

The Beast laughed in response. Once he stopped cackling like a hyena, the Beast looked me dead in the eye and said, "You are good, real good. Normally, I'd be inclined to believe what you had just said… If I hadn't already been alerted to The Young Prince and your impending arrival. Well, that and we had this very same conversation mere hours before."

"Prince?" I exclaimed, genuinely confused.

The Beast cackled again, this time even louder. "Clearly, you believe what you are saying. You shall soon see just how mistaken you are about a great many things."

Seemingly on cue, the only door in the room knocked twice. The Beast threw up his arms in frustration, revealing hastily written words scribbled up and down his arms. "Oh, come on! I was just getting to the good part!"

There was silence for a few seconds, then a now-familiar voice said from beyond the threshold, "Time's up, my turn to play." The Beast sighed in discontent at the Dwarf's words, slumping his shoulders, and quickly exited the room.

A welcoming silence followed the Beast's departure. The only sounds were the drip-drip behind me, accompanied by a hushed conversation that lay just outside my range of hearing.

With what little peace I had, I looked around to take stock of my surroundings. The area seemed damper than any of the rooms I had seen prior. Perhaps we are close to the core? The only source of light was a solitary torch that hung close to the door. The door itself seemed to be made out of some sort of reinforced metal. Not getting past that without a key. I sighed.

Finally, I gave my restraints a good tug, no dice. My legs were bound to the chair. The chair seemed to have been carved directly from the asteroid itself.

Feeling a sense of desperation more than anything else, I tugged at my arms. Again, no dice. The cuffs that bound me were of an unknown make. Shame.

Without warning, the talking beyond the door stopped, and instantly, my entire body tensed up, remaining that way as the door slowly creaked open, as if from some old horror video. Much to my non-surprise, "she" stepped in, a huge grin plastered onto her face. In her bulky arms, she held what looked to be a cattle prod. I shivered in sheer terror at what I saw. "Yes," she started, seeing my apprehension. "You will tell me... everything."

Without warning, millions of volts surged through my body. Pain like nothing else before poured out of every cell. I opened my mouth to scream, and most likely did. I could not hear it, for at that moment, my mind knew only one thing... pain.

After what seemed like an eternity, I returned to sanity. "She" was there wearing that same dumb grin as before. Only this time, it looked to be wider; however impossible that was.

Is she in... ecstasy? This seriously cannot be turning her on, I thought to myself with disgust. What kind of monster would employ such a creature? Oh... that's right.

"You ready to answer my questions?" The Dwarf said between gasps of air.

"Yes... Yes, I am," I said, hanging my head down in utter defeat.

The response she gave me was not one of elation but one of detest. "But I wanted to play some more!" the Dwarf said. Seemingly in a fit of rage, she pumped me with millions more volts straight into my body.

"I WAS READY TO TALK!" I cried in desperation.

"I don't care," the Dwarf said as she whacked me upside the head for good measure...

This time, everything came back with one sharp intake. Judging by the fresh torch, a couple of hours must have passed. Things looked the same, but they felt different overall. I gave my cuffs another slight tug for posterity's sake. They, too, felt diff... no... familiar. Why? I thought to myself. Wait! These cam... I continued, my thoughts being interrupted by sounds from the outside.

"Playtime is over; we need to move forward with the plan," an unknown yet still somehow familiar voice said from beyond the void.

"But sir, before we..." the Dwarf protested, or at least she tried to until she was stopped by what could only be the sound of a man's fist smacking her face.

"I said..." The man continued, his voice rising in anger, "Playtime... is OVER!"

After some very hurried footsteps, the door finally opened. In walked... Anders with a syringe, no less. And he's wearing my old uniform! I thought in shock. "Oh, I didn't realize you were awake," Anders said, quickly pocketing the needle. "That would have been HELPFUL TO KNOW!" he yelled that last part back at his subordinates before turning his gaze towards the upper corner of the room. That's probably where the camera is.

"My apologies, Jayce; good help is so hard to find in these not-so-troubled times," he said, looking me over. His eyes drank in my disheveled state. "I see you like the uniform; I figured something familiar would help jog some of your more... dormant memories." Laughing, he once more pulled out the syringe, staring at it for a moment before turning his gaze back upon me.

"Let's make this simple, Jayce. I'd honestly rather not use this, but I will if I have to," Anders said as he walked up to me, syringe still in hand, kneeling to my level, yet still somehow above me. "Where were you planning on taking the Prince?"

I looked up at him, dumbfounded. "Prince?" I asked, truly at a loss for words. Anders stared back at me for a long moment, seemingly not sure how to react.

Without warning, he burst into a fit of laughter. "You don't know!" Anders said between gasps for air. "You truly do not know." He then pointed towards the northeast corner. "That boy, that brat you travel with, he was... once upon a time, the Crown Prince of Shinkar. The irony here truly is strong."

"What?!" I exclaimed, jumping up from my seat in a mixture of shock and confusion. The cuffs quickly did their job, yanking me back into it. These cuffs… I pondered—an idea taking form inside my mind. I did not have the time to dwell on this notion, for my brain was still coming to terms with what had just been said to me. "He can't be. Elrick would have had him killed at first sight."

"He wishes he had, every single day," Anders said with a sigh. "Despite your best efforts to abandon them both, our once Queen is more resourceful than even you or I combined." He paused to take stock of my reaction. At this point, I had taken on a stone face, so he got nothing.

Disappointed, he continued with his spiel. "She found passage off of Mars and has eluded capture ever since," Anders said. Again, he paused, this time for dramatic effect. For the second time, I gave him nothing in return.

Taking my stoicism in stride, he proceeded to look me straight in the eye and say, "Do you know where she is?" Anders said after yet another pointless pause. No wonder this fool failed drama school.

At that, it was now my turn to laugh. The bellows echoed throughout the small room. "I thought you knew me better, Anders! I haven't seen that bitch since the night I fled the capital."

He didn't respond at first, preferring to look me over instead, pondering how to proceed, looking down at the syringe that was still in his hand. He then looked over at me. Our eyes truly met for the first time in forever, eyes still radiating with the same jealous rage I was all too familiar with.

Tensing up in preparation for him stabbing the syringe... somewhere, I was surprised to hear the sound of glass breaking. I opened my eyes to see that Anders had tossed it behind me. "Guess we won't be needing this, then." His next move was an about-face, followed up by a brisk march towards the door.

"Huh?" I said in complete confusion. "That's it? What now?"

In response, Anders crooked his head back in my direction. A sneer that he considered to be a smile split his face in two. "You are of no use to us, Jayce. What do you think happens to useless things?" Anders replied. Cackling in delight, he timed his last word to line up exactly with the closing of the door. That door closed with an extra loud THUMP. With it went all hope I may have had left in me.

"Damn drama que…" I started to say, suddenly overhearing Anders talking to the guards outside.

"… done here. I'll be back in 30 minutes. When I return, I want this holding cell clean. Understood?" Anders said, practically yelling, oddly enough.

My time is short. This can't be the end of my story, I thought, reassuring myself while I gave my cuffs another tug, a fit of frustration overtaking me. Pausing for a moment, I proceeded to give the cuffs one last tug.

This time, a flash of recognition hit me. I know these cuffs! The realization washed over me like a warm glow. How a set of standard-issue Royal Guard handcuffs found their way onto my wrists was of no consequence to me at this moment. Weirdly convenient, but I'll take it!

Wasting no time, I quickly and quietly set out, engaging the series of mechanisms that had been designed to open the cuffs—a design that I had specifically requested but had only partially been granted. With a very satisfying CLICK! the concerns I raised 15 years ago were validated, and my freedom was once more in my hands. But what to do now?

My answer came in the form of the Beast entering the room, cattle prod in hand. His muzzle formed a twisted grin. "Time to finish what started earlier."

With the Beast slowly approaching me, my window of opportunity to come up with a plan was ever so slowly closing in on me. My wrist blade's venom had been spent on the previous encounter. My bag of tricks was pretty much empty. I concluded that my fears about the survivability of the situation were growing larger by the moment. Remembering the cuffs that had been dangling from my wrists this entire time, my heart surged, filling up with a foreign feeling called hope.

"Unfortunately, we seem to have run out of time together, Mr. Lamont," the Beast proudly proclaimed. His salivating jaw betrayed his actual intentions, pointing the cattle prod over my crotch area for full effect. "Let's make the most of what we have left, shall we?"

"Yes... let's," I roared. With all the swiftness I could muster, leaping from my chair, I swung the cuffs around his neck, choking that little doggy for all it was worth.

The Beast writhed in agony, thrashing about in a failing attempt to throw me off of him.

"Where is the Kid?" I yelled straight into the Beast's ear while dodging his claws.

"Fu…" The Beast replied, or at least he attempted to, before I dug further into his neck.

"Answer the question, asshole; I may even consider letting you live," was my retort, obviously enjoying this a bit too much. The Beast proceeded to cease struggling for just a moment.

He pointed a claw towards his left. "Cell... nine," he said between gasps for air.

"Thanks," I replied, giving the cuffs a final tug. The Beast's neck made an extremely satisfying snap while the last bits of life left his eyes. "Whew, you were a tough son of a bitch!" I said to what I believed to be his corpse as I undid the second cuff from my wrist.

With not another moment to waste, I grabbed the Doggie's key card, gun, and a cattle prod. Upon exiting my room, the stale air greeted me, as if to welcome me back to freedom.

The air was not the only thing that greeted me. For on either side of me was what looked to be an endless hallway of doors. Looking up, the number on my cell could be found sticking up above the door: 616. "Well, at least I'll be getting in my cardio for the day," were my words, a nervous smirk besieging my face while I set off into a jog towards where I believed the Kid's cell to be.

I was about two-thirds of the way there when I heard a set of familiar voices. What was weird was that one of those voices I had not heard since... the colony!

"Isss eeeeverythiiiing goiiiing accordiiiing to plaaaan?" The Inquisitor... inquired, its voice dragging in the usual places. Why is it here? My mind asked itself while my body shivered in utter terror. Frozen with fear, I cowered behind a nearby corner.

"Y... yes, sir. Lupan almost went too far, but it ended up not mattering in the end," what could be no one else but the Dwarf replied, her voice uncharacteristically throbbing in sheer panic.

"Gooooood," the Inquisitor replied with the usual drag to its speech. The thing's voice seemed to slither with glee. "Ssssee that things keep on raaaailssss. The Emperor would be mosssst dissspleassssed with meeee if it did not." It paused for a moment. From my perch, I saw it brush its hand along the Dwarf's cheek, looking upon it. I watched as the Dwarf shook from head to toe. She seemed to be overcome with constrained panic.

Its cracked lip broke into a twisted smile while it said, "You do not want thingsssss to roll downhill, you ssssack of shhhhit. Understand?" All the Dwarf could do in response was put her head down. Seemingly satiated, the Inquisitor turned and walked away without saying another word.

The Dwarf continued to stand there motionless. For a moment, I thought she had passed out. But, to my... relief? She finally snapped her head up and walked back into the darkness. From my perch, I could just make out the faint sounds of... sobbing?

I stood there for a few seconds, pondering why exactly I felt... mercy for my abuser, shaking my head to clear it of such nonsense. I have a job to do, my instincts reminded me. Promises to keep. Promises? What a... nostalgic notion. Knowing that my lax attitude had its upper limits, my legs quickly slipped themselves into a rather strong stride. The Kid's cell can't be too far ahead.

Upon reaching the cell, my brain became an empty void of thoughts and emotions. Not sure what to do, I just stood there, paralyzed by choice. I have to do something; I've come too far just to lose it all. Deciding to throw caution to the wind and wing it, I pounded on the door.

"I DON'T KNOW THE LOCATION OF THE REBEL BASE! PLEASE... JUST BELIEVE ME, ALREADY!" Standing there, hearing the Kid's broken cries of desperation, left me shattered in a million pieces. They have broken him. That one thought repeated itself in my head on an endless loop. In the process, my body became awash with both sorrow and pity.

"Kid, it's me," I said, my voice losing any sort of idea of security and going as loud as it could. I tried to use my voice to convey a sense of strength for the Kid's sake, sadly failing miserably.

"Ju... Virgil, you came for me!" The Kid cried in exhilaration, his voice swelling up with hope for what probably was the first time in a great while.

"Kid," I started saying, trying to make things quick. "First off, we can dispense with the code names 'cause they know." Taking a breath to gather both myself and my thoughts before continuing, "Secondly, I'm here. I got a key, and we will get out of this together. Do you trust me?" My hollering echoed across the halls. They most certainly will hear my ruckus.

Waiting for the Kid to respond, my confidence dwindled with each passing second. A cone of silence descended to envelop me while I waited for him to decide our fate. For too long, my only sonic companion was a constant drone coming from the air filters.

Finally, as if to break the tension—or perhaps he actually meant it?—The Kid simply said one word, a word that I desperately needed to hear.

"Yes."

Letting out a huge breath that I had not realized was held, I said, "Okay, when I open this door, it will be go time. I need you by my side. No quips, no complaints, nothing. Do you understand?"

Another moment of silence was shared between the two of us. This one, thankfully, was much shorter than the last. "I do," was all The Kid said in response.

I swiftly swiped the key card. Next thing I knew, I had an armful of Kid clenched tightly around my waist.

"Thank you!" he exclaimed, between gulps of air and waves upon waves of tears. Just as quickly as he embraced me, he disengaged, adopting a more dignified persona. "So... where to next?"

Not really sure what to say, I just replied with, "Ah, good question." My mind a void of what to actually do. Just keep winging it, Jayce. "This way."

While I obviously had an idea as to the layout of this rock, I felt that I could reason out the rest in order to find our way out. Trusting my instincts, the Kid and I brute-forced our way through the maze of corridors. Things seemed quiet until…

"The Prince has escaped, sir," the Dwarf said from around the corner, seemingly into her comm, probably trying to alert the Inquisitor. She took a sharp intake of breath, indicating that the Dwarf was most likely about to ask a follow-up question. She never got the chance to ask that question as The Kid tripped over a rock and fell forward, straight into her line of sight, in the most raucous display of failure I have ever seen, thereby blowing our cover.

"What should I do... sir?" she finally said, looking straight at us. For what could only be an eternity, the

Dwarf's eyes and mine locked into place. It felt as if the jig was well and truly up. I started to turn my head in the direction of the Kid as the Dwarf turned hers in the direction of her comm. She whispered a reply to an order that had been inaudible to the Kid and me.

She then looked down at the comms in shock at what she seemed to have been told. Then, to my complete shock, she looked at me, blew a kiss,... and walked off.

"What the actual fu…" That was all I could manage to say in reaction to what had just transpired before my voice trailed off. I crouched there, dumbstruck and at a total loss for words. My mind was still attempting to process exactly what had just transpired.

"Jayce, I... I think we should press onward," the Kid said to me, breaking me free from the mental prison that I had placed myself in.

"Yeah, of course," was the only thing I could say, seeing as how my mind was still wrapped in fog—a thin fog, but a fog nonetheless. My voice was still shaking when I followed up with, "We need to stay vigilant. Something's not right; nothing adds up."

Upon hearing my words, the Kid tilted his head like some sort of dog. Then, much to my chagrin, he laughed—laughed at me! "You just figured that out?"

Returning his look with one of my own, this one contained pupils that burned with the heat of a million suns. Now properly cowed, I motioned for him to follow me.

Thankfully, at this point, the scenery had started to look a bit more... familiar. This godsend allowed me to retrace my steps back through the hallowed halls I had previously endured.

Where is the security detail? I wondered, my mind racing faster than my heartbeat. The notion echoed back and forth in my brain, gnawing at me, clawing at me. From hallway to empty hallway, we continued. The worry on the Kid's face was growing in tandem with my own.

"Ow! Why did you hit me?" the Kid squealed when I tapped him on the back to indicate where we were going. I had to extend my arm downward in order to stop him from speaking any further, "accidentally" hitting the Kid upside the back of his head in the process. His cries were only silenced fully when I was able to cover his mouth with my free hand.

"Shush! We're getting close," I whispered to the Kid. My eyes shot daggers at him in an attempt to keep him quiet. This time, he seemed to take the hint. Thus, my attention was refocused on that fateful hallway.

No Warwolf this time. I took care of that, my mind recalled in an attempt to reassure itself.

The cries of my past failures continued to flood my brain, drowning out anything close to a joyous notion. I did my best to push those long-term residents aside and bring in more helpful thoughts. The Dog may be gone, but the Dwarf and Anders are still in play. Yeah, that should do the trick.

I scrambled to form a plan. While I may once have been a leader of both men and women, a strategist, I certainly was not. Still, I had no choice but to try. "Anders is probably in the control room like the coward he is," I muttered under my breath. The Kid, of course, caught wind of my words and looked up at me in confusion. One look was all it took to prevent another disaster.

With the Kid quelled, my mind once again returned to the task at hand. Anders is in the control room. That's for certain. As for the Dwarf? Could she be looking to make history repeat itself? Deciding to tempt the fates and risk everything on my hunch, I quickly whispered my plan into the Kid's ear. He looked up at me, seemingly bewildered. In response, I did a quick jab to his gut and pointed at my ship, glistening like the diamond it was, at the end of the hallway. Once he recovered, he stood up short and proud, shrugged, and quietly whispered, "Whatever."

With that issue solved, the Kid and I broke into a brisk trot. The gap between us and our freedom was getting shorter with every step. Risk is part of the package, I reminded myself. My mind may have been filled with doubt, but my heart was filled to the brim with determination. This will work. It... HAS TO!

Nearing the threshold of our liberation, I took in a deep breath—surprisingly, the first one in a while. This is it. "Now!" I shouted, abandoning my stealth in addition to signaling the Kid to slide in tandem with my own. Both of us glided over the threshold to the docking bay.

Right on cue, a giant club, a very familiar club, whizzed past my nose. Not giving The Dwarf a chance to react, I slammed a cattle prod, one that the Doggie had so graciously provided me, deep into her side.

The Dwarf, in turn, let out a cavernous roar—so loud that she soon fell over, accompanied by a giant THUD. Her cries of pain echoed throughout the halls for a few seconds afterward.

The Kid and I quickly got up, training my pistol on her while the Kid looked around, clueless as to what to do.

"Um, Jayce, now what?" the Kid asked me. His head continued to whip back and forth, frantically in search of a purpose.

I looked over at him with a dumbfounded expression. He, in turn, stared back at me with his signature piercing gaze. To break the tension, I pointed at the Evantide and yelled, "Start that ship up!" yelling louder than I probably should have to release my frustration.

The Kid finally snapped in my direction. He seemed to have at last landed back in reality. Twisting his head towards me, his mouth formed into a snarl, and then he growled at me. "I am a Prince, not a pilot."

I looked at the Kid and then back at the Dwarf, my mind trying to process what he had just said. Is he serious? Can someone truly be this out of touch with reality? Seeing that the Dwarf was beginning to rouse, I knew our time was running short. "The computer will handle the worst parts. Just tell it what to do, and you will be fine. Now go!" I roared, the pressure from the moment beginning to break me.

"You do realize your landing gear is bolted in, right?" Anders called out, his voice booming over the loudspeakers.

I looked up, staring straight into one of the many cameras in this room. "I do," I said, smiling while saying those simple words—simple yet oh-so effective. A stillness enveloped the landing pad, our only companion the ever-increasing revving of The Evantide's engines.

Suddenly, like a hot knife through butter, a squeal broke through, utterly shattering the silence. "G... G... GET HIM!!" Anders cried, his voice reeking with desperation.

The Dwarf started to stagger her way over to me. "Not so fast, Dwarf," I yelled. The engines had now reached their zenith.

Ignorant of the danger, the Dwarf continued to push forward. "I have a name," she said, much to my surprise. Her eyes were trained on me the entire time—well, they were… right up until I pointed a gun in her face.

"I don't care," was my reply—a completely truthful one at that. Smoke began to spew from the ship's exhaust, signaling that the thrusters would soon ignite. "Time's up... Dwarf. In your defense, Anders fell for the exact same trick on Drifter Colony 17. Bye-bye." I winked at her to achieve maximum douchebag effect.

I backed up the ramp, the gun still pointed directly forward for my safety. "A.I., get us out of here!" I yelled back into the ship, charging up the entry ramp while it shuddered shut behind me, and finding my way onto the bridge as the ramp finished closing.

"Landing gear is still locked in place; cannot comply," A.I. replied to my query.

"Override," I yelled back, not having time for its crap. I slammed my hand onto the front console for confirmation.

"Please find your nearest seating and strap in. This will get... bumpy," A.I. replied. The ship groaned in sheer pain as she broke free.

"Did A.I. just make... a joke?" The Kid asked, looking me straight in the eye with a bewildered expression.

"Just go with it," was all I could say in response, letting out a sigh of exasperation. The ship's groans grew louder as we remained in place. Then, in a burst of motion, we flew from our perch and out into the great unknown.

"Are we there yet?" the Kid asked, seemingly eager to jump the gun. His tone indicated that he thought himself to be the first one in history ever to say that.

I decided to respond with another stock answer, rather than simply saying "Not yet." I got up from my seat and marched towards the forward console, demanding, "E.T.A. to slipstream?"

"Current estimated time till slip engagement is five minutes," A.I. spat out with its usual cold demeanor, as A.I.s tended to do.

"Frack me!" I screamed in frustration, the Kid covering his ears as I did so. Without any other hesitation, I walked up to the entrance of the bridge. I placed the palm of my hand upon a panel at the side and tossed the Kid one of the Hyper Visors from said panel, keeping the other for myself.

"What's this?" the Kid asked, his eyes not leaving the device, holding it up like it was radioactive.

"It's called a Hyper Visor," I said, starting to explain to the Kid, rolling my eyes for having to go over such a basic device. "A.I. says it will take five minutes for the FTL to spool up. In the meantime, we've got some Imperial Buzzards to fend off."

Sitting down at the comms console, I threw the Visor over my eyes. "Jaycen Lamont, Captain General," I said into the mic to give it my pre-programmed voice print. On cue, the screen snapped into place. The words ID CONFIRMED flashed before my eyes.

Having synced up with the Visor, I prepared myself. The screen was hazy to start. My view was a mesh of static while it finished pairing with my drone. At last, the oh-so-familiar sight of empty space greeted my eyes.

"Orion Shinkar, Crown Prince," the Kid spoke into his own Visor, giving his voice print after seeing me do it and deciding to mimic my motions.

I turned down the opacity on the Hyper Visor to look over at him. My head turned to face him, my ears picking up the faint chime of confirmation emanating from his Hyper Visor.

So they did program him in, after all… I thought, marveling at what was obviously the Queen's handiwork. Much to my surprise, he was staring right back at me, more than likely looking to gauge my reaction, I surmised, my mind rationalizing this obviously odd interaction.

Looking into his eyes, I could see his desperation, his pleading, and most importantly, I actually felt sorry for him. "Don't look at me. We've got five Imperial Buzzards about to breathe down our necks," I shouted over to him, focusing my attention back on the task at hand.

Snapping the Hyper Visor back onto my face, I looked over the readout of what exactly the Kid and I had to face: five likely low-skilled pilots flying rejected designs. Even in the face of an obvious win, never take your victory for granted. My old flight instructor's words rang loudly in my mind.

My musings were quickly shattered by the sharp ping in my ear, alerting me to an impact on my aft shield. "Oh no, you don't!" The roar of my voice was in lockstep with the groaning of my drone doing maneuvers it was never designed or intended to do.

I gazed on in wonder as my returning muscle memory swung the drone around to meet my challenger, the enemy pilot not immediately reacting—must have been shocked at the turn of skill that I put on display.

I wasn't going to waste such a lapse in attention, landing just a single shot at the base of its neck, a tiny sliver where the silver shroud that covered its neck met with the rest of the craft. It's a tough shot for sure, but one well within my skill set.

That shot was all it took; soon my efforts were rewarded with a familiar but still very satisfying ping. Said ping was shortly followed up by a series of small explosions. Those explosions eventually culminated in one last beautiful display of destruction.

"WOO HOO!" I cheered, pumping my fist in the air for good measure. The celebration was sadly cut short, though, with the sight of another Buzzard entering my 3 o'clock. I fired off a few shots to test the mettle of this new foe. The response I received was the sight of shields absorbing my hits.

"Mother fracker!" I cried out, my frustration boiling up to the surface. It was then that a memory of a past battle entered my brain. In the final battle of IO, those hicks flew Buzzards better than these fools. I smiled as I recalled my past glories.

With posthaste, I engaged the emergency booster. Swinging in under its belly, I fired a round of shots straight toward the cargo bay—well, to be more specific, the hinges. Of course, my shots hit their marks. As a result, the cargo bay doors shot off their remaining handles, rapidly depressurizing the entire craft. I chuckled as I watched it collapse, like a tin can.

"Yeah!" I cheered, leaping out of my seat while screaming in utter joy. "That's how it's done... SHADOW HAWK STYLE!" The expected query from the Kid soon followed my fervor.

"What's Shadow Hawk style?" he asked, right on cue. My mind instantaneously formed several snarky snapbacks. Sadly, before I could say even one of them, I was forced to tell him…

"Kid, behind you!" I yelled, trying to get his attention. It ultimately proved pointless as I was forced to watch a Buzzard sneak up behind him, hoping to get a cheap kill. I figured this was the end of the Kid's run. I had started to queue up my thrusters to meet this fool when, much to my shock and amazement, the Kid flipped his drone around. With a speed that could even rival my own, he fired off a series of shots toward the Buzzard's cockpit.

Miraculously, or perhaps ironically, the Buzzard did not currently have its front shielding engaged. It paid for that mistake. I watched in glee as the cockpit window cracked and then burst clean open. "I got one, Jayce. I got one!" the Kid said with glee; this time it was his turn to stand up and cheer. He's definitely got the touch, I thought to myself.

My admiration for the Kid's skills had to be sadly cut short, gazing on in helpless horror while another Buzzard swooped in behind his former companion and fired off a single seismic torpedo. That charge detonated mere meters from the Kid's drone, obliterating not only him but me as well, for I got caught up in its wake. My drone slammed into the ship.

"SON OF A BI…" the Kid and I both said in unison, both of us tearing off our headsets at the same time. Our actions were only to be stopped dead in their tracks when we glanced over at one another, realizing what the two of us were doing. Thankfully, our awkward silence was quickly cut short when one of the Buzzard pilots started lighting up our squawk box.

"Evantide! By right of Imperial Authority, you are to be escorted back to the checkpoint. You have thirty seconds to comply." The Kid's eyes went wide in reaction to the pilot's announcement. My reaction was to walk up to the forward console calmly, activate the ship's weapons, and then finally turn on the outbound connection, pausing for dramatic effect before simply saying,

"Did they tell you who I am?" There was a pause on their end, most certainly not for dramatic effect.

Upon the pilot's return, her voice was a bit shaky.

"No" was the only thing she seemed capable of saying.

"My name is Jaycen Lamont," I started saying into the squawk box. "Disgraced Captain General of the Royal Guard. Former leader of the Shadow Hawk Squadron."

Glancing back to confirm my suspicions, and indeed, the Kid was staring at me. "What?" I hollered back at him, perplexed. "You had your secrets. I had mine." I paused for a moment, this time to regain my composure, before flicking back on the switch to the squawk box.

"If the pair of you do not immediately flee, I will have my vengeance in this life... or the next," I said, switching off the outgoing transceiver for the squawk box.

Exhausted, I leaned back in my chair... and waited. For what seemed like an entire eon, the two ships in front of us just stayed in place— locked in a silent stare-down, each of us waiting for the other side to "blink."

Getting tired of this stalemate, I reached towards the console. "How about we turn this cold war hot?" I taunted over the squawk box like the smartass I thought I was, pressing the button to prime the ship's targeting systems.

"It's still two to one," was her only response, the voice cracking towards the end. I loudly chuckled upon hearing their pathetic attempt at intimidation, keeping the comms open to make sure they heard my mirth.

"I have the superior craft, the superior set of weapons," I stopped; my speech stuttered so that the pilots could hear the computer chime in.

"Targets... locked. Would you like to fire?"

With that announcement, I gave it a moment to sink in before finally adding, "Oh, and I am most certainly the superior pilot." Another round of silence; I used this opportunity to fine-tune the ship's targeting readouts, making dead certain my shots would find their mark.

Without any prior notice, one of the Buzzards broke off and tore out in the direction of the checkpoint. Like clockwork, the other Buzzard broke rank as well, heading back to the checkpoint with its proverbial tail between its legs.

I leaned back in my chair, adopting a more relaxed posture, just sitting there in stunned shock. The Kid looked over at me, his expression aghast at what I had done.

"I can't believe that actually worked…," he said to me, our mutual silence broken by the steady beep of the Nav Computer, indicating the ship was ready for its jump. Not wanting to stick around another moment longer, I swiftly pulled the lever and was thrown back as we made the jump to Slip Space.

"Anything you can walk away from, right, Jayce?" the Kid said as he got up from his chair and stretched.

"No," was the only word I seemed able to muster. The weight of everything was beginning to swell up inside me, alongside pent-up anger now that the danger had passed.

"What do you mean?" The Kid's voice faltered with apprehension as he spoke.

"No, we are not friends. One moment of bonding does not undo fifteen years' worth of pain and regret," I responded, rising from my chair to head back to my room, completely and utterly done.

"I don't have any regrets about what has happened," the Kid said, completely naive to what was actually going on. Stopping at the threshold, dead in my tracks, I looked back at the Kid. My eyes filled with liquid sadness as all of my choices hit me at once.

"I do."

6
What Is Love?

The time had finally arrived. Word had just come down the line that Elrick and his contingent of revolutionaries were currently on their way to charge the palace gate. My position at the time placed me near the head of the table. Only the Queen sat closer to the King than I did.

To my immediate left was the sniveling weasel, named Corfis Anders. How he had wormed his way into the number three spot on the Royal Guard was a mystery to me. Sitting just across from me was my trusted second-in-command, Fuir-Ey Jackson. It was almost difficult to make him out in the dim light of the room. The dark clothes we wore, recently converted to battle mode, blended in with our skin almost seamlessly.

I wished for something to drink, but given the state of alert we were in, we couldn't afford to waste anything. As per tradition, we all stood up as the King entered—that is, everyone but the Queen. Her hands were busy tending to the King's newborn son. The King walked to the end of the table with as much grace as a regal robe over pajamas could allow. He was further along than I thought. I gasped mentally upon seeing his appearance.

"What's the situation?" the King brazenly asked while sitting down. "I am not pleased to be taken away from my deathbed." A small puff of air escaped from beneath him as he sat on his throne.

"Your Majesty," I began, my voice quivering with uncertainty after seeing the King's frail state. What am I doing here? The thought once more entered my head. I was born a warrior. I still walk that very path, just as my forefathers did. Why am I here, playing the aristocrat? Shaking my head to rid myself of any doubts, I cleared my throat and continued. "As you are aware, news of your failing health has not been taken well by your subjects."

The King's head shot up, stirring him from his stupor. Mere moments before, he'd looked to be on the verge of oblivion. Now, the King's eyes showed the very fire his ancestors had used to found the kingdom. "Ungrateful, the lot of them. I built the very society they live in!" the King yelled, not realizing that he did not build the Shinkar Kingdom; his forebears did. It was only after his outburst that he saw the faces of his "subjects." Realizing the gravity of the situation, his mind finally returned to reality with the words, "Please continue, Jayce."

I took a sharp breath to collect myself. The King's tenuous grasp on our plane of existence would make holding onto things that much more difficult. Deciding just to pick up where I left off, I went on, "Your son, Elrick, has raised an army against you, believing himself the rightful heir."

The King burst into a fit of laughter at what I had said. He leaned over and kissed the Queen on the forehead. The Queen winced at his contact, her eyes looking at me in horror. The King either ignored her transgression or was oblivious. Either way, he pointed at the Kid and proclaimed to the whole room, "But I have an heir! He's right here."

"Be that as it may, Your Majesty," Jackson chirped in at the most crucial moment—a move that he was infamous for. That man would have made an amazing Captain General; why he never stepped up was a mystery to us all. I shot him a glance to thank him. He glanced over at me, nodded, and then continued. "Elrick's forces are quite considerable."

The King froze in his tracks at what Jackson told him. You could see the fire go out of his eyes in that instant. Immediately, the King returned to looking a hundred years older than his actual age. He looked over to me, his face desperate for respite. I tilted my head down in shame and just shook it. He then looked over at Jackson and asked the most important question of his reign: "How many?"

Jackson fiddled with his datapad. What he intended as looking up the actual number was painfully obvious to us all as a stall for time. After he could delay no longer, Jackson looked up with tears in his eyes and said, "Three hundred and sixty…" The man hesitantly took a breath, not wanting to finish the response. The King took his pause as a finish, his eyes gleaming with hope, a feeling that had been absent from the palace for months. The brief moment of salvation was shot down when Jackson could no longer delay the inevitable. He swiftly said, "Thousand," then got up from his seat and left, mumbling something about preparing the defenses. While I did not doubt that the man was speaking the truth, I knew he actually left because the weight of the situation was proving unbearable.

The man we called King looked up towards the skylight. The ruins of Earth and all its failings shone brightly down upon us. "Oh," he said before promptly collapsing on the table. Each one of us knew better than to check for life inside that royal husk. No one said a word. Their King, the very man their existence revolved around, lay dead on the command table. Readouts of strategies and maps of every inch of the palace were quickly being covered in the king's bowels—an apt metaphor for what was to come.

Gathering up what strength I had remaining, I pushed my chair out from under me. "We have a palace to defend!"—everyone looked up at me when I spoke—"The King is dead; long live the King."

My words seemed to affect them. At once, they all stood up and looked at me. "The King is dead," they yelled in unison. Then, looking over at the Kid, their voices took on a more noble vigor: "LONG LIVE THE KING!"

Seeing that display and knowing the stakes, a switch flipped inside me. At once, I felt sick, like I wanted to vomit my entire soul. Promptly taking my leave and exiting the room, I flagged down a nearby aide, pulling her aside and whispering into her ear, "Prep the Evantide; we need an exit strategy."

She looked up at her superior as if for the first time, not believing what she'd just heard. "Are things really that bad?" she quietly asked me, her huge eyes seeming to go even wider with her words.

I scooped up the aide into a big hug, unsure if it was for her benefit or mine. "You don't need to have the engines running. Just take care of all the pre-launch stuff, okay?"

She nodded in response to my attempts at reassuring her. Then, without saying anything else, she swished away, her skirt flowing, and headed off in the direction of the launch pad. As for myself…

"Jayce!" the Queen cried out, breaking me from my concentration. I turned over and looked at her. Not even the low light could diminish her beauty, her violet eyes shining out in the darkness. She was still holding onto her son for dear life.

I took two steps towards her, then stopped. Not wanting to, once again, be caught in her emotional snare, I stood my ground. "You should find shelter, Your Highness; we have this covered."

She scoffed at my remarks, stomping the ground for dramatic effect. "That is not my way. My place is with you-you and the rest of the defenders."

I sighed, feeling the truth in her words. "I know," was all I could say, not sure which part I was agreeing with or perhaps agreeing with both parts. The woman had been an enigma ever since I first set eyes upon her. She seemed more at ease among the warriors than she did among the aristocracy. But what could you expect from an Ascended?

"Jayce?" My name was uttered for a second time. However, it now seemed to be coming from a combination of sources. One was undoubtedly the Queen herself, but the other? This was different yet somehow still familiar. I took myself out of the haze that was my internal conflict to focus on the moment at hand—the realm of the real.

I turned my back on her, sadly not for the last time, and said, "I must go; I have a job to do. Act as you must…" Breaking out into a sprint, I looked to put as much distance between myself and that woman as possible. The guilt of my upcoming choice had already begun to seep into my conscience. Even though I could not see the woman, I felt her eyes still burning into me. At any moment, I expected her to cry out.

"Jayce?" My name entered my ears for a third time. But this time, not from the Queen. No, this time, it came from the Kid. Confused as to what was happening, I opened my eyes. What greeted me was the same sight I had become accustomed to over the past fifteen years: the royal bedchamber, rather, what had been the royal bedchamber. Now, it was a mess of tools, mementos, and the undergarments of women I had not spoken to in over a decade. "Jayce! We really need to talk!" the Kid cried out to me for what had to have been the fourth time.

Not wanting to be reminded of my name for a fifth time, I, at last, got out of my bed for the first time in a good, solid week. Clad in nothing but my skivvies, I hobbled over to the door. I did not bother to open it; instead, I gave the thing a single pound to let the Kid know I was there. "Kid, what the hell do you want? Can't you see I'm busy wallowing in my self-hatred?"

A moment of awkward silence hung between us. Finally, he found the courage to speak up. "Why didn't you read the packet?" he asked, the Kid's voice soft and unsure. "It had all the information you needed for this mission."

Against my better wishes, I chuckled—the first genuine moment of mirth in who knows how long. The Kid had somehow figured out the perfect icebreaker. "Because I'm a cowardly SOB who can't face the facts," I answered, the honesty now just sliding out from me. "Even when it's annoying the ever-loving Hades out of me."

"I don't believe you." Another thump—this time it was the Kid's doing. By the sounds of it, he must have slumped on the floor. "The Jayce I know came back to rescue me after freeing himself, especially when he didn't have to."

Faced with my altruism, it was now my turn to slump to the floor. "I was given a job to do; that is all—deliver you safe and sound. It's the obligation that drove me, kid, not benevolence." The Kid responded to my deflection by pounding what had to be a metal rod into the door, somehow finding the perfect spot so that the sound would slam straight into my eardrum.

"You had another job once—an obligation to me!" the Kid roared in what even I had to admit was a righteous fury. He stopped for a split second to collect himself. "Jayce, which is it? Are you, or are you not, a man of your word?"

He's hitting me with the tough questions, I thought to myself, shocked at his audacity. Straight to the point, just like his mother. Now, looking inward, probably for the first time since I had fled the capital—fled from my old life, from myself. "I…" I choked on my words, not being used to this level of introspection. "I want to be. It's not that easy, kid. What I did to your mother—what I did to you— that's unforgivable!"

"My mother once told me a man has two great spiritual needs: one is for forgiveness, the other is to do good," the Kid replied with a certain maturity I had not thought he possessed. She never lost faith, least of all in me… Slowly, I rose from my pit of despair.

"Your mother—did she ever speak of me?" I asked the Kid, leaning my forehead against the door. He didn't respond at first; he was probably combing his memories.

"A few times," the Kid said after what felt like an eternity. "The way she talked about you, she hated what had been done, Jayce. But she never—not even for a moment—hated you." Silence hung in the air after the Kid's revelation, like a bad fart that nobody wanted to admit to. Sensing the tension, the Kid decided to pipe in with a fateful anecdote. "Hey… uh, why don't you come outside? I'm sure that you need to check the Nav or something…"

"The Auto-Nav! How could I be so stupid!" I said, cursing myself. The Auto-Nav was the only thing standing between an uneventful journey and certain doom. With it being left unattended for upwards of three weeks, there was no telling where we could be! Not even bothering with clothes, I rushed out the door, flying past a very confused kid and straight onto the bridge. "A.I., generate Auto-Nav readout!"

The volume of my voice did not affect the commands I gave to the A.I.; I was just in such a frantic state of panic that I couldn't be bothered to care. After about three agonizing seconds, the Auto-Nav spat out the log. Snatching it up, I quickly went down the list of the routes it had chosen, promptly feeling my stomach sink to the floor in the process. Dread washed over me, probably for the first time since we'd hit the checkpoint. That feels like it was another lifetime.

Looking back, I saw the Kid still sitting by my door, looking more confused than ever. "Kid, get over here and strap in!" I roared, pausing as I looked down, remembering that I was still in my underwear. You don't want to crash-land half-naked, do you? "Actually, before you do, go inside my room and grab me a set of clothes; whatever is lying on the floor, take your pick."

Thankfully, by this point, the Kid had learned enough about me to know when to shut up and do as he was told. Before I could finish punching in the exit codes, he was already by my side with a change of clothes—clean ones, too. "Thanks, kid, that actually helps," I said to him, sincerely grateful that at least one thing in this emerging dung show was going correctly. "You'd better strap in. Things are about to get rough."

"Which port are we landing at?" The Kid's naïveté was still in full effect. Swiveling in my seat to meet his unknowing gaze, I wanted to laugh at his failure to grasp the state of things, just like all the times before. But I found that this time I couldn't. Perhaps the rock had changed me, or perhaps it had awakened something inside of me I long thought dead.

Leveling my eyes at the Kid, no longer looking down on him but instead looking at him, I said, "We will not be landing at any port. We will be crash-landing onto the surface of Venus."

He had no response to that—no pompous quip, no attempt at being witty, nothing. The drastic notion of what we were about to partake in overwhelmed his ability to process reality. "We… will… will we be okay, Jayce?"

I didn't answer at first. Instead, I turned my back to him so that I could attend to the emergency exit from Slip Space—a maneuver so monumentally moronic that it's literally discouraged on day one of flight school. I mean it; they tell you right after informing everyone where the bathrooms are. Is it that important? Here I was, about to break the first rule of space flight: NEVER, EVER MAKE AN UNPLANNED EXIT FROM SLIP SPACE! EVER! My instructors called me a madman from afar, but even they could never fathom me being this stupid. But here I was, pulling the lever to take us out.

As expected, the ship lurched forward upon our return to normal space—well, as normal as you can get with the second rock from the sun taking up the entirety of your viewport. I think I even heard the dampeners snap. I just replaced those suckers a year ago! I remembered, shaking my head while I fired up the sublight engines.

"Okay, we're still in one piece. That's a good sign, right? Now let's get the frick out of here!" the Kid said, his head darting back and forth to check on the condition of the ship. He looked back at me after a few moments, appearing to have noticed that we hadn't moved a millimeter. "Um, Jayce? Why aren't we going anywhere?"

I didn't bother to reply, having other, more pressing matters to attend to—first among those being the enormous gravity well we now found ourselves in. Like gnats caught in a web, the two of us were helpless to resist its pull. The ship's engines were the best money could buy twenty years ago, but their power was still considerable. Sadly, even the Evantide's mighty thrusters proved incapable of breaking us free.

Knowing the inevitability of the situation, I decided to stop fighting the raging pull and instead swim with the current, plotting a course that would set us down in a valley I was at least somewhat familiar with. Oh, and by "set down," I was referring to a rather rough landing that had a sixty percent chance of ending in a giant ball of fire and death—you know, just another day in this lovely hellhole.

Finally getting the chance, I stole a glance at the Kid. My face was not even bothering to put on its usual mask of assholery. Feeling scared beyond belief, I could not in good conscience hide that from him. Conscience—now that's a concept you haven't pondered in some time, since that night, I believe. Well, you certainly did afterward—ruined two sets of sheets with your incessant tears.

Then, almost as if on cue, every light on the forward console lit up at once, breaking me from the respite of this waking nightmare. Looking around, it was as if the ship was screaming at me in pain—a sight that was just about too hard to watch. But watch I did, the ship careening straight into the welcoming womb of Mother Venus. Up until this point, I would consider my performance in landing the ship to be adequate at best. Sadly, that was before we hit the atmosphere.

A brick wall of carbon dioxide and sulfuric acid greeted me at the gates of the goddess of love—the Roman version, anyway. Its seductive pull lured the ship ever closer to its eventual demise. If I were

lucky—or, to be more accurate, properly skilled—
skilled-the ship would crash-land into a barren field
of volcanic ash, with acid rain coming along to wash
away any trace of our presence quickly. Yes, landing
would be just the first hurdle to overcome, albeit one
of the most important.

"Brace for impact, kid!" I hollered back, unsure
how much good it would actually do. At the same
time, the ship seemed to be following along the
path I had charted. I found the journey towards it
was filled with pockets of lighter oxygen,
something that definitely did not help matters.
"Hold on to anything!" With the final three
hundred kilometers closing in, my attention turned
towards our landing angle. It was then that I
realized we were off by thirty degrees. At this
angle of entry, we were more likely to act like a
skipping stone than a proper starship.

Given the amount of fuel we had left, we could
possibly correct it to fifteen degrees. "Even that
won't be enough!" I shouted into the ether, the
words somehow echoing in a pocket of silence,
fitting in somewhere between every alarm the ship
had ever been fitted with, each one going off in
unison. Looking through the viewport's reflection, I
saw two things: one was the readout indicating that
we now had 200 kilometers until impact, and the
other was the Kid's face contorted into an
expression somewhere between extreme confusion
and outright terror.

"Wha…" His screams were drowned out by all the alarms, which somehow found a way to be louder and more numerous. I'm not sure how that's even possible… We were now down to the last hundred meters, and I knew things were now or never. Slamming the forward console with my fist, the ship seemed to understand what I wanted to achieve. My ambitions had been made a reality when I heard the sputtering of the sublight engines' desperate attempts to push us back on course.

With judgment now a mere fifty kilometers away, I felt every single cell in my body tense up at once. Up until this point, I had avoided looking at the meter displaying the landing angle. With the knowledge that no more could be done, I cautiously looked over—eighteen degrees, nowhere near optimal. It would have to do. With our fates now sealed, I closed my eyes. I was fully conscious of the fact that the next time they opened, I'd either be in the afterlife or still here, on Venus. Both outcomes were now on the table. With that thought, I relaxed, feeling the impact beneath me, the landing heralding our descent into the true darkness…

7

Please Don't Hurt Me

"Warning... warning... hull integrity at 46 percent..."

Is this my hell? I wondered, the A.I.'s never-ending updates buzzing in my ear. A constant loop of hope, only to be dashed by the ship crushing around me?

Upon my arrival on this pockmarked planet, I seemed to have made a new friend: crippling nihilism. A debilitating ideology that devours the very soul. Normally, I wouldn't be one to fall so easily into such a curse. One doesn't reach the heights I had by believing nothing matters. Sadly, in circumstances like this, even the strongest wills find themselves vulnerable to its charms.

"Ju... Jayce? Are we there yet?" The Kid cried, shaking me from my spell, if only for a moment. Even in the direst situations, he finds a way to annoy me. Honestly, in a time like this, I can't be mad at him.

Sticking my neck out to look over at The Kid took some effort, not to mention a great deal of pain. Thankfully, he seemed to be in one piece. Aside from a few scrapes and cuts, it looked like only his ego was seriously hurt—an injury we seemed to share. "Yes, yes, we are. We can't stay here long, though."

The Kid responded to my words by unbuckling his straps and then immediately falling to the floor.

Something inside me awakened at the sight, all negative thoughts vanishing from my mind in an instant. I leaped from my seat, scooping The Kid up into my arms. "What hurts?" I asked, surprising myself at how much I cared.

Raising his head to meet mine, he gave me a look of complete bewilderment. "You mean besides everything?" he responded, trying to bring forth his cutest smile and failing miserably.

Not having the time or the patience for his BS, I shot him a glare—one that he was quite familiar with at this point. The Kid got the point and quickly followed up with, "My left leg; it's what hurts the most."

I looked him up and down and raised him onto his good leg. Indeed, there was a piece of tubing sticking out of his thigh. "This is gonna hurt, okay?" I told The Kid before, quickly yanking it out of his leg.

Right on cue, he howled in pain. I couldn't fault him too much for that. If it had been me getting a large piece of plastic yanked out, I, too, would be calling out for my mother—Gods rest her soul. "I thought you were going to count to three or something!" The Kid cried once he had finished yelling.

"No time. The ship could collapse at any moment!" I fired back, looking around to take stock of our seemingly dire situation. I ran to the med cubby, grabbed some collapsible crutches, and tossed them over to The Kid. "Use these to grab whatever supplies you can while I try to send out a distress signal. Oh, and hurry!"

I didn't have time to make sure The Kid got acquainted with his new best friends. My fingers were occupied flying across the forward console, queuing up a distress signal on all emergency frequencies. "This is Jaycen Lamont, Captain of the Evantide," I began once the console signaled that the transmission was ready to be broadcast. "My companion and I have crash-landed on the surface of Venus. Our current coordinates will be included in the sub-data of this message. After this goes out, we will be seeking shelter nearby. Please come to our aid if you are able. Gods bless."

I turned back to look at The Kid after flipping the switch to send out our Hail Mary. "What?" I asked, not sure what to say to him.

"You do realize the Empire probably heard that," The Kid replied, his nose finally reclaiming its former lofty position. I didn't respond at first, instead choosing to walk past him and out to the foyer. He didn't immediately follow me, probably expecting me to engage him further. Once The Kid realized he wouldn't be getting any attention this way, his crippled legs hobbled out as fast as they could propel him, exiting the craft just as the exit ramp finished its descent.

When I saw that The Kid had finally decided to join me, I tossed him two shield discs. He looked down at them in complete confusion. "Are these supposed to be food rations or something?" he asked, holding them close to his mouth. Again, I decided not to take his bait. Instead, I placed the shield disc above my right pec and gave it a good slap to activate it. Almost instantly, my entire body was covered in a purple, shimmery glow.

"Shield Discs," I said, hating to play instructor but knowing The Kid's life depended on my proper explanation of such basic equipment. "These are standard issue in the military. They disperse the impact of projectile weapons, but each one only has a certain capacity." I looked at The Kid to see if any of that got through to him. I was rewarded with the sight of his blank, wide-eyed expression, as if his entire body had shut down and was struggling to reboot. "They'll protect us from the acid rain, but only for so long."

Like a light switch, the Kid's expression instantly returned to that of a superior being. "Oh!" he said, acting as if he had known this all along. "Probably should have led with that one, Jayce."

Not having the time or the patience to deal with his issues, I just shrugged and made my way down the ramp. "Whatever," was my only response to the madness at hand. Looking back, I was glad to see that, thankfully, The Kid had gotten the message and activated his disc.

Stepping out onto the surface, my ears were greeted by the deceptively familiar pitter-patter of rain hitting the shield. Letting the nostalgia wash over me, I breathed in a long breath of stale, filtered air. The disc removes any toxins from the air, leaving little else. Bringing my wrist up to check the display, I could tell we did not have long. "Kid, the topographic map shows a cave system about two kilometers north. We should hurry. Oh, and take this." I tossed him a blaster, which he barely caught.

He held up the gun as if it were radioactive, his face contorted into a look of intense disgust. "You sure about this?" he asked. To be perfectly honest, I wasn't, but seeing as anything could happen at any moment, I wasn't left with much choice.

And so, we set off toward shelter. Barren craters soon gave way to rocky outcrops. The entire time, my mind was going through the list of creatures that called this planet home. "Cockatrice, Drowners, and there's one more I'm missing. They usually hunt solo, too…"

My thoughts were interrupted when I ran into The Kid, nearly knocking him over, but surprised by how firmly he stood. It seemed as if every muscle in The Kid's body had frozen solid. "What's got you so scared?" I asked, mostly in jest but with a hint of frustration. We had maybe ten minutes left on our current shields, and I wanted to get to the caves without having to use the backups.

With his body still stuck in place, The Kid lifted his arm and pointed upward toward the nearest outcropping. Atop it stood a shadowy figure, its piercing red eyes the only thing that had actual form. As if on cue, a fork of lightning streaked down between us, landing just shy of twenty meters ahead. In this brief flash of luminosity, I caught sight of a creature I had once thought existed only in the darkest corners of my imagination.

A mixture of toad and turtle, legions of warts covered every millimeter of its scaly yellow skin. The creature's domed shell glistened in the low light. The dome was a dark shade of green, while the ring that bonded it to the main body was dark black. It opened its mouth in what looked to be a yawn, but only a series of clicks came out. Those clicks soon coalesced into a slow but low-pitched yowl. "Kappa," I whispered, not wanting to believe what I was seeing.

Though The Kid couldn't hear me, he must have seen my lips, correctly guessing that I had identified the creature. He looked over at me, his eyes saying the words his mouth could not: "How screwed are we?"

My only response was to motion for him to take up position behind the rocks to our right. From there, he would probably be hidden and perhaps able to help me, though I had sincere doubts about the latter. Thankfully, the Kid did as he was told. Years of being on the run must have taught him the proper way to hide from one's enemies, I thought, grabbing my gun from its holster and sliding the safety off. We were well beyond caution at this point.

The Kappa had known our position for some time. It just stood there atop the cliff, studying us as I prepped for what was to be a very tough fight. Once I drew my gun, it knew I was ready for combat. Gracefully leaping from one outcropping to another, the Kappa held its head straight so as not to disturb the drinking bowl atop its forehead.

You see, Venus once had many raging rivers, but over the centuries, mining efforts and other extractions had made them scarce. Those rivers were the creature's domain. A Kappa needs water like I need air, so without the rivers, they evolved to collect rainwater. It's their one weakness.

Once the creature landed in front of me, I gave it my most formal bow. Despite being a savage beast, the Kappa was oddly formal. I hoped to curry some mercy from it. Sadly, formality was not its only defining trait, and the Kappa went against its instincts, refusing to return my bow. Instead, it chose to circle me, its eyes probing for any sort of weakness or opening.

"You don't need to do this. We have no quarrel with you," I pleaded, but the Kappa ignored my cries, obviously picking up on the desperation in my voice. "Fine," I said with a sigh, raising my gun to end this. "We'll do this the brutal way."

Now it was the Kappa's turn to act in desperation, realizing that, while I was desperate, I was no easy prey. With a roar that shook the entire valley, it leaped at me, its poison-tipped claws aimed straight at my heart.

Knowing I would get only one opening shot, I dived out of the way. As I sprang up, I managed to fire two shots at its belly; one of them actually hit its mark. The Kappa yowled in pain for a moment, causing me to almost pity the creature. It seized on this moment of weakness, tackling me to the ground while digging its claws into my shoulders. "Shoot her!" I cried to The Kid between yelps of agony.

I tried to pull my gun on it, but found my hand empty. The gun must have flown out when it tackled me. Now, only the rocks around me served as any kind of defense! "Shoot her!" I cried again. This time, I could hear The Kid struggling with his gun.

BOOM! A shot rang out, but sadly, it went clear over the Kappa's head by a wide margin. The attempt was not entirely in vain, however. The creature snapped its head over to see The Kid standing atop his former hiding place, pointing a gun at it and wearing the stupidest grin I had ever seen. "Get away from my friend, or the next shot hits your head!"

I knew The Kid was bluffing. He wouldn't have shot near me if he had been attempting a warning shot. No, he missed. While I was wise to his bluff, the Kappa was not, lifting a single paw from my shoulder and freeing one arm from its current peril. I have to do something really stupid, I thought, wincing as I felt the poison begin to work its way through my body. Unfortunately, I have no other choice. Looking up, I could see the distraction would not last much longer. If I were going to do something, I'd best act quickly.

Grabbing one of the nearby rocks with my now-free arm, I swung it in an arc, putting in as much force as I could muster. Unlike The Kid, my aim was true, hitting the creature square across the temple. The creature's water spilled out.

The Kappa instantly doubled over, gasping for breath. "Gun, now!" I yelled to The Kid. My Shield Disc screamed warnings of low power as the hard-won battle had drained it of what little juice it had left. Not to mention, the poison was beginning to take its toll. I needed a Cure-Pen.

At first, The Kid did not toss it to me, instead giving me a look of disdain. "You beat it, Jayce; there's no need to kill it," he said, looking at the Kappa with... pity?

I turned to him, showing him the blinking red lights of my disc and my ripped shirt with green veins popping up. The shields had blocked most of the poison, but they couldn't hold back everything. Hopefully, he was getting the gravity of the situation. "Gun, now!" I roared, having just about lost my patience with everything.

Whether he finally understood or simply didn't want to argue further, The Kid tossed me his gun. I grabbed it with one hand, flipped it into firing position, and looked down the sight. The Kappa stared back at me, its eyes pleading.

I knew it was not the creature's fault. It was only doing what it thought needed to be done, unaware of the destruction its choices caused. That sounds familiar… "I'm sorry," I whispered to the beast, feeling an odd kinship with it, but firing a single shot between its eyes. The beast's body went still, as did my beating heart.

The Kid walked up to me, slamming another shield disc into my chest right as the other one was about to expire, using a bit more force than necessary and knocking the wind out of me in the process. "What the Hades was that for!?" I asked him. "I just saved our fricking lives! Be grateful for once."

He just stood there and stared at me before grabbing his pack and walking right past me. When he realized I wasn't following, he turned to stare at me, his eyes full of seething hatred. "You're a monster."

Long past done with everything, I rushed past him. Every muscle screamed in agony as a result of the Kappa's poison, but at this point, I couldn't care less, smiling as I shoved The Kid face-first into the gravel as I passed him. "That's what everyone says. Now, if you'll excuse me, I'm going into that cave. If you ever decide not to consort with monsters, feel free to join me," I said, a wicked smile on my face. The Kid tried to get up and say something, but I pushed him down again. "Otherwise, piss off!"

I didn't bother looking back at The Kid, my legs carrying me the remaining distance to the cave. I was grateful to see it was exactly where I had seen it on the map before setting out. At this point, I no longer cared if he followed me or not. That idiot couldn't even shoot a large creature from three meters away! Completely useless; how he survived this long, I have no idea. Except I did know exactly how he survived. My heart sank, along with any morale I once held.

Reaching a large, empty cavern, I put my green-tinted hand into my pack to pull out one of the fire lamps I had packed. It feels a bit pointless now, but whatever, I thought as I activated it. The warmth it gave actually felt pretty good. My body reacted well to the comfort; the rate of my infection even started to slow down, but the crushing inevitability of it all seemed to cancel everything out. Looking down at my gun, I considered doing something I had almost done on the Drifter Colony before…

"Hey, Jayce! Can you help me with this thing? It weighs a ton! No wonder it crushed you!" Looking toward the sound of The Kid's voice, I was shocked to see the Kappa I had previously shot. He had somehow managed to drag it to the cave! I noticed his shield disc was blinking, too; his timer was about to expire.

Jumping off my perch with renewed vigor, a sudden surge of adrenaline canceled out any effects the poison still had. I slapped my chest to reactivate my shield. "Stand aside, I got this," I told The Kid, shoving him into the cave at the exact moment his shield would have blinked out. At first, he looked up at me in anger, but once he noticed the disc was out, something seemed to click inside him, and he looked at me as if for the very first time.

Dragging the beast into the cave wasn't easy. Dealing with the smell would be a difficult task, even in the best of circumstances. "Please tell me you know how to cook this thing, Jayce," The Kid said to me, covering his mouth with his sleeve. "I want it to be used for something. It deserves a better fate than just being a rotting corpse."

I was never a good cook, but like most men, I'd had a living-single phase where I was forced to learn either to cook or die the death of a thousand frozen dinners. Luckily, my mother had been gracious enough to send over her recipe folder. One of the recipes was a dish that got me laid every time I made it: Kappa soup. "You're in luck, Kid. You're about to experience some of the best cuisine this side of Titan!"

"Wait!" he cried out as I began to hobble around. At this point, if the poison were going to kill me, it would have done so already, but without treatment, I wouldn't be at my best.

"Ow, what was that... oh, thanks," I said, confused at first as I felt The Kid stab me in the back with something. The sudden feeling of relief that flooded my body told me he had given me a Cure-Pen. "Thanks…" I said to him, unsure of what else to say.

The Kid just stood there, acting sheepish. "I knew you were too proud to ask for help or even to help yourself." Looking down at the syringe and then back at me, he quipped, "So I took matters into my own hands."

I shook my head and walked past him. The Kid didn't say anything else while I set to work, choosing to study me with a gaze reminiscent of his mother's. While I found his stare unnerving, I had become quite experienced in ignoring it by this point. It used to drive his mother crazy! Still got the scar from that one time she 'accidentally' shoved an ice pick into my arm.

Once our meal was finished, I blasted some nearby rocks with my pistol so we could use them as makeshift bowls.

Handing The Kid his bowl and a ration of water, he looked up at me again—this time with thankful eyes. "How can someone so skilled be so brutal?" he asked me upon tasting my cooking, his face lighting up with genuine happiness.

"Practice, and lots of it," I replied, taking a taste for myself. Would have been better with spices, but as is, it's not bad. Between bites, I glanced over at him. His soup was at his side, completely forgotten. The Kid's head was tilted as if he were some sort of dog. "What now? I fed you, so don't say I never do anything for you, Kid."

He sat there in silence, studying me. At last, he opened his mouth, asking me a question I wasn't prepared for. "Why do you hate me so much?"

My body froze at his query. I wasn't used to such deep introspection. Setting my soup down on the ground, I looked inside myself for the first time since that night. For too long, I had retreated behind walls built upon a volatile mix of anger and self-hatred. Anger was a great salve for burning away grief, but it left little in its wake. "I don't. If anything, I hate myself," I finally answered, being honest for the first time in fifteen years.

For a moment, things were still, the only sound being the raging storm outside our cave. For some reason, its ferocity seemed to have lessened from just a few moments before. The Kid looked at me. I expected to see pity from him, but instead, it was something far more impactful: understanding. "My mother never failed to make me understand that a person is the sum of the choices they make," The Kid began, getting up from his seat to sit on the floor next to me.

My body couldn't hold back the laughter that followed his words. "You're not helping! I've made so many bad choices, you being first among them!" Not wanting to confront this, I took off my disc and marched toward the mouth of the cave. Even half a step more, and I would melt into a puddle within seconds.

Alarmed by my outburst, The Kid stood up, sprinting toward me. "Was your mistake picking up my contract?" he asked, his tone conveying genuine worry about my safety.

"No," I replied, weighing my options. Figuring we would both die on this rock, I decided to go for ultimate candor. Turning my head to face both The Kid and my destiny, I finally admitted the truth, going straight to the crux of my entire being. "My first mistake was abandoning you all those years ago. Not only did I leave you behind, but I also left my honor and my very sense of self…"

Peeking a toe out to test my next step, the leather almost immediately dissolved, leaving only the steel toe to protect my foot. Seeing this, the Kid attempted to pull me back from the brink. Given that he was half my size, the attempt didn't amount to much.

"Jayce, please!" he pleaded, trying desperately to reverse years of self-loathing.

Snarky comments and dickish behavior may have gotten me this far, but after being confronted with the consequences of my actions, I could no longer lie to myself. The truth was now plain as day.

"You are not a monster!" The Kid answered, somehow reading my thoughts. Finding a strength he probably didn't even know he had, he pulled me back onto the ground of the cave before I could take another step. Looking over at him, I could see he was done idly standing by. "We're going to talk about this! Get back to your seat."

Internally, I felt a cross between amused and pissed as hell. The Kid was like a Chihuahua who suddenly thought itself a Doberman. Figuring it would help pass the time while also wondering how far he would take this, I got up straight in his face, our noses practically touching. "You sure your ass can back up what you're saying?" Recalling my counterintelligence training and ready to really nail down my point, I unholstered my gun and pressed the barrel against his temple.

He winced only once, feeling the barrel press against him, but The Kid never broke eye contact with me. This kid either has balls bigger than mine or prior training—probably both. With a face bearing no expression whatsoever, he responded with the seasoned chill of a trained spy. "Yes, shoot me if you must. You've probably considered it before."

The Kid's strength took me aback. He definitely got that from his mother. "Once or twice," I said, withdrawing the barrel from his temple and returning it to its holster. "For the record, there are professionals who couldn't BS with a gun to their head nearly as well as you just did."

"It helps that it wasn't my first time. Now, shall we?" The Kid replied, gesturing toward the circle of rocks I'd put together.

Not really having much choice anymore, I complied, picking up my soup and setting it on the now-dimming fire lamp to warm up with what little power it still had left.

"Jayce, I want you to answer one more question, and I promise to get off your case."

I laughed at the very concept of The Kid following through with such a thing. "Don't make promises you can't keep, Kid." I paused, looking at his face. It had now adopted a forlorn expression, as if he felt all the progress was about to evaporate. "But ask away."

He seemed to brighten up at that, feeling hope return to him. Adjusting his position on the rock, The Kid looked me straight in the eye and asked, "Why haven't you dumped me somewhere? You've had plenty of opportunities to do so."

I certainly wasn't expecting that one, I thought, my mind racing for an answer. Why hadn't I? The Kid had been a pain in my backside and caused nothing but trouble the entire time. Figuring the easy answer was best, I responded, "Simple: the money was too good." Nonchalantly taking my soup from the lamp, I indulged myself with a sip or two. Still not good enough, I thought, my body shuddering in mild disgust.

With a long sigh, The Kid got up from his seat and moved to the one next to me, looking straight at me as if peering through to my soul. "No," he began, "you could have dropped me off anywhere, especially after the events at the checkpoint. Why didn't you?"

Like a bolt of lightning, I shot up. "Because I gave my word! Once upon a time, it actually meant something!" Realizing what I had said, I looked around in shock. The Kid just stared at me as if he was seeing me for the first time—and, oddly enough, I think he liked the person he saw.

He rose from his seat and met me in an embrace—an embrace of equals. "It still does. That person never left you, Jayce; he's just been in hiding." Feeling the truth of his words, the walls inside me began to crack.

Sadly, a reevaluation like this was not enough to overcome fifteen years of self-imposed trauma. "You're still an insufferable little try-hard," I told him, returning his hug in kind. "We should probably get some sleep. No one is going to show up till morning, if at all."

Nodding in agreement, The Kid unfurled the bedroll he had managed to grab before leaving. I, on the other hand, had the pleasure of sleeping on a sheet—a dirty one, at that. "Someone needs to keep watch, and you certainly aren't up to the task," I said once I caught The Kid smirking at my choice of sleeping arrangements.

"You're correct on that. Night, Jayce!" he chimed, taking way too much pleasure in this and falling asleep as soon as his head hit the pillow. Some things can't change, no matter how hard you try.

Looking out at the mouth of the cave, I let myself get lost in thought at the absurdity of the situation. Sleep was not far behind. My mind went numb just as two points of light flashed by the mouth of the cavern…

8

A Tangled Web

Mars, the New Earth, once a red wasteland, is now a vibrant display of royal might. From the viewport of my craft, I could see the entire northern hemisphere. The green forests gracefully gave way to concrete canyons that made up the capital. I took it all in with a sharp sense of trepidation in my heart. For not even sixteen standard hours beforehand, I was the section chief of the Shadow Hawk Squadron—an elite strike force made up of the best pilots in the Sol System. With me as their leader, we engaged in countless successful missions.

Now, the time has come for me to move on with my career. Well, at least that's what my father had thought. Recently ascended from the Warrior caste, he had much to prove. Using these new connections alongside a few of his old ones, my father managed to secure me a post as a captain of the Royal Guard. "You will constantly be three steps from royalty, son," my father's words rang out to me. "A position most envious to all; use this privilege wisely." I sighed as I recalled his words, being perfectly content with where I was, not being part of his plan.

As if on cue, the ship shook violently, signaling that it had entered the upper part of the atmosphere. Probably no more than ten minutes out, I thought to myself with dread. Realizing these would probably be the last moments of true privacy I would get for some time, I decided to spend them on familiar ground. Reaching into my pack to retrieve my tablet—or, more precisely, the farewell message contained in it—I smiled to myself.

The screen burst to life, and I gazed upon my brothers and sisters in arms. At the time, I was only three doors down, busy gathering up my things. The orders had come so suddenly, not giving me much time to say any sort of goodbyes. The squad, being the stand-up fellows they are, took it upon themselves to take care of that.

"I realize you are some big shot now, Jayce," Nileia, my second in command, was the first to speak. Best to show respect and address her by the title she has earned, I thought. Chief Nileia spoke straight into the camera, already taking on the mantle of a leader like it was a second skin. "Don't you go forgetting about us. We're family and always will be." A wave of nostalgia washed over me when I heard those words. It hadn't even been a day, had it? I shouldn't be yearning for simpler times already.

Each of my former squadmates took their turn saying farewells. Every single one of them said something from the heart. I honestly will miss this bunch. Sadly, my musings were cut short by the rush of air that accompanied the landing hatch opening.

Raising my hand to shield myself from the onslaught of light, I did my best to take stock of my new home. To put it simply, my new post was… beautiful. More garden than spaceport, my eyes and nose were filled with every possible flower I could imagine, along with several dozen that I couldn't even imagine.

Standing at the base of the ramp was the most immaculate flower of them all. The Queen, while dressed more casually, was still the best-dressed person in the system. Her dark forest green leather jacket looked freshly polished, its shine almost blinding. The gold trim was buffed to a perfect sheen. Her pants were of similar material, tight enough to show off her curves but not enough to be obscene. The Queen's outfit showed her to be an expert in riding the line between nobility and commonality.

Her face lit up once she saw me, giving me a practiced smile that she had surely given a million times before, but each person who received the gift thought it was just for them. "Captain Lamont! I hope your journey was a comfortable one," she said to me when I reached her. Her voice conveyed a soft strength.

Walking down the ramp, my squadron jacket slung over my shoulder, I looked around. "Where is the King?" I asked, a bit insulted by the reception I was given. "Isn't it a tradition for the King to receive any new officers in his court?"

The Queen paused for a moment, giving an odd reaction. One side of her lips furrowed into a "how dare you ask questions" sneer—the obvious reaction of a royal being questioned. The other side, though, oddly cracked into a bit of a "you are brave for asking questions" smile. I was not expecting such a divided response. There is definitely more to her than what the court sees.

I sadly didn't have time to indulge my curiosity about the Queen. She quickly filled the dead air with some hot air of her own making. "The King is feeling ill today. He asked me personally to be here. Do you have a problem with that? If so, you can always get back on the ship."

The gall of that woman! I like her! my mind thought as I could not hold back a chuckle. "Honestly, this has been pretty entertaining. Lead the way, Your Highness."

The Queen did not start toward the castle; instead, she walked straight up to me, then around me, taking a look at my squadron jacket. "Your jacket—it's from your old squadron, right?" she asked me. I nodded in response. "Lose it. Only loyalty to the crown is allowed here."

Flabbergasted, I did not reply. I really lacked any sort of response to what she had just said to me. Snarky or honest words eluded me. She seemed to take this as a form of resistance, gesturing to one of her guards, who snatched away my jacket. "Box it and store it on the fourth floor," she said to the guard before he disappeared off to the side.

"Hey! What gives?" I roared. The Queen gave me a look in response. Her mouth curled into a sneer, but her eyes were filling with... pity. What is going on with this woman? "You guys asked me to be here, remember?"

The Queen twirled around to face me, looking me up and down to take me in fully. Her eyes finally met mine. I swear I caught a hint of an approving smile. Approval for what? I was unsure. "We did indeed ask you to be here, Captain," she said, walking right up to me. The top of her head did not even reach my chin. Looking up at me, I suddenly forgot that I could overpower her with just my pinky. The look she gave me disarmed any thought I had of noncompliance. "And we can ask you to leave just as easily. Understood?" I nodded, now completely cowed.

Seeing me buckle beneath the sheer force of her will, the Queen did not smile. Instead, a scowl scarred her lips, as if the woman did not enjoy wielding power thrust upon her but did it anyway. "Follow me, Captain; you must be tired after journeying from the front lines. Let me show you to your room so you can rest before being formally received by the King."

We walked up to the castle in relative silence—the scurrying of countless servants our only companion. At several points, I tried to breach the silence with small talk. Each attempt was met with a grunt and a dirty look slung my way. It took four of these for me to finally get the message that I was to remain silent. The irony is that the final glare was given just five steps from the entrance to the castle.

Once we were all inside, she dismissed all but her bodyguard, a mousy young lad who seemed joined to the Queen's hip—a feat he likely performed without being told.

"We may now speak semi-freely. Even so, I advise you to watch your tongue. The castle has long suffered a rat problem," the Queen said as the three of us climbed the stairs of the grand hall.

Not being one for small talk, I cut straight to the chase. "Is the King in good health?"

Not even bothering to break her stride or turn back to look at me, the Queen responded plainly, "He's as healthy as a dried-up King who has seen over sixty-eight cycles can be. Fill in the rest as you will." Standing at the top of the stairs, she gestured toward the left hallway. "Your chambers are down this hall. The door has been marked with your name. Personal effects have already been set up. Just make sure you are presentable by dinner."

With her task done, the Queen set off in the opposite direction. "Come, Anders, our newest Captain can handle tucking himself in." Figuring this little tiff was finished, I set off toward my room. My mind was looking forward to getting in a few hours of rack time.

"Jayce!" Like a slap across my face, the Queen called out to me. Confused, I looked over to see her across the hall, giving me a look of actual warmth. "Welcome to the Royal Guard. I'm sure you'll perform with distinction."

Not really sure how to reply, I answered with a simple "Thanks." Parting ways with her, more confused than ever, I found relief in the fact that my worn body reached my room easily. Just as she said, my personal items had been moved in and set up with the speed that only well-trained servants could achieve.

The one shocking thing, however, was what I saw hanging above my bed in a shadowbox, no less. Looking up, I saw the uniform I had worn as a member of the Shadow Hawks. Not only had she failed to destroy it, but in the time it took us to walk back, she had someone mount it in a nice display on my wall for all to see! A note sat beneath it, resting atop my nightstand.

Jayce, you probably have already heard me say this, but welcome, the letter began, her handwriting a beautiful script. As you will soon learn, this castle is a battlefield. One must adopt many faces in order to survive. Looking up at my uniform and the care taken to preserve it, her words began to sink in. Your record shows you to be an honest man. Honest men die quick deaths here. I implore you to be anything but.

Looking around at my new surroundings, I wondered what exactly I had gotten myself into. "This is not who I am!" I said, about to crumple the letter in my hands before deciding I might as well hear the rest out.

But do not lose sight of your true self. If you do, then you may never come back.

Folding the note, I tucked it behind the shadowbox. "No turning back now. My Pa would skin me alive," I muttered to myself, tugging off my boots. The bed welcomed me into its embrace. I could feel myself slowly drifting off…

"Jayce!"

Again, my name rang out. Again, my face stung as if slapped. This time, the voice was not that of the Queen, but of…

Shooting up from my cot, my body was awash in cold, dirty water. Dim light covered the small steel room I found myself in. Looking over, I saw a lanky woman standing over me. She had an empty wooden bucket in her hands and a full one on the floor, just begging to be used. While small in stature, I knew better than to try anything. With a huge knife at her side, she shouted at me to sit up and shut up. Pirates. I have fallen in with pirates.

Slowly, I did as I was told and sat up. My body was still weak from being out for who knows how long. "Where are we?" I asked, figuring these were the ones who found my distress signal. Though why a band of pirates would leave me alive confused my already addled brain.

"Old Earth," she responded before walking to the door and opening it up. "Come, the lady wishes to see you once you have awakened."

Now more confused than ever, I looked down to see a set of slippers. "Who?" I asked while putting them on, having a feeling what the answer would be.

The pirate smiled. "She said you'd probably figure it out. If not, you'll see soon."

I never thought I'd meet her again… I thought. My mind finally got everything together.

It had been so long since I stepped onto that ship, never to see her again. Well, that is, until now, apparently. So much time had passed; would she be a different person? Am I a different person? The recent events have caused me to question everything I once held sacred.

"Jayce!" The Kid's voice cried out when he saw me enter the room. In my reflective haze, I must have lost track of where I was, operating on autopilot the entire way. The Kid practically tackled me; he was so happy to see me. Oddly enough, I returned his warm embrace tepidly.

It was only then that the realization hit me. I care about this kid. Our journeys had somehow endeared me to this pompous, empty sack. He doesn't realize what he does. The Kid's obviously been sheltered his entire life.

This somewhat joyous reunion was swiftly interrupted by a cough. A very… familiar cough. Looking over, I saw Nileia glaring at me, now twenty years older. Not that her face had aged a single day in the interim. "Jaycen Lamont, you have no idea how surprised I was to hear your voice over the squawk box."

Rising from her chair, she looked down at my pathetic sight. Clad in a set of drab khakis, she seemed satisfied that I was put in my proper place. Walking up to me, her stride conveyed the same confidence that I had fallen for all those years ago. The frizzy ponytail was new, but seeing as how she hasn't had to adhere to military regs for a few decades, it made sense that she'd style it however she saw fit.

Even though I was taller than her by a noticeable margin, the way she looked down at me left no doubt that the difference between us still did not matter in the slightest. "You wanna know why I saved your sorry ass?"

I knew this line of questioning would end up somewhere. Not really enjoying it, but I didn't really have a choice in the matter. "For old times' sake?" I replied with a shrug.

The next thing I knew, I was on the ground clutching my gut. The woman had smacked me in my solar plexus before I even had a chance to realize what she was doing! "Yeah, old times' sake, something like that."

Seemingly satisfied with her burst of rash actions, Nileia walked to the side of the room, punching some buttons as the screens came to life. "You haven't lost your edge," I said to her, my left arm bracing against the table so I could have a hope of standing upright.

Nileia looked over at me, visibly scoffing at what she saw. "And you've grown soft. I assumed your time in the Alpha Centauri system would keep you hard, but it seems not."

At that point, the monitor had warmed up. It was showing my ship sitting atop the surface of Venus. Its outer hull was almost completely eaten away by the acid rain. "This was the ship when my crew found it," she said. She clicked forward to the next frame, showing it in a much better state. By the looks of it, much more work was still yet to be done, but I was honestly just happy to see the ole girl still kicking. "This is a live feed from the Ford Field docks."

So we are in the remains of Detroit, good to know, I thought to myself, filing away that nugget of potentially useless information. Though the question remained… "So, if you hate me so much, why are you doing so much to help us?" I asked Nileia, the Kid looking over at me as I said this. I blinked in shock as I realized it was probably one of the first times I had referred to him and myself as a single unit.

My former second-in-command didn't respond— at least not vocally—choosing to switch over to the next image, another live feed. This one showed some sort of lab. I could make out the nanite tanks very clearly. "Ah, you wanted my hull so that you could culture your own Nanatose," I said, finally figuring out her play.

"That's part of it—a big part, mind you—but still just a part," she said, flipping over to what would be the final image: a map showcasing a section of Mercury's surface. Circled in what looked to be bold red ink was a single base in the lower right corner. "As much as I hate to say this, I need you."

Dumbfounded, I looked over at Nileia. She returned my gaze with a shrug of her own. "This research outpost was abandoned about six months ago when some idiot knocked over the algae tanks." She then pressed a button, and the same woman who slapped me awake entered. "Caroline, tell them what kind of equipment they used at the outpost."

Caroline looked at Nileia and nodded. Turning her attention to me, her mouth broke into a sneer. "Well, besides the solar shielding and communication equipment, the outpost was researching cutting-edge enigma breakers." She paused for a moment to catch her breath, her disdain for me having let up in the meantime. "Shortly before you had me torch the tanks, they had a breakthrough. With this new technique, no code is safe."

Throughout all this, the Kid tried to keep up, but after a while, he decided to fall into old habits and pretend that he understood. I looked down at the Kid as Caroline finished up her briefing. "Thank you, that will be all," Nileia said to her, nodding as she spoke.

The Kid looked back at me, his face practically screaming at me, 'What the hell did she just say?' All

I could do was shrug in response. Nileia picked up on our wordless conversation right away, laughing as she shut off the monitor. "Didn't realize you and the Prince had gotten that close."

Disgusted, I pushed the Kid away from me. "I don't care about him. He's the reason I am who I am!" His back made an audible thud as the Kid slammed against the wall. It didn't knock him out, though. The Kid shot me daggers with his eyes as he got up.

Nileia looked over at my display with a mixture of amusement and frustration. "Obviously," she said while pulling down her goggles to get a better look at us. "Tell you what, why don't you and the boy go for a walk around town and hash out… whatever this is." She chuckled as she made her way out the door. "Make sure to be back before dark. The area is… mostly clear of monsters. Talk to Caroline if you have any questions!"

With that, the door closed behind her, leaving the Kid and me to stare at each other in heated silence. Choosing to break the brick wall of tension between us, I at last said, "So… about that walk?"

To no one's surprise, the Kid was not pleased with my suggestion, throwing a pitcher of water at me to show just how displeased he was. While I easily dodged the pitcher, the water it contained was another story entirely. Standing there drenched, a whole other thought occurred to me. Maybe the Kid is mad at me for saying I didn't care about him, undoing everything we have experienced together up to this point… He wouldn't be wrong.

"Look, Kid," I began, putting my hands up in a gesture of peace. He had grabbed one of the stone cups. Judging by the way his arm was cocked, he looked ready to launch it at me. "What I said, I said in anger. Doesn't make it right, but it doesn't make it true either."

What I had said must have gotten through his thick armor. The Kid now seemed to have abandoned his anger, putting down the cup. He was just standing there, looking at me with a confused expression. "Then why say it, Jayce? I thought honor meant something to you?"

It was now my turn to dive into anger. But instead of throwing things like a child, I walked to the wall, pounding it with my fist while screaming like the mature adult I am. "It means everything to me!"

He certainly didn't take my hypocrisy well, running straight up into my face and digging his finger into my chest. "Then why forsake it like you have? Why abandon me in my greatest hour of need? I demand answers!"

Not having an immediate answer and suddenly desiring some new air—well, any kind of air—I slipped under him and opened the door. "Why don't we go for that walk?" I suggested, motioning for the Kid to follow me. "Probably do us both some good."

Saying nothing in response but falling in line behind me regardless, we made our way to the place Nileia told us we could put on our outside gear.

While Earth was not completely uninhabitable, centuries of a society being wasteful and treating its home like a cesspit certainly took its toll, leaving the atmosphere toxic to all but the most vicious of beings. Thus, any normal person who wished to set foot on its surface needed to protect themselves, both by wearing an air filter and covering every part of their body.

A vacuum seal was not needed. The covering protected the wearer more from stray particles than anything else. Still, there's a reason Earth had yet to be completely resettled. Sure, there were some outposts here and there, such as this pirate compound we found ourselves in, but those types of settlements proved themselves a rare and resilient breed.

One would think that with the number of valuable artifacts on this planet, there would be a more concerted effort to salvage some of them, but no, the groups are either too lazy or too poor to pull it off properly. Thus, Earth… is Earth, no better or worse off since the Exodus nearly a thousand years prior.

"You two ready for this?" Caroline asked us, shaking me from my midday musings.

I looked up at her and then out the window in front of us. Beyond six inches of ancient steel lay a wasteland—a once-bustling metro teeming with life. It still teems with life, just a different kind now. I thought, a lump forming in my throat. Fighting my fear, I managed to squeak out a single word. "Yes."

The woman just shrugged before flipping the switch to the landlocked position. "It's your funeral. A little tip: if you two get lost, just look for the pair of stadiums. We run them both."

The air that greeted us was warm and sticky. The Greenhouse Effect had done a number on the planet. There wasn't a spot on this rock that dipped below thirty degrees Celsius. Lucky for us, Detroit was toward the northern end of the planet, so we stepped out into the brisk winter weather. The heads-up display on our goggles indicated that it was currently thirty-five degrees outside. "This is Earth?" the Kid asked as we both looked around in wonder.

"It was at one point," I responded. My neck started to hurt from my head darting back and forth. One would think the former Captain General or even the ex-Squadron Leader of the Shadow Hawks would have visited Earth at least once, but no. I was too busy with one thing or another to see the system that I had been sworn to uphold. Not even my betrayal could free up the time to allow me to come here.

Come to think of it, my duties with the Royal Guard prevented me from a lot of things. Perhaps that's why Nileia hates me… I wasn't there for… I wondered, standing there just a bit past the threshold, lost in the choices I had made.

The Kid got about five meters ahead of me before noticing that I wasn't following. "Are we actually doing this?" he hollered back at me.

Shaken from myself, I looked over at him. "Of course, the stadium shouldn't be too far from here." Breaking into a stride, I easily sailed past him. "I'm kind of eager to see how the repairs on the Evantide are going."

With a shrug and a sigh, the Kid followed suit. He was easily matching my pace. It was clear he could overtake me if he wished, but for some reason, he did not. The two of us marched like that for a little while. The sounds of a decrepit, long-abandoned wasteland were our only companions. To be honest, I think this is what we both needed—a quiet, peaceful moment that we could share between us. At this time, nothing else really mattered. We were just two people enjoying a good run.

"Wait, did you hear that?" I asked The Kid, raising my arm to stop us both in our tracks. My ears picked up an ominous rumble in the distance.

The Kid shrugged in response. "I don't know, could be anything, really," he said. His body displayed a sense of calm while his eyes began betraying a growing concern.

Not wanting to ignore my instincts, I bent down and touched the ground. "There was definitely something out there," I said. Looking over at The Kid, I could see his concern slowly turning into outright terror. "Something big."

It was only now that I actually paid attention to my surroundings. Looking into the dark and dingy alleyways, I saw something I was not expecting—something that filled even me with dread. Webbing, and lots of it. I thought to myself with a shiver. We've stumbled into its lair. "Quickly now," I said to The Kid, waving him forward. "We need to find shelter before it passes."

He tugged at my sleeve as I attempted to rush him forward, his face betraying a sort of panic. "Before 'what' passes, Jayce?" he asked. A look was all I could spare him, and a look was all I needed. For The Kid saw the fear in my eyes and instantly knew what was at stake. "Lead the way," he said with a whimper.

Looking around, I could not help but notice how limited our options really were, despite being literally surrounded by buildings. Only a few of them weren't already caved in. Of those few, only one still had any sort of coverings. "Let's hide out in Judy's!" I said, pointing to the long-since burned-out neon sign.

The two of us shuffled over there as quietly as we could, jumping over a part of the sign that had fallen down centuries ago. Our efforts at stealth seemed wasted as, upon our entrance, I could hear the monstrosity pass us by. It follows...

"What was this place?" The Kid asked, looking over the rows of curtain rods and rusted mattress springs. "Some sort of inn?"

"Something like that," I responded, not having the heart to tell him we were taking shelter in a former brothel. Why do I care what sort of stuff he's exposed to? I wondered to myself as we both looked around for anything useful. Why do I suddenly feel so protective of the brat?

Our search was sadly cut short by the rumbles of the monstrosity. Its steps were getting increasingly loud as it moved in closer. "Upstairs!" I shouted, the two of us needing a place to both see and not be seen.

Upstairs looked a little more intact, a dormitory of sorts. Not being picky but more importantly pressed for time, the two of us entered the first room on the left. It looked to be a sparse affair. You could tell the person didn't have much by how little there clearly was to begin with. The only thing giving it personality was the name "Kiro-Enforcer" written in old English script on the door.

"We should be safe here for a moment, just don't touch anything," I said to the Kid, peeking out from behind the wooden blinds.

Of course, as soon as I said that, The Kid began rummaging through things—items that probably hadn't been touched in over a thousand years. It gives him something to do, at least, I mused to myself, still keeping watch, my eyes glued to the eight legs currently walking past our window. I don't know how long we waited there, the sounds of The Kid's curiosity my only companion. Everything came back into focus as the sounds of his search came to a screeching halt. "Jayce," The Kid said, holding out an old photograph to me. "Why is this woman holding my mother's sword?"

"What?" I exclaimed, not really believing what I was hearing. Snatching it from his grasp, I almost dropped the thing as I saw what it displayed. "Windseeker," I whispered.

There are two swords sacred to the Shinkar family, one of which, the sword known as "Windseeker-The Last Blade," was wielded by The Queen. That very sword sat at the hip of a young blonde woman.

Next to her was a Samurai, clad in traditional armor. Why this warrior was in more modern times, I had no idea. But what I do know is that the sword he wielded was very familiar to me. Staring at the photo, I had no idea what to make of it. I knew both blades were special, but none of us knew their origins. "Jayce, what does this mean?" The Kid asked, his eyes ablaze with wonder.

"It means…" I choked up, my past once again coming to haunt me. My nostalgia was thankfully cut short as I heard a crash in the distance. It's found us. "It means we gotta get the hell out of here!" The two of us barreled down the stairs, not caring if we were heard or seen. The building behind us collapsed in on itself just as we exited. Looking down, I saw The Kid still holding the snapshot. Only one way out of this. "Come on, let's head to the park," I said, itching for a final fight.

I hadn't kept track of where we were running, being reminded of that fact when I found myself giving some face time with the concrete. You see, in the haze of bonding we found ourselves in, I didn't take into account that my path led me straight into a giant stone fist. Future research would tell me it was a memorial to some long-dead boxer. I had certainly granted it another TKO. The Kid definitely enjoyed this, cackling up such a storm that the window on his mask began to fog up.

Fully embarrassed and completely disheveled, I managed to pick myself up and dust off what I could with at least a degree of dignity. "What?" I called out to him. "Never seen a guy trip over a two-thousand-year-old statue on a planet that hasn't been relevant in half that time?"

To his credit, the Kid bowed his head in shame. "Sorry, it was just nice to see you be the fool for once."

For once? I thought to myself, his comment catching me off guard. What does he mean… oh… OH!

Ignoring the pain in my ankle, I rushed over to the Kid and scooped him up in my arms. He seemed shocked that I would make such a gesture. Frankly, I was, too. Perhaps the old me was beginning to reawaken?

It was truly hard to say. My mind had not been given a chance to come to grips with recent events. Going catatonic after realizing you had been carting around your greatest shame for the past month tends to do a number on a person's psyche. "Don't say that… ever again."

Looking up at me, his eyes were flooded with embarrassment. "But… I am. I see your reaction every time I screw up." His words somehow got past my thick walls and pierced the very core of my heart.

It just so happened to be my turn to cry. Breaking down in front of the Kid certainly wasn't on the list of things I was hoping for. It wasn't on any list. But here I was, bawling like a bloody baby in front of the being whom, just a month prior, I was considering tossing out of my airlock. "Just… Ori… Kid… Dammit!"

I broke away from his embrace. The sudden rush of emotions proved much more than I could possibly handle. "I… can't… do this!" I continued, backing away from my greatest shame. My mind paid no heed to the obvious nest I was backing into. The Kid's face looked horrified—at first for what I had just done, then quickly shifting to what I was about to do.

My first notification of how badly I had screwed up came in the form of a squishy snap—a distinctive sound that could only come from my boot crushing bodily remains, remains that had been covered under copious amounts of webbing. The second and final warning was the sensation of my sides being caught between the mandibles of a Servine Spider.

Servine Spiders are common throughout any trash world. They lie in wait for any scavenger who dares try to sift for plunder—or, in my case, some dumbass just to stumble in. What's that saying regarding a free lunch? I thought to myself, trying to go for my pistol. The spider's venom turned out to make quick work of my will, sapping any hint of resistance.

A fleeting thought did enter my brain. Just yell at the Kid to shoot it? It's an easy enough shot. But memories of the kappa told me such an action would be a foolish endeavor. Besides, I could hear the clicks of the spider's webbing, swiftly turning me into a packed meal. Won't be long now… The Kid is probably halfway back by now…

That's when I heard it. BOOM! The sound of the Kid's firearm, followed by a beastly scream. BOOM BOOM! Two more shots and an even bigger scream followed the first. Did he? My mind reeled, trying to understand what was going on. The spider's venom in my system made it hard to focus.

The answer to my question came to be in the form of me suddenly falling out of the arms of the spider. Its webbing shattered upon my return to the ground. Sadly, it did nothing for the fall itself. A large pain instantly shot up my side. This did have the side effect of shaking me from my haze, if only enough for me to become semi-functional again.

Standing up was an effort, but I did manage. Still clutching my sides, I looked over at the creature. Three clean holes marked the monster as dead. These shots had hit the spider in its vital organs—the kind of hit that can only be done by knowing where to shoot. "How did you know the correct spots to hit?" I asked the Kid after inspecting the spider.

The Kid returned my query with a sheepish grin. "Just because I was sheltered doesn't mean I didn't study. Quite the opposite, actually," he replied, pushing his luck a bit too far when he attempted to twirl the gun between his fingers. It made about a quarter revolution before the gun had enough and decided to make a break for it, flying halfway across the pavilion.

With a sigh and a slump of my shoulders, I carefully made my way toward the gun. I guess the battle with the spider must have scared off any other nearby creatures, as I did not encounter anything else.

Gun in hand, I made my way back to him. My mind processed what had just occurred. The Kid learned from his mistake. There just might be hope for him yet.

The Kid wasn't able to meet my eyes when I handed back his firearm. The embarrassment seemed to be too much for him. "Sorry, you didn't have to do that, Jayce." Like you didn't do worse things when you were his age!

For some reason, seeing the Kid like this really wasn't sitting right with me. For the first time in what seemed like forever, I reached out and placed my hand on his shoulder. Gods. I feel like my father—well, when he still cared about me. "Kid, that was some good shooting back there. You were certainly taught well."

His head shot up, first glancing over at the hand on his shoulder and finally looking up at me. His eyes filled up, not with sorrow this time, but with pure joy. "You bastard! From day one, I hated your guts, but now that I have your approval, it feels like my life is complete. Why do I feel this way?"

Not sure what to do, I fell back on instinct, surprisingly finding myself scooping the Kid up into my arms again. A few weeks ago, I would have just shot him. Now, I'm treating him as if he were my own. What gives? "Emotions are complicated, Kid… I'm living proof of such."

What I said seemed to have satisfied whatever need he had. The Kid soon broke from our embrace, moving faster than winds could carry the nasty fart I had just set loose. "I assume that's where we will be going?" the Kid asked, pointing to the horizon. From my perspective, his fingertips lay just atop what had been Ford Field.

"Yeah, it is," I replied, looking around to make sure there were no more surprises. Thankfully, to my eyes, there were none. "We should probably make our way over there; it'll be getting dark soon." I shoved the canteen into his arms as I passed. "Drink. We don't want to be out here after dark. Trust me."

We were making our way downtown, threading between the concrete canyons. Some streets seemed to have succumbed to disrepair and were completely impassable. Others looked virtually untouched.

The Kid looked around, his mouth gaping in wonder, much wider than mine was at the time. "Have you never seen ruins before?" I asked, more out of a desire to break the silence than any actual interest.

In response, he bent over and picked up a thin sheet of metal—a "license plate," if I remember correctly. "Nothing of this scale," he said, staring at the plate intently and taking in every detail he could. "You're a learned man, Jayce, so tell me: what would cause a society so advanced to collapse so spectacularly?"

Asking me the oldest question, I thought. It was honestly something I had long pondered myself, the answer to which I settled on even before my betrayal. Perhaps those beliefs are what brought you here. Shrugging, I acknowledged that my conscience had a point, as consciences tend to. Jayce, just wing it. Let your heart do the talking.

My heart was a bit out of practice with this sort of thing, as it had only recently begun beating again. The walls that strangled it had crumbled, lying beneath the acid rains of Venus. I sighed, then let myself loose. "We are our own greatest foes, Kid; what makes us great is the same thing that ultimately seals our fate," I said, gesturing to the strafe marks all around us—something that could only come from aircraft artillery. "For war… war never changes."

He had the plate just about in his knapsack when I finished my spiel. The Kid's head snapped to attention as he realized what I had just said. A huge grin broke out on his face. "Never figured you for a Fallout fan. Honestly."

Scooping up a nearby white ball with black stitches in it, I tossed it up and caught it. "There's a lot of things you don't know about me. Such as… THINK FAST!" I yelled before chucking the ball at a nearby Rotgul, hitting it dead in its midsection.

The bird landed next to the Kid with a squishy thud. "That wasn't funny!" he said, picking himself up after hitting the dirt. He is way too good at that…

Much to his dismay, I was unable to hold back my laughter. "It is to me!" I said, tossing my head back and laughing in a way that I forgot I was capable of. So much at once, it's starting to dizzy me. "Hey, enough of this!" I roared, flipping the switch and retreating into myself. "It's almost dark, and we still have a ways to go! No more talking."

He was now looking at me like I was some sort of wounded animal. He mouthed the words "So close" before falling in line behind me. Given that I had laid down the law, unburdened from my growing feelings, the rest of the trip was completely uneventful. Not a word was spoken between us. Oh, how I have missed this… but do I really mean that? I wondered before shoving those thoughts down, along with all the other uncomfortable notions.

Sadly, I never really developed a fondness for North American history. My passions belonged to Europe and its grand tradition of chivalry. However, even I knew that Ford Field had once been a great sports arena. Though like most of its ilk after the first Great Collapse sometime in the early second millennium, it fell into a routine of shoddy repair and maintenance. Once the Kingdom had been founded, they began their second lives as havens for all sorts of scoundrels.

Most of the doors had long since been welded shut. I figured the pit would be the only point of entrance. My suspicions were proven correct when no sooner had we gotten in sight of it than a loud voice boomed from all four corners. "Halt! Identify yourselves… oh wait, it's just you two. Captain Bonny is waiting for you in the ready room."

A loud crack followed the announcement, the wide doors swinging open to let us in. Fresh air rushed between the Kid and me. Neither of us wanted to get yelled at for wasting perfectly good air, so we rushed in. The doors closed behind us just as quickly as they had first opened.

"They certainly don't build 'em as big as they used to," I quipped upon entering the main hangar. What was a "football field" had now been repurposed to serve as a hangar. Dozens of ships, each in different stages of repair or disrepair, filled the space. The Evantide, which sat at the far end of the field, trended more toward the latter end of that scale. It was plain as day now that we could see the damage with our own eyes.

The ship probably wouldn't have lasted another hour under that rain, I thought, looking over the damage. The outer hull had been completely removed, exposing the insides of the ship to the outside world—probably for the first time since leaving its space dock all those years prior.

"You guys are lucky to have Nanatose plating," Nileia said. My head swiveled back to look at her. "One: the ship would have been eaten up in the first hour. Two: the fact that I can now cultivate my nanites is the only reason I am willing to help you two fools."

Spinning around, I met her with a stare of my own. A stalemate ensued. Neither of us could ever best the will of the other. It's probably the reason we ran the Shadow Hawks so well… In this case, though, will was not a factor. She held all the cards; we both knew it. "Just tell me what I need to do so that we can get this over with."

Nileia smiled one of her crazy smiles—an expression she reserved for only the most ludicrous of schemes, ones that had a fifty-fifty shot of getting you killed. But you did them anyway because her instinct was hardly ever off. "Walk this way, gentlemen," she said before setting off without another word.

The room she took us into was smaller than the one in which we had initially met. In the center was a table with various objects on it. Behind the table was a map of the compound. "I've already briefed you on the broad strokes, so I'll keep this short," she began, her hand hovering over a switch by the door. "I bet you are wondering why I need you for this mission in particular?"

"The thought had occurred to me," I replied, having a feeling where this was going. "Surely, you've had enough of my charm to last a dozen lifetimes?" I continued my spiel, wanting to see how it played out. Best to keep your cards close to your chest when you can.

To the gal's credit, she chuckled at my remark. "On that, we are in agreement," she said, finally flicking the switch. Ancient motors hummed to life, driving the shutters to reveal what lay beyond their obstruction. "Bet you never thought you'd see this again."

My jaw hit the floor at what I saw. It can't be… "Holy sh— I… I thought they were all destroyed?" I asked, my mind still coming to terms with the fact that before me waited a Pillbug Stealth Transport— one of three such transports allotted to the Shadow Hawk Squadron. Its purpose was to ferry various things across enemy lines: goods, strike teams, or the occasional banned substance. Its stealth generator is even better than our Raven Stealth Fighters.

Nileia simply shrugged at my reverence. "Not all of them. After the fall, I managed to smuggle out two fighters, one of which was your old ship." She paused for a moment to let that last part sink in. While I was definitely shocked, my mind still hung on the idea that a single stealth craft existed, let alone three. "This one came up on a Black Market Auction a few months back. Let's just say we… smoked the competition."

"Let me guess," I chimed in, my mind finally getting back on track after the sheer shock I had received. "You need a co-pilot, and I am the only one qualified to do so?" Nileia simply nodded at my words, waiting for my next response. "Well, fine then, but the Kid comes with us."

She definitely didn't like my reply. "Ah, hell no!" she said, closing the blinds. "This mission is too delicate for him to come and gum it up." Looking over at the Kid, he instantly buckled under her glare. "He stays here."

It was now my turn not to like what I had heard. Putting my arms over the Kid's shoulder and drawing him close, I noticed him looking up at me, his eyes saying, 'What the Hades are you doing?' Turning my attention back toward Nileia, my body suddenly filled with stubborn determination. "I've been contracted to transport this Kid to the Spartans safely. I will not forsake that."

Nileia burst into a fit of laughter at my words. "You haven't changed a bit, Jayce—lawfully stupid till the end." She then walked over to the table and scooped up what looked like a pair of watches. "I figured you'd say that. Put these on," she said, handing them to both of us.

I shrugged to the Kid, putting mine on with him quickly following suit. Looking down, I could see a set of biometrics and comm options. "Are these Bio Bracelets?" I asked, pretty much already knowing what the answer was.

Her eyes lit up at what I said. Her body language showed that I had finally asked the right question. "Yes!" she said with excitement. "These will allow you both to monitor each other's current condition, even if you are on separate ends of the system!" Taking a few breaths to calm down, she then followed up with, "So, will you come, Jayce? I still hate your ass, but I don't really have a choice. Neither do you, really."

Looking down at the Kid, I could tell he knew what I was going to say. "Just promise to be safe, okay? I'm kinda starting to like you," he said to me.

Instead of giving him a straight answer, I just ruffled his hair. "When do we leave?" I asked Nileia.

In response, she dashed to the door. "We leave now."

9

Now We Weave

"Coming out of Slip Space in 3...2...1!" Nileia cried before flipping the switch. Our ship made a smooth exit from FTL. She was always good at this stuff, I thought, my mind wandering back nostalgically. Looking down below us, I could see the red-hot dot that was Mercury.

More of a blight than Earth ever could be, it was a completely inhospitable planet. That didn't stop some mad lads from setting up little outposts of civilization. For research, they claimed at the time. Personally, I think they just wanted to scratch an itch that only exploration could soothe. It seems they at least kept their promise, judging by the pictures on the screen.

Poorly made and hastily constructed—that was the story of almost every station on this hellscape of a planet. Thankfully, to people like Nileia, that made each of them ripe for exploitation. "...Patrols won't be around for another two days. Are you even listening, Jayce?" Nileia said, flicking my forehead and rousing me from my wandering, bringing me back to her best-laid plan.

Looking up at her, I could see she obviously had little patience for me. The reputation I had garnered as her superior and one-time lover had long since evaporated. Now, she gazed down upon me as if I were her student, full of broken promises and little else. "Yeah… sorry. It's been a while since I operated in any… official capacity. Carry on."

She rolled her eyes at my attempt at being professional. She sighed, knowing she at least now had my attention, and continued. "Let's just cut to the necessary bits: upon our landing, your job will be to enter the facility and first assess the condition of the power supply. If it can be jump-started, our mission will continue. Yes, what is it? You don't need to raise your hand."

Feeling rather sheepish at the awkward way I had gotten her attention, I slowly put my hand down in shame. Probably making me look even more like an ass, I thought. "I get that, but what will you have me do in the meantime?"

Her eyes lit up at my words. For the briefest of moments, I swear she saw her old commander. "Ah, so the booze hasn't eaten up all your brain cells just yet. It's probably the only reason you're even alive— the very thing that got you off Venus. It's for that reason I need you."

This time, it was my turn to look shocked. Nileia Boony, once commander of the Shadow Hawk Squadron, now a feared pirate needed me? It was almost too much to bear. "Why do you need a washed-up turd like me… oh… OH!" I said to her. Chuckling at first, the mirth slowly faded to melancholy as I looked over at the console—or, to be more specific, the stealth controls situated in front of the co-pilot's chair, the very chair I was currently sitting in.

"Now he gets it!" Nileia replied, patting me on the head like the good boy she saw me as. "I didn't have a choice to begin with; you and I are the last of our kind." She bowed her head as she finished her words. My jaw soon followed.

Am I the cause of every bad thing in this solar system? I wondered to myself. My mind was still reeling from the bombshell she had just dropped on me. "No! What about Torchfire? The one you said helped you take the ships from the nest?" I asked in desperation, knowing the answer but still wanting some sort of hope, even if only for a few more moments.

Nileia looked over at me. Our ship had been still since its exit from Slip Space. We were at risk of being detected by a sensor sweep, but at that moment, she didn't seem to care. "Killed…" she replied, choking back tears. "He was shot during our escape and died in my arms after we landed."

From what I had gathered in the years between my transfer and now, the one known as Torchfire had been recruited to fill the spot left empty by my absence. He even piloted my old ship to great distinction. Shame I never got to meet him… even though I once had the chance to… I thought, shaking off these bad feelings and turning my attention back to the present. "We should probably cloak. A sweep could pass us by at any moment."

With a look of forced, grim determination,

she nodded. "Prepare for stealth!" she declared. Her usually stern voice was reduced to a series of squeaks.

Knowing my job, I quickly looked at our surroundings and did the calculations in my head. Stealth wasn't some magic cloak that draped over a ship. No, it was an advanced camouflage field that had to be manually calculated to match its exterior precisely.

A computer automated most of it, but the initial engagement could only be done by hand. Even one slight deviation could cause us to stand out more than we would have otherwise. At that point, it would have been better not to engage it at all. "Input complete!" I said, the process flowed from me as if it had never left.

The entire process usually took about five minutes. Still, since Nileia and I were both seasoned vets with a former relationship, we fell easily back into old habits and managed to get it done in three.

Seeing the familiar yellow hexagons envelop the view screen was a more comfortable sight than I realized. Not that Nileia seemed to notice. I guess you can't be nostalgic for something you never abandoned, I mused. The woman acted as if the war had never left her, which most likely was the case. "Reentry in ten minutes. Recalibrate," she called out, once again showing that command was her home.

As I put in the numbers, I couldn't help but wonder: Is this the fate that would have awaited me had I stayed? The very thought both scared and exhilarated me.

A life of debaucherous wandering had been all I knew up until a month ago. Now, something much scarier lay ahead of me: reconciliation with my past sins, now laid bare. No longer could I hide behind pride and a mountain of pills and booze. The only thing I knew for certain now was that I wanted to return to the man I once was, when everything made sense and all was right. But could I go home again?

A sharp pain in the back of my head broke me from my misery. "Hey, jackass! We're entering the atmosphere. Recalibrate!" Nileia barked at me, her right hand still poised to strike in case I didn't heed her call.

Giving my former partner a stern look, I said, "You were never this rude when I knew you." But my curt words didn't match my actions; my fingers were flying across the numpad, inputting calibrations I had long since committed to muscle memory.

Nileia returned my look with one of her own. This one was made of pure fire and determination—a fire that had never once gone out. "And the man I knew had a backbone. Guess that's what happens when you abandon everything that made you. At least some things are eternal, though." Her eyes wandered downward to my fingers, which had been perfectly inputting the codes without me even realizing it. The idea that she was throwing an ounce of praise my way caused me to let out a slight yelp. My fingers still managed to keep to their task, thankfully.

The ship shook violently as we entered the atmosphere—something small ships like ours tended to do when re-entering. The shields took the heat, and the kinetic stabilizers absorbed most of the outside forces, but one can only cheat physics so much.

The worst of it lasted for about half a minute. Thankfully, Mercury didn't have much of an atmosphere to speak of, though that didn't mean it lacked one entirely. Clearing it, we both looked down to see our target—a mid-sized research facility. The place definitely looked recently abandoned. That much of the briefing was correct. As for the rest, I was sure to find out soon enough.

Continuing to look down, I pulled up the map and flicked it onto the view screen. "We should probably land here," I said to Nileia, pointing to an alcove on its eastern side. "Not only is it right next to a side entrance, but it's in the shadow of the hangar, so we should at least have some shading against any surveys."

"Very well, good advice is good advice," Nileia replied, punching in the landing coordinates I suggested. "Even if it does come from a washed-up jackass," she added, unable to stop herself from getting in one more jab.

Getting through re-entry was the hard part. With that over, the cloak ran at optimal levels, and landing was a breeze. The Pillbug touched down gracefully, its size allowing it to slot easily into the alcove I had picked out.

"Alright, Jayce, let's get this over with," Nileia said, disengaging from her restraints and making a beeline for the vac-suits. "Never thought I'd meet someone who smells worse than I do."

Unfortunately for Nileia, putting on the suit was a two-person affair. Her nose was painfully scrunched tight the entire time. "Remember: start the power, then meet me in the hangar. Once you return to the ship, we can go from there. Understood?" she told me, knocking on my now-snug helmet for good measure.

Giving her a thumbs-up to show I understood, I quickly followed up with a generous helping of the bird and made my way over to the airlock. "Very funny, Flyboi," Nileia said over the comms. It wasn't until the airlock shut behind me that I realized she had addressed me by my old moniker.

That thought left me stuck in a void between air pressure and the pull of the task outside. "Don't forget we're on the clock," she said as I heard her press the button to suck out the oxygen in my chamber. My suit quickly picked up the slack.

"Jayce, be careful in there," Nileia chimed in, the outer door opening before me and, this time, dropping the insults in favor of more reasonable concern. "I don't know if you'll run into any dead zones inside, so watch out. You might be on your own for a bit."

Stepping out onto the planet, the first thing to greet me was the sun. Since Mercury is the closest planet to the sun, its horizon was all but filled with the yellow giant. Thanks to my quick decision, the side entrance was only ten meters from the ship.

"Don't worry, Bonny, I've got the need!" I said to her, pulling down on the handle. On the way out, she had informed me that in the event of a power collapse, all the locks would be disengaged. "The need… to bleed!" I grinned as I heard her growl at my attempt to dredge up an old joke. The door opened to blackness.

Flicking on my forward light illuminated only the surrounding fifteen meters in front of me. Honestly, the darkness had no bearing on me when my heart had been plunged into emotional blackness for the past fifteen years. I had only recently come up to the surface, gasping for air. A quick dip back into familiar surroundings was nothing.

Sadly, Nileia's accomplice had only been able to provide me with a partial, hand-drawn map—still better than nothing, I thought to myself, giving myself little comfort. According to the map, the power room lay on the exact opposite side of the facility from where I had entered. Clutching my pistol tight, I moved forward cautiously. There was no telling what had taken up residence in the short time this place had lain abandoned.

The halls, of course, were as silent as the grave, which was to be expected. What I definitely didn't expect were the tiny specks of light dancing like fireflies under the glare of my lights. My rudimentary knowledge of interstellar physics told me these were random debris left in the air after it was displaced. My presence was the catalyst for their disruption. By now, they should have settled into a fine film on the walls… someone had been here in the interim.

My hand was on my wrist in an instant, activating the comms so I could call out to Nileia. "Hey… um… has there been anyone else here since the place was last occupied?" I said over my wireless Squawker. She didn't reply immediately. A few moments stretched into an eternity as I waited for her response. With my heightened senses, I picked up… something—a sound I thought I could identify, at least at first.

"…No?" was her reply, seemingly as confused as I was. "Jayce, what's going on in there?" Her voice started to get a bit shaky toward the end of the sentence.

Figuring at this point that the silence had me staring at specters of my imagination, I said, "Nothing, I'm probably just being crazy. Don't worry about it. I'm almost there anyway." The only part of the statement that was actually true was that I now stood in front of the entrance marking the power room. The large doors easily split apart, their locks having been disengaged weeks ago.

In a mid-sized facility such as this one, instead of having everything spread out, all the controls for the various utilities were centralized in a single room.

This, of course, made any servicing that needed to be performed that much easier. As I made my way up to the console that controlled the power, I let myself feel relief, thinking that soon I would let there be lig…

Staring down at the console, my heart sank to my shoes. "Umm, Nileia… we have a problem."

I could hear her rush to her squawk box. Swearing, I heard the sound of her belt being fastened in haste. "What kind of problem? Talk to me, Jayce!"

I'm not really sure how to describe it, so I decided to tell it straight. "The keys are clean."

"So?" she shouted back, her frustration beginning to boil over. "This isn't the time for humor!"

I sighed a long sigh. She really doesn't get it, does she? "You know how, when you leave a space alone for a long time, dust settles everywhere?" There was silence between us; I took this as confirmation of understanding and pressed on. "Well, there's dust everywhere—except for the very keys I'm currently standing in front of."

"Oh…" was all she could manage after a long pause. "Anything else you see that's out of place?"

Walking over to the circuit breakers, I could see that they, too, lacked a layer of dust. "The breakers are clear, too. It looks like they've been serviced recently." I ran my glove over the hinge that bound one of the sets together. When I held the glove to the light, I saw it was covered in very expensive grease. "The grease is still pretty fresh. I think an assessment crew was here within the last week or so."

Over the comms, I could hear her let out a huge sigh of relief. "Thank the gods. I tried to time this so we arrived after they came through." I heard a flurry of keys as she looked up the tutorial. "Getting the power back online should be easy then."

I made my way back over to the power console, my mind swimming with this new information.

"Hey, Nil, don't you think it would have been a good idea to tell me something that important?" She's not one to hold back information from her colleagues. "Imagine if I had run into one of them."

In response to my very valid concerns, I could hear Nileia laughing at me. She wasn't even trying to hide it. "But did you?" she asked. I didn't respond at first, unsure what to say. She took my silence for agreement and continued her tirade. "Honestly, Jayce, I expect better of you. Now listen up, I only want to go through this on—"

"You've changed!" I shouted at her through the comms. "And not for the better either! I see shades of the woman I once loved, but she's buried under a thick pile of sass and cynicism."

"You believe you're any different, Jayce?" she fired back. "I see glimpses of the man I once looked up to, but there's no way the person I'm talking to now is the man I once considered my equal. The person I'm talking to now is much too whiny and broken.

The Jayce I knew would never act this way!"

She was right, of course; neither of us was the person we once were—an impossible task, really. "Fifteen years of near-constant turmoil tends to change a person."

She seemed to take a moment to consider what I'd said. "Yes, it most certainly does." An awkward silence fell between us as we realized how far apart we had become. Thankfully, Nileia decided to be the better person and threw me a bone. "Shall we continue?"

Grateful and relieved, I bent over to flip the switch that lay to the side. At once, the reserve power flooded in, and the console hummed to life. Its screen flooded the chamber with an amber haze. "It's booting up now," I said to her, my voice starting to return to its current level of confidence.

After a few clicks, Nileia returned to the mic. "Once it boots up, you're going to look for the tab labeled 'prestart.' Is that too much for you?"

With a grunt to tell her I understood, I quickly found the proper tab. Clicking it, I could hear the engines around me humming to life. "What was that?" Nileia asked me. Apparently, the suit's mic was more sensitive than I'd realized. "Did you do something?"

I couldn't help but crack a smile—something only I would see. Regardless, it felt good. "Yeah, I engaged the prestart sequence." I stopped for a moment to bask in her surprise before really nailing home my competence. "In about thirty seconds, the generators will have spooled to eighty-six thousand RPM, thus allowing me to start the system in earnest. Did you get that, or is it too much for you?"

More silence was her immediate reaction. Once she had finished what I assumed was collecting her brain matter from all the corners of the ship, she came back on, trying to play it cool—but that was impossible for a firebrand like her. "You seem to be an expert on this, so I'll leave you to it. Contact me when things eventually go pear-shaped." With that, she cut off contact, leaving me all alone in a room now tastefully lit by the blue glow of the generators. The luminousness indicated it was ready to be utilized.

All that was left was for me to push the normally sized red button located near the top of the console. I snickered, pushing it, knowing the placement was meant to feel like launching a missile. Whoever said engineers don't have a sense of humor? I thought to myself, looking around in wonder as these once unsettling and foreboding corridors were filled with the light of hope. "Power's on. Heading to the hangar now," I said to Nileia over the comms once I made sure everything was running properly.

"What?" she replied, seemingly caught off guard. "You couldn't have done that so quickly!"

My ego replenished, I strutted out into the hangar, noticing the door controls were on the other side. "Don't you remember who my father is? What he does for a living?" I said to her as I made my way over.

"Oh… isn't your aunt running the company now?" Nileia shot back. At first, I thought she meant to demean me, but the way she said it sounded almost… concerned. For a moment, I drifted back to my childhood. As the heir to Lamont Aerospace, I was groomed to take over, which manifested in learning every aspect of the business. Of course, that meant I gained a passing knowledge of electrical engineering.

Coming back to the present, I looked at the panel that held the switches for the roof. Emblazoned at the bottom was the current logo for the company my grandfather Leon had bought. "Camilla forced my dad out not long after I fled the capital in an imperial-backed coup," I said to her, letting out a long sigh as I flipped the switch to open the roof. "Anyway, you'd better get the ship started. I just started the sequence."

The next little bit was spent in silence. Nileia was preoccupied with landing the ship in the hangar while I found myself lost in a tainted web of nostalgia and the choices I could have made to prevent it. I was so far gone that I didn't even hear the ship land mere meters away from me. What ended up awakening me from my musings was Nileia's voice. "Jayce? I'm literally looking right at you! JAYCE!" Her cries snapped me back to reality, and the gravity of the situation soon flooded back in.

Now fully back in the present, I marched up to the ship. I slammed the button to close the outer door once I had cleared the ramp. The now-familiar whoosh of air followed. Green light began to flood my temporary quarters, indicating that the pressure had stabilized with the interior of the ship— basically, it meant I was now clear to remove my helmet, which I promptly did, breathing in the same stale air I'd been ingesting for the past few days.

Nileia was in the center of the ship. She had pulled up the conference table from the floor. A holographic map of the entire facility flooded the ship's interior. Buried among the lines were three points of interest marked by different-colored dots at various points on the map.

"These first two are pretty easy," she began, pointing out the purple dot in a small room— undoubtedly the manager's office. The other dot was black and situated smack-dab in the cold storage section—a bioweapon of some sort. "You'll grab these, then head back to the ship. Once you return, I'll provide a hover lift so you can finally grab the Enigma Breaker. Any questions?"

"Just one," I said. Nileia looked over her shoulder as I pointed to the view screen at the top of the ship. "Shouldn't we be concerned about that?" I asked while the unmistakable roar of three Wyverns buzzed the entire ship.

She simply looked back at me and shrugged. "Probably not. They must have gotten an automated alert when the power came back on. I imagine they'll get lazy, call it a glitch, and go back to base."

I didn't really share her optimistic outlook. Not having much choice in the matter, I held my tongue and put my helmet back on so I could once more enter the fray.

With power restored and the light returned to its normal state, navigating the halls would now be a simple task. Time was the only remaining barrier to my success. If the dice were cruel and the pilots circling above us didn't subscribe to the usual nonchalant attitude of their peers, we'd have only a short window to grab things before being rendered unable to escape. Either way, the exit was sure to be a brutal one. That was an issue for future Jayce; current Jayce needed to focus on getting what had been asked of him.

Lifting my wrist to call up the map stored in the memory of my suit, I could see that the office was only about a hallway and a half ahead of me. Making my way there, I made it a point to keep an ear out, not for anything inside the base. No, with the power now restored, I'd done an internal scan before leaving the center, finding no life forms other than Nileia and me residing anywhere close.

The real threat I was keyed into came from outside the walls. To my horror, the familiar drone of Wyverns had not abated. It had definitely lessened, but hadn't left entirely. That's not a good sign, I thought to myself, absentmindedly turning the handle to the office.

Obviously, in my travels, I'd seen many things. I'd witnessed firsthand the best and worst of my species. But nothing—and I mean nothing—could have prepared me for the sight of my weeks-dead cousin, his assailant lying dead on the floor next to him after having done his job. "Nileia, were you aware that my cousin Michael Hunter was the commander of this facility?"

"You just found his corpse, didn't you?" Nileia began, and I could hear actual remorse in her voice. "Please believe me when I say I didn't know it was him. I only met him once, but he seemed nice."

"A better man than his father ever could be," I said, trying to hold back tears. Walking up to him, I could see that he'd died a fearful death. The facility was his responsibility; the destruction of the algae would have thrust great shame upon him—a feeling I was very familiar with. "And yes, I do believe you. Just tell me where the item is so I can get out of here."

Nileia seemed relieved at what I said, though she chose not to vocalize it. "Look for a plaque above his desk. It has a couple of things you should recognize."

With that description in mind, it wasn't too hard to find the item. Sitting above the desk was a small shadowbox that indeed held something very familiar to me. "How the hell did both of our wings make it all the way out here?" I asked Nileia once I'd pulled the box down and gotten a better look at it.

"I don't know," Nileia said matter-of-factly. "Caroline just told me she spotted the wings in the GM's office. She didn't mention yours were there as well."

Looking down at my now-deceased cousin, it suddenly all made sense. "You've got it in reverse, Nil," I said to her over the comms, feeling myself on the verge of tears yet again. "My cousin was displaying my wings; yours were the bonus." Once I finished crying, I reached down and grabbed Michael's dog tags in addition to his gold beaker pin. Nileia never said I couldn't grab a few mementos of my own.

"Alright, one down, two to go. Heading to the lab now," I chirped—more as a formality than anything else. I was never really a fan of this kind of work, always preferring a tense firefight to a terse treasure hunt. Thankfully, the lab wasn't too far from the office, even being in the same section!

While my next target was so close, that fact did absolutely nothing to make the walk any less dull. One generic beige hallway gave way to another, each door colored the same monstrously monotonous stone gray.

Things were so boring that I almost walked straight past the door to the Experimental Genetics Lab, the place where the DNA vials I sought resided. "Heading into the lab—any updates on our friends upstairs?" I said to Nileia over the comms.

"They're still flitting about," she replied, giving me the news we both didn't want to hear. "I believe at this point they've narrowed their search to the valley we're currently in."

Damn, we don't have much more time! Cursing myself, I dashed over to the fridge. Sensitive samples usually had their own internal refrigeration, activated upon a power loss—obviously. From there, they had a shelf life of approximately one month before spoiling. We're well within that window, I reassured myself. Just grab the pod and go!

I did just that, fortunate to find the correct one in the first fridge I searched. I quickly put it with the others in my satchel. Making a mad dash for the hangar, an occasional roar had now joined the drone that was slowly becoming ever-present, announcing that the Wyverns were closing in on their prey—us.

I was all but out of breath when my eyes gazed upon the now-familiar sight of the hangar. The outer door to the Pillbug opened as soon as I was in sight.

"Could this airlock go any slower?" I yelled in frustration once the outer door finished taking its sweet time to close. I tried jamming the button, but, of course, that did nothing but shorten its lifespan.

Finally, after what seemed like an eternity but was in actuality the same time as always, the inner door opened. Nileia already had the hover lift ready for me. "How close are they?" I asked once I'd slammed the satchel onto a nearby seat.

Nileia stayed silent at first. Her eyes conveyed the dread we both felt as she gestured to the view screen. There, I saw the patterns the Wyverns had taken over the past few hours, showing an ever-tightening circle. "N… n… not long," she said, her voice struggling to get out the words. The last time I'd heard her like this was when she came to me after crashing her first training craft, almost killing her instructor in the process. "The computer estimates we have about forty-five minutes before they find us."

Grabbing the hover lift, I made a beeline, smashing the button to vent the airlock before I even had a chance to put on my helmet. Desperation certainly makes for a wonderful motivator, I thought to myself, clearing the hatch in what could only be record time.

Sadly, this time, luck wasn't on our side. The crate holding the Enigma Breaker was in the warehouse, a room that lay on the exact opposite end of the building. Getting to it wouldn't be a swift process, nor could I speed things along in any meaningful way. This time, only the steady march of progress was my ally.

Ironic how it had been my enemy a mere month prior, I mused to myself. My thoughts were now my only companion. With the Wyverns coming ever closer, Nileia thought it best to go radio silent—an idea I was wholly receptive to, if for no other reason than to get her condescending tone out of my ear.

She has good reason to hate you, I thought. My mind wandered back to the memory of when I'd been possessed to give them an award.

Couldn't have been helped. You were on exercise, I justified. The guilt of such a snub still haunts me to this day. Shaking my head, I reminded myself that I couldn't afford to waste even a moment, no matter how seductive it might be.

Not wanting to get distracted by past failures, my mind instead turned to the task at hand. Looking at the map, I could see there were two-thirds of the distance left to cover—well past the time I should have returned my full focus to the present.

One couldn't help but wonder, though, what kind of damage Nileia could wreak with such a device, given the Enigma Breaker's power. No code, whether current or in the near future, could withstand its might—a powerful tool for a powerful woman. But was she the right woman? These were a few of the fleeting notions that flung around in my head as I turned the handle for the warehouse.

Finding the crate wasn't too hard a task. If the empire loved anything better than subjugation, it was order. Provided with its storage number, it became easy to locate its precise position.

Lo and behold, the number proved true. In front of me was a crate that not only bore the digits in my nav but also the name "Enigma Breaker- PROTOYPE." Bingo! Now to load this up and get bac—

"SCAVENGER SCUM!" A harsh voice broke into my ear. There was no doubt about who it could be. "You will open the doors to the mining facility and surrender at once!" Hades! I cursed to myself. They found us… alrea… wait… did they say 'mining facility'?

Not wanting to waste this gift that had been given to me, I quickly loaded the crate onto the hover cart and rushed it out the door, running as fast as my legs could take me. "Nileia!" I roared over the comms, no longer caring who could hear us. "Please tell me you caught the same thing I did?"

There was no response for a little while. She's probably pondering whether to respond. Logic swiftly faded with each step. No sooner had I passed the T-junction that marked the halfway point than Nileia got back to me. "I did, but they won't make the same mistake again—especially after what your dumbass just did." She paused, hoping I'd make some excuse. When she got none, she continued, "But it's done. Please tell me you're close, Jayce."

Instead of words, I let my feet do the talking, kicking open the doors to the hangar and rushing toward the already-opening airlock. "Please tell me you have a plan?" I asked in desperation.

What surprised me was the hug I received once the airlock shut tight. This wasn't just some "relieved to see you" hug—no, this was most definitely a "glad you've returned alive" hug. I guess she still does care somewhere in there. Once the vac-suit was fully removed, she pointed to the gunner's seat and said, "I always do… Captain."

Having an idea of the gears turning in her head, I complied and took my place in the gunner's position. The Pillbug was a transport and thus not heavily armed. That didn't mean it was defenseless, though—just that its defenses were minimal. "You've kept yourself busy," I said to her once I spotted her plan.

Looking back at me, she smiled a smile I was all too familiar with. "When I give the word, shoot the stack in that direction. I'm sure you'll know when to shoot the ones on the right."

That I did, I squared my sights on the pile of canisters to my left, listening as Nileia gave one of the best bullshit performances of her life. "Alright, you got us. However, please be aware that we inadvertently tripped some gas lines. Any attempt to incinerate us could result in the destruction of every base in this quadrant." Flipping off the outgoing transceiver, she looked over at me and roared, "Now!"

Doing what I was told, I shot a three-round burst at the stack of biohazard canisters Nileia had hastily propped up. A tiny explosion followed, and a plume of neon-green smoke wafted up to the roof, quickly eating it away. Once the gas had done its job, I could see the three Wyverns circling above us, their mouths filled to the brim with fiery plasma death— the very thing they were known for.

They held their fire, for even they weren't stupid enough to ignite a noxious fume like this. "Scumbags, you may have bought yourselves a half hour at most. If you surrender before the gas breaks, we promise not to kill you—on the spot, at least."

Nileia sent me a sly smile, one I was quite familiar with. It's almost like old times have come again. There was a brief pause before she turned her attention to the other pilots, flicking on the outbound comms. "I have a better idea. How about we just get on with it? You know, really… ignite our passions."

The pilots didn't respond, unsure how to reply. I sure did, though; that was the signal I'd been looking out for. I swiveled my guns toward the second stack, this one made of excess ship fuel. I couldn't help but cackle while pulling the trigger. "Fire in the hole!" I roared, not caring who heard. At this point, I doubted Nileia did either.

Her attention was suddenly elsewhere—namely, navigating out of the giant ball of fire that had been the facility mere moments prior. Bracing myself, the ship quickly went skyward. Knowing the plume could only mask us for so long, I re-primed the weapons. Cloaking would be all but useless by the time they were ready.

As expected, the towering inferno carried us into the mid-atmosphere. Upon our exit, I wasn't surprised to see the two remaining Wyverns circling below us. Thankfully, they hadn't spotted us just yet.

Deciding to take advantage of this momentary grace, I announced our position in the best way possible by shooting an entire volley of fire at one of the Wyvern's necks—its most vulnerable point.

My aggressive play soon bore fruit. I watched with childish glee as the neck separated from its body, the ordnance being held there igniting soon afterward. "Woo-hoo!" I cheered. "I haven't felt this alive in forever!"

Still at the helm, Nileia threw her head in my direction. "That's great and all, Jayce… but THERE'S STILL ONE MORE!!"

Right, I thought to myself. Kill now, celebrate later. I knew the standard tactics of Wyvern pilots were to climb above their foe and rain plasma fire down below. Shock and awe were the keys to their effectiveness—but against the very people who tested the initial design? Completely and utterly useless.

Indeed, the pilot displayed absolutely no imagination whatsoever, igniting its afterburners so it could climb above us. Wasting no time, I met its climb with a series of well-placed shots against its now-exposed underbelly. You'd think a ship known solely for dive tactics would have its most-often-exposed side heavily armored, but no. Budget cuts can be a cruel mistress, it seems, I pondered while watching every one of my shots hit home.

In a beautiful symphony of destruction, the landing gears went first. Miniature explosions gave way to slightly larger ones as the thruster system imploded in on itself. With nothing to keep it in the sky, the ship fell like a brick, returning to the cradle of fire from which we'd emerged.

Now fully out of the woods, relief washed over me at first, soon followed by… regret. I hadn't realized how much I missed this—the fight. Unhooking myself from the gunner's seat, I made my way to the front and took my rightful place at Nileia's side. "I now know why you never stopped."

That caught Nileia dead in her tracks, halting her jump calculations to look over at me. "Oh, you do now, do you?" she said with a mixture of confusion and amusement. "Enlighten me, oh wise sage."

Instead of answering her, I stared blankly, choosing to look out the front window into the vastness of space. My eyes eventually fell on the flight controls. From there, it all fell into place. "We're soldiers, and like all soldiers, we need a fight. No, 'fight' isn't the right word. We need… purpose."

Nileia froze. What I'd said seemed to resonate with her. "I've felt more myself in the last thirty minutes than I have in the past twenty years," I continued, now looking her straight in the eyes. "I'm a creature of the sky, same as you."

The woman just looked at me. Judging by the way her eyes widened, it felt like Nileia was finally staring at the man she once knew. "There you are, Captain," she said, confirming what I'd thought. "So, what are you going to do now?"

I smiled. "Well, first we run," I said, pulling the lever that launched us into Slip Space. "The next step is to get the Kid to the Spartan Alliance."

"You still can't call him by his actual name, can you?" she asked between smiles, her voice taking on a tinge of sadness as a result.

Unable to look her in the eyes, I got up and stared at our new cargo. "Just because I had a breakthrough—just because I've decided I want to be my old self…" I replied, my head turned down in shame. Swinging around to look at her, I could feel my eyes begin to well up with tears. "That doesn't make me whole again. If only things were that easy."

Not knowing what else to do, I went over to the rack and sat on it. Silence hung between us as she manually navigated Slip Space, and I stared at the ceiling. After what seemed like forever, I felt the lurch that announced our return to Earth.

Turning to get up from the rack, I was greeted by none other than Nileia, on her knees so we could look at each other as equals. "It's the pursuit that matters, Jayce," she said, giving me a tender kiss on the cheek. "And in this moment, you are the man I fell in love with."

She then got up and moved to the back. Looking over at me, her hand over the button to release the ramp, she said, "Now come on, our Prince is waiting for you."

10

A Drink To Our Youth

"You don't have to go, you know?" Nileia's words rang out to me just as clearly now as they did back then, when she said them just as I was placing the last of my luggage onto the transport. This ship would shuttle me from everything I had known straight toward the great unknown.

I remember putting on a brave face for everyone. Inside, my mind was split down the middle. One side wanted to remain where I was, where I felt comfortable. The other side yearned to push myself, to raise my status as high as it could reach. Ambition had carried me this far. It seemed logical to continue the winning trend.

Nileia stood beside me, surveying the remaining boxes and acting as the last barrier for me to overcome. She would prove to be the most challenging one. Having been my second-in-command for so long, we had, of course, grown... close. "Jayce, I just don't think you understand."

That's a new one, I thought to myself, dropping the box I was holding. In my shock, I hadn't accounted for where the box would land. To my chagrin, it landed right atop my left foot. Pain quickly shot through my body. "Mother fu—" I swore, catching myself before it went too far. "Nil, I just dropped a very heavy box on my foot. Sit with me, and you can explain whatever in Hades you mean."

The girl smiled, helping me up and over to a nearby bench. She... smiled at me! She knows I'm weak to her smiles. Dammit! "Command comes easily to you, Jayce," she began, easing me not only into this conversation but onto the bench where we both sat. For a long moment, the two of us just watched the Royal Pages scurry about, doing the jobs assigned to them. Not unlike what you're about to do, I reminded myself. "I don't know if I'm ready to fill your rather large shoes."

Chuckling at Nileia's put-down, my mind looked back at the relationship we had built over these six years. Insults and retorts were our stock-in-trade. A pilot only had so much ego to go around before they became unbearable. "No one is ever truly ready for new responsibilities," I said to her, my gaze fixed on the Royal Crest adorning the transport. Who am I really talking to here?

She quickly caught where my eyes had wandered, staring at the crest with me; I could see her expression soften ever so slightly. "How old were you when you signed up?" she asked me.

Personal questions as deep as that were rarely broached between us. The very nature of our job kept us focused on the present. With such a drive, it seemed pointless to open up our pasts. We certainly had enough issues in the present to keep us busy. What would be the point of reopening old wounds?

Still, though... This might be the last time I see her. If this isn't the time for full transparency, then when is? "Sixteen. My Pa made sure I went straight to command school."

She pulled back, horrified. And why wouldn't she be? The minimum age of enlistment was nineteen. To go in at such a young age was unheard of—unless your father had recently ascended to the aristocracy, using his newfound influence to ensure that his only son and heir attained a prestigious position. That same influence now tore me from the only family I dared call my own. "It... it all makes sense now," she said, laying her head on my shoulder.

The hardest part is leaving... this... behind, I thought, my heart nearly splitting in two from the ache. "Pa has great ambitions for me. Doesn't matter if I'm on board or not," I replied, my hands rubbing her back in an attempt to comfort the only woman I had ever loved. "Nileia, you're going to be a great leader."

My words seemed to touch something inside her. At once, she sat up and looked me straight in the eyes. Her expression told me that the Nileia I had fallen in love with was back in the building. "Of course I am! It'll take a few weeks to waft your stench from the barracks, but I think I'll manage."

With both of us feeling at least somewhat relieved, I stood up, taking Nileia by the hand and leading her to the entry ramp. Upon seeing us, the pilot ceased his conversation with the newbie-the one taking my spot—and made a beeline for us. "Sir Jayce, your things have been loaded, and we're ready to leave at your command," he said to me before taking a bow and heading up the ramp onto the ship. "That's my port call," I said to Nileia. Somehow, we had found ourselves locked in each other's embrace.

Looking up at me, the wetness in her eyes hinted at the sorrow she hid so well, but not from me. There are no secrets between us. Not anymore, I thought to myself. "You'd better have us over there soon. You're a captain! If you can't arrange a flyby, what good are you for?"

Cracking my most devilish smile, I looked over at her, convinced she knew what was coming. "I can think of one thing," I said, drawing her in even closer and giving the lady a deep, passionate kiss.

As usual, time stopped. Our worlds shrank to encompass just the two of us. For the briefest of moments, our existence stretched out into infinity. All was right, and everything made sense. To be honest, the only thing that ever made sense to me was her love... until I met—no, not now. This needs to be savored.

Sadly, like all good things, this too had to come to an end. Our lips parted from each other in unison. Little did I know that this would be the last time the two of us would ever be fully in sync. Stealing one final glance, I turned my back on her and marched up the ramp to the ship.

The inside of the ship was as sterile as the royal reputation that preceded it. But just like the royals, when one looked into the shady corners—the places the higher-ups hardly paid attention to—you could see the dirt on full display.

Jumping at the sound of the door closing behind me, the soles of my boots hit the bottom of the door on its way down, all of this shaking me from my anguish.

"Sir, you might want to sit down. We're almost fully prepped for launch," a royal page said to me when he noticed me standing there.

Doing as I was told, I took my seat behind the currently empty pilot's chair. Deciding to keep my mind busy, I took stock of the tech presented before me. It was obviously on an entirely different level than what I was accustomed to. The royals get all the best toys, I thought, starting to get a little pissed off.

It wasn't the fact that the ship was more advanced than the Shadow Hawk fighters. No, that was to be expected. What really got me was the degree of the gap. The tech in front of me couldn't be less than eight years ahead of what I'd been flying for the past six. "You should see what kind of stuff they're putting in the Royal Starship retrofit," the pilot chirped in from behind me, obviously noticing my study of the controls. "Makes this thing look like a trash heap."

Taking his place at the head of the ship, the skipper turned to look at me once he had settled in. Looking me up and down, I could tell he was about to say some demeaning remark. He even opened his mouth in preparation to cut me down.

His piehole closed as quickly as it opened when he noticed my Maverick Medals—an award given only to the bravest of flyboys for gallantry in combat. I had three such chunks of metal pinned to my chest, to his zilch. You can't cut down that which is taller than you, I recalled my instructor's words, smiling not only at myself but at this fool who now played taxi driver. "So…" he said after a bit, probably struggling to find words to say. Idiot. "Do you want to get out of here or what?"

Those words hit me like a twelve-ton truck. Here was the knife's edge; the next thing I said would decide my fate. "No… but I don't have much of a choice anyway," I said to him. The weight of the decision I had made practically suffocated me. "Fly."

"So, do you actually want to go or what?" Nileia said, snapping her fingers in my face and breaking me from the recollection of a similar event. Many of the players were the same, but the circumstances behind the choices made were certainly different.

It had been two days since Nileia and I's life-changing field trip. Aside from recovery and the subsequent relaxation, neither of us had really talked much. The first words we exchanged were when she burst into my room, telling me the repairs on the ship had been completed.

Looking at the ship, they had indeed done an amazing job. It takes great skill to regrow first-generation nanites. "She looks better than when I first laid eyes on her," I said, glancing over at Nileia with awe in my eyes.

In response to my comment on the reconditioning, she chuckled. "It's better; we have the woman who designed her as part of my crew."

I wasn't sure exactly how to take this. Picking up on that, she put her hand on my back and steered me toward the back of the ship. I was even more shocked to see The Kid helping the pirates load up our stuff like some sort of commoner. "Elrick would never be caught dead doing such a thing," she said, her eyes still fixed on the display in front of us.

My head snapped to her in an instant. "You clearly have something to say to me," I proclaimed, knowing that Nileia only beat around the bush when she was unsure if she should say what was actually on her mind. "So say it and be done."

Both of us watched The Kid labor. He's definitely trying his hardest, I acknowledged, a hint of a smile creeping onto the edges of my lips, even to the point of keeping up with the rest. Finally, my former second-in-command and now equal in arms hugged me. "Your cause has merit, Jayce," she whispered into my ear, her words sending shivers down my spine for some reason. "As before and as now, I stand with you till the bitter end, Captain."

Breaking from her embrace, I looked at her with new eyes. Now, she could see what she had truly become. This woman was me, but from another timeline—one where I'd made a different choice. I gave her a nod—not of subservience, but of respect. "Captain," I said, returning the grace she had given me.

There was no kiss this time around. While the flame between us had certainly not died out, it was currently buried under our mutual mountain of duty. Instead, she returned my nod. No more words needed to be said between us. She knew her role in this, and now so did I.

The Kid ran up the moment his eyes found me, hugging me with a deep fondness that could only be born from mutual trauma. "Jayce!" he said, looking up at me, his eyes filled with happiness. "We're all loaded up; I even helped!" he said, as if doing back-breaking labor was a feat worthy of a feast. "Are you ready to go?"

I felt a bit annoyed at his ignorance. To be fair, I was honestly just glad to be moving forward again. Ignoring the Kid's naiveté, I chose instead to walk up the ramp, though I stopped midway. The parallels are becoming too obvious. Best just to get on with it, Jayce, I thought. Heeding my own words, I turned to face not only The Kid but the entire room. With a slightly booming voice, I said, "Yes... Yes, I am!"

I waved to everyone as the doors closed behind us, finally leaving The Kid and me on our path. Gods, Jayce, you are such a tourist!

Turning away for a final time, I made my way to the bridge with my head held high. To my shock, The Kid was already in his seat and buckled in. "I had the A.I. begin pre-launch procedures. I hope that's okay."

It wasn't really the action I found odd, but rather the very notion of The Kid taking any sort of initiative. "Yeah…" I replied after pulling myself back into the moment. "That's fine. How long till the engines start?" I asked after mentally picking myself off the floor. He's picking things up so fast. Every day, it's like looking at a new person.

"About thirty seconds," he said to me once I had buckled myself in. Looking around, it seemed they had put things together just how I'd found them—well, as I had found them fifteen years ago, that is. They must have the original design docs.

With a bump and then a huge roar, the ship came to life once more beneath my feet. Welcome back, girl. I thought I'd lost ya, I thought to myself, patting the console before taking the controls.

The Kid and I sat in silence while we broke the atmosphere. I guess, given all that's happened in the past few weeks, some silence could do us both some good, I mused. No sooner had I thought that than we crested the edge of the atmosphere, an endless ocean of possibilities spilling out before us. It was at this moment that The Kid chose to tear apart the blanket of silence that had settled between us. "So, where are we going?"

My palm instantly embraced my forehead, both parties emitting an audible smack as they met. "Europa," I said once I had regained my composure. "It's the last stop before we'll be able to head to Spartan Base Alpha." The Drifter Colony feels like a lifetime ago, I thought, taking stock of all that had brought the two of us to this moment.

Silence again took hold between us. Setting up our departure in a comfortable, quiet, at some point, I couldn't help but look over at The Kid. I expected to see him with his head down in solemn contemplation. Instead, I was shocked to see him calmly staring out into the void, his expression showing he was lost in thought. "What's on your mind, Kid?"

Much to my glee, he practically jumped out of his seat. Like some lost puppy, The Kid let out a very audible yelp. By my estimation, he must have cleared a full meter. "Yeah, yeah, laugh at my expense!" he said as soon as he plopped back down.

He stared at me with frustrated fury. The Kid looked like he was about to say something when I stopped him. I gave him a moment to take in what he was about to say. He then changed his mind, opting instead to sit down and ask a question he felt was more pressing. "Why do you refuse to call me by my name?" he asked, making it my turn to be caught off guard. "I get that you were guarded at first, but now that we've been through metaphorical hell together, I thought you'd open up more."

I didn't answer him at first. To be honest, I wasn't sure if I could. Instead, I chose to pull back the lever, launching us into Slip Space. The transition pushed us back into our seats suddenly, reminding me of an old memory. A game I used to play about an amusement park. Wait, I believe those things on Earth were called 'roller coasters.' It's been a while since I played that Tycoon game.

The Kid continued to stare at me while I put the finishing touches on our journey. He seemed eager to hear what my response to his question would be.

The computer estimated that our journey would take two days. Therefore, I'd need to check the logs every four hours. Sounds doable enough. Probably get minimal sleep, but should be…

"Ow! What gives, Kid?" I yelled, my head hurting from the smack it had just received on the upside.

He just stood there, staring at me—well, as best as a 1.7-meter boy could stare at a 2-meter man. "Like I said before, and as I say now, my name is Orion. Say it!" he demanded, looking at me with something fierce behind his eyes.

Gazing downward, I reluctantly met his stare. "No," I told him, his face at once breaking down. The expression transitioned from ridiculous anger to deflation and depression. He honestly doesn't get it, does he? I thought to myself in confusion.

Not wanting to bother explaining my life story, I walked past him without another word, hearing the sounds of choked-back tears as I exited the room.

When this journey started, I would have taken perverse pleasure in his pain. Now? Indifference bordering on slight concern. I no longer hated the boy, but I was still a long way from liking him. He doesn't understand…

Finding my way to the galley, a swift search revealed that my secret stash of booze remained intact. Thank the gods! "Small mercies still exist," I said to myself with glee, pouring out some whiskey. The noxious liquid filled a cheap tin cup—something made for the servants who were to staff this ship. I found that fact oddly charming.

Sadly, peace was not to be found here either, for The Kid was quick to track me down. "Why do you hate me, Jayce? What is it that I represent to you?" he asked, standing at the threshold of the door, seemingly unwilling to let me escape this time. No more running from the truth, I guess.

With a shrug, I turned to face my greatest mistake, my hiding place still perched between my fingers. "I don't hate you, Kid," was all I could manage to get out. "I hate the idea of you." His face showed no recognition of what I had just said. I simply shrugged and elaborated. "You are a walking embodiment, a reminder of all that I've done wrong."

I shouldn't be having this conversation sober, I thought to myself, finally raising the tin cup to my lips to drink in its toxic goodness-or at least I would have, if The Kid hadn't gently taken it out of my hands. Perhaps a part of me wanted him to? "Jayce, you can't BS me, not anymore. We had this same conversation on Venus. Do you recall?"

Oh, I most certainly did. The events of that night had been playing on a constant loop in my head ever since. "Of course, I just don't know what answer to give you, Kid."

His eyes bulged at my continued insistence on the 'Kid' moniker. "Orion! My name is Orion," he screamed, his face now completely red with anger. "Why do you refuse to call me by my name?" He paused, stopping to take a breath. He's really hung up on this…

Still staring up at me with incensed eyes, he continued. "We've made so much progress together! Yet you act like I'm still nothing to you."

"That's where you're wrong, Kid," I replied, emphasizing that last part for his anger and my pleasure. "On so many levels. First off, I don't hate you—well, not anymore. Secondly, the key thing you fail to understand is that a few good moments don't erase a decade and a half's worth of trauma."

A glimmer of recognition flashed in his eyes. He's starting to understand. There's hope for him yet. "Alright, but where does that leave us in the here and now?" The Kid said, finally asking the right questions after all this time.

Not having a valid answer right off the cuff, I didn't reply. What I did instead was toss the tin cup aside. The Kid smiled at this, probably thinking I was abstaining. He was at least partially correct. I wasn't about to drown myself in lonely liquid comfort. No, this time, I'd be changing the context and the company.

Reaching into the cupboard, I retrieved two crystal goblets—reserved for the most special of ceremonies among kings and queens: weddings, christenings, or even passing an excessively large deuce. You know, the important stuff. He was both shocked and confused when I put them on the table. "Um, Jayce? What's going on?" he predictably asked.

With only a wink and a sly smile to satiate his curiosity, I dived head-first into my liquor stash. There's only one bottle that suits this moment, I thought to myself, the memories of that day flashing before me. "Ah, found you!" I said with glee, my hands grasping a familiar bottle.

With a flourish, I fished out a partially drained bottle of Phobos Reserve—an extremely rare and expensive liquor that only goes up for sale every twenty years. "We're gonna drink... that? It's already been opened!" The Kid protested. He, of course, knew nothing about booze, nor was he aware of the significance of this particular bottle.

"It's only been drunk from once, Kid," I said to him, the expression on his face still not changing. "Fifteen years ago." His face instantly shifted to a more interested expression. Now that I had his undivided attention, I continued. "The King and I shared a toast with this bottle to your birth." His jaw dropped to the floor as I finished.

Pouring a generous helping into both goblets, my mind considered what I was about to do. If you really mean to go down this path, Jayce, you might as well declare it. "I propose we do a toast of our own," I said to him, handing a goblet to his outstretched hand.

The Kid gingerly took the goblet into his grasp. From the looks of it, he had never handled something like this. It's not surprising, really. He's only fifteen. "To what, then?" he asked, staring down at the opaque liquid, studying its depths.

Raising my goblet high, I cleared my throat and roared with a firm voice, "To our partnership—we don't have to like each other, but we can get through this... together." The Kid's eyes showed some recognition of my words, though I got the feeling he'd heard such proclamations before. Feeling the need to assure him, I added, "I won't let you down, Kid. You have my word."

That definitely caught him off guard, his head shooting up so fast his drink nearly spilled. "The one thing you still value... okay, I believe you now," he said as he stood up, raising his goblet to meet mine. "To our partnership!"

Our glasses clinked, our throats moistened, and a union was sealed. "And for the restoration of my honor…" I whispered to myself after we had drunk—a personal pledge I had every intention of seeing through.

"I heard that," The Kid said with a wink and a smile of his own.

"Heard what?" I asked, trying and failing spectacularly to play dumb.

The Kid sat down and took another swig of his booze. "Oh, nothing of consequence, I suppose," he said, not taking his eyes off me for a moment while taking another sip. "This is some good stuff, though. Strong, but good."

Shaking my head, I downed the rest of my share in a single gulp. "I should probably check the logs," I said, looking for any excuse to get away from this cheeky bastard. The trip ahead was set to take three weeks—three weeks alone with this smart-ass prince. I couldn't help but smile inside, though. He reminds me of myself when I was his age…

11
The First Contact

Europa, the manufacturing and trading hub for the entire Jupiter sector, was where the minerals mined on Io, the goods farmed on Ganymede, and the research conducted on Callisto all converged. The moon does have its own resources, chief among them its ample supply of water, but commerce was its primary import and export.

It was this same commerce that now found me standing outside customs, the Kid by my side. Both of us gazed around in awe, like a pair of clueless tourists. "Have you ever been here before?" the Kid asked me, his voice a blend of its usual naïveté and genuine curiosity. I had to admit, seeing him take real interest in his questions, rather than asking something just to fill the silence, was refreshing.

Glancing at the boy, I couldn't help but smile, marveling at how far he'd come. The last time we'd traveled on land, he'd worn a garish outfit adorned with gold. Now, he was dressed in dark blues, his usual flair subdued by the need for anonymity. "Surprisingly, no," I replied. "The King never thought to visit such a dump, go figure." We shared a chuckle at that.

Pushing forward, we reached the first square, where the path split ahead of us. To the left lay the comfort district, offering beds for all durations. To the right was the commerce district, a place where every need could be met—food, weapons, even a foe's death, for the right price, of course.

I wasn't sure which way to go, and the Kid picked up on my hesitation. "You didn't read the packet again, did you, Jayce?" he asked, posing the question I'd hoped to avoid.

There's the Kid I know! I thought with a flash of indignation. The pompous know-it-all never faded. "Not yet!" I shot back, straightening my back to look less foolish. "I've just been waiting for the right time, that's all."

He wasn't buying it, rolling his eyes as he reached into his satchel. "One of us has to be prepared for these situations," he said, handing me an envelope sealed with wax that carried a familiar scent—lavender and gooseberries, though I couldn't quite place why.

The letter inside was simple, written in an elegant hand:

Jayce, I cannot imagine the hardships you will face on your way to Europa. If you do manage to make it, you are instructed to place the memento I gave you in the dead drop listed below. Then and only then will someone reach out to you regarding our meeting. For your protection, they have been instructed to refer to you by your code name, "Virgil." Stay safe—both for your sake and the Prince's, Scarlet "Fur" Kokori.

I stared at the letter longer than necessary, absorbing the care in her words. If only I could've spoken to this version of her, not the one I met, I thought, my chest tightening with an unfamiliar pang. "This is great and all," I said to the Kid, eager to shift focus, "but without the memento, we're truly SOL."

The Kid grinned and dug into his satchel again. What I expected to take seconds stretched into an agonizing wait, likely deliberate, just to irk me. "Honestly, Jayce, how did you survive without me?" he smirked, handing me a box containing the gift.

"Quite well, actually," I retorted, snatching it from him and sticking out my tongue childishly. "Since when did you become so prepared?"

This time, no witty comeback followed. Instead, he lowered his head. "Nearly perishing on the barren wastes of Venus tends to change one's outlook on certain situations," he said softly, his gaze still downcast.

I gritted my teeth, striving to stay strong. His words struck deep, but one of us had to hold it together, and as the elder, that fell to me. "Fair enough," I said, my voice shaky yet firm. "Let's just press on, okay?"

He looked up at my feeble attempt to lead, his eyes showing confusion rather than doubt. "How did a blubbery mess like you get chosen to protect the king?" he asked, a curl on his lips hinting he was half-joking, aiming to provoke me.

"Hey!" I snapped, giving him what he wanted. "I did my job to the best of my ability!" I could've stopped there, but I decided to rein him in before he derailed us. By "rein in," I mean I literally shoved him into a wall with my side—not hard, though. Once, I might've broken a bone; this time, only his ego took the hit.

He tumbled easily, the crowd parting around him without a glance. "There's the man I was told about!" he said, standing up, his eyes gleaming with triumph. That's when I saw his game.

"Well played," I conceded, grabbing his arm and pulling him along with a grin. "You wanted the hard-ass; you got him." My mopey air shifted—not to rage, but to sternness. This feels familiar—the good kind, I thought. "Shall we press forward?"

The Kid nodded, his compliance a strange but welcome change. The dead drop, per the map, was twelve blocks away, in a rougher part of town. The directions were clear, so off we went.

The trip was straightforward. The Kid corrected my map-reading a few times, and I yanked him back from near-death encounters—apparently, stepping into truck paths was a lesson he wouldn't learn. Still, we arrived faster than I'd expected alone. The dead drop was a derelict, decommissioned mailbox, unused for decades—perfect for this. I placed the memento inside.

No one seemed to notice, or at least they didn't react. No one's collecting it if you loiter like an idiot, I thought. "Hey, Kid," I called out.

While I'd been busy, he'd fixated on a nearby statue. "I saw a cheesesteak place on the way here. Why don't we—" I started, but my words faltered as I saw the statue's subject.

"Is that… my father?" he asked, his eyes brimming with tears. It hit me—he'd never known the man. This might be his first glimpse of him.

Unsure what else to do, I placed a hand on his shoulder. "Yes," I said plainly. "This is Aerys Shinkar the Third, your father." He nodded, transfixed. "Kid, we should move. No good comes from staring at a usurped king's statue."

He didn't fully grasp it, but he let me guide him away, eyes locked on the statue until it vanished from view. Then he turned to me, resolute. "You will tell me about him," he said, his gaze icy.

Sighing, I kept a hand on his back, steering him from his birthright. We'd have this talk eventually, I thought, sighing again. Might as well be now, while we've got time to kill.

We didn't speak much en route to the restaurant. Our unspoken deal was that he would remain silent in exchange for information about his father once we sat down. That held as I ordered, paid with my scant funds, and settled with our food.

Eager, he broke the quiet. "So spit it out already!" he demanded, ignoring his meal.

I was mid-second bite, realizing I hadn't eaten in over twelve hours. "My food?" I mumbled, pointing to my full mouth.

He rolled his eyes. "No, dumbass, my father, the King! Well, the former one, anyway."

He didn't just say that aloud, did he? I thought, shocked, clapping a hand over his mouth. "First, not so loud, okay? Want to get us killed?" His eyes widened, then softened as he got it. I let go. "Second, it's hard to talk about him. He was… something, alright."

"Something good?" he asked, hopeful.

I looked down, knowing he'd hate this. "Sometimes, but mostly not. The King cared more for himself than anyone or anything." His jaw dropped. Seizing my chance to vent years of pent-up truth, I added, "He kind of brought the succession crisis on himself with his own negligence."

He shot up to argue, but a hooded figure interrupted. "Virgil Alligries?" they called, more for my sake—they clearly knew me.

I stood as the Kid sat, a darkly funny routine. "That's me," I said.

"Here. Don't be late," they replied, handing me an envelope. Their eyes lingered on the Kid before they melted into the crowd.

Fancy for a rogue op, I mused, opening it. The Kid peeked over my shoulder. "What's it say?" he asked before I could read the ornate card.

"It's an invite to a street fair," I said, flipping it to reveal scribbled notes. "With directions to a food tent and a time."

He tilted his head, cheesesteak dangling from his mouth. "Do we have time to finish our food?" he mumbled, manners clearly unheeded.

I shook my head, sitting back down. He took the hint, grabbing his cheesesteak and devouring it like it might be his last, which, given his life, wasn't far-fetched.

That hit me hard. My life had been tough, but his was another level. You had anonymity, Jayce, I thought. He never did. The Emperor's forces could've stormed his door anytime. Then it clicked: Being with me might be the safest he's ever been.

"Want dessert, Kid?" I asked. Sweets wouldn't erase his trauma, but it was a start. "We've got time before we head out."

His head perked up, then sagged. "I don't know, Jayce," he said, torn between desire and duty. "I've seen your funds—we don't have much."

Ignoring the cost, I waved over a waitress. "We'll be fine this once," I said as a cute redhead approached. "My boy and I will share a banana split."

She was too young for me, but perfect for him. Sure enough, they exchanged shy glances, each thinking they were subtle. To me, it was obvious.

Blushing, she dashed off. "She's cute, huh?" I teased, grinning wide.

He floundered. "Uh... I... yes?" he stammered. Romance was clearly new to him—

maybe his first crush.

With little time before she returned, I pulled him close. "You know we're going to a street fair, right?"

He nodded. "…Yes," he said, still clueless.

"And what do people do at fairs? You should know this," I pressed, patience thinning.

He pondered, then gave a lazy, "They have a fair tim—Oh! Stop that!"

"They dance, idiot!" I corrected, smacking his head. His flush deepened—maybe from me, maybe from the waitress returning with our dessert. Her neckline dipped, angled at him, not me. I grabbed a spoon and dug in, avoiding any creepiness.

My mind blanked beyond the taste. Sweets were rare—money too tight to splurge. With the Kid joining in, we polished it off fast. "Ah, that was good," we said together, then laughed.

"Stay here while I pay," I told him, standing. He needed a breather, and I needed to chat with the waitress—win-win.

She rang me up, the only staff left in a dimmed diner. "Sorry for taking so long," I said, feeling guilty.

She giggled. "It's okay," she said warmly. "We don't see many good father figures here—it's nice."

"Father figure?" I echoed, startled.

"You're his dad, right? You act like it," she said, confused.

Thinking fast, I played along—it could work in our favor. "Yeah," I lied. Her face relaxed. "Recently, though. His mom and I only had one night. She died a month ago, so I'm still adjusting."

Her relief turned to pity. "I'm so sorry!" she said, hugging me. "You're doing great, for what it's worth!"

Arms pinned, I patted her back with my elbows. "Thanks…" I said, baffled. The Kid laughed at me. "Actually, you could do something—not for me, for him." His eyebrows shot up.

She released me, beaming. "Name it! Your kid's a cutie!" The Kid buried his red face in his hands.

"You know the street fair?" I asked. She nodded. "It'd mean the world if you danced with him." He mouthed "No!" shaking his head. I ignored him.

Her eyes lit up. "Can I be honest?" she whispered, leaning in. "I fancy your son. I was gonna ask that." She struck a cute pose.

"When can we expect you?" I asked after a beat. She slipped a paper into my hand.

"That's my comm code," she said, handing me the receipt. "You're our last customers—I'll be there soon." She waved at the Kid, who blushed impossibly deeper.

"You didn't have to do that," he grumbled once she was out of earshot, his anger shallow, ears still red.

"Nonsense," I said, handing our tickets to the fair attendant. "You deserve happiness more than anyone."

He scowled. "You just want to see me flop."

He's not wrong, I thought. "That's part of it," I admitted, eyeing the bustling square. "Say she's not attractive, and I won't call her."

He stayed silent, so we wandered, waiting out the twenty minutes. My mind drifted to life pre-Kid. I'd guarded a client at a fair on Centauri Six a year back—revolution got them kidnapped right in front of me. Hope this goes better.

With six minutes left, I called, "Hey, we should head to the food tent—it's in the cen—Kid? Kid! Damn it!" He'd bolted like a rabbit, but I found him, entranced by a techno-rock band.

"Hey! Your destiny's in four minutes!" I shouted.

He looked up, swaying happily. "Thought you set me up with the waitress, huh, Jayce?"

Fair point, I thought. The stage aligned with the tent. Two birds, one stone. "Fine," I said. "Stay here. I'll call her to meet you. Don't move, got it?"

He swore on his mother's grave, so I left, phoning her en route. She sounded thrilled. Love on a battlefield—go figure.

Inside the tent, myriad smells and stares greeted me, but I focused on one. "Vodka Cranberry, shaken, not stirred," I told the barman, per the note's code.

"You're not a super spy, you know," a voice replied—the countersign. A hooded figure, familiar yet different, emerged.

I passed her the drink. "I know, I just like saying it," I said, finishing the check.

She eased, gesturing to a table. I sat, ensuring I could see the Kid. "You're risking a lot, giving him that leash," she chided, noticing my glance.

"I know, but he deserves some joy after… everything," I said, peering at her hood. "Where do I know you from? We've met."

She scanned the crowd—no eyes on us. "Better view, bucko?" she said, lowering her hood to reveal a plain, pretty woman with short black hair.

I've met her, but where? Frustration grew. "Sorry, I know you—I can't place it."

Sighing, she handed me something. "This should help," she said. "In another time, another place, gifts showed goodwill to clients."

In my palm sat a painted wooden heart—a drifter colony courtesan's gift. "It's you!" I gasped, recalling her threat to scalp me. Knowing now, it was clear; without the hint, I'd have missed it. "You changed your hair."

"Not quite," she chuckled. Her hair grew before my eyes—brunette bob to blonde curls in seconds.

Speechless, I squeaked, "I I-how… what are you?"

"A Chameleon," she said, reverting her hair. "We adapt." Her eyes flashed neon pink. "Or blend entirely." She vanished, space warping around her.

I reached out, only to be smacked by nothing. "Wow!" I exclaimed. "Where can I learn that?"

She reappeared, done showing off. "It's not taught—at first," she said, locking eyes. "We're made this way. My partner and I are infiltration units. You met her today."

Advanced tech, I thought. "Alien?" I asked aloud.

She nodded, dissolving her left hand. She guided my wrist to the stump—real as it looked. "Fuir-Ey hates public displays," she said, regrowing it. "But I thought you'd like it."

Impressed, I latched onto a name. "Fuir-Ey? As in Fuir-Ey Jackson?" Another nod. Pieces clicked. "He's Spartan Prime, isn't he?"

She didn't answer, sliding me an envelope instead. "Data chip—coordinates and codes for Spartan Base Alpha," she said, all business. "DNA-locked to you and Prince Orion. Only you two can access it."

Task done, she bowed to leave. Not wanting this rare positivity to end, I tugged her arm gently. Her face flared with anger, poised to snap at me. "Wait," I pleaded. "Stay for a drink? I could use good company."

Her anger held, but my arm stayed intact. She checked her watch, then the Kid—dancing with the girl, her head on his shoulder. I'd kill for that again, I thought, heart aching. "Fine, lucky we have time," she said, sitting and ordering us drinks.

She sized me up. "How does a disgraced Captain-General end up guarding what he fled?" she asked, sharp despite the casual turn.

Her question stung. What am I doing? Honor nagged me. You lost that when you left him on the pad. "I don't know," I admitted. "Flying by the seat of my pants."

Pity filled her eyes. "You're lost," she said, offering a drink. "But not forgotten. Drink."

I took it, hesitating. "To what?"

"Yourself," she said, studying me. "What's broken is mending. It's clear to me, and should be to you— and your… companion." She glanced at the Kid, giggling with his date.

Why'd she pause? "What aren't you saying?" I demanded, eyes darting between them. "It's about the Kid—spill it!"

Her eyes widened, caught. "I… shouldn't have—" A red dot appeared on her forehead, growing, then bleeding.

Panic erupted as she slumped dead. My heart clenched—not just for losing a rare confidante, but because she was targeted. The Kid or I could be next. Kid! I thought, scanning.

He was gone from his spot. The fleeing crowd muddled my search—three exits from the square. The first, our entrance, was empty; no one retreated that way. If I lose him, all this is for nothing.

I marched to the second gate, where guards failed to hold back a crush of people. Three… two… one… The gate groaned, then cracked under the weight. No Kid—his plain clothes cursed me now. If only he had something—like her hair!

I scanned for the redhead. Not here, I sighed, turning to the last gate—quieter, orderly, and crawling with Inquisitors. Panic rose; I shoved it down, searching. There! Hope surged, then crashed. The Kid and his date were cuffed by Imperial Demagogues—Elrick's elite, answering only to the Emperor and the Inquisition, who'd chased us since the drifter colony.

Hiding behind barrels, I sought the Inquisitors. Demagogues need a leash. Two stood ahead, fixated on the Kid. "Yesss, take themmmm to holding," one hissed. An officer relayed it, and the Kid's captor yanked his leash with a toothless grin.

The Kid snapped up to retort, then saw me. "Jayce! Over here!" he yelled, hope flickering.

No turning back, I thought, charging with my weapon—only to lose it instantly. A bag shrouded my head. "Eh! What gives?" I shouted.

"Quiet! Lucky they didn't spot you first," a voice said, rifle butt cracking my skull, lights out.

12

A Second Chance

Once again, Life Week was upon us. The rite is one of the holiest in The Faith of the Pantheon, a yearly celebration of what we have and what we should be. My father had pulled some strings to give me the extra leave time I needed so I could be home for the holidays. Word had reached me of something important he had to discuss.

Apparently, what he and I thought of as "important" were two very different things. For here I was, on the seventh and final day of the celebration, sitting on the couch—the centerpiece display in my family's spacious living room. With the fire roaring and music playing, I even had a cute blonde to chat up—probably yet another setup by my father, I surmised. She was nice enough, and the conversation proved far from boring, but there wasn't really any spark between us. It didn't help that, at the time, no one outside my squad knew I had secretly been dating Nileia, my second-in-command. Now, there's a firecracker!

I knew Father would never approve of Nileia. While she and I belonged to the same caste, she was on the lower end while I was on the higher side—so high that my old man had even ascended to the aristocracy a few years prior. The bastard was certainly a man of ambition. That ambition extended to his family, and thus, I found myself merely a pawn in his machinations.

"So there we were, our exit point taking us right behind the Shoulders of Orion. That's the name of the asteroid cluster, by the way," I said, regaling her with one of my favorite war stories. She nodded in tacit approval. It was clear by her expression that she had no clue what I was talking about. Her feigned interest was merely to elicit my approval—a sentiment I had grown all too accustomed to.

The lady had more than likely been spurred on at the behest of her overbearing parents. Like everyone else, they were looking to increase their station in life. Her parents and mine probably found each other at the intersection of convenience. Arranged marriages were common at my level of influence. Those who had power obviously sought to maintain it, even from beyond the grave if need be. Coincidentally, infidelity was also frighteningly common among people of my station. I'm sure you can put the rest together…

Sensing my emotional drift, she put her hand on my lap, jolting me from my dour thoughts. "These places are so noisy," she said with a coy smile. "Perhaps we could go somewhere a bit more… private?" she asked, abandoning any hint of subtext. It was obvious her appeal to my heart wasn't working, so she decided to make a play for a different part of my anatomy.

This certainly was not the life I wished for myself, I thought, looking down at her perfectly manicured hand. If flying had taught me anything, it's that a life devoid of passion is no life at all. I had witnessed firsthand the lack of love between my parents, oftentimes bearing the brunt of their schemes. "I would love that, b—"

"Jaycen, my boy, would you be so kind as to join me on the balcony?" my father said with his usual perfect timing, tapping me on the shoulder before I could even have a choice in the matter. He made sure to send a sharp glare at the girl. She got the message loud and clear, slinking away with a huff and soon disappearing into the dim light.

Placing a hand on my left forearm, he led me away, guiding me toward his chosen destination with his typical mixture of charm and firmness. We, of course, had the twenty-meter-wide balcony all to ourselves. No doubt he had made the arrangements prior to calling me. Looking out over the balcony, the sights never ceased to take my breath away. My father handed me a spyglass. "Check that out," he said, pointing toward the spaceport.

Once again doing what I was told, I put the spyglass to my eyes and peered through it. "What am I supposed to see, Father?" I asked; the only thing I could perceive was standard ships docked in their usual bays.

My father did not respond—at least not in the way a usual father would—choosing instead to smack the miniature telescope in his desired direction. "How about now?" was all he said, leaving me to the wolves yet again.

Sighing, I continued my search. The same ships filled my field of vision until… "Father," I said once I had spotted the ship that, in twenty years, would become my home. "Is that The Evantide?"

He nodded in approval. "Yup, the King just left our estate," he said, his face practically beaming as he told me.

Nearly dropping the spyglass in shock, I turned to look at him. "The King?" I replied, a bit more stunned than I probably should have been. "Here? What did he want?"

The old man paused for dramatic effect, letting me stew in this scrap of information. Finally, when he'd had his fill, he walked up to me, placing something in my palm. "He wants you, Jayce," he told me as my eyes looked down to see what he had handed me.

In my palm now rested a silver badge—a badge designating the rank of Captain, Captain of the Royal Guard of House Shinkar.

I didn't know what to say. It was as if everything I had once known was sucked out at once.

My father looked down at me, waiting for a response. "Father, I don't know what to say."

"You can thank me once you become Captain-General and have the King's ear," he said, betraying the true intentions behind my new posting.

My gaze instantly hit the floor. I should have known better, I thought to myself. Since when has the man done anything that wasn't to his benefit?

From my core, a fire began to brew—one that would take a few years to fully ferment, but in this moment, I sought to finally test the strength of my chains. "And if I refuse your oh-so-generous offer, Father?"

Instead of getting angry like a normal sociopath, he laughed in my face, as if the very idea of me not doing as he asked was humorous to him. "Oh, Jayce, your time with the Shadow Hawks has really left you with the gift of jest," he told me. Then, all of a sudden, the laughter ceased. My father's face grew cold and detached as he narrowed his eyes upon me. "I'm sure I don't need to remind you of the price of my displeasure, do I?" he asked.

Automatically, my eyes drifted downward toward the long-abandoned doghouse at the foot of the stairs. These stairs led to our least-traveled back entrance. Here lay the man I once called my brother, the dried blood still clinging to the collars. He had been reduced to nothing more than the family plaything after daring to get a tattoo. It was here that he wasted away for weeks until, one day, a maid discovered his hanging corpse. My father had at last disposed of him with the rest of that week's trash...

"Of course not," I replied, my survival instincts quickly overriding any sense of rebellion I had. "I am honored by the opportunity. When do I leave?"

His face returned to the jovial mask it usually wore in an instant. "That's my boy!" he cried, slapping me on the back so hard I stumbled forward. "You leave a month after your return to the Hawks." With that, he turned and made his way back to the celebrations. "Don't say I never did anything for you," he said, slipping in a final jab before disappearing into the party and leaving me alone—my usual state.

Downing the rest of my drink and tossing it over the railing, I resigned myself to return to the party and enjoy the display of opulence my father had put on for the people who wanted him gone more than anything else.

"Is he dead?" an unknown voice said from beyond the veil. By "veil," I mean the black one I currently wore over my head. I had been wearing it ever since it was placed over me at the rally—or rather, the remains of it, anyway. One long van ride had eventually led me to my current perch, sitting in a government-issued chair. Not tied up, thankfully, but judging by the putrid smells wafting toward my nostrils, I was flanked by two very underpaid pieces of meat.

Turning my head in what I thought was the direction of one of them, I adopted a crooked smile—something only I could see, of course. "Not yet, anyway," I replied, enjoying the sound of them both jumping up in surprise. "Is anyone going to tell me what this is about? You obviously want something from me, or I'd be dead already."

From the far end of the room, I heard a door open. Judging by the sound of expensive work boots, I could tell this one was probably the boss. They didn't say anything as they walked around me, mumbling some judgmental remarks under their breath, before finally taking their seat at what I assumed was their desk.

At long last, he spoke. The voice that reached my ears rang all sorts of bells. "You are as quippy as ever, Jayce. Remove the hood."

Light filled my eyes, and I couldn't immediately identify the familiar voice. When my vision adjusted, I looked over at a person I thought I'd never see again. "Elias!" I shouted, unable to believe my eyes. He looked much the same as the last time I saw him, just older. "So, you're an Elf now?" I asked, stating the obvious.

His pointed ears definitely marked him as such—genetically modified to be better in every way, a short-lived experiment quickly shut down by humanity's insecure egos. I never forget a face, especially those of my friends, no matter how far they fall—or rise, in this case.

"No more than that brother of yours," he said, my normal human ears perking up at that revelation.

"Jacob's alive?" I asked, not knowing what else to say.

My once-commanding officer walked up to me, his limp visible to all. "We were in the same batch together," he said while approaching. Once he stood tall in front of me, he cast his eyes down upon me—not with malice, but with graceful pity. "Look how far you have fallen," he said as he placed the tip of his cane under my chin. "Up," was all he said.

Rising to meet him, I could see his history playing out in those all-too-familiar eyes—the abuse he suffered at the lab, the torment my former commander must have endured to become an Elf. "I have so many questions," I said, still taking it all in.

With a wave of his hand, he dismissed his guard, leaving only the two of us in what I now realized was his office. "I'm sure you do," he said, beckoning me to take a seat in front of him. "But we only have time for the essentials, unfortunately. Tea?"

I nodded with eager acceptance, a fond nostalgia guiding me. He turned his back, pouring a cup of tea and handing it to me after. Taking a sip, I was surprised by the taste that greeted my lips—Earl Grey, my favorite. He remembered!

"Alright, Elias," I said, deciding to take the situation in stride, knowing what was truly at stake. "You're obviously not aligned with the Emperor; otherwise, there'd be no need for a pro-government insurgency." He smiled at my words, confirming my suspicions. "You said 'just the essentials,' so let's do that. What's my mission?"

"Your time in the Royal Guard has done you well," Elias said, grinning like the lovable bear he always was. "I'd say it's fortuitous you're here, but this mess is precisely due to your arrival—with the Crown Prince in tow, no less."

His knowledge took me by surprise more than I realized. "Someone's well-informed," I said. He simply nodded in approval. "I assume you know what went down at the festival—probably better than I do."

My oldest friend reached behind him and turned on the monitors. "You were followed, and not just by the Spartans," he replied as my exploits were displayed before me. In each one, a figure clad in black could be seen sneaking in the shadows.

"The redhead—was she a plant?" It was the first thing I thought to ask with this new info.

The chief gave me a confused look, seemingly taken aback by what I chose to focus on. "No, she was merely an innocent bystander," he said. One of the monitors flipped to show her being dragged away alongside the Kid. "A bystander who'll become a casualty if nothing's done."

The stakes were now laid bare. "What would you have me do?" I asked, ready to be proactive instead of reactive.

His response was to slide a thin folder across his desk. "That's all we have on any known co-conspirators."

Opening it, I was greeted by a single sheet of recycled paper. "The only thing in here is contact info for some trinket dealer," I said, unsure how to make sense of it.

With another click, a screen shifted to a series of net posts. "Chatter about the event's been quiet. We assume a gag order's in place. We also guess he didn't get the memo."

Looking at the address, I compared it with the Nav on my wrist. It's only sixteen blocks from here. "What do you expect me to learn from him?" I asked, trying to gauge what I was getting into.

"Whatever you can," Elias said with a shake of his head. "This is literally the best we could come up with on such short notice." He stood and walked to me, offering his hand. "Keep us in the loop, will you?"

Taking the hint, I stood and shook his hand. "Just one more question, then I'm gone," I said, taking his silence as consent. "How did you survive the torment?"

For a moment, sorrow filled his eyes as memories flooded in, but it was quickly replaced by a mysterious glee. "You're asking the wrong question, Jayce."

Unsure how to respond, I asked, "What's the correct question, then?"

"'How I' is what you need to know; 'Did I' is the tree you should be barking up," he chuckled, pushing me out the door and onto the street, slamming it behind me.

Great, just great, I thought, looking at the paper and wondering what I'd do when I found him. Well, it's a bit of a trek; plenty of time to formulate a plan.

"You've had a long day, Virgil," a voice said from the shadows.

Turning toward the sound, I saw a familiar woman cloaked in darkness. "You're the one who told me where to go!" I said. She nodded. "I'm sorry about your partner," I added quickly.

Through the shadows, her head bowed in remembrance. "She knew the stakes," the shadow said, sorrow tinging her voice. "For both our sakes, let's not let her sacrifice be in vain."

We shared a moment of silence for her fallen partner. Knowing why she was here, I broke the tension. "Let me guess, you want to know what the Chief and I talked about."

"Indeed, I do. You could say I have a vested interest in your success," she said, flourishing her cloak to reveal the slave branding on her wrist.

Opening the folder to show her, she leaned in. "I'm heading there now. Just stay out of my way, okay?"

From her hood, I heard a click—likely capturing an image of the file. "I figured," I said. "As you wish. I won't be far behind, though. Promise to bring the boy back, okay?"

She cares about him more than she should, I thought. "Of course. If I didn't care, I'd be long gone. What is he to you?"

Even in the shadows, I sensed her hesitation. Choosing her words carefully, she finally said, "Someone who cares very much… about the Kingdom. Yes, let's go with that. Good luck, sir!"

With that, she melted back into the darkness.

Now alone in the alley, I shrugged. "This job's getting weirder by the second," I muttered before hightailing it out of there.

By the time I arrived, I had a plan. The "there" was a three-story, run-down shack. The store was on the bottom floor, with the upper two likely storage and living spaces. The windows hadn't seen a squeegee since installation, and inside was a maze of junk.

Undoing the clasp on my holster, I knew whoever was inside would see me before I saw them. It was as much about show as skill—fear was the game, and for the next twenty minutes, I'd be its master.

With a cliché ding of the doorbell, I entered. My nose was assaulted by centuries-old mildew. My earlier observations of junk towers were understated; it was like stepping into another world built on relentless hoarding. Everywhere I looked, electronics, parts, and supplies greeted me.

At the center sat a short, lanky, bald man, his skin paler than any moon. He looked like he'd never seen the sun. Upon my entrance, he sat up, giving me a judgmental stare and a sneer. "We're closed," he said, his vocal cords struggling—clearly seldom used.

Ignoring him, I put my hands behind my back and marched forward. "I have some questions for you, Frank" I said. He returned to his tablet.

Okay, I see how you want to play this, I thought, stepping back into a zen state. Returning to the entrance, I locked the single bolt loudly, ensuring he knew.

"Yes, you are closed," I confirmed, walking back, hands still concealing my trump card.

He finally put down his tablet and looked up. "What gives, bro?" Frank demanded.

"What gives?" I affirmed, slamming my pistol's muzzle against his skull. "You'll give me all the information you have on the Inquisitor Insurrection, or I'll give your skull a high dose of plasma. Clear?"

Like the coward he was, his demeanor changed. "Hey, I don't know a damn thing, bruh!" he stammered.

"Sure about that?" I asked, cocking the primer. His body trembled. Almost got him.

He looked me in the eyes, bloodshot pupils staring into my soul. "I... I don't know anything. I swear!" he pleaded, his eyes darting right. Gotcha!

"Way wrong answer!" I roared, moving the pistol to his left knee. A jet of plasma followed.

His head rolled back, mouth agape, howling in pain. "Next lie, I take another cap," I told him, my pistol over his right knee. "Tell me what I need, and we can both get this over with."

Staring at his burnt knee, he weighed his options. "Fine, you win," he said, exhausted. "I'm low-level; I don't know much."

"Tell me all you know," I said, pressing harder, eyes locked on his.

"Okay, jeez! You're hardcore, bruh," he sobbed. "There's a rally at some factory ruins. Password's Rosebud."

That's something, I thought. "Is that all?" I pressed harder.

"Yes… yes, it is," he said. He's telling the truth. Still, I destroyed his other knee. "Arrrrrrghah, why?! I told you what I knew!"

Rising, I shook my head. "That's for choosing the wrong side."

Instead of sobbing, he switched to fury, glaring up. "I could say the same about you, bruh," he spat. "Long live the Emperor!"

I jammed my gun in his face, but he didn't flinch. He handles death better than I could, I realized. Knowing death would be a reward, I withdrew, holstering my pistol and leaving.

"Enjoy the party!" he jeered. I didn't respond—better to let him have the last word. I had bigger concerns.

Back on the street, the world seemed darker. I'd sunk lower than ever, all in the name of "doing what's right." What's the point of fighting the system if I become it?

No time for philosophy—my goal was to report to Elias. After distancing myself from that memory, I opened my comm, ensuring the call was recorded.

"Alright, old man, I've got something for you."

He responded instantly. "What did you learn?" he asked, skipping pleasantries.

"Your contact was a fanatic, but a stupid one," I began. "Still, he gave me a rally location. Coordinates are in the message. I'll head there after a few stops."

"Hope you didn't shoot the messenger," Elias said, noting my dead eyes.

I couldn't meet his gaze. "He's alive," was all I could say.

"What did you do?" he pressed, unconvinced.

Lacking the stomach to face myself, I killed the call and sent the recording to the hooded lady before pocketing the comm. Then I headed to the shopping center—I couldn't show up as I was.

I had to become someone else.

One brisk shopping spree later, I was ready to blend in with the riffraff, clad in a nondescript brown hoodie and dirty jeans. Cheap black aviators hid my eyes. With only forty-five minutes left, a cab would do.

"Wabash and Lake, and step on it," I told the cabbie, handing her my cash card.

She eyed my outfit, marking me as the stereotype I intended. With a shrug, she swiped what she thought was mommy and daddy's money.

"I hope you know what you're getting into, kid," she said condescendingly. Internally, I was amused— she was at least ten years my junior, I thought.

When I didn't respond, she slammed the gas, pushing me back. "You Secondary kids have it so good. I'd kill three people for what you have." Is she serious? I wondered. I thought people like her died with Old Earth.

Thankfully, we arrived before she could force a reply. "End of the line, sonny boy," she said, parking.

Her spot was perfect—ten meters ahead were two guards at the entrance.

I handed her a silver piece—a vintage Shinkar Mark with King Aerys's likeness. "Hey! Where'd you get this?" she cried, my gift working.

Feeling smug, I lowered my glasses dramatically, revealing eyes that had seen horrors. "It was given to me," I said, whispering, "Long live the Kingdom."

"Lady doesn't like Imperials," a guard hollered as we watched the cabbie speed off.

I shrugged and approached. "Something like that," I muttered. Up close, they had shock sticks, no armor—just black boots, slacks, red belts, leather jackets, red shirts, and imperial badges. "This the place for the rally?" I asked with phony confidence.

They sized me up. "Depends if you know the code," the left one said.

"Well, of course—Rosebud," I smiled.

Unexpectedly, they stared, confused. Finally, the left guard's eyes flashed with recognition. "One moment, sir, I'll tell the gatekeeper to open up."

He gave the other a look and turned the corner, leaving me with one guard. That bastard gave me the warning code! I realized—the junk shop owner had tricked me.

A lamb for slaughter unless I acted. You prepared for this. "Hey, got the time?"

"Yeah, it's…" the guard began, but I clocked him in the jaw, grabbing his shock stick and card. I slid through the gate, quick as I could after leaving him slumped against the wall.

Inside, the warehouse was barren, with hasty structures and a giant stage. Behind it, a maze. Somewhere in there, I'll find what I need.

Time to act—they'd soon hunt me. Solution: don't match the description.

Five meters in, a shivering Spacie in shorts and a beater crossed my path. "Hey, want my hoodie? It's a Kartina Kotor," I called.

He grinned, three teeth glinting. "Sure," he said, eyeing more. "I like the sunglasses and hat."

"They're yours, friend," I said, handing them over, slipping into a crowd. Halfway across, his cries rang out—they'd found their guy. Pity gnawed, but he was a necessary sacrifice, I justified, swiping the card and slipping through the door.

The unseen parts were best maintained—halls of reinforced bio-plaster. Find the control room, I thought.

Idle thoughts crept in. Unbelievable that I'm here, saving the Kid. The hero in me wouldn't let go.

"Well, hello, what do we have here?" I said, stopping at briefcase bikes. Knowing I'd need one, I grabbed it.

Propaganda guided me through the maze. At its apex, a common area—reception. To my left: the control room. I swiped the card—nothing. Deactivated.

Cover blown, I chucked the bike at the glass, shattering it. Alarms blared. Go time. Pistol drawn, I stepped in, unsure what to look for. Tablets—yes! One opened easily—too easy, but it had what I needed.

"Clevvver boy, you are, Misssster. Lamooooonnt," a slippery voice said—the one who killed her.

"It'sssss jusssssst me, Jayssssssss," the Inquisitor said. Its serpentine speech patterns slithered through an otherwise empty room. It was indeed all alone. As was I, judging by the lack of shadows outside the window. I could tell there was no one beyond the door. No backup for either of us.

Noticing where I had been staring, it looked back there before returning its gaze to me. Staring into my soul with its cold, dead eyes. "You think I would compliment you with a full set of guards?" it said, drawing its weapon. A long, black plasti-dagger. "No, today the honor of your death belongs to me." Its voice filled with an uncharacteristic amount of rage. Setting down the bike, I slipped the tablet into my satchel before drawing a weapon, the shock stick I had recovered earlier from the guard out front. I could have used my pistol, but the fact that we were in a closed space gave me enough pause not to do so.

Remember, these snakes are quick, I reminded myself, having only faced one of its kind before. A prototype made in the waning days of the Kingdom. It had me flat on my ass within five seconds. I had every reason to believe these newer models would be just as good, if not leagues better. They aren't the only ones who have gotten better, I thought, trying to psych myself up. Still, though, I had best be cautious.

The fight began as most do, with us circling each other, sizing up each other's might. "You know the outcome of this, Jayce," the Snake said to me in an attempt to psych me out. Its speech now oddly coherent. "Just give up now and I promise to be gentle… ish."

Looking into the slits they called eyes; I could tell it believed what it said. But do I? I wondered. Refusing to give in so easily, I yelled, "Is it now?" before lunging at it, taking the initiative back into my own hands.

It seemed to have expected my move, at least somewhat, using my momentum to sloppily throw me across the room and onto the wall of monitors that sat on the other side. Sparks flew everywhere. People had to have heard that, I realized. It was then that the stakes became perfectly clear.

This is a vanity fight, a show. There is no way they'd allow one person, albeit a highly skilled person, to go in and apprehend someone of my stature solo, not unless they thought they had this— well, me—perfectly in the bag. They want a show; they'll have one, I thought.

Inside of me, I could feel a mental dam bursting. Over twenty years of pain, resentment, and regret bursting to the surface. The thick wall of sorrow that once contained them could not hold back the tide any longer. With a flip, I was back on my feet, shock stick held proudly. "If you want me, come and claim me!" I roared, giving the stick a squeeze, sending sparks flying for dramatic effect. This display had no effect on it, of course. Little did it know it was for my benefit and not its.

"How quaint," it said with a yawn, shrugging one of its bony shoulders. "Oh well…" it started to say before rushing to meet me, its body becoming a blur. I just barely managed to raise my stick in time to meet its outstretched dagger. Another second too late and that thing would have been buried in my chest. "…This makes things more fun anyway," it said, mouth twisting into a swirly smile.

The thing was so close I could probably guess the contents of its dinner. Week-old Birdrat? I wondered, trying not to puke right then and there. It looked at me, seeking any signs of weakness. I gave it none, instead elbowing the bastard in the face, using the momentary freedom to make an attempt at thrusting the shock stick straight into its abdomen, ending things right there and then.

"Not bad," it said with a giggle, easily jumping backward to avoid my attack. Its vocal patterns returning to their usual slur. I must be getting to it. "You might actually be a challenge," it said before taking a more serious stance, signaling to me that playtime was over.

Or was it? I sneered in my head, remembering these things' one fatal flaw. In one quick motion, I jumped onto the table in front of me. The snake just stood there, not sure how to take my unexpected move. "I bet I would be. Unfortunately…" I said, then with a flourish, swung the shock stick upwards, landing smack dab on one of the security cameras.

The combination of physical impact followed by a sudden surge of electricity quickly set alight all of the shoddy wiring that permeated this wasteful place. Light began flashing on and off around us, the electrical systems failing all at once, the rhythmic display paralyzing my opponent's lizard brain.

Seizing upon its seizure, I flipped down from the table and jabbed the stick into its stomach, sending 10,000 jolts of energy on an express lane to its brain. The thing then went limp.

I waited a moment for the voltage to pass, then checked its mouth and nostrils to make sure it was indeed still alive; I had to be sure. "No matter what they say, you are not a killer," I thought, unholstering my gun and pressing the barrel against its unconscious head, knowing what was up ahead. Not unless you have to be.

I knew what I had to do, then and there. With its body slung over my shoulder, gun in one hand, and the Briefcase Bike in the other, I set out to what was sure to be an interesting encounter. "Hey y'all, look what I found!" I screeched, yelling at the top of my lungs, kicking open the door and bursting out onto the stage.

The music stopped instantly, everyone turning to look at me. "My name's Virgil Alligries, and you have a friend of mine," I declared, looking down at my once-foe then back out onto the crowd, giving them all my cheesiest smile. "How about a trade?"

Only another Inquisitor remained. "Noo prisssonersss," it said. "Giiiivvveee theemm tooo meee and waaalk ffreeee."

The Kid's not here, I thought. "Meet me at the entrance," I said, loading the bike. "I'll drop him blocks away. Follow, and he dies."

They didn't stop me. Blocks away, I set my captive down, pity rising. Empathy—or weakness? I sped off. To save the Kid, I'd need help—something I swore I'd never ask for again.

13

The Third Strike

"Well, it looks like you'll end up at the old Orville Aerospace factory," the tech said, handing me the tablet stolen from the Inquisitors just a few hours prior. Her gaze never left mine as she did so.

The chief looked it over and then glanced back up at me. "You definitely have your work cut out for you on this one," he said before turning to everyone and simply stating, "Leave us."

The two of us remained silent while the techs filed out. The woman who had spoken to me did give me some sort of flirty glance, but I was long off the planet before I realized as much.

When they all had left, the chief pulled up the schematics on the big screen. "The Inquisition seems to have converted the three lower levels into a makeshift prison," he began, pointing out the first and third levels in particular. "Thankfully, the main security hub lies on the first basement level, with the holding cells on the third."

Looking over what lay ahead, I could not help but feel a bit concerned. "So, how is this going to play out?" I asked, not used to being the one who was given orders. In my years, I had grown comfortable in the role of shot caller. To take them felt like becoming a boot all over again. *You've already broken yourself down,* I reminded myself. *Now is the time to build yourself back up.*

"Section Op Jeremy Coffey whipped this up for you," the chief said, handing me an access card. "It should get you as far as the security room."

Not liking where this was going, I asked, "And what will we do when we get there?"

He chuckled at my query. "What you will be doing is disabling any and all security, thereby clearing the way for us to sweep in and arrest them."

"You're sending me in without backup?" I roared, slamming the key card on the table. Pissed off and not really thinking straight, I followed up with, "Screw you! I'd rather do all this on my own," making my way to the back door.

Grabbing the key card and running up to intercept me, Elias put his hand on my shoulder, grabbing my attention. "Hey, understand the position I'm in. I could very easily have turned you in," he said, handing me back the card. "Instead, I am helping you, at great risk not just to myself but this entire department."

He's right, of course, I thought, a wave of guilt washing over me. What right do I have to demand his help with all the things I have done? Pocketing the card, I looked up at him and offered my hand. "You're correct. But after this is done, I want you to tell me where my brother is."

"Deal," he responded, taking my hand into his.

With nothing left to go over, I exited and made my way to the other side of the alleyway where my bike had been stashed.

"What did the old elf say?" the Chameleon said to me as she emerged from the darkness. Her sudden appearance, while expected, still caused me a bit of shock.

Looking over her, from what little I could glean, the girl looked tired. Her cloak was now dirty and frayed—more than likely the result of too many nights sleeping in it. What little patches of skin I could see were marred with cuts, scrapes, and bruises. Reaching into my pack, I retrieved a water pouch and handed it to her. "When was the last time you drank?" I asked, actual concern pouring forth from my lips.

"Much too long," she said, snatching the pouch from me and proceeding to drain it in just three gulps.

Looking down, I noticed her legs had stopped shaking. Feeling a bit better, I continued with our conversation. "I'm to assault the old Orville Aerospace factory alone."

"Like hell you are!" she said, hopping on my bike and starting the engine.

I immediately shut it off. "Look," I said. "If we are going to do this, we must trust each other. I'm Virgil."

The Chameleon paused for a moment. She was unsure of what to do. Finally, the girl just shrugged and removed her hood. What greeted me was a youthful face with eyes of emerald green—eyes that you could tell had seen countless unspeakable horrors. She currently had her hair styled short in a dark auburn.

Finally able to look me in the eye, she met my gaze and smiled. "Since we are using assumed names, you can call me Kaya."

"How would you know Virgil isn't my real name?" I asked, mounting the bike and starting the engine.

She just smiled at me as the two of us zoomed off. The short distance we had to travel was done in relative silence. When only a few blocks remained, she finally said to me, "Your Adam's apple twitches when you lie." Then, without another word, the Chameleon flew upward, her line catching onto the top of a building. But not before twisting the knife with, "I once knew a guy who did the exact same thing."

Shaking my head, I collapsed the bike into its briefcase form and hid it behind a nearby dumpster.

The side entrance was now in sight. Plugging the earpiece into my comms, I gave it a test tap. "I hear you loud and clear," the chief and Kaya said at the same time. There was a pause, then they both laughed at what just happened, confirming that they both knew about each other.

The door was guarded by what looked like just two sentries. "Kaya, if I take care of one of them, can you handle the other?" I asked. A series of two beeps was all the confirmation she gave me.

Looking around, weighing my options, I decided to pick up a piece of nearby rubble, chucking it as far as I could. "Hey, you hear that?" the first sentry said to the second. It nodded in agreement. "I'm going to go do a sweep. Be alert," it said before marching off.

Knowing Kaya had that one, I quietly snuck behind the second sentry, shocking it unconscious. Not wasting a second, I swiped the card. Knowing I didn't have any time to waste, I slipped inside. Kaya followed immediately after me.

"Wow, this crew certainly works fast," I said, gazing up at the different yet still familiar surroundings. In the brief time I was gone, they had managed to erect an entire system of fully stocked shelves, effectively turning what was a party space into what appeared to be a functioning warehouse.

Kaya was having none of my wanderlust. "Come on, Spacer, we've got people to save, and I have a sister to avenge," she said, elbowing me in the stomach and ejecting the breath from my lungs.

Before I could react or even retaliate, Kaya jumped up. Leaping from side to side, she easily scaled the high shelves, eventually landing perfectly on top. "Try and keep up," she said, once again disappearing into the shadows.

Shaking my head, I drew upon my previous memories of the place to guide me where I needed to go—that, and according to the tablet I swiped, the entrance to the underground prison lay in the back.

I made my way as quickly and as quietly as I could; the guards patrolled every other row. Once or twice, I got lucky and came across a guard Kaya had already dealt with. They were pretty easy to spot, usually out cold and propped up in some kind of compromising position. The final two lads I came across on the last row were put in some sort of sexual position—"wolfy," I believe it was referred to.

Thankfully, the door to the basement level was unlocked—another pity present from my "partner." The stairs leading down looked to have been carved straight from the permafrost itself. I'm not sure how they kept the whole thing chilled; I just had to hope that it would hold strong.

Immediately, when crossing the threshold into the underground, I was struck by that bitter chill. Being built directly through the ice shelf, coating the surface, it made sense that the walls would be of a similar composition. They were colored through with a near-infinite number of generations passing through its walls. The few electro-torches that were actually lit gave the space an eerie vibe.

The control room, thankfully, lay just a stone's throw away. Its entrance was just a few steps from the upper warehouse. Crouching down, I walked slowly over to the door. I gently opened it with my shock stick.

Peering in, I could see that two people manned it—the first one being close to the door, his back to me and his mind occupied with whatever was on his tablet—an easy mark, I thought. But the other one… that might be an issue.

That other guard was on the other end of the room. She would surely hear me knock out the first, no matter how silent my takedown was. I guess I'll have to do it the old-fashioned way.

Decision made, I took a deep breath and tiptoed through the threshold. It's much warmer here, I noted. That certainly made sense; as an area commonly used by people, it would need to be made comfortable to work in. The distance between the guard and me was now only a span and a half. Forcing all other musings from my mind, I raised my shock stick, placed the long end against his throat, and squeezed.

Not being a fan of killing, I turned away from what I had to do, focusing my attention instead on the other person in the room. She hadn't noticed me yet, but with my target's moans growing louder by the second, it wouldn't be long.

I could see his strength waning. Just a little bit longer, and this torture will be over, I reassured myself. Contrary to what you may think, killing was not in my nature. One would imagine that being born a member of the Warrior Caste would give me a certain disposition to the act. That kind of broad brushstroke thought died with Old Earth.

"Juan Paulo, what did I tell you about jerking off on du…" the female guard said, turning to face us. The man named Juan Paulo's groans reached a crescendo right before he expired. "Wh… who are you?" she asked, stammering her words. Clearly, she was more scared of me than I was of her.

Reading the situation, I put the baton up, making a point to aim it in her direction. "This doesn't have to end in bloodshed," I said. Honestly, I didn't want to kill her, especially if I didn't have to. "Just leave and forget you saw anything, okay?" The girl was shaking like a leaf; she wouldn't be a threat to anybody.

"O… okay!" she said, her disposition changing immediately. Getting up from her seat, she actually bowed to me! "You Spartans aren't half as bad as the propaganda makes you out t…" She said to me, her beautiful words being tragically cut short by the sudden appearance of a metallic spike in her abdomen.

The girl looked down at her demise, then looked right at me. "to…be…," were her last words before collapsing to the ground in a lifeless heap. Standing behind her was Kaya, the bloody spike retracting back into her. I couldn't help but notice that the blood was still on her hands, even as everything else changed.

"What the hell?" I screeched, voice cracking as I stood up to face her. "She was clearly leaving peacefully."

Kaya just gave me a look, wordlessly telling me how much of a moron she thought I was. "You don't know that," she said, turning away from me and putting her attention on the security console.

"She could have just as easily warned the guard."

Aghast, I just stared at her. Is this how the Kid sees me? I wondered. This woman was ruthless in her actions, not caring who she stepped on to achieve her goals. "You could have just as easily incapacitated her."

"Whatever," she replied, not even bothering to look at me while she stripped the guard of her uniform. "You might want to do the same. Things are about to get real crazy down here."

Looking at the monitors, I noted the number of guards posted all around. Once we flip that switch, all Hades will break loose, I concluded. Looking at the bottom monitor, I noticed the cell where the Kid was being held. Of course, he was in the bottommost cell. He looked to be comforting the girl. Good on him. The cell in question had the number 7-C—the seventh cell in cell block C... shouldn't be too hard.

While I was formulating the plan, Kaya finished putting on her outfit. She was now indistinguishable from any other official. That will certainly help her once she flips the switch, which just so happened to be right now. "Good luck," she said to me before dashing out the door and disappearing amongst the crowd.

The first thing to go was the lights. What replaced them was the strobing emergency lights, preceded by a loud groan filling up the space. Joining it would be the sound of every door being unlocked at once, unifying the soundscape into a single roar. Afterward, there was silence. Clearly, no one knew what to do at first. The peace didn't last long, however; the silence was almost instantly broken by the pitter-patter of thousands of people rushing to the door. I probably should put on the outfit, I concluded. Wouldn't want to get shot by accident.

Reluctantly, I donned the uniform of the man whom, mere moments ago, I had murdered. I would need its cover for what I had to do next. The Kid's cell was at the far corner of the bottommost level. That meant trekking through two more floors of confused guards and crazed former inmates. It wouldn't be easy.

Ascending to the second floor proved easy enough; the mob had yet to reach that high. That luck ran out right away. The horde and I finally met one another. My disguise instantly proved useful. People parted around me like I was some sort of repellent. This might be easier than I figured, I thought to myself. It sure would have been if not for…

"Juan Paulo!" screeched a voice from down the hall. I did not know it, but judging by the authority behind it, I was pretty sure the person was an officer. "What in the nine hexagons of Hades is going on here?"

She must think I am him, I thought. Scheming on the fly, I tapped my helmet to indicate my transmitter was out, pantomiming a message that it had been busted in the scuffle.

The officer looked down at me like I was crazy, but she got the message all the same. "I see. Where are you heading?" she asked me, her tone indicating she was getting suspicious. I held up three fingers and then put my fingers in the shape of a gun. "Good idea, grab an extra rifle for me while you are at it," she told me, confirming that my gamble had paid off. I knew weapons were usually stored in the most out-of-reach place of any given facility. I took an informed stab in the dark and thankfully made it out in one piece.

Descending the stairs to the third level, I was surprised at the stillness of it all. Sure, some stragglers were fleeing all around me—there will always be looters in this kind of thing—but it struck me as odd how peaceful things had been now that the initial rush had died.

That's when I realized it; upon reaching cell block C, that all of the cells were still locked up tight. Must be some sort of failsafe, I figured. I now found myself frantically searching for some sort of manual release. The clanging of over a dozen cells filled my skull.

Of course, the thing was in the last place I looked—obviously. It was even a big red button mounted on the side of the wall so that all but the most special of fools would have easily seen it. Apparently, I fell into that category. I slammed my fist onto it with the fury of one bested by an inanimate object.

The cell doors popped open, and the inmates wasted no time rushing out. At first, they were hesitant around me. Once all had realized I was doing nothing, the group rushed past me, not a thought for anything but their freedom.

With the Kid's cell being the absolute last on the block, it stood to reason that he would be the last one out. I was practically on my tiptoes in an attempt to catch sight of him. After failing him so spectacularly, this is the least I could do, I thought. The affection I showed for him in my thoughts had not been lost in the shuffle.

When you started this trip, you hated his guts, my inner self reminded me of all that had come to pass. Now look at you, craning your neck trying to catch even a glimpse of the bastard! My neck was not the only thing hurting, though. My heart had begun aching to see him.

As the last few people passed me by, I felt a sudden urge of panic wash over me once I realized the Kid wasn't among them. Having had enough, I walked over to cell #7, and wouldn't you know, there was the Kid. A jailbreak was going on, and he was the only one to stay behind.

To be fair, that last statement wasn't entirely accurate. Beside him was the redheaded waitress, her arm around the Kid's shoulder—not just out of affection but also to prop up her injured left leg. Blood dripped from it onto the floor.

"Hey, we've got to go!" I yelled out to the pair. They both looked up at me. The Kid, in particular, had a certain amount of fury painted over his face. "You have no power here, not anymore," he said to me, pointing at the open bars as if to indicate something. It was only then that I realized I was still wearing the guard uniform—that he had no idea who he was talking to.

Stepping toward him, I raised my hands to take off my helmet. "You don't understand…" I said before his fist made a connection with my face and grounded me flat on my ass.

"No, you don't understand!" the Kid said as he and the girl made their way out. "We're leaving, and there's not a damn thing you could say to make me stop."

I trained him well—too well, I thought, my brain still a bit fuzzy. Sitting up, I hollered at him, "Where'd you learn to punch like that?"

Not breaking his stride, the Kid looked back at me and said with the smuggest of smiles, "Let's just say an old man taught me the ways of the world."

What? How dare he! "I am not that old!" I said, ripping off my helmet. No longer being bound to the voice changer, the Kid could hear clearly the person behind the words.

He stopped dead in his tracks, setting the waitress on a nearby bench before turning to look at me. Once he saw my face in all its exhausted glory, his eyes began to well up with what I assumed to be tears of joy. "Jayce?" he said, choking on even my name.

I didn't even have time to respond before he ran up and bear-hugged me. "You came! You didn't give up on me!"

Much to the Kid's surprise, I returned his affection, embracing him as someone of value. "Did you ever have any doubts?" I asked.

The Kid broke his hold on me, looking me dead straight in the eyes before saying, "Honestly, yes. The only person I ever trusted is dead. The rest sold me out as soon as it was convenient to do so."

I sighed, his words hitting home. I know that feeling all too well, Kid. Extending my hand out, the Kid took hold and raised me up. "Stay sharp; we ain't out of the woods yet," I told him. While it was great to have the band back together, there were stormy seas ahead. It would take all four of us to get through this. Four? Wait, where did that girl go?

It was only then that I noticed that the Chameleon had slipped away at some point. The action made sense, seeing how our goals were only loosely aligned.

Motioning with my head, I drew my pistol and took point, leading this trio up the levels to the surface. By this point, the subfloors were devoid of anyone important—only ourselves and the looters remained. Thus, the journey upward was a quiet one. The Kid tried to engage me on several occasions, but I silenced him every time.

Once we reached the final stairs, I called the Kid over. "Look," I said to him in a whisper. "I don't know what we might encounter up there." Pointing to the stairs, we could see flashes of light and sporadic bursts of noise coming from above. A battle was surely going on ahead. "Whatever happens, I need you to focus on getting to safety." Reaching into my pocket, I handed him a card. "If anything happens to me, seek out this man. The old elf is a friend of our cause."

He nodded and took the card. "Our cause?" he chided before pocketing it. "Don't tell me you are a true believer now?"

Am I? I asked myself—another question for another time. There were more important things I had to focus on, such as…

"We are getting out of here. Follow my lead," I said to both of them, the commander in me coming out to play. The pair nodded, taking positions behind me. Marching up the stairs, I felt a foreign sensation—something I forgot was ever known to me: fear. In an instant, my throat went dry, my knees began to shake, and my vision tunneled. I am going into battle.

What lay atop the surface was as I expected. The police had been alerted as soon as the security dropped. Of course, the Insurrection wasn't going to surrender peacefully—they only needed to hold out long enough for the Emperor to land. It was a battle to see who could set the narrative, and so far, neither side looked to be doing very well. As for ourselves, we just had to make it out unseen before we were…

"Founnnnnd Theemmmm!" a voice yelled out, a call that could only belong to the other Inquisitor. Leaping down from its perch atop the nearest shelf, it made a perfect landing in front of us. "My brother is in the hospital, thanks to you!" it said to me, this time with perfect cadence.

"So you're telling me that drawl is just for show?" the Kid quipped, for what I could only imagine to be the first time.

Its only response was to stare daggers at him while keeping its gun continually trained on me. "His Excellency will be here soon," it said, fishing a knife from its pocket and then pressing it against my throat. "He said you were to remain unharmed, but I no longer care for that particular order." Slicing across my chest, it said, "My brother is clinging to life because of your actions," as the remains of my shirt fell to the ground.

"That's not entirely accurate," Kaya said from below the stairs. All of us stopped to turn and look at the source of the disturbance. The other Inquisitor's head flew up and landed at its partner's feet. "Not anymore, anyway."

All of us on the ground floor stood there stunned. The Inquisitor, who still lived, picked up its "brother's" head. "Why?" was all it said, taking a few steps back, looking up at Kaya, eyes pleading for an answer.

Beneath her hood, I could see Kaya smiling; it was obvious that things had been playing out exactly as she planned them to. "It's simple, really," she said, her grin somehow getting even bigger. "A brother," she continued before flipping up and making a perfect landing in front of the Kid and me, "for a sister."

"But it was I who killed her," the Inquisitor responded, its expression turning from sorrow to pure hatred.

In a flash, she crossed the distance between her and the Inquisitor. "I know," she said with a sort of manic glee. It was only then, after the menace had realized the full amount of its suffering, that she buried her knife into its abdomen.

"Our master has trained you well," it said, doubling over in pain. Looking up at her, its eyes filled with some sort of understanding. "He has perfected what he began with us." Its last message given, the creature rolled over and accepted the hand fate had dealt to it.

What the hell did it mean by that? I wondered, walking over to the corpse to inspect it. Despite the fact that its death was a mere moment ago, its body had already taken on the resemblance of month-old mud. "Any idea what it meant by that?" I asked.

The Chameleon simply shrugged. "I dunno," was her response, a response that I could tell was a lie. "I'd get out of here if I were you. The place is crawling with pro-Imperial cronies." She then followed her own advice, disappearing into the shadows.

Her words could not have been more prophetic. No sooner had she gone than an entire squad surrounded us, seeing the corpses of their former masters and, obviously, connecting the murder to us. "Down on the ground!" said what could only have been the head of this motley crew.

The three of us, not knowing anything better to do, complied with their actions. The entire group converged on us, weapons drawn. It was clear they planned to avenge the death of their masters, right here, right now. Bracing for the inevitable, I closed my eyes and…

"Oh, I forgot to mention," Kaya said… from somewhere, her voice seemingly coming from everywhere and nowhere at the same time. "I set some charges above and below. They should be going off in, oh, three minutes? Good luck!" the Chameleon bellowed, then, with an intentional swish of her cloak, she was gone.

Now that survival was more important than capturing us, the squad scattered to the wind. "Now's our chance!" I said to them, grabbing the Kid by the wrist and pulling him along. He didn't really need to be told to do so, but a guiding hand certainly helped.

This place was more packed than I thought, realizing we probably would have never gotten out without Kaya's foresight. Behind every row was at least half a dozen more guards, all now running every which way. The news of the bombs traveled quickly through the ranks, sending everyone inside straight into panic mode.

None of them bothered us, thankfully—they all had to worry about escaping themselves. But how long do we have left? I wondered, looking down to check the timer I had begun when Kaya first announced her explosive exit. According to my not-so-accurate timer, we had less than a minute to get clear. The bikes were parked a block away. If we all rushed, then the three of us could just make it.

Showing them the timer on my wrist, I could tell that they thought the same thing I did. As one, we burst from the doors and out into the alleyway. Freedom was not quite ours, though; that would come only once we sped away.

We were making our way across the moldy side street. The panic of the others had begun to set in with me as well. Would we make it? I asked myself. Will this be all for naught? Realizing such queries only exacerbated the undesired outcome, I banished such thoughts from my mind.

By the time we reached the bike, I was back to being my hyper-focused self. In fact, I felt more like myself than I had been in some time. Is the old Jayce coming out to play at long last? I wondered, slamming the bike onto the ground. The Kid and his companion got on before it was even fully formed.

"You two, hold on," I said while revving up the engine. "It's about to get bumpy."

The three of us zoomed off. No sooner had we cleared the alley than the warehouse exploded. At first, all I heard was the sound—the booming reverberated through the cheaply made dwellings that permeated this district.

After the sonic boom, the change in air pressure caused a shockwave that almost kicked us off the bikes. Thank the Gods this thing has a good set of dampeners. Everything that had happened so far occurred in only a split second. The real show was just about to begin.

At last came the light; by this point, it was early evening, but you'd be hard-pressed to guess that, as currently the block was lit up as if it were half past noon. "Close your eyes!" I yelled back at the couple. Since we were so close to the blast, I worried it might blind them. For my part, I squinted my eyes for a few seconds as the light's wrath was brought down upon us.

All in all, the whole ordeal lasted less than ten seconds, but let me tell you, in the thick of everything, it felt more like an eternity. In that short time, we had maybe traveled two blocks. True escape seemed imminent—or at least it would be if we weren't halted by a checkpoint—a checkpoint headed up by the local city watch.

"Halt!" said the one at the front, her left hand raised high, pointing where to park with her right.

"You three are under arrest!"

Looking back, I saw the Kid go for the pistol at his side. "Not here," I said to him, shaking my head, knowing how quickly things would go south if he escalated things. "Do as they say. It's the only way we can come out of this alive." Thankfully, the Kid got the message and dropped his hand to his side while I put mine up in the air.

We all stayed still as six officers of the Watch approached us—we apparently had two apiece between us, guns drawn and just looking for an excuse to fill us up with plasma. "Off the bike and hands behind your head. All of you!" the leader said before the rest of them approached us.

Doing as we were told, the three of us stepped off the bike and laced our fingers behind our ears. One by one, we were bound by laser cuffs, the blue light surrounding our wrists, preventing us the use of our arms.

The group then began herding us into the two squad cars—the Kid and I went into one, and the waitress into the other. Of course, the Kid was having none of this. I had to jab my elbow straight into his stomach before he could settle down. "We'll find her later," I whispered to him. His only response was to look at me with those pleading eyes of his. I really hate it when he does that.

"Now, can I talk?" the Kid asked, his frustration still at the surface.

Probably mics everywhere recording our every word, I thought. Looking around, I could definitely spot several divots that very likely would be where the microphones were placed. "Yes, but be careful. Our ears aren't the only ones listening in."

For once, he seemed to pick up on the hint, looking around for himself, spotting the same spots that I had. "Is this the end of the line?" he asked after taking a moment to gather his thoughts.

Is it? I wondered. All things considered, we were in a bit of a pickle—the two of us in the back of a car belonging to the City Watch, heading to who knows where. To top it all off, the Emperor would be exiting from Slip Space any moment! "I wouldn't be so sure," I told the Kid, choosing to put on a brave face for both of our sakes. "You never know what lies just beyond the next door."

The answer to which was to be revealed sooner rather than later. The car lurched forward, making a sudden stop, clearly indicating that we had arrived at whatever this place was to be. "Whatever happens, I want you to know that…"

"Virgil, so good of you and your son to join us!" Elias said, opening the door and screaming inside. "Come, come, we don't have much time!" he added, practically dragging me from the car.

Huh, guess we won the fateful jackpot, I mused. Before us was a hangar, and in this hangar sat not a prisoner escort ship but the Evantide, prepped and ready to go by the looks of it. "How?" I asked, my mouth still hanging open in astonishment.

"I apologize for the rough way you were brought here," Elias said, unlocking our cuffs. "This was the only way we could get you here without raising suspicion. You definitely did us a favor by killing both Inquisitors."

Feeling the spots where the cuffs once were, I looked up at my old friend. Looking past him, I could see a familiar hooded figure lurking in the shadows. "Thanks, but it wasn't our do…"

"Where's Fiona?" the Kid blurted out, running up to Elias as soon as his hands were free, putting a finger in his face.

To the old man's credit, he simply smiled at this display. "Oh, you mean your companion? We sent her to a girls' home," he said to him, putting a calming hand on his shoulder.

That seemed to have done the trick, for the Kid instantly backed down, though still close, pressing for more info. Seeing this, he elaborated, "After the ruckus you dragged her through, she'll need to lie low for a bit. The girl will be safe. You have my word."

Seemingly satisfied, the Kid retreated to my side. "So, is everything ready to go?" I asked, not wanting to stay on this rock a moment longer. But as I said that, a thought crossed my mind, and so too did a shadow between Elias's shoulder blades. She wants to talk, I thought. "Actually, hold it for a moment," I told him before disappearing into the shadows myself and leaving them just as confused as I felt.

"Is he okay?" was the first thing she asked me once I was within whisper distance.

"Who exactly are you talking about?" I replied, confused as to her choice of priorities.

Kaya grabbed me by the waist, spinning my body around, using my hand to point at the Kid. "Oh, him," I said, finally realizing whom she was having me point at. "He's a bit shaken but otherwise fine." She seemed to relax at hearing that. Odd, I thought. "I thought you helped me so that you could avenge your slain sister."

"A person is capable of doing more than one thing," she said, shoving me back toward the group and ending our conversation—well, that is, if I didn't have something to ask her.

Pushing back, I looked her straight in the eyes and said, "We're heading to Spartan Base Alpha. You're coming with us, right?"

She looked at me, glancing at the Kid before quickly turning back to me. From underneath the hood, I could see a hint of a frown cross her face. "I wish I could, but Master needs me for a mission," she said, placing her hand on my cheek. "Thank you for your help. We will meet again."

Just as soon as I registered the warmth in her touch, she was gone, returning to the only place she must feel comfortable.

"What was that all about?" Elias asked me once I had returned to the light of the group.

"Nothing of any importance," I replied, still rubbing the part of my cheek where her hand had once been.

The chief looked at me for a moment, not exactly sure how to take what I just said. "Okay," he said after a long pause. "You two need to blast off posthaste. The Emperor is due to break out of FTL any second now."

With the fire now lit under our butts, the Kid and I practically ran to the ship. "Thanks for everything!" I yelled back at the last minute. The man just smiled and waved to us as the ramp closed up.

"A.I., begin emergency startup procedures!" I screamed as we entered the bridge. The ship usually needed a few minutes to get going properly, but in rare moments such as these, it could be done almost instantaneously. The procedure definitely wasn't a good idea to make a habit of—doing so would cause irreparable harm to not just the engines but possibly the entire ship.

With the engines humming to life below us, I took my place. "Kid, take a seat at the aft console," I screeched at him, not having time to be nice. "I need you to watch my back."

He smiled as he took his seat, realizing that I was putting trust in him, that I needed him. "Yes, sir!" he said proudly, taking his place at my side.

"Engines ready. Shall we launch?" A.I. asked, the readout on my console confirming as much.

"Yes!" the Kid and I said in unison. The ship accepted our command, launching us into the sky. The two of us were sitting in silence as we went through the atmosphere, occasionally stealing glances at one another.

Finally, after what felt like an eternity, but in reality was only a few minutes, the alert went off, signaling our imminent arrival into outer space. "A.I., prepare Slip Space jump to these coordinates," I said to the console, inputting the numbers given to me by the slain Chameleon.

"Input confirmed," A.I. said after I finished putting them in. "Launch in three minutes."

Leaning back in my chair, I breathed a sigh of relief. Almost there, I thought. Looking back at the Kid, I was surprised to see him staring out the window with a look of abject terror. "What is it?" I asked. His only response was to point out the window.

Turning back to the viewscreen, what I saw almost caused me to relieve myself of any waste that I had in my system. It's him, I thought, the terror I hadn't felt since my teenage years grasping me tight. "A.I.!" I screamed, panic gripping my throat. "Enter limp mode until launch!" If we lower our thermal trail, he might not see us, I thought, my mind grasping at any possible way we could get out of this.

Sadly, it was the only thing I could do. Looking out, I marveled at the sheer size of the Emperor's capital ship—the comparison in size would be like a flea gazing up at a cruise liner. It just boggled one's mind.

"Will we make it, Jayce?" the Kid asked, our ship bellowing the two-minute warning.

Looking over at him, I wasn't sure what to say. "Maybe," I replied, choosing to be honest. "Depends on if the…"

"Evantide! Cut your engines and prepare to be boarded!" a harsh voice came from the squawk box. At the same time, the computer signaled that it had less than a minute till launch.

I can do this, I thought. Steeling my will, I flicked the switch for the outgoing transceiver and put on my best poker face. "What seems to be the problem, sir?" I asked, my voice not having a trace of fear in it.

There was a pause as I'm sure the tech took a moment to contemplate my gall. I could hear him about to respond, but then there was what sounded like a scuffle. When the voice spoke up, it wasn't the tech any longer but Anders. "Listen here, shut down that trash heap before we send it back to the scrapyard!"

Oh, this is going to sting, I thought. The alert went off to signal that the FTL was ready. "No," I said before punching the button, hurtling us away from trouble and toward the last leg of this story.

14

A Spark Of Hope

"It's a trap, sir, no doubt," I declared to a group of people not interested in hearing the truth.

Fuir'ey, a Captain of the Royal Guard and His Majesty's chosen representative, was the first to look my way, not with anger but with curiosity. For I am sure he thought…

Captain Caster was be the second person to look my way. Though he out of all of them was the least qualified to judge me. With a record so disastrous he had earned the nick name Caster The Grave Digger. I smiled as he sent his glances my way.

"Who the Pluto is this little pipsqueak that thinks themselves worthy of our time?" said Admiral Timothy DiMare, the head of the Royal Navy.

My commanding officer, Elias Hargreaves, put his arm around my shoulder and said to the superiors that filled the room, "This here is Jaycen Lamont, my Backwing. You treat him with the same respect you treat me. Understood?" He stared down the blimp of a man in the process.

Any sensible person would have backed down after such a display. But this peacock did not. Instead, he seemed to get even wider. How that was possible, I will never understand. "Get that little shit out of here!" he roared like the wounded sea lion he was.

Without waiting for Elias to tell me, I walked away, throwing my arms up in protest as I left. "You all want to get ambushed? Be my guest!"

Once in the hallway and thus free of those stooges, I put my arm against the wall to brace my collapse. It was not in my nature to speak so out of turn, but what they had planned was beyond stupid.

The plan in question involved a frontal assault against Warlord Murg, set against the moon of Io. What my bosses could not see is that a small army could hide in the shadow of that moon and strike our forces when we least expected it.

Now that I had a chance to catch my breath, I continued my walk of shame. I had barely gotten halfway down the first hall when, much to my surprise, the door to the war room opened up. Out stepped Elias. "Sir, I will not apologize for something I believe to be right. What they have planned…"

"Is bullshit, I know," he said, stopping my tirade dead in its tracks. "But what is it you propose we do instead?"

I hadn't really thought that far, to be honest. "If I was the one making the call," I said, Elias nodding for me to go on, clearly seeing I was flying by the seat of my pants with this one, "I'd say get behind that moon first and strike our foes before they can do the same to us."

Elias stood there for a moment, mulling over what I had just said. "You know, that's actually not a bad idea. It's simple but elegant." He smiled and then put his hand on my shoulder. "You've got a mind for this stuff, Kid; I certainly made the right call in having you as my second in command. Wait in your quarters while I smooth things over. I'll come grab you later."

"Thank you, sir, you won't regret this!" I replied before practically skipping down the rest of the hallway.

"I already am!" he retorted, half-joking to me as I rounded the corner and fled from his sight.

This being a carrier ship, the trip back to my quarters was not too long. Usually, the squadron was based on the moon of Titan, the place I once called home. Being in an active rebellion, it was more advantageous for the entire squadron to be mobile, which is how we found ourselves guests upon the RSS Macarthur. Joining us were the WarStar Sackoff and Heavy Spacer Shenzhen.

"You pissed them off that quickly? Must be a new record for you, Jayce," Nileia said, teasing me as I entered our quarters.

Unlike the armies of the past, fraternization was not only allowed in our modern military but encouraged to a degree. Through the millennia, we found that people will fight harder when motivated by love. Thus, two people in an active relationship with one another were allowed to live together, even if they were deployed in the same unit. Nileia was that person for me. We may have been from two entirely separate worlds, but we found unity in our disdain for overbearing parents.

"That plan Carver cooked up is ridiculous," I said, lying down beside her. Looking into her loving eyes reminded me that everything would be alright.

Returning my loving gaze with one of her own, she placed a soft hand across my back. "What did Captain Hargreaves say?" she said, concern flooding her face.

Taking a deep breath, I savored the moment. One never knew when everything they held dear could be ripped from them in an instant. "He said he'd smooth things over," I said at last.

I could see the joy and relief wash over her. "My little leader in the making, if Cap told you that, then there is…"

"Nothing more to worry about, Kid," Captain Hargreaves said, bursting into our room, shattering the peace between us. "Suit up, both of you. We leave in ten." Then, as quickly as he entered, he left. The man had a million other things to attend to.

We nodded to each other and silently went to our individual lockers. The time for love had passed. Now was the time for war. From here till the end of the mission, we were to be completely different people.

Like a scene out of some movie, each pilot of the Shadow Hawk Squadron exited their quarters in unison. As one, we strutted down the hallway. Our purple and black jumpsuits clashed spectacularly with the dull white interiors of the ship. Together, we marched in formation, me at the front with Nileia right behind me. In this unit, we marched as one, we fought as one, we died as one.

Captain Hargreaves smiled as he saw us march into the hangar, full of swagger and confidence. "All crew present and accounted for, Captain," I said to him, saluting him before the others followed suit. "I trust the planning went well, sir."

His smile grew wider, leaning in and whispering, "The others are on board. Rally the team, Jayce. Your plan, your speech."

I had never been given such an honor, but I was not about to squander such an opportunity. Looking out over the squad, there were nine of us in total, not counting our fearless leader, of course. "Comrades, our plan is simple. The battle will take place around the moon of Io. There, Murg plans to make his final stand."

I knew I had the entire lot eating out of my hand. Don't jinx this, Jayce, I reminded myself. Someone's probably recording this. "We will be assisting the Fighting Vipers in their assault. They'll be taking poi…"

"Bullshit!" cried someone in the back. "Why do they get to take all the glory?"

"I'm glad you asked!" I replied, throwing the holopuck Elias had palmed me before I began to speak. It lit up in the center of the crowd, illuminating not just Io but also the positions of where all the ships would be. "Now, I don't need to tell an entire squadron of hardened stealth strike operatives just how important the dark side of this moon truly is."

That seemed to have gotten their attention, I thought, looking over them, seeing the wheels turning in their heads. Finally, the same person from before spoke up again. "So what would you have us do?" they asked.

"Next still," I said to the puck. At once, the view shifted, showing the side of Io cast in shadow. Purple dots represented our ships, and the warlord's vessels were shown in red. "Flynn means to ambush our forces by hiding in the void. Our plan is simple." I smiled, knowing it literally was that simple. "We ambush the ambushers."

"That works!" hollered the person from the back. That seemed to be all the approval the group needed. No sooner had they spoken than they began banging their helmets onto the ground—a sacred pre-raid tradition of ours. "You have your orders, people," I said above the rabble. "Break a wing!"

"Break a wing!" every one of us said in unison. All of us then broke off to set up our fighters. I chose to hang back in order to catch my breath, leaning against a ship. The rush had now left me.

Elias walked up to me, a smile splitting his face in two. "Command suits you, Kid," he said. "You'll be my eyes in the void. Think you're up to that task?"

Looking up at him, my eyes beaming with pride, I said, "Sir, I was born for it!" Without waiting for a response, I hopped into my ship and began the pre-flight warm-up.

Tapping his earpiece, Elias said to me, "Remember, I won't be too far from you. So if you screw up, I'll be quick to give you an earful, understand?"

I chuckled at his jest. The closing canopy cut me off from any sort of response. Turning my attention to my ship, I punched in the coordinates. Turning on my squawk box and setting it for all users, I simply said, "Let's go make history."

"Evantide, you are cleared for landing," the friendly lady said over the squawk box. "Welcome to Spartan Base Alpha."

The coordinates provided to us by the late rogue agent had led the Kid and me to a no-name rock in the asteroid belt. It was a perfect place to hide Spartan Base Alpha, the main hub of the Spartan Alliance—a resistance group formed from the core of the former Kingdom's special forces. Getting started no sooner than the fall of the old monarchy, their goal was to usurp the usurper.

For too long, the would-be Emperor Elrick had been allowed to run roughshod over the solar system. At least, that's their party line. For myself, I wasn't quite sure exactly where I stood.

"Jayce, are we going to be landing anytime soon?" the Kid asked, snapping me out of my internal monologue.

I nodded to him and then looked at the console. "A.I., begin landing procedures." Turning my head back to him, I noticed a look of concern was now painted on his face. "What? Got something to say? Say it!"

"What's on your mind?" he asked, seemingly sensing my trepidation. "You've been quiet the whole ride here."

Brushing him aside, I made my way off the bridge. "None of your concern," I said, not wanting to have this discussion. Not now, anyway, I thought. Not when you are at the precipice of this journey. Turning back to the Kid, I dug deep and put forth my old jerk smile. "Besides, after tomorrow, you won't have to deal with me ever again."

Promptly leaving the bridge, I didn't want to stick around for any possible moping that might occur. Why do they always get so attached? I wondered, absentmindedly fingering the token I had received on the drifter colony. It feels like that was a lifetime ago. Like I was a different person.

I could not dwell on such… nostalgia. No, not the right word. That implies you miss who you once were. Either way, I had a job to do—a job that was almost over. Once I had confirmed that the Kid was in a safe place, I was free to leave.

In my room, I packed up enough clothes and other sundry things to last me the few days I expected to be on base. While I could always come back and grab more, it helped to have things on hand for when they were needed. Not that I expected anything of note to actually happen. It's just that some old habits die hard, like my honor.

The distant chime alerted me to the fact that we were now on rocky ground. Bursting out, duffel bag slung over my shoulder, I was surprised to see the Kid standing where the top of the ramp was soon to be. He looked even more nervous than I was. "Stand up straight, Kid. They are expecting a Prince. Time to start acting like one!"

The Kid's head instantly snapped over in my direction, his mouth agape, the surprise too much for him. "I believe that's the first time you have referred to me as such."

Stopping dead in my tracks as the realization hit me. He's right. Not wanting to dwell on this revelation, I took my place at the Kid's side. "Just trying to help you along," I said, slapping him on the back. I then leaned in close and whispered into his ear, "You will refer to me as Virgil while here, understand?"

He nodded just as the doors opened and the ramp extended downwards. Greeting us was a middle-aged man in some sort of fancy military officer's garb. Flanking him were two gruff dudes who obviously belonged to his security detail.

"The Prince and his Pauper!" the man exclaimed, running up and embracing the Kid in a very awkward hug. "When we heard the news of your return, we celebrated for an entire week straight!"

"I thought this was a resistance movement and not a social club," I quipped, earning myself a stern glare from the woman.

Walking up to me and getting in my face, he stood about half my height on his best day. "I am Jacob Benedict, or Spartan Designate, chosen by Spartan Prime to guide in his absence." He then tried to poke me in the ribs. His hand instantly recoiled in pain. He only let that weakness show for a moment before quickly covering it up with, "And who are you exactly?"

Brushing him aside, I walked over, grabbing the Kid's two enormous bags. "The Muscle," I replied with my best shit-eating grin, having easily taken one bag under each arm. Without waiting for his approval, I walked down the ramp.

He did not like this one bit. He looked at the Kid to see if the reaction he wanted was justified or not. To his credit, the Kid just shrugged and followed my lead. I had just earned an enemy and couldn't care less.

"We are a resistance movement founded on… principles!" Designate said to me, trying desperately and failing to keep up. He probably would have been able to if he hadn't chosen to wear such elaborate boots. He finally caught up to me once I had set down the bags at the foot of the ramp. Not a bead of sweat had broken from my body in the process. "One of which is respect for your superiors!"

I looked him straight in the eyes. "Look, I'm a gun for hire. The only one I answer to…" I then looked up at the Kid, shooting him a wink before saying, "…is him."

"You know these wild types," the Kid said, prancing down the ramp like he now owned the place. In all fairness, he kinda did. "You can only point them where you want them to go and hope for the best." As he passed by me, he returned the wink I had given him prior.

Looking around, I could tell right off the bat that the movement was well-funded. While they certainly didn't have the latest and greatest tech, it was all well-maintained and clean-looking—a far cry from Nileia's ragtag operation.

The hangar, like the rest of the place, I assumed, looked to be carved directly out of the asteroid itself. Given that this was the first area most saw, I was surprised to see that they hadn't bothered to cover the exposed rock face. Perhaps things aren't quite as they seem, I wondered, as Designate led both of us away from the landing pad.

Once removed from the hangar, the base took on a more normal appearance. The exposed rock face was now covered in metal, most of it painted white. I say "most" because there were parts where the paint hadn't been maintained, and now the bare metal lay exposed before me. "We are a small operation, Merc, but a passionate one," Designate said to me once he caught me eyeing the flaws.

"What exactly are you fighting against?" I asked, genuinely curious. "The Emperor is corrupt, sure, but so was the last guy."

Upon hearing what I said, Spartan Designate stopped dead in his tracks, causing the Kid to run into him. He barely even flinched. "How… DARE you speak ill of our king!" he screeched. By the looks of it, he wanted to get in my face again, but knew better this time around. "The Emperor allows thieves and bandits to run amok in his domain, not caring in the slightest as long as they pay their tribute!"

Sounds like the only difference is that Elrick made the king's indifference state policy, I thought to myself. I could have said as much to him, but people were beginning to crowd us, and I simply wanted to move things along. "Of course, Spartan Designate," I said, giving my most pompous bow. "Where will you show us to first?"

Seeing me cowed before his eyes seemed to calm him down a bit. "The first place the Prince will be shown is our command room. Try and keep up," he said with a swish of his ceremonial sash, turning his back to me and heading off the left fork. The Kid just gave me his trademark sly grin as he passed. Clearly, he was enjoying every second of this display.

I must be rubbing off on him, . When I first met him, the boy was as naive as he was green. Now, here he was, enjoying a good mouthing off. Kinda makes me wish I had kids of my own… kinda.

The halls we went through were as nondescript as one could be—probably to confuse any would-be invaders, I concluded. Still, though, it was not impossible to get a lay of the land, something I had been doing in my head since the moment we arrived. Taking the long way to their control room, , making my judgment based on the fact that we had just now seemed to be getting close to the heart of the facility.

My suspicions were soon proven correct when Designate proudly flung open the doors and showed off what had to be a third-rate tactical center. My Gods, I thought with horror. Some of this tech is older than me! While everything inside looked functional and well-maintained, based on the narrow view I had from the back, the newest piece of gear I could spot was at least twenty-five years old. It's stuff that would be considered outdated even in my Shadow Hawk days.

"Not to your liking, Merc?" Designate asked me, picking up on my obvious disdain.

"Nah," I responded, trying and failing to maintain a straight face. "Just let me know when the next junk moon raid is." The Kid and I burst out in laughter at this, neither of us able to hold it back any longer.

"Out!" he screamed, pushing me beyond the threshold. "You will be escorted to your quarters. The Prince will meet you there shortly," he said, motioning to one of the guards before slamming the door in my face.

"Is he always like this?" I asked my chaperone, who simply nodded before putting their hand on my shoulder to lead me away from this mess.

The place is smaller than I thought, I noted. The distance from the Control Room to the personal quarters was only eight kilometers. The mismanaged white walls gave way to just the metal underneath. I guess they only dress up areas the "public" sees—typical.

"These quarters will belong to you and the Prince for the duration of your stay," the guard said as we got to the room, Q42 being the number on the door.

"Thank you. I'll begin unpacking at once," I said to her before ducking inside.

Much to my joy, the door did not lock behind me. So I am not their prisoner… yet. Having no idea how long it would be before the Kid would arrive, I decided to forsake unpacking and just take a nap. It had been a long journey to get where we were, and I was looking forward to having some time to myself. This will do for now…

"I don't know what you are paying him, but I can guarantee you that it is way too much," Designate said, poking me in the ribs to wake me up.

Rolling over and opening my eyes, I was greeted by the loving sight of Designate and the Kid standing over me. Designate looked as surly as ever, and the Kid was doing everything he could not to laugh. "Oh! That tour didn't take too long," I said, looking up and giving her a surly smile.

"It's been three hours, Virgil," the Kid said to me, looking like he was about to succumb to the giggles.

"Well, it's been a long journey," I said, springing up from the bed. "I guess I'll take care of it after dinner. Which is when exactly?"

Having had about enough of me, Designate turned and walked out the door. "Dinner is currently being served. But afterward, you two are to meet us in the conference room," she said before turning to look at the Kid with a measured amount of disdain. "He insisted." Then, without saying another word, she returned whence she came.

The two of us stood in silence after the door closed behind us. I was bewildered by what had just transpired, and the Kid looked a hair's breadth from laughing silly. "So?" I said, my frustration beginning to boil over as I broke the silence. "What happened?"

It seemed he couldn't hold it in any longer, falling to the floor. The room echoed with the sounds of his amusement. "You should have seen it, Jayce!" he said in between gasps of air. "The tech didn't get any better. In fact, it got worse!"

"That's great and all, but did they inform you of what their plans are?" I asked, beginning to pace back and forth. "It's not every day the Crown Prince shows up at one's doorstep."

"No, they didn't," the Kid said, his laughter instantly ceasing. Looking up at me, I could see the gears turning in his head, figuring out what I was getting at. "What do you think is going on?"

"I don't know," I said, looking out the window in the door to make sure there weren't sentries posted at our door—there were. "Something ain't right; that's all I can figure at the moment."

I expected him to scoff at my suspicions. Much to my shock, he walked up and hugged me. "You've gotten me this far. I trust you'll see me through to the end."

"I made a promise, didn't I?" I replied, pressing the button to open the door. The sentries outside made their way inside. "Once upon a time, promises meant the world to me." I then put my hand on his shoulder. "Now, they matter even more than before. Come on, Kid, we've got a show to catch."

We had three guards assigned to us. Guess they are taking him seriously, . Then I noticed it was me their eyes paid attention to. Or perhaps it is I they are not taking a chance with. None of them really had much to say. I tried to engage them in some light banter, only to be rewarded with several types of grunting for my efforts. Thus, we marched in relative silence.

The mess hall must be at the back of this place, I thought. Judging by the distance we traveled, that was the only conclusion I could come to. After a bit, the sweet smells of cooked food began to waft toward my nostrils. About time I tasted some good food. My stomach was waking up, rumbling at the notion of cooked food. The ship rations were okay, but in my line of work, being able to sit down and eat a cooked anything was a true rarity.

At this point, I could have used my nose to find the rest of the way. Not wanting to cause even more of a scene, I followed along. When we got to the front doors, they stopped, taking posts on either side. "End of the line for us," one of them said. Due to the helmets they wore, I couldn't tell which. "From here out, you both are on your own." As one, they then opened the door and ushered us inside.

The base must have housed a lot more people than I originally saw if the mess hall was anything to go by—a cavernous place. The space it took up had to have been at least a third of the volume that made up the asteroid. Way at the back was a stage, so this space obviously doubled as a meeting place or entertainment venue.

The food lines were, of course, at the front of the hall, and that's where the Kid and I made our first port of call—getting in line behind the ones in front of us, quickly causing a stir among the ranks as each looked behind them and saw exactly who was in line. The Kid was starting to get a bit sheepish at all the sudden attention. "They've been waiting for you to come along, Kid," I whispered into his ear. "How would you feel if all your hopes and dreams suddenly came waltzing into the cafeteria one day?"

This seemed to calm him down, and the line quickly followed suit. We picked up our trays, waiting till it was our turn. Once it was, we were saddled with a slice of mystery meat, a starch, and some sort of vegetable mush. It was hot, though, and that was all I really cared about. The Kid, on the other hand, was not looking too pleased with what he was given. His grimace was short-lived as I'm sure he recalled what he had been eating before this day.

As we made our way down the line of tables, I was shocked by the number of people who didn't want to sit with us—the percentage being one hundred. Whether through shaking their heads, pointing elsewhere, or just outright no's, not a single person desired our presence. "Hopes and dreams, huh?" the Kid quipped, looking up at me with a sneer.

"This doesn't make sense," I muttered. "Nothing has made sense since we lef…"

"Something on your mind?" the Kid asked, picking up on my distress.

Our path getting here has been too easy, I thought. Anders gave me up too quickly on the Drifter Colony, those damn cuffs at the checkpoint—that's not even mentioning the little resistance the Inquisitors gave me! Looking at the Kid, happily munching away at his meal, I did the same, if only for appearance's sake. "No, nothing, just eat your food."

"I hope our rations are a lot better than 'nothing,'" said Designate, creeping up from behind us. She pointed down the cavern at a set of oddly placed red doors. "Once you two are finished, we will speak beyond that side exit."

She then left us to wonder what in Hades had just happened. The Kid and I exchanged glances to that effect. We both were thinking the same thing, but neither of us wanted to say it. "Did we make the right call?" the Kid asked me, finally saying what was on both of our minds.

"I don't know." That was all I could say at first. Looking at the door, I said to him, "For now, it's probably best we do as the Romans do." The Kid, of course, did not get my turn of phrase. "We'll follow along for now," I said, simplifying it so that even he could understand. The Kid just nodded, getting up as I did to throw away our trash before heading over to those fateful doors.

"You two sure took your sweet time," Designate said as we made our way through the doors. The room itself was neither small nor big—somehow falling into the median of the two. A small square table sat not far from the door, with two chairs set up on either side. On the right sat Designate and one of her guards. The other chairs were empty, awaiting our butts to fill them.

Designate looked us over as we sat down. She was judging us like county fair beef, and for the Kid, she sneered, giving a look of complete disdain as if she was gazing at the foulest thing ever to exist. As for myself, she had no judgment whatsoever. To her, I was beneath any sort of judgment—nothing better than walking, talking furniture. It's an odd way to greet one's "savior."

"When will we meet the true person in charge, Spartan Prime?" I said, trying to take charge of the conversation as soon as it began.

I got an interesting reaction out of my question, watching with interest as her nose flared up rather dramatically. She was looking ready to go on a tirade, but a hand on her shoulder from the guard was all it took to get her to back down. "Spartan Prime… is out… right now," she said, looking like she wanted to say more but was using every ounce of willpower not to do so.

"That's odd," I replied, my confusion deliberately put on full display. "Do you know when they may return? A resistance leader isn't usually away from their group for very long."

Something I said must have triggered her. She shot up from her seat, said seat being flung across the room in the process. "We'll… talk about this tomorrow!" she said before marching out of the room in a huff.

"Our apologies; she's under a lot of stress as of late," said the guard, attempting to give some type of half-hearted apology. "You have the run of the base," he said before getting up to exit.

"And if we want to leave?" I asked, surprising not just the guard but also the Kid… and myself.

He just looked at me for a second, eyes darting back and forth. "Unfortunately, due to a solar storm, no ships are able to leave for the next three days," he replied, then swiftly left the room, leaving the Kid and me staring at each other in utter confusion.

"This… is… bullshit!" I yelled after a very awkward silence. My loud voice bounced off the walls, magnifying its intensity. This can't be real, I thought. Everything that has led me to this moment has been paved in suspicion, but now that it's all coming to roost, I'm left feeling unsatisfied.

The Kid stepped up from his seat and looked around. "What are we going to do now, Jayce?" he asked, fear creeping back into his expression. "Was it a bad idea to come here?"

"There's no way we could have known beforehand," I said, getting up from my seat, walking past the Kid, and putting my hand on the door. "As for what the two of us will do? We'll discuss it back in our room. For now, just act natural."

He nodded to me as I opened the door. Both of us exited wearing the fakest of smiles. Somehow, no one picked up on our plastic emotions. To them, we looked sufficiently whipped. In the end, that's all they seemed to actually care about. Since our outward appearance was that of subservience, no one even glanced our way as we made our way back to our rooms.

"So what now?" the Kid asked as soon as the door to the assigned quarters closed behind us.

Looking around, I couldn't see any observation or listening devices. Still, though, , my sense of caution at peak tinfoil hat. Best to act like we are being watched. "You stay here," I told him. His reaction was one of immediate disappointment. "I'll take care of this."

I immediately started grabbing some stuff I needed. I'll need to make a stop in the ship first. The Kid did not look happy at what was said to him, but he did as he was told. "Do you have my back, Jayce?" he asked, uncertainty coating his voice. "After all this time, do you actually care what happens to me?"

His question froze me in my place. I wasn't expecting that, I realized. My next thought was whether I actually did care. Together, we had fought through hell, and both came out better people. I believe the choice is obvious. I was about to exit for my task, but before I leaped once more into the breach, I turned around to face my friend. "Yes," I told him, surprising even myself with the answer.

Once outside the door, I sighed before getting back into character. I put a smile on my face as I marched back over to the hangar, an empty satchel slung over my shoulder. While I made my way there in complete silence, the gravity of what I was about to do weighed on me with every step I took. It's not like you're guaranteed to push the red button, I said to myself in a failed attempt to calm myself down.

"We'll kill them both at dawn," said a voice from beyond the door I was passing at the time—a voice I now recognized as belonging to Spartan Designate! "How dare he bring up that false prophet!" he screeched. "We made it fifteen years without this brat; we don't need him to get us the rest of the way."

My body froze at this revelation. The Kid isn't their savior. He's their albatross. Things certainly were clearer now, but by no means did everything suddenly make sense. It does explain our cold reception, but there's no way they could have engineered our countless close calls. Those thoughts had nothing on how the Chameleons assisted us. If they really wanted him dead, they could have killed him in countless ways back on Europa.

An investigation for another time, I concluded, sneaking my way past that fateful door and trying my best to look casual as I walked up to the lone guard barring my passage. "Hey, I forgot to grab some things from my ship," I said to him, holding up my satchel. "Mind if I sneak past you?"

The guard looked me up and down. He had a "You serious?" look on his face, surprised at my boldness. Sensing his dismissal, I quickly followed up with, "Do I look ready to dash off?" I said, gesturing to my very casual attire. "Besides, the Brat's not with me, and it's not like I could get anywhere with this storm."

The guard weighed the options in his head. He then shrugged and stepped aside, realizing he didn't actually care one way or the other. "Thanks!" I said to him as I passed by.

At this ungodly hour, the hangar was deserted, the only soul crazy enough to be here being me. The Eventide stood proudly in its center. In and out—a place like this has to have an active patrol schedule.

Walking up to my chariot, the thing that had not just been my home for the past fifteen years but had also ferried me to wherever I needed to go. Of course, by now, I had an attachment to the old girl; such things were inevitable, given enough time. Not unlike these feelings bubbling up for the Kid.

I flipped the emergency release lever located next to the entry ramp. It fell with a rather loud THUD. If there weren't anyone who cared about such a thing within a kilometer or two, I would have been in deep trouble.

Sneaking about my ship, I was happy to see that they hadn't ransacked it yet. Probably waiting till after they kill us so as not to arouse suspicion, I thought, the reassurance bringing me little comfort. Knowing I was now under a clock did nothing to help things along. Still, I knew what I had to get and where I kept them. This portion of my task was the easy part. I was not looking forward to what was to come next.

Stepping off my ship, I put the ramp back up. It was a bit difficult, seeing as how I was now weighed down by a side satchel full of heavy and very volatile things. But I managed, honestly, not having much choice in the matter. Either I take what I have and sneak deep into the base, or die trying.

Slipping past the guard, I clung to the shadows like a man possessed. Getting to the core of things would not be easy, but it's either I do something or watch everything blow up in my face…

15
Starting The Fire

Nothing. Three hours later, the squad still sat in their fighters, waiting for our adversaries to arrive. Something's not right, I thought. The Aux Force should have materialized by now. Frustrated, I checked my scanner. Nothing...wait. I said to myself, looking at the battle as if for the first time.

The Royal forces were effectively in the middle of the fray. To their "right" was the main attachment to the rebellion. Both sides were currently in active engagement. It was then that I noticed the "left" side was completely devoid of forces from either side. At once, the enemy's true plan was revealed to me.

"Captain, I was wrong," I said over the comms. "The enemy isn't going to pop out from the shadow of the moon. It's going to ambush them from our left flank." There was silence among us. A few groans coming from some of the junior members were the only responses I got at first. "Check the scanners if you don't believe me."

While our fearless leader checked out my claim, I launched a deep space pulse. If anything were to exit Slip Space in the near future, that pulse would detect it. The sad part is that it would take a few minutes to get any sort of response.

"He's right," Elias said, confirming my suspicions. "The question now is, what do we do?"

Right then, my pulse bounced back to me, revealing that "Enemy squadron preparing to exit on the left flank!" I said to everyone. "Permission to take point?" I asked, firing up my engines.

"Granted," he said to me, zooming off to coordinate from afar. The man knows when to take a back seat. It's what made him such a good leader. I would have never risen so high otherwise.

As we blazed across the expanse of the moon, our engines set to full burn, we began to see the ships materialize out of Slip Space. A momentary portal followed by a flash of bright white light. That's all it took for nearly a dozen fighters to appear out of nowhere. "Hold your fire until my mark," I told the crew, priming my weapons for the fight to come.

You see, they didn't know we were right on their exhausts. To them, their plan of setting up a surprise pincer maneuver was well underway. "Fire volley one!" I commanded, spoiling their otherwise well-thought-out plan.

The entire squadron scrambled after our initial burst. One shot wouldn't break our stealth, but any more than that certainly would. "Dandelion Formation!" I called out, telling the crew to form a haphazard sphere. That way, shots would come in from all sides, hiding both our numbers and actual position, allowing us to scramble away before engaging like normal fighters.

Our initial burst did quite well. Three of the enemy fighters could not dodge in time, exploding into trillions of pieces almost instantaneously. That tipped the scales slightly in our favor, leaving nine ships left to our eleven. Not bad odds, I thought, before reminding myself of the skill level our opponents possessed. These people were battle-hardened vets even before they followed their general in rebellion.

Once my fellow Shadow Hawks were in the proper formation, I waited. We had fired our first shot; it was only sporting that we give them the same courtesy.

They seemed confused by what had just happened. Their ships turned every which way in search of us. After they had seemingly determined that they could not ascertain the origin of the attack, they pressed on like the knuckle-brains they were. "Cap," I squawked out to him in a shortwave pulse. "It doesn't seem like the main fleet notices the new pieces on the board. When we break stealth, could you get them on the horn and inform them?" Two beeps followed, confirming my request.

Okay, here goes...well, everything. I reveled in that sliver of peace one felt before the hell of battle breaks out. "Fire!" I commanded. Each ship broke its stealth to fire the second shot, then scattered to the solar winds. Winds of change, it seemed. The tide of battle has now shifted back in our favor.

Before we engaged, the main fleet was having a rough go at turning back the enemy forces. Now, with the shock and awe of seeing one's plans turn to literal dust, their morale had broken; it wouldn't be long before this day was won.

The rest of the battle was mostly cleanup work. Those who did not run stood and covered for the rest, carrying on bravely, as expected from someone of their station. "Backwing," Elias called out once we were nearly done mopping the floor of the stragglers. "Seems like brass wants to pin some metal to our chests. An award ceremony is to be carried out on deck; be sharp."

Medals, huh? I thought to myself. And here I thought they were going to just throw the book at me. It still is, but a different kind of book.

Getting in line behind Elias, we flew in single-file formation back onto the carrier. A group of officials was already waiting for us near the landing zone. This should be exciting.

What was not exciting was the gaggle of flashbulbs going off as we jumped out of our ships. Each one is trying to capture that perfect moment that would, in turn, go viral and make their career—for the next week, anyhow.

"Ladies and gentlemen," the crier said to his crowd, waving his arms wildly in our direction, "I give you the men and women of the hour: the SHADOW HAWK SQUADRON!!"

Most of us had never experienced such adoration. The bulk of the crew walked awkwardly to the podium. Being the son of a military contractor does have its advantages, I mused, walking up to the stage with every ounce of phoned-in confidence I could muster. They seemed to have bought my display, cheering me on as I stepped atop the podium, taking my place next to Elias's side.

The awards started with the lowest-ranking members, as was the tradition, before making their way up toward the front of the row. By the time they had gotten to the last two members, the chief and I, a crowd had formed. They were erupting into cheers as each merit was pinned to our chests.

"I guess none of us would be here if it weren't for you," Jackson said once he had gotten to me. "Your actions today deserve something special," the man said as he reached into his pocket to pull out a different medal. This one was made of gold, as opposed to the others, which were cast from silver.

It felt so surreal to be recognized in such a way. For once, I was being applauded for something of my doing, not my father's. My family's name had nothing to do with the hunk of shiny metal being pinned to my chest. "The King has been informed of your actions today," he whispered into my ear. "From now on, the Royal House will be watching your career with great interest."

If only all battles could go as well as that one.

"Proximity warning!" blared the alarm, coming from every speaker in the room, jolting The Kid and me awake. Both of us had slept through the first wave. I had only gotten back a few hours prior. He, on the other hand, had no such excuse.

By the time the second wave of alarms hit us, I was primed to bolt upright upon the sound—something that was certainly the last reaction I ever wanted to have. "The Imperial Flagship is in range. This is not a drill!"

Of all people, he is here, I thought with dread. The Kid and I exchanged worrisome glances. Both of us knew this could only mean bad things ahead. "Pack up whatever you can," I told him.

"Are we leaving?" he asked—a reasonable question, but one I currently had no answer to.

Looking around, I took stock of what we could leave behind, which, thankfully, was pretty much everything. The only thing worth grabbing was the packet I had received at the beginning of this journey. It still remained unopened.

Despite the constant pleas from me for us to just leave, The Kid had to grab one thing: the picture of his mother, held in a locket I had given her in a hidden-giver arrangement, oh so many years ago. She was so quick to figure out that it was I who had given her that. I remembered my thoughts drifting nostalgically back to a much simpler time. She never told anyone, though—truly a light in that cavern of darkness.

Pocketing the fruits of last night's labor, The Kid and I set out into the hallways. The lights flashed red and white. Everyone was running around in a panic, yet somehow also with purpose. They all knew their tasks and what they were supposed to be. Where was our place? I wondered, watching everyone move around with the kind of confidence I once had. The hangar should do, I suppose.

So off we went toward the epicenter of my actions. There wasn't anywhere else we could escape to, so the frying pan would have to do.

I wasn't overall too concerned about our prospects. Inside my pocket was our escape plan—the consequence of a long night twisting myself between various tubes and sprockets.

The Kid, of course, looked scared out of his mind. Looking up and seeing me calm confused him to no end. "What do you have up your sleeve, Jayce?" he asked, clearly catching on.

"It's not my sleeve you should be concerned about," I told him, patting my pocket where the escape plan was held—though not too hard, lest I accidentally set it off too early.

He opened his mouth to say some witty retort. Thankfully, before he could get anything out, the two of us were whisked through now wide-open hangar doors. The rest followed along shortly after. Much to all of our dismay, the doors shut and locked themselves behind us.

So, remember when I said that this hangar was huge? Imagine that same ginormous cavern but with a mere transport ship taking up two-thirds of it. Several ships were sacrificed in the process to ensure it had enough room. The Evantide, thankfully, was not one of them, but only just.

Our speck of a ship nested mere millimeters from the exit ramp to the ship.

Upon said exit ramp stood...him, The Emperor, Elrick. He may go by the last name of Shinkar now, but I knew him for who he really was: The Usurper—an illegitimate son of a much-reviled King. Born out of wedlock, the boy was raised with the legitimacy he would never actually have. The best schools, resources, training—whatever he needed, all were at his disposal.

The people loved him. He had inherited all of the King's former good looks as well as the last scraps of his cunning. The throne would have been his...if not for the inconvenient arrival of The Kid. Born in the twilight years of Aerys's reign, The Kid was a miracle child. Such a notion followed him till the present day. As it was definitely a miracle we had made it so far, hopefully his luck lasts us just a little bit longer.

"My citizens!" Elrick yelled and strutted down the ramp as if he had already won. "I come to you all in a forgiving mood." As he got to the bottom of the ramp, he looked around, noticing The Evantide almost instantly and staring at it, muttering something under his breath before looking over the huge crowd that had now formed.

"I realize that life can be hard," he said to a now-captive audience, his favorite kind. "People and things are bound to slip through the cracks of such a huge bureaucracy." No reaction from the crowd.

Most were probably still processing that the Emperor was here. "But I am a generous leader. Any who kneel for me now will be given clemency, no questions asked."

At once, half of the crowd knelt. What the? I thought in confusion, never having seen such a sight before. Those who had bent the knee were herded onto the ship. Elrick somehow shook the hands of each and every one of them. "As for the rest of you…," he said once his new loyalists were aboard, "I am now inclined to be less forgiving."

"This wasn't part of the deal!" screamed Spartan Designate, leaving the entire hall in stunned silence.

Elrick turned to face his accuser. A smile splashed across his face. "You're right, it wasn't." Looking over the crowd, he then bellowed, "This one contacted me a month ago. She said she had a proposition for me."

The crowd stood there frozen, no one knowing exactly how to take this. Designate, for his part, ran up and began screaming in his face. None of us really understood exactly what it was he said. His cackles echoed off the walls, resulting in a true mess of incoherent ideals.

The Emperor just stood there and took it. One would be remiss if, at this point, they did not understand why he was sovereign.

All of a sudden, he embraced him, scooping him up into a big bear hug. Then I spotted a flash of something metallic, soon followed by Designate slumping to the floor, a knife sticking out of his back. "He would have betrayed every one of you, especially you, Jayce."

Did he just…? I wondered. The crowd looked around for the person he had just called out by name: me. "Yes, Jayce, I made you as soon as I stepped off my transport. The False Prince, too." Motioning to the Evantide, he then said, "You think I wouldn't recognize my father's starship?" From there, he extended a hand to beckon us forward. "Come, he's half the reason I am here."

"What's the other half then?" I asked, the guards not being pleasant with how they brought us forth.

Elrick circled us like a predator encasing its prey. "When Anders told me that he had encountered you at the Drifter Colony, it'd be a lie if I didn't say there was some…confusion." He stopped in front of me, staring straight through me. "I thought you cowed, so I wondered what could possibly bring you back onto the board after so long away from it."

He then moved over to The Kid, who, after refusing to look up at him, was grabbed by the scalp and forcibly lifted to his level. "The answer, in hindsight, was obvious. Thus, I did what I did best…schemed."

"It's been you this entire time!" I growled, revelations hitting me like a ton of bricks. The checkpoint, Europa, even here—all of this…

"You played exactly to my design, Jayce," Elrick said with a slight cackle. "I'll admit, some of my subordinates got a bit...overzealous," he continued, releasing from his grip as he finished. Finally, turning to the crowd and bellowing, "Does anybody have anything to say?"

"Yeah, I do," I said, reaching into my pocket so that I could finally pull out the one card I had to play.

Elrick turned to look at me. "This should be good," he said, his smile somehow growing more... sinister.

That smile soon turned to a frown as he saw what I had pulled out: a detonator. "I've had a feeling that something wasn't right for some time," I said with a smirk, waving the switch over the crowd. I could not help but take a sense of perverse pleasure watching them recoil in fear.

Serves them right for how coldly they received us. "Last night, I overheard Spartan Designate detail his plan to kill us." No reaction. Damn the entire lot! A cold fury started to fill my heart—a toxic warmth that had kept me going in my darkest of hours. Now a changed man, it served as only a momentary source of strength. "So I took matters into my own hands, rigging up the generators with explosives."

A single man let out a wail of fear. The rest of the crowd quickly followed suit. "This, of course, has a dead man's switch in case one of your snipers was thinking of taking me out," I said to Elrick. His composure was slowly returning to him.

"A clever gambit," he said, a sly smile forming around the corners of his mouth. "I would expect nothing less from the Hero of Io."

Flattery—the man must truly be desperate. "I want free passage out of here, for me," I told him, first leveling my eyes on him, then, "and the boy."

He, of course, scoffed at my impossible request. "You think I would go to this much trouble just to let both of you go?"

I smiled, a reaction he was not expecting. "No, but I needed time to prime the detonator," I said, raising it high for all to see before pushing the button.

A crash could be heard from deep inside the asteroid, followed by a small flash of light coming from the door to the hangar. Said light would be the last as everything was soon plunged into darkness, the amber emergency light only partially taking its place.

Everyone stared at me in stunned silence. No one could have foreseen the drastic action I had just taken, least of all Elrick, his mouth now agape. "Do you have any idea what you have just done?" he asked.

"Why yes," I answered, glancing down at my wrist to double-check the time before continuing, "By my estimation, we have about 4 minutes and 42 seconds before the air runs out. Chop chop!"

The orderly crowd instantaneously turned into a chaotic mob when my news broke. Everyone scrambled to get into anything with a pressurized interior. A large crowd massed around Elrick's ship, demanding to be let in. The Emperor's guards quickly moved forward to usher him away, much to the protest of the mob. Two shots and ten bodies later, the rest realized that this was a bad idea.

"You're coming with me, Your Highness," I said to Elrick, stalking toward him, my pistol trained on him.

He was confused, but he did as he was told. "What do you need me for?" he asked as he walked forward, hands up in the air.

"Leverage," I told him, putting The Emperor—a man many believed a god—into a headlock, dragging his sorry ass back to my ship. "Your ships wouldn't dare shoot down the craft that has their leader on board, would they?"

He didn't respond, instead choosing to remain silent as we got on the ship and began the startup sequence. He didn't utter even a peep as The Kid tied him to the aft chair. "You make one wrong move, I'll blow your brains out," I said to him, my pistol pressed against his forehead. "Your Highness."

Elrick did as he was told. I smiled as I saw the ship hum to life. It feels good to be standing for something again, I thought, looking over at The Kid. My wistful thinking was interrupted by his insistent shouting and pointing. "What? What's the matter?" I said, snapping at him a bit harsher than I probably should have. He didn't say anything in particular; he just kept pointing and shouting. Following the path he pointed out, I could see exactly what had caused him alarm.

"Weapons, A.I., we need weapons!" I shouted, my mind desperately trying not to panic. In our mad scramble to get the frack out of here, I had forgotten one very key fact: the roof, our only way in or out of this rock, was currently sealed shut.

"You idiot!" Elrick cried. "Now that you cut the power, this place is soon to be a meat grinder."

He's right… about the present state anyway. "Kid, slap the Emperor, please."

The Kid smiled at my request. "With pleasure," he replied before reaching over and smacking him upside his cheek.

"As before and as to come, we will make our own way," I said to the Emperor with a smirk. A scowl was his only response. Turning my attention back forward, I pulled up the weapons menu. "Proton Salvos," I called out.

Elrick's eyes popped out when he heard my choice—clearly knowing what I intended. "Are you mad?" he said, panic again filling his voice. "You'll kill each and every one of us!"

"Only when I need to be," I said, my head facing forward. Full attention was devoted to the two shots I was about to fire off. With luck, they would melt the blast doors by the time we hit them ourselves, allowing us to just breeze on through. If I misfired and were off by even a single meter, we'd hit a solid wall of fire, becoming such ourselves and crashing down into an already panicked crowd, killing them all in an instant.

Let's not do that, I thought as I fired off the salvos. The point of this is not to kill anyone.

I would not know if my plan had worked until I was already in the thick of it. My eggs are now in the proverbial basket. Dread filled my body as I pulled down on the lever controlling our thrust. Each of us was thrown back as the acceleration hit us. With each passing moment, the wall of red got ever closer. My mind only thought about one thing: Will this really work? Not knowing which way the dice would land, I closed my eyes. For when I opened them...

I'd breathe easy, the darkness of space greeting me like an old friend, proving that my gambit had paid off. "Now I can see why you rose up the ranks so quickly," The Emperor said with a solemn voice. "Tis a pity you lost yourself. With instincts like yours, The Empire would have no equal."

Lost..., I thought, the Emperor's words mulling in my head. But have I been found? The thought rang in my head unanswered. It would have to remain that way for some time. For now, the cronies were calling.

"Evantide!" came a voice over the squawk box— a voice that more than likely belonged to an Imperial officer. Their ships are now dotting my screen. I didn't bother to count them, but just at a glance, I could tell their number was in the hundreds, at least. "Power down your weapons and prepare to be boarded!"

Smirking over at the Emperor, I flipped on the outgoing transceiver, and with the biggest shit-eating grin, I said, "That's probably not a good idea."

There was silence on both sides as I waited for a reply, and then as they figured out what to say, clearly not being used to having their might challenged. "M... may we ask why?" they said after a few not-so-tense moments.

"You may," I said, enjoying the role reversal. "But I believe it would be better if you heard the reason straight from the source."

Turning my chair to face him, I extended the mic in his direction. "This is Emperor Elrick," he said, his voice cracking with every sentence he spoke. "I have been kidnapped. Do as he says." Slumping back into his chair, the man continued to shoot daggers at me with his eyes.

This may seem easy, but you are still walking a very tightrope, Jayce, I reminded myself. "Here's what is going to happen," I said over the comms, my voice much more serious and on point now. "We are going to spool up our FTL." I did just that, flicking the right switches to start the process. "Before we disappear, we'll stuff your glorious Emperor into a standard escape pod." I grinned like the madman I was as I shut off both ends of the communication, not giving them even a chance to protest.

Feeling pretty good about myself and my plan, I leaned back. All it took was a cackle from Elrick to shatter my peace. "That's your plan?" he said, still laughing in a manic glee. "There is nowhere you can run that we won't find you!"

I was out of my seat in an instant, and the next moment, my gun was pointed under his chin. "What do you mean?" I demanded. "Tell me!"

"We hid a tracker in this ship at the checkpoint," he said, still smiling from ear to ear. "Venus, Luna, Europa, and finally...here. You were never far from our clutches."

Cocking the primer, I pressed the pistol further into his neck. Any further, and I would begin to tear the skin. "Where? Where did you put it, Elrick?" I yelled. The Kid sank into his chair as he observed my brutality.

"You shouldn't have run, Jayce," Elrick replied, trying to avoid the question. "You would have done great under my rule—much better than that sycophant Anders."

"You're stalling," I said, my patience beginning to wear thin. "Tell me where the Dwarf hid it, and I promise not to kill you."

He smiled; the cold-hearted bastard smiled! "You'll never find it," he said, savoring every syllable. "It's in a place you never look."

Lowering my weapon, it was now my time to crack a smile. "You just gave it away." I then bowed to the man who had handed me our salvation. "Thank you... Elrick."

Quickly dashing away to the storeroom, I didn't have time to see his expression, but I was positive it had been one of confusion. "Wait, no, I didn't!" he said, completely lost in his denial, at the same time confirming what I had thought.

The man who called himself Emperor, Elrick Commodus Bowles, knew me all too well—or at least he knew the person I used to be so long ago. The only common link between the soldier I was and the man I am currently trying to become is the importance I put upon honor and shame. There was only one thing—or, to be more precise, one article of clothing—where both intersected. It was the only thing I could never get rid of. The very thing I could never stand to see again was my uniform.

It was stuck in a footlocker deep in the storage area—always close by, a reminder of who I once was. It was a shame, a stain I could never remove. Only recently have I learned it is better to wear that stain and own up to it. Hiding past sins only served to deepen their impact.

The footlocker was under a few layers of assorted crap. I flung things around, dreading the inevitable cleanup. The Imperials will only wait so long, I reminded myself. It doesn't matter if I have the Emperor. Wait too long, and they'll just shoot us and be done with it.

Looking down at my prize, trepidation soon filled my heart, instantly turning it to lead. This thing hasn't been cracked open in fifteen years, I thought. One can only imagine the smell! I wouldn't have to imagine for very long. As soon as the footlocker was cracked open, a decade and a half's worth of mildew came spilling out. The assault on my nostrils was relentless in its ferocity. I had to tear off a huge piece of my sleeve, dip it in some nearby oil, and put that against my mouth. The oil smelled terrible, but compared to the horror coming from the locker, it might as well have been a basket of roses.

The place I first checked was the most obvious, so, of course, the tracker wasn't in any of the pockets. Then, moving on to the insides of the clothing—nothing. "Dammit!" I yelled, the frustration becoming too much to bear. "Do I have to strip this ship down to the metal...wait! Medal!"

It was then that I realized exactly what Elrick meant. My uniform was certainly my greatest shame, but it wasn't what I shied away from the most. What is the thing a man who has forsaken his honor avoids the most? His greatest triumph! I concluded, tearing through the locker in search of my medal case, and finding it in a compartment at the bottom.

As I opened the box, a light quickly enveloped me. It had no light source of its own, but the medals were so shiny that they managed to reflect what little light there was. Having accumulated a fair number of medals in my time with the Shadow Hawks, there were many to sift through. Thankfully, the one I sought stood large among them.

In the middle sat a large golden disc. Laser-etched onto its surface was a cascade of roses: The Rosary Ring. They were given only to those who displayed the most exemplary service to the Kingdom—an award given to me after my last-minute tactics and decision-making saved our hides. They called me "The Hero of Io," I remembered, thinking back to that time and how it had set me up for my role in the Royal Guard. If only I had stuck out a little bit less, I wouldn't be here now.

Knowing that it was a therapy session for another time, I flipped over the medal. Sure enough, a blinking green light greeted me. I detached the tracker from its hiding place and pocketed it before heading back to the bridge.

I must have still been sour from dwelling on my inner conflict, for when I entered, Elrick took one look at me. "Didn't find it, did ya?" he said with a smug smirk.

"Oh," I said, my spirits lifted when I realized he had just set me up. "You mean this crappy little thing?" I asked, reaching into my pocket to pull out the tracker, lifting it so he could see it before I tossed it to his feet. "What's the status of the FTL?" I asked The Kid, who still had his gun trained on Elrick. That's the spirit.

The Kid glanced over at the screen—by the looks of it, for the first time since I had left. He's learned so much, I observed. There may be hope for him yet. "Looks like we're ready whenever you are," he replied, staring up at me, his eyes hoping for some sort of approval.

"Splendid! You did good, Kid," I said, this time giving him what he deserved. Looking back at Elrick, I watched him shrink back in his chair, fearing the worst. "As for you," I said to him, drawing this out as long as I could, "your departure is shortly at hand."

I can solve all of this, I thought, my mind going to a very dark place—right here, right now. Drawing my pistol and pointing at The Emperor, The Usurper—the man who is responsible for every bit of my misery.

"Jayce, what are you doing?" The Kid asked as I pressed the muzzle of my gun against Elrick's forehead.

"Ending this story," I said, pushing back the primer. The fear in Elrick's eyes grew with my words. He knew I was not bluffing.

"You think killing me will end things?" he said, not really helping his case. "It will go about the same as if I had done nothing after I found out my old man was on his deathbed."

That last part did give me pause, causing me to lower my weapon temporarily. He was just a baby when Aerys died, I recalled, looking over at The Kid. At the same time, he had grown so much in our time together. To say he was ready to lead a kingdom when I met him, let alone when I first left him—that would be unthinkable. "Can you imagine the mess that would have followed had I not stepped up?" Elrick said, seizing upon my hesitation.

"Can you say with a straight face that this is any better?" I said, again raising my pistol, this time fully prepared to do what I thought needed doing.

"No, I can't!" he said with a straight face, meeting my intense stare with his own. "But kill me and find out if you truly are correct."

I should, I really should. My finger tightened on the trigger. It would be the easy way…

"Jayce!" The Kid cried, breaking me from the moment. I looked back at him, shocked to see he had his gun trained on me! "Don't stoop to his level. You said to me you wanted to be better, so be better!"

He... he's right, I thought, lowering my weapon before ultimately holstering it. The Emperor let out a rather long sigh of relief. "A.I., get the Imperial Flagship on the horn," I commanded, feeling myself return to a more normal state.

Walking back to the forward console, I looked over to see The Kid putting away his sidearm, a cheesy grin on his face. Good won this day. Glancing over at the Emperor, I saw he had put up his persona again. But will it win the war?

"Is the Emperor still alive?" the comms attendant asked, panic flooding their voice.

Straight to the point—part of me can't help but respect it. Shooting a glance at Elrick to tell him he was up, he leaned forward and said, "Yes, yes, I am."

I then motioned to The Kid, who, by now, had guessed what my plan was. He grabbed the Emperor and dragged him in the direction of the escape pods. "We'll be blasting off shortly. You'll have your fearful leader back in no time."

Looking at the cameras, I was shocked to see Elrick offer no resistance. One would think this would be the perfect time to try something, but he didn't. Perhaps he wants this over as quickly as I do.

With the man secure in his escape pod, I was about to press the button to eject him. It was only then that I realized the tracker was still lying where I had tossed it. Getting an idea, I grabbed it and scooted over to where The Kid had taken him.

Both were surprised to see me show up. The Emperor expected to be off the ship by now. "You forgot something," I said, tossing the tracker into his lap. "This should help them find you easier, anyhow."

The Kid and I smiled as I slammed the button to seal up the pod. "Together?" I asked him, gesturing to the big red button that sat right next to the one I had just pressed. With glee, he reached up and put his hand on it. I then put my hand on top of his.

As one, we pushed the button, releasing The Emperor of The Shinkar Empire out into the void like yesterday's waste.

"What now?" The Kid asked as we rushed back onto the bridge. We only had a few moments before they would pick up his trail. Once he was secure, our safety would not be.

Good question. Looking at the star charts, nothing immediately jumps out at me. "Let's just get out of here and then figure out the rest later, okay?"

He nodded, taking up his place at my side. The FTL had long since been spooled up. With nothing else holding us back, I pulled back the lever, launching not just the ship but myself. In my rush to escape, I had forgotten to secure myself. As a result, my entire body was flung toward the back of the bridge. Thankfully, nothing was bruised besides my ego.

"Whoa, you okay, Jayce?" The Kid asked once things had stabilized, and we were successfully in Slip Space.

"Yeah," I responded with a bit of labor, making the walk of shame back to my seat at the front of the ship. Once I was secure in my place, I was surprised by a set of arms that suddenly wrapped themselves around me. The Kid was hugging me.

"Thank you! Thank you so much!" he said with a gleeful zeal.

Shrugging him off, I looked at the routes available to us. That place near Uranus might work. "Just part of my job, Kid."

"No, it wasn't," he said, still standing next to me. "Your job was to take me to the Spartans safe and sound. You did that; rescuing me from The Emperor was not what you were paid for."

He's right, I thought, the realization hitting me like a ton of bricks. From here on, I'm off the clock. Looking up at him, there was only one thing I could say: "Oh."

16
Something Begins

So here we are, the Kid and I. Me sitting in this booth, the Kid laying his head down, long since having fallen asleep. We had ended up at a place called Gravy Goodness, a greasy spoon sitting on the edge of the Pit Stop, a refueling station sitting atop the rings of Uranus. I would have preferred to press on farther, perhaps even to someplace near Neptune, but a lack of gas prevented us from going any further. Hell, I had to sell most of my guns to some sketchy pawn shop in order to afford this meal alongside half my ship's tank. This is going to be a…

"Rough night?" the waitress said as she came by to refill my cup for what had to have been the fifth time.

"Something like that," I replied, looking up at her. I could see the pity in her eyes. In a rush to get to the hangar and then to run away, neither of us had had a chance to sleep or even bathe for about three days. So yeah, we looked like hell. "I didn't order this," I told her.

Before I could protest, she placed a slice of pie on the table in front of me. "On the house," she said with a smile. "You look like you could use something good."

"You're not wrong!" I replied, my mouth stuffed with a mixture of fresh apples and blueberries. I thought these fruits went extinct long ago. "Where did you find these?" I asked once I had managed to chew my food.

She gestured down to her wrist. There, I could see a barcode tattoo, indicating she once belonged to the various penal camps that dotted the system, several of which were not too far from here. "We had a garden back where I served my time," she told me, her head down while she spoke. It was clear to me that this wasn't some distant memory. "I managed to smuggle out some seeds after I got out. We then started a truckers' dome when I landed here."

After her confession, she stood there in solemn thought. Then, like a wind-up toy, she shot up, as bubbly as ever, giving me a sort of emotional whiplash. "So, how long have you two been on the path together?" she asked, gesturing to me and the Kid.

Deciding to answer in half-truths, I replied, "About a year now. He kind of fell into my lap after his mother died."

"I'm sorry it didn't work out between you two," she said, putting her hand on mine. "You're doing a great job. As far as I am concerned, you and your son can stay here as long as you need."

Wait...did she just? "Ummm, yeah, thank you," I said, confused at first but deciding it would be safer just to play along. Satisfied, she gave me another smile and wandered off.

This has gone too far and for too long, I thought to myself, looking down at the sleeping prince. He was correct; I did my job. I got him to where he needed to go. Seeing his peaceful face stirred something inside me, feelings I had never felt before. Why am I still here?

Running through the possibilities, I knew the option to just turn him in to the Emperor was still on the table. He'd still be pissed as all Pluto but might go easy on me after I delivered him his prize—a possibility, but not a good one.

I could always just leave him here, go out on my own, and continue my life as a merc. Can a snake truly crawl back into its skin once it has been shed? So yeah, that was out, too.

The days of me not caring about others had long since set. If this journey has taught me anything, it's that I need to be the man I was before.

That left just one choice, the hardest one of them all: take the Kid with me and find our place among the stars together. A life on the run? That's no life for a kid. But then again, what choice do either of us have?

So, we have options A or C: either I turn the Kid in or go on the run with him, I thought, playing both scenarios in my head. Each one calls to a different path. Would I follow my head or my heart?

"Waitress, could I ask you a favor?" I said, raising my hand to get her attention.

"What is it, darling?" she asked as she walked up, smile still on her face.

I took a breath before asking what I knew would get shot down. "I need to head back to the ship and look over some stuff. Could you watch him for a bit?"

At once, her entire demeanor changed. Where once a smiling, bubbly waitress stood, now a fiery dragon took her place. Placing her hands firmly on her hips, she looked down at me and said, "Do I look like a babysitter? Do you know how many people abandon their kids here? Here's a hint: you'd be the third this week."

Reaching into my pocket, I pulled out a golden crown, the last one I had. "Will this help?" I asked, placing it into her palm.

She looked down at it and then back up at me. Her face was now filled with awe. I guess she's never seen so much in one place. "You got one hour. A second more, and I call security on your ass."

"You won't regret this!" I said, jumping up and giving her a peck on the cheek. It was clear by her sour expression that she already was. Thankfully, the lady didn't say anything as I rushed out the door.

Once back on the ship, I made a beeline for my room. There was only one thing I had to look at: the packet. The little manila envelope contained all the information I was supposed to need for the mission, information I had never even bothered looking at in the intervening time.

Picking the thing up from the nightstand I had left it on, I flopped onto my bed, turning the thing over and dumping its contents onto the floor. Information that I already knew, maps, bios, keys— all that and more fell before me. Things that would have greatly aided not just me but the Kid in our quest. But in my ignorant arrogance, I declined it all. Oh, what an idiot I was, I thought, the last item hitting the floor. Nothing new to be had. No last-minute insight, no wisdom would I gain.

"Why am I doing this?" I yelled to no one, tossing the now-empty packet across the room in a fit of despair. It's only a matter of time before we are tracked down, I thought, glancing down at my hip where the pistol rested. What's the point of even con— wait, what was that?

My thoughts had been interrupted by a strange clattering sound. In a flash, I fled from my bed, pistol in hand, ready to investigate. The search only took a second. As soon as I turned on the lights, I saw what had made that noise: a plastic data wafer, and an older one at that. Apparently, I had not been as exhaustive in my emptying of the packet as I had once believed.

Picking it up and turning it over, I saw the words To Jayce inscribed on the wafer with a very familiar hand. I know this hand. Just can't remember where. The intricacies of said handwriting burned bright in my mind.

I know I have a holo player around here somewhere, I reminded myself while searching for it, finding it in the corner after a quick scan. Tech like this had been outmoded for some time, but then again, the ship hadn't been the pinnacle of cutting-edge tech for some time now. My fingers remembered the weave to thread the player's wires into the ship's systems.

So, I put the data wafer in...and waited, the thing taking its sweet old time to remember that it still functions properly. Finally, the blinking light turned green... and still nothing. "This is pointless!" I said again to no one. Well, not exactly...

"Jayce, long time," came a voice from behind me. "Still no see, I guess." No, I thought as I heard that sweet laughter. It can't be... Turning around, all my wildest hopes and fears were confirmed at once: it was her.

"Brianna," I said, my voice going up an octave and a half. Standing before me, in holographic form, was Queen Brianna Shinkar, the Kid's mother and my former... well, that's not important right now. Her beauty had not diminished in the slightest. While the years had certainly worn on her, by no means had they broken her. The woman who stood before me was just as defiant as she had been all those years prior.

"If you are viewing this, Jayce, I am more than likely dead or worse," she said, her voice not wavering in the slightest. "I wish things had not gone down the way they had, but I guess we both made our own choices that night." Her eyes somehow found me, staring directly into my soul like they always had. "No sense dwelling on what has been done."

How? was all I could think, collapsing back onto my bed. "This message is a contingency; you are the contingency, Jayce," the Queen continued, her voice finally starting to crack. "I have instructed… my… son Orion to seek you out."

It was then that she began to break, tears streaming down her holographic cheeks. All I wanted to do at that moment was to scoop her up and hold her tight. But I could not, and that is what finally broke me. "You are the only one I can trust to bring him safely to where he needs to go. He is our… our only hope, Jayce."

I could see her knees shaking, but she held firm like the giant oak she was. "Please keep him safe. I'm so sorry we never got to meet again. Goodbye...my love."

With that, she was now gone from my life, forever this time.

Not able to hold back the flurry of emotions that had been welling up inside me, I screamed. I screamed a scream of unimaginable pain. I had lost, lived, and now lost all over again. This is why I retreated into myself in the first place, I thought, the one notion that stood out among the storm.

This time, I could not retreat. The dam had been busted, and there was no building it back up. Now, I was forced to feel it all: guilt, regret, shame, agony, and above them all, despair. It was no longer a choice of A or C. Now it was either him...or my gun.

Is it really even a choice? Do you want to throw away everything you and that boy have built together? Getting up from my place of dying, a new Jayce had arisen—one who knew exactly what he had to do.

I walked into the diner to see him chatting up the waitress. The Kid had somehow ordered some food in the short time I had been gone. "And then my old man put his arm around him and said, 'Leverage.'" They both laughed at this, the waitress enjoying what she believed to be a tale.

"What have I told you about telling stories?" I yelled as I grabbed him by the scruff of his collar and dragged him off, tossing the waitress more credit sticks than were needed to pay for my meal.

"But I was just getting to the good part!" the Kid said before catching on to what I was getting at. "Besides, I was about to eat the special."

"You don't want that," I told him, opening the ramp to our ship. "Last one I heard order the special, their chest burst and danced on the counter!"

The Kid looked up at me as we rushed inside. "You sure you aren't the one telling tall tales now?"

"I'm serious," I replied, the two of us making a beeline for the bridge. "Top hat, cane, the works!"

He said some other stuff, but I wasn't listening at that point. My mind focused on where we would go.

"If we push it, we could probably make it back to Nileia," I muttered to myself.

Confused, the Kid tugged on my sleeve. "Ummm, Jayce, what's going on?"

I did not bother to answer, my mind being focused on this single task. "I better send a pulse beforehand. Otherwise, she just might kill me."

His frustration at a boiling point, the Kid kicked me in the shins, screaming, "Jayce, just tell me...What are you doing?!"

No point holding this off any longer, I thought, turning to face him and falling onto the floor, my knees bending before me. Looking up at him, I said the fateful words.

"Protecting you...my prince."

The End

Lost Kingdom Glossary

Aerys Shinkar: The last King in a line that had up to that point lasted over 300 years. An old man at the time of the fall. Aerys had always had problems conceiving a child. Little did he know it would lead to his destruction.

Alpha Centauri System: What started as a project to expand the reaches of the Shinkar Kingdom before the fall has turned into the only lawless place known to man. Existing on the farthest edge of the known space. This is a system for people who truly want to disappear.

Auto-Nav: A system devolved to help automate the navigation of Slip Space. What once was done by hand could now be done with a simple device. An imperfect system, one must manually check the logs lest they go to far off course.

Backwing: The name given to the 2nd in command of the Shadow Hawk Squadron. Usually, the person chosen is the one being groomed to eventually take over the leadership position.

Battle Of IO, The: The decisive battle that ended the Kapf Rebellion. It's where Jayce first distinguished himself and caught the eye of the royal family.

Bio Bracelets: One of the many medical advancements that have made life after The Old Earth Better. These devices can monitor the health between one or more people. It's transmission can be picked up from vast distances.

Brianna Shinkar (The Mother): Hailing from the ancient House of Spencer. Brianna has found herself as the young Queen to a very disinterested king. The Last Sword to Jaycen's First, Brianna is meant to be the final line of defense of the king. Wielding Windseeker as proof of that.

Briefcase Bike: A piece of compact transport. It's meant to fold up to the size of a briefcase, hence the name.

Buzzard: What was once a ship designed solely for scrapping has been repurposed to a cheap and easily replaceable fighter. While its weapons may be weak, they attempt to make up for that in sheer numbers.

Captain-General: Head of The King's Royal Guard. The Captain-General is the highest position one can have as a member of the Warrior Caste. Often sitting higher than many of the Aristocracy Caste.

Caste: The system of social hierarchy that governs everyone. You have Labors at the bottom, then Artisans/Scientists, and finally at the top you have the Warriors/Aristocrats. While it is defiantly possible to transcend your caste, it doesn't happen as often as most people would want it to.

Chameleon: When you need something done, and done right, and you absolutely want no one to know about it, you bring in the Chameleons. With the nanites grafted into their very being, they can become anyone or anything and can produce and reproduce almost any solid object.

Coms: The main means of communication between people of the 'Verse.

Corfis Anders: Being the third Captain of The Royal Guards, Anders has always been a spiteful shrew. Always looking for his next way up. He will screw over anyone or anything to get on top.

Crown Prince: A title given to the next in line for the throne. Currently held by Orion Shinkar.

Detroit: What was once a shining city on the river has been reduced to a pile of rubble. Only stone and steel remains of what was once The Motor City.

Drifter Colony: While most see junk, the people who made the Drifter Colonies saw treasure. A Venn diagram of different types of junk mashed together. Floating through the cosmos. The people who live here are the height of ingenuity. Often by necessity.

Dwarf: For those who lived hateful lives then passed down their spite. Eventually over the generations a group of people emerged. Dwarves. Small, spiteful little cretins. Nothing is ever their fault, and they are always the most important person in the room. At least that's what they think.

Earthbringer: An ancient sword which once belonged to The 2100 Samurai. It now serves as the blade of The Captain General, the first sword its enemies meet. Lost to the general public since the Usurper War, it is believed to still be in the possession of Jaycen Lamont.

Elias Hargreaves: Here you have a man who at one point led the Shadow Hawk Squadron with Jaycen as his Backwing. He then disappeared for years, reemerging as an E.L.F. and Chief of Police on Europa.

Emperor Elrick Shinkar: Born a bastard, Elrick was raised with all the privileges of a Crown Prince, only without the title. Even without the rights, the public still adored him. That's why when the King fell ill, the status of his only legal heir fell under heavy suspicion.

Enhanced Life Form (E.L.F.): An experiment by some long-forgotten lab led to these beings: a group that was never meant to get out. Creatures of enhanced intelligence, stamina, and fortitude, the only thing keeping them in check is their low numbers and low birth rates.

Eventide, The: First ordered to be the King's Royal Starship, it has since served as personal transport of Jaycen for the past 15 years. A well equipped ship, if not a bit behind on it's repair schedule.

Europa: What looks like a working class backwater planet turns out to be exactly that. The thin layer of salt that covers the planet makes everything a bit... hazy.

Fallout: While much of the media of The Old Earth was brought over in The Exodus, little of it caught on like this video game series, its themes reflecting a humanity many sought in themselves.

Faith of the Pantheon, The: Once there were many religions. Now there are two. One of these is The Faith of the Pantheon, a religion encompassing all of the Old Earth's heroes, including but not limited to Jesus, Buddha, Zeus, and Batman.

FTL: Short for "Faster Than Light". It's a means of traversing the stars in a rather expedient way.

Ford Field: Somehow this structure built in the very early 20th century is still standing. What was once used as an area for local gladiators is now used by thieves and pirates. Located on the banks of the now dried up Detroit River, this space was where they fought Lions.

Great Collapse, The: Taking place around the 2200's. The world as everyone knew it just could not function anymore, leading to over 300 years of desolation. The reasons for the collapse are yet unknown.

Hypervisor: Worn over the eye's, these are just one part of a system to remotely control fighter drones. Allowing someone to defend their ship without the risk of actually being in it.

House Shinkar: Founded shortly after the settling of Mars, House Shinkar took advantage of the unrest caused by The Interstellar Spring to establish a kingdom that ruled over the entire Sol System. Lasting for over 300 years, it was only toppled upon the death of the elderly Aerys.

Imperial Guard: Formed from the ruins of the Royal Guard, these people are much more...direct in how they protect their emperor.

Inquisitio Insurrectionis: Operating in twos, these men with their hands of blue are the secret police of the empire. Feared by all and having almost unchecked authority, they are people you don't want to be on the bad side of.

Jaycen "Jayce" Lamont: The former Captain-General General of the Royal Guard. Before that, commander of The Shadow Hawk Squadron. Jayce now lives in the bottom of his next fix, chasing jobs in the hopes that he might one day outrun his immense guilt.

Jackson Fuir-ey: A man led by his principals. This former #2 Captain of the Royal Guard now leads the resistance to the Emperor. Styling himself as Spartan-Prime, he will stop at nothing to see justice done.

Judy's Pleasure Palace: A long-forgotten brothel. operating in the early 22nd century. Not much is known about it. Some say it changed names. Others say it harbored a legendary Samurai. Nobody really knows.

Kappa: What was once considered a creature of myth was found to be true on the harsh surface of Venus. A vicious creature, not much is known about them since any attempt to study the beast ends with the scientist in shreds.

Kappa Soup: One of the rarest of delicacies. This dish is hard obtain due in large part to the hassle in acquiring its ingredients.

Lamont Aerospace: The premiere ship builder for the Kingdom (now Empire). Success has allowed the current head to ascend to the Aristocracy Caste.

Leon Lamont: While not the first Lamont, he is the first of note, being the one who bought out the struggling Orville Aerospace. Leon created a power base that extends to this very day.

Mars (aka New Earth): When The Old Earth fell, Mars became humanities new home. Quickly becoming the most terraformed and adapted planet in the Sol System. Mars is the beating heart of the Empire.

Mercury: The first planet of the Sol System. Mercury is hell space that only the bravest are bold enough to step upon. Mostly used for research bases and putting things you would rather be forgotten.

Nanatose: Similar to Nanites, albeit in a more processed and refined form. This is what most people think of when the substance is mentioned.

Nanites: Probably one of the few substances in the Sol System that are confirmed to be of alien origin. Nanites are an illy understood tool. What was once used to power Bi-Opts in the early 2000's now is used mostly as armor for spaceships.

Nileia Bonny: The last to lead The Shadow Hawk Squadron and the first to lead The Raven Squadron. Former lover of Jaycen. She will always hold a candle for her former boss.

Noodle Boodle, The: Some said the House of Waffles would be the one to outlast Earth, but it turns out that The Noodle Boodle became the premiere fast food of the Sol System, its reach extending as far as Alpha Centauri itself.

Old Earth: Long since abandoned and hardly habitable. Earth has become a haven for plunders, pirates, and any other sort of outcasts.

Orion Shinkar (The Kid): The supposed child of King Aerys and his Queen Brianna. (Or at least that's what's claimed to be the case anyway...) Having lived most of his life on the run with his mother. He still seems to have all the Royal arrogance one would expect of him.

Orville Aerospace: An aerospace company that dates back to well before the founding. Orville was eventually bought out and turned into Lamont Aerospace.

Phobos Hellfire Whiskey: When people want to get drunk, and get drunk quickly, they chug the hellfire, a potent swill that has led many marines to their doom.

Pillbug: One of the now banned Stealth Ships, geared towards transport and reconnaissance, it is a bit larger and requires two pilots to operate.

Queen, The: Born Brianna Spencer, this woman was given everything in life. Including the keys to the Shinkar Kingdom. Married to an old man who shows little interest in her, rumors suggest she found solace in the arms of another...

Raven Squadron: Forged from the ashes of The Shadow Hawk Squadron. This team lives as outlaws, plundering from the more fortunate so that they may eke out a life for themselves.

Royal Guard, The: The King's personal army. All who serve swear to defend him and his castle to their last breath. Breaking said oath is not one does lightly.

Samurai, The: A figure rooted in myth and superstition. Known to have operated around the year 2100. No one knows where he came from, or what eventually happened to him.

Servine Spiders: The corruption of the Old Earth led to many abnormalities. One such was the Servine Spider, a vicious thing that feeds off of anything dumb enough to pass by its traps.

Shadowhawk: A now highly illegal type of space fighter. Designed with the ability to cloak itself and become basically invisible, thus allowing them to do hit and run strikes.

Shadowhawk Squadron: When the king needed something done, and done quietly, he sent in the Shadowhawk Squadron, an elite group of pilots centered around the use of the Shadow Hawk Stealth Fighters. They were disbanded shortly after Elrick's Evolution.

Shadow Hawk Style: A method of attack oft-attributed to the Squadron it is named after. Characterized by a series of quick hit and run tactics followed by a hasty retreat.

Shield Discs: Personal protection device. Meant to be used and consumed. Rated for hours of protection, that time can be less if under heavy stress.

Shinkar Mark: The base denomination which the Imperial Currency is based off of. A single mark is enough to by most basic things.

Shock Stick: This weapon is often used by the most lowly and cowardly foot soldiers. A simple stick that emits electricity at the end. One poke is enough to make almost anyone compliant.

Slip Space: Discovered not long after the Exodus of Earth, Slip Space is a sort of sub space where the rules do not apply; a veritable spider-web of ever shifting tunnels. It's one that takes specialized training to properly navigate.

Spartan Alliance: Formed not long after the end of the Usurper War, this group is dedicated to taking down the Emperor and restoring the monarchy. While they have so far had middling success, rumors suggest that a fracture has taken place near the top.

Spartan Base Alpha: Headquarters of all Spartans. This secret base is known only to a few.

Spartan-Prime: The leader of The Spartan Alliance. Currently held by Jackson Fuir-Ey.

Split The Root: A technique used to open up the drone controller. It is referred to as such due to the root-like shape of the device.

Squawkbox: The main device used for communication in the 'Verse. Best for both short and mid-range distances.

Sol System: A name given a long time to the collection of 8 plants most people currently live on. Most people have no idea who Sol is. Most people don't even care.

Titan: One of the many moons of Saturn, this hunk of rock is home to most of the system's elite and upper class.

Vac-Suit: It's a space suit, but newer. Nuff said.

Venus: This lovely planet is actually a hellscape that not even outlaws dare to venture onto.

Warrior Caste: One of the upper levels of the caste system. Most here do not live long enough to see the fruits of their labor. This is the caste Jaycen belongs to.

Warwolf: Something that started out as an experiment during a long-forgotten world war thousands of years ago has evolved into a race of humanoid canines. Shunned by most of society, they tend to live in their own enclaves unless requested elsewhere.

White Claw: While the exact age of this drink is not known, what is known is that it dates back to the Old Earth, its formula somehow finding its way onto the data banks of The Exodus. Now as common as sand, everyone says they hate it, but everyone still drinks it.

Windseeker: The first blade of the kingdom. Once belonging to the 2100 Samurai itself. This Katana is now traditionally wielded by The Captain-General Of The King's Guard.

Wyvren: A heavy assault fighter, its armor is thick. Designed for close engagements, it will dive-bomb the enemy and engulf them in a thick fiery death.

CRITICAL BLAST PUBLISHING
SOUTHERN KNIGHTS
FLARE
ARCHIVES VOLUME 1
CAPTAIN THUNDER AND BLUE BOLT
ARCHIVES VOLUME 1
ARISTOCRATIC XTRATERRESTRIAL TIME-TRAVELING THIEVES
LEAGUE OF CHAMPIONS
Criticalblast • com

www.ingramcontent.com/pod-product-compliance
Lightning Source LLC
Chambersburg PA
CBHW062110290726
48975CB00001B/174